Books by Jonathan Kellerman

FICTION

ALEX DELAWARE NOVELS

Victims (2012)
Mystery (2011)
Deception (2010)
Evidence (2009)
Bones (2008)
Compulsion (2008)
Obsession (2007)
Gone (2006)
Rage (2005)
Therapy (2004)
A Cold Heart (2003)
The Murder Book (2002)
Flesh and Blood (2001)
Dr. Death (2000)

Monster (1999)
Survival of the Fittest (1997)
The Clinic (1997)
The Web (1996)
Self-Defense (1995)
Bad Love (1994)
Devil's Waltz (1993)
Private Eyes (1992)
Time Bomb (1990)
Silent Partner (1989)
Over the Edge (1987)
Blood Test (1986)
When the Bough Breaks (1985)

OTHER NOVELS

True Detectives (2009)
Capital Crimes (with Faye Kellerman, 2006)
Twisted (2004)
Double Homicide (with Faye Kellerman, 2004)
The Conspiracy Club (2003)
Billy Straight (1998)
The Butcher's Theater (1988)

NONFICTION

With Strings Attached: The Art and Beauty of Vintage Guitars (2008)
Savage Spawn: Reflections on Violent Children (1999)
Helping the Fearful Child (1981)
Psychological Aspects of Childhood Cancer (1980)

FOR CHILDREN, WRITTEN AND ILLUSTRATED

Jonathan Kellerman's ABC of Weird Creatures (1995)
Daddy, Daddy, Can You Touch the Sky? (1994)

VICTIMS

JONATHAN KELLERMAN

VICTIMS

AN ALEX DELAWARE NOVEL

DOUBLEDAY LARGE PRINT HOME LIBRARY EDITION

BALLANTINE BOOKS

NEW YORK

Published in the United States by Ballantine Books, an imprint of The Random House Publishing Group, a division of Random House, Inc., New York.

BALLANTINE and colophon are registered trademarks of Random House, Inc.

ISBN 978-1-61793-710-1

Printed in the United States of America

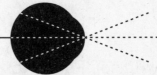

This Large Print Book carries the Seal of Approval of N.A.V.H.

To Libby McGuire

VICTIMS

CHAPTER

1

This one was different.

The first hint was Milo's tight-voiced eight a.m. message, stripped of details. **Something I need you to see, Alex. Here's the address.**

An hour later, I was showing I.D. to the uniform guarding the tape. He winced. "Up there, Doctor." Pointing to the second story of a sky-blue duplex trimmed in chocolate-brown, he dropped a hand to his Sam Browne belt, as if ready for self-defense.

Nice older building, the classic Cal-Spanish architecture, but the color was wrong. So was the silence of the street, sawhorsed at both ends. Three squad cars and a liver-colored LTD were parked haphazardly across the asphalt. No crime lab vans or coroner's vehicles had arrived, yet.

I said, "Bad?"

The uniform said, "There's probably a better word for it but that works."

Milo stood on the landing outside the door doing nothing.

No cigar-smoking or jotting in his pad or grumbling orders. Feet planted, arms at his sides, he stared at some faraway galaxy.

His blue nylon windbreaker bounced sunlight at strange angles. His black hair was limp, his pitted face the color and texture of cottage cheese past its prime. A white shirt had wrinkled to crepe. Wheat-colored cords had slipped beneath his paunch. His tie was a sad shred of poly.

He looked as if he'd dressed wearing a blindfold.

As I climbed the stairs, he didn't acknowledge me.

When I was six steps away, he said, "You made good time."

"Easy traffic."

"Sorry," he said.

"For what?"

"Including you." He handed me gloves and paper booties.

I held the door for him. He stayed outside.

The woman was at the rear of the apartment's front room, flat on her back. The kitchen behind her was empty, counters bare, an old avocado-colored fridge free of photos or magnets or mementos.

Two doors to the left were shut and yellow-taped. I took that as a *Keep Out.* Drapes were drawn over every window. Fluorescent lighting in the kitchen supplied a nasty pseudo-dawn.

The woman's head was twisted sharply to the right. A swollen tongue hung between slack, bloated lips.

Limp neck. A grotesque position some coroner might label "incompatible with life."

Big woman, broad at the shoulders and the hips. Late fifties to early sixties, with an aggressive chin and short, coarse gray hair. Brown sweatpants covered her below the waist. Her feet were bare. Unpolished toenails were clipped short. Grubby soles said bare feet at home was the default.

Above the waistband of the sweats was what remained of a bare torso. Her abdomen had been sliced horizontally below the navel in a crude approximation of a C-section. A vertical slit crossed the lateral incision at the center, creating a star-shaped wound.

The damage brought to mind one of those hard-rubber change purses that relies on surface tension to protect the goodies. Squeeze to create a stellate opening, then reach in and scoop.

The yield from this receptacle was a necklace of intestines placed below the woman's neckline and arranged like a fashionista's puffy scarf. One end terminated at her right clavicle. Bilious streaks ran down her right breast and onto her rib cage. The rest of her viscera had been pulled down into a heap and left near her left hip.

The pile rested atop a once-white

towel folded double. Below that was a larger maroon towel spread neatly. Four other expanses of terry cloth formed a makeshift tarp that shielded beige wall-to-wall carpeting from biochemical insult. The towels had been arranged precisely, edges overlapping evenly for about an inch. Near the woman's right hip was a pale blue T-shirt, also folded. Spotless.

Doubling the white towel had succeeded in soaking up a good deal of body fluid, but some had leaked into the maroon under-layer. The smell would've been bad enough without the initial stages of decomp.

One of the towels beneath the body bore lettering. Silver bath sheet embroidered *Vita* in white.

Latin or Italian for "life." Some monster's notion of irony?

The intestines were green-brown splotched pink in spots, black in others. Matte finish to the casing, some puckering that said they'd been drying for a while. The apartment was cool, a good ten degrees below the pleasant spring weather outside. The rattle of a wheezy

A.C. unit in one of the living room windows was inescapable once I noticed it. Noisy apparatus, rusty at the bolts, but efficient enough to leach moisture from the air and slow down the rot.

But rot is inevitable and the woman's color wasn't anything you'd see outside a morgue.

Incompatible with life.

I bent to inspect the wounds. Both slashes were confident swoops unmarred by obvious hesitation marks, shearing smoothly through layers of skin, subcutaneous fat, diaphragmatic muscle.

No abrasions around the genital area and surprisingly little blood for so much brutality. No spatter or spurt or castoff or evidence of a struggle. All those towels; horribly compulsive.

Guesses filled my head with bad pictures.

Extremely sharp blade, probably not serrated. The neck-twist had killed her quickly and she'd been dead during the surgery, the ultimate anesthesia. The killer had stalked her with enough thoroughness to know he'd have her to him-

self for a while. Once attaining total control, he'd gone about choreographing:
laying out the towels, tucking and align-
ing, achieving a pleasing symmetry.
Then he'd laid her down, removed her
T-shirt, careful to keep it clean.

Standing back, he'd inspected his
prep work. Time for the blade.

Then the real fun: anatomical exploration.

Despite the butchery and the hideous
set of her neck, she looked peaceful.
For some reason, that made what had
been done to her worse.

I scanned the rest of the room. No
damage to the front door or any other
sign of forced entry. Bare beige walls
backed cheap upholstered furniture
covered in a puckered ocher fabric that
aped brocade but fell short. White ce-
ramic beehive lamps looked as if they'd
shatter under a finger-snap.

The dining area was set up with a
card table and two folding chairs. A
brown cardboard take-out pizza box
sat on the table. Someone—probably
Milo—had placed a yellow plastic evi-

dence marker nearby. That made me take a closer look.

No brand name on the box, just *PIZZA!* in exuberant red cursive above the caricature of a portly mustachioed chef. Curls of smaller lettering swarmed around the chef's fleshy grin.

Fresh pizza!
Lotta taste!
Ooh la la!
Yum yum!
Bon appétit!

The box was pristine, not a speck of grease or finger-smudge. I bent down to sniff, picked up no pizza aroma. But the decomp had filled my nose; it would be a while before I'd be smelling anything but death.

If this was another type of crime scene, some detective might be making ghoulish jokes about free lunch.

The detective in charge of this scene was a lieutenant who'd seen hundreds of murders, maybe thousands, yet chose to stay outside for a while.

I let loose more mental pictures. Some fiend in a geeky delivery hat ringing the doorbell then managing to talk himself inside.

Watching as the prey went for her purse? Waiting for precisely the right moment before coming up behind her and clamping both his hands on the sides of her head.

Quick blitz of rotation. The spinal cord would separate and that would be it.

Doing it correctly required strength and confidence.

That and the lack of obvious transfer evidence—not even a shoe impression—screamed experience. If there'd been a similar murder in L.A., I hadn't heard about it.

Despite all that meticulousness, the hair around the woman's temples might be a good place to look for transfer DNA. Psychopaths don't sweat much, but you never know.

I examined the room again.

Speaking of purses, hers was nowhere in sight.

Robbery as an afterthought? More likely souvenir-taking was part of the plan.

Edging away from the body, I wondered if the woman's last thoughts had been of crusty dough, mozzarella, a comfy barefoot dinner.

The doorbell ring the last music she'd ever hear.

I stayed in the apartment awhile longer, straining for insight.

The terrible competence of the neck-twist made me wonder about someone with martial arts training.

The embroidered towel bothered me.

Vita. Life.

Had he brought that one but taken the rest from her linen closet?

Yum. Bon appétit. To life.

The decomp reek intensified and my eyes watered and blurred and the necklace of guts morphed into a snake.

Drab constrictor, fat and languid after a big meal.

I could stand around and pretend that this was anything comprehensible, or hurry outside and try to suppress the tide of nausea rising in my own guts.

Not a tough choice.

CHAPTER

2

Milo hadn't moved from his position on the landing. His eyes were back on Planet Earth, watching the street below. Five uniforms were moving from door to door. From the quick pace of the canvass, plenty of no-one-home.

The street was in a working-class neighborhood in the southeastern corner of West L.A. Division. Three blocks east would've made it someone else's problem. Mixed zoning allowed single-family dwellings and duplexes like the one where the woman had been degraded.

Psychopaths are stodgy creatures of routine and I wondered if the killer's comfort zone was so narrow that he lived within the sawhorses.

I caught my breath and worked at settling my stomach while Milo pretended not to notice.

"Yeah, I know," he finally said. He was apologizing for the second time when a coroner's van drove up and a dark-haired woman in comfortable clothes got out and hurried up the stairs. "Morning, Milo."

"Morning, Gloria. All yours."

"Oh, boy," she said. "We talking freaky-bad?"

"I could say I've seen worse, kid, but I'd be lying."

"Coming from you that gives me the creeps, Milo."

"Because I'm old?"

"Tsk." She patted his shoulder. "Because you're the voice of experience."

"Some experiences I can do without."

People can get used to just about anything. But if your psyche's in good repair, the fix is often temporary.

Soon after receiving my doctorate, I worked as a psychologist on a pediatric cancer ward. It took a month to stop dreaming about sick kids but I was eventually able to do my job with apparent professionalism. Then I left to go into private practice and found myself, years later, on that same ward. Seeing the children with new eyes mocked all the adaptation I thought I'd accomplished and made me want to cry. I went home and dreamed for a long time.

Homicide detectives get "used" to a regular diet of soul-obliteration. Typically bright and sensitive, they soldier on, but the essence of the job lurks beneath the surface like a land mine. Some D's transfer out. Others stay and find hobbies. Religion works for some, sin for others. Some, like Milo, turn griping into an art form and never pretend it's just another job.

The woman on the towels was different for him and for me. A permanent image bank had lodged in my brain and I knew the same went for him.

Neither of us talked as Gloria worked inside.

Finally, I said, "You marked the pizza box. It bothers you."

"Everything about this bothers me."

"No brand name on the box. Any indies around here deliver?"

He drew out his cell phone, clicked, and produced a page. Phone numbers he'd already downloaded filled the screen and when he scrolled, the listings kept coming.

"Twenty-eight indies in a ten-mile radius and I also checked Domino's and Papa John's and Two Guys. No one dispatched anyone to this address last night and nobody uses that particular box."

"If she didn't actually call out, why would she let him in?"

"Good question."

"Who discovered her?"

"Landlord, responding to a complaint she made a few days ago. Hissing toilet, they had an appointment. When she didn't answer, he got annoyed, started to leave. Then he thought better of it because she liked things fixed, used his key."

"Where is he now?"

He pointed across the street. "Recuperating with some firewater down in that little Tudor-ish place."

I found the house. Greenest lawn on the block, beds of flowers. Topiary bushes.

"Anything about him bother you?"

"Not so far. Why?"

"His landscaping says he's a perfectionist."

"That's a negative?"

"This case, maybe."

"Well," he said, "so far he's just the landlord. Want to know about her?"

"Sure."

"Her name's Vita Berlin, she's fifty-six, single, lives on some kind of disability."

"Vita," I said. "The towel was hers."

"*The* towel? This bastard used every damn towel she had in her linen closet."

"*Vita* means 'life' in Latin and Italian. I thought it might be a sick joke."

"Cute. Anyway, I'm waiting for Mr. Belleveaux—the landlord—to calm down so I can question him and find out more about her. What I've learned from prelim snooping in her bedroom and bathroom is if she's got kids she doesn't keep their pictures around and if she had a computer, it was ripped off. Same for a cell phone. My guess is she had neither, the place has a static feel to it. Like she moved in years ago, didn't add any new-fangled stuff."

"I didn't see her purse."

"On her nightstand."

"You taped off the bedroom, didn't want me in there?"

"I sure do, but that'll wait until the techies are through. Can't afford to jeopardize any aspect of this."

"The front room was okay?"

"I knew you'd be careful."

His logic seemed strained. Insufficient sleep and a bad surprise can do that.

I said, "Any indication she was heading to the bedroom before he jumped her?"

"No, it's pristine. Why?"

I gave him the delivery tip scenario.

"Going for her purse," he said. "Well, I don't know how you'd prove that, Alex.

Main thing is he confined himself to the front, didn't move her into the bedroom for anything sexual."

I said, "Those towels make me think of a stage. Or a picture frame."

"Meaning?"

"Showing off his work."

"Okay . . . what else to tell you . . . her wardrobe's mostly sweats and sneakers, lots of books in her bedroom. Romances and the kinds of mysteries where people talk like Noël Coward twits and the cops are bumbling cretins."

I wondered out loud about a killer with martial arts skills and when he didn't respond, went on to describe the kill-scene still bouncing around my brain.

He said, "Sure, why not."

Agreeable but distracted. Neither of us focusing on the big question.

Why would anyone do something like this to another human being?

Gloria exited the apartment, looking older and paler.

Milo said, "You okay?"

"I'm fine," she said. "No, I'm lying, that was horrible." Her forehead was moist.

She dabbed it with a tissue. "My God, it's grotesque."

"Any off-the-cuff impressions?"

"Nothing you probably haven't figured out yourself. Broken neck's my bet for COD, the cutting looks postmortem. The incisions look clean so maybe some training in meat-cutting or a paramedical field but I wouldn't put much stock in that, all kinds of folk can learn to slice. That pizza box mean something to you?"

"Don't know," said Milo. "No one admits delivering here."

"A scam to get himself in?" she said. "Why would she open the door for a fake pizza guy?"

"Good question, Gloria."

She shook her head. "I called for transport. Want me to ask for a priority autopsy?"

"Thanks."

"You might actually get it because Dr. J seems to like you. Also with something this weird, she's bound to be curious."

A year ago, Milo had solved the murder of a coroner's investigator. Since then Dr. Clarice Jernigan, a senior pathologist, had reciprocated with personalized attention when Milo asked for it.

He said, "Must be my charm and good looks."

Gloria grinned and patted his shoulder again. "Anything else, guys? I'm on half-shift due to budgetary constraints, figure to finish my paperwork by one then go cleanse my head with a couple of martinis. Give or take."

Milo said, "Make it a double for me."

I said, "Was significant blood pooled inside the body cavity?"

Her look said I was being a spoilsport. "A lot of it was coagulated but yes, that's where most of it was. You figured that because the scene was so clean?"

I nodded. "It was either that or he found out a way to take it with him."

Milo said, "Buckets of blood, lovely." To Gloria: "One more question: You recall anything remotely like this in your case files?"

"Nope," she said. "But we just cover the county and they say it's a globalized world, right? You could be looking at a traveler."

Milo glared and trudged down the stairs.

Gloria said, "Whoa, someone's in a mood."

I said, "It's likely to stay that way for a while."

CHAPTER

3

Stanleigh Belleveaux's house was as meticulous inside as out.

Cozy, plush-carpeted place set up with doily-protected too-small furniture. The dollhouse feel was heightened by a brass étagère filled with bisque figurines. Another case bore photos of two handsome young men in uniform and an American flag paperweight.

"My wife's thing," said Belleveaux, wringing his hands. "The dolls, they're from Germany. She's in Memphis, visiting my mother-in-law."

He was black, fiftyish, thickset,

dressed in a navy polo shirt, pressed khakis, and tan loafers. A fleece of white blanketed his scalp and the bottom half of his face. His nose had been broken a few times. His knuckles were scarred.

"Her mom," said Milo.

"Pardon?"

"You called her your mother-in-law rather than her mom."

"Because that's how I think of her. Mother-in-law. Worst person I know. Like the Ernie K-Doe song, but you probably don't remember that."

Milo hummed a few bars.

Belleveaux smiled weakly. Turned grim and wrung his hands some more. "I still can't believe what happened to Ms. Berlin. Still can't believe I had to *see* it." He closed his eyes, opened them. No booze on the table before him, just a can of Diet Coke.

Milo said, "Change your mind about the Dewar's, huh?"

"It's tempting," said Belleveaux. "But a little early in the day, what if I get a call and have to drive?"

"Call from who?"

"A tenant. That's my life, sir."

"How many tenants do you have?"

"The Feldmans down below Ms. Berlin, the Soos and the Kims and the Parks and the other Parks in a triplex I own over near Korea Town. Then I've got a real problem rental down in Willowbrook, inherited from my dad, a nice family, the Rodriguezes, are there now but it's been tough because of the gangster situation." He rubbed his eyes. "This is my best neighborhood, I chose to live here, last place I thought I'd have . . . a problem. Still can't believe what I saw, it's like a movie, a bad one, a real horror movie. I want to switch to another channel but what I saw won't budge out of here." Placing a thumb-tip on his forehead.

"It'll fade," said Milo. "Takes time."

"Guess you'd know about that," said Belleveaux. "How much time?"

"Hard to say."

"It's probably easier for you, this being your job. My job, the worst thing I see is a bat in a garage, sewage leak, mice eating wires." Frowning. "Gangsters in the Willowbrook place, but I keep my distance. This was way up close, *too* close."

"How long have you owned the property across the street?"

"Seven years eight months."

"That's pretty precise, Mr. Belleveaux."

"I'm a detail-man, Lieutenant. Learned precision in the army, they taught me mechanics, a little mechanical engineering, I didn't need a college degree to accumulate adequate knowledge. Later when I was out and repairing washing machines and dryers for Sears, what the army inculcated in me came in handy: Only one way to do a job: right. Machine needs three screws, you don't put in two."

I said, "The same goes for boxing."

"Pardon?"

"Your hands. I used to do karate, you pick up the signs someone else is into martial arts."

"Martial arts?" said Belleveaux. "Nah, none of that for me, I just did a little sparring in the army, then a little more when I got out, light welterweight, used to be skinny. Busted my septum three times and my wife, she was my girlfriend back then, said Stan, you keep scarring yourself to the point where you're ugly, I'm going to go find myself a pretty boy. She was kidding. Maybe. I wanted out anyway, what kind of life is that, getting knocked around, feeling dizzy for days? The money was terrible."

He drank some Coke. Licked his lips.

Milo said, "So what can you tell us about Vita Berlin?"

"What can I tell you," Belleveaux echoed. "That's a complicated question."

"Why's that, sir?"

"She wasn't the easiest . . . okay, look, I don't want to be speaking bad of the dead. 'Specially someone who—what happened to her. No one deserves that. *No* one, no matter what."

I said, "She had a difficult personality."

"So you know what I'm talking about."

I didn't deny it. "Being her landlord could get complicated," I prompted.

Belleveaux picked up the soda can. "Does what I tell you go in some kind of record?"

Milo said, "There's a problem with that?"

"I don't want to get sued."

"By who?"

"Someone in her family."

"They're difficult as well?"

"Don't know," said Belleveaux. "Never met them. I just believe in being prepared, ounce of prevention and all that."

"No particular reason you're worried about being sued."

"No, but those kinds of things," said Belleveaux. "Traits. Orneriness. Runs in families, right? Like Emmaline. My mother-in-law. Her sisters are all like her, scrappy, always ready to tussle. It's like stepping into a cage of badgers."

"Vita Berlin threatened to sue you?"

"About a million times."

"What for?"

"Anything that bothered her," said Belleveaux. "Leaky roof, she doesn't get a call-back in an hour, I'll sue you. Torn carpet, I'm at risk of tripping and breaking my neck, fix it fast or I'll sue you. That's why I got irked when she demanded I show up for the toilet and wasn't there when she said she'd be.

That's why I decided to use my key and go in there and fix it. Even though I knew she'd call me up and bitch about entering the premises without her permission. Which the landlord association says I can do at my discretion for just cause. Which includes reasonable repairs requested by the tenant. Turns out the toilet was fine."

Milo said, "You went into the bathroom?"

"I listened while I was looking at her. I know it's crazy but I couldn't move for a few seconds, just stood there trying not to hurl my breakfast. And it was quiet, toilet's out of whack you hear it. So I thought about that: It wasn't even broken."

I said, "Vita enjoyed giving you a hard time."

"Don't know if she enjoyed it, but she sure did it."

"Did you try to evict her?"

Belleveaux laughed. "No grounds, that's the way the law works. To get evicted, a tenant's just about got to . . ." He stopped short. "I was going to say they've got to kill someone. Oh, man, this is terrible."

I said, "Seven years, eight months."

"I bought the building four years five months ago, she came with it. I thought that meant good, long-term stable tenant. Then I learned different. Basically, she thought she owned it and I was her janitor."

"Entitled," I said.

"That's a nice word for it," he said.

"Cranky lady."

"Okay," he said, "I'll come out and say it: She was a miserable specimen, didn't have a good word for anyone. It's like she had bile in her veins instead of blood. My guess is you're not going to have too many people crying. Disgusted, yes, scared, yes. But not crying."

"Disgusted by . . ."

"What happened to her." Belleveaux's eyes clamped shut again. The lids twitched. "Man, *no* one deserves *that.*"

"But no one's going to mourn."

"Maybe she's got some family who'll mourn," he said. "But no one who had anything to do with her is going to say they miss her. I'm not stating that for a fact, I'm just guessing, but I'd put money on my guess. You want to see what I mean, go over to Bijou, it's a coffee shop on Robertson. She ate there from time to time, made their lives miserable. Same for the Feldmans, the downstairs tenants. Nice young couple, they've been here a year, are ready to move 'cause of her."

"Neighbors' dispute."

"No dispute, she harassed them. They're on the bottom floor, she's on top but *she's* the one complaining about footsteps. Actually made me come up to her place to listen a bunch of times, all I heard was her bitching, she's saying, 'See, hear that, Stan? They're clomping around like barbarians.' Then she lies down puts her ear to the carpet, makes me do it. That position, maybe I pick up a little sound but nothing serious. But I lie, tell her I'll talk to them. Just to keep her out of my hair, you know? I did nothing about it, she dropped it. The next time, it's something else—they fill the trash bins too high, they park their cars wrong, she thinks they snuck in a cat and it's a no-pet

building. What happened was there was
a stray cat came to the back door,
looked like it was starving, they gave it
some milk. Which is the human thing to
do, right? Now the Feldmans are going
to leave for sure and I'll have both units
vacant. Should've put my pension money
in gold bars or something."

Milo said, "Sounds like Vita was a little paranoid."

"That's a word for it," said Belleveaux.
"But it was more like she wanted attention and being mean was a way to get
it."

"She have any friends?"

"None I ever saw."

"And you live across the street."

"Part of the problem. She knew where
to find me. Here I was thinking the building would be perfect, convenient, no
need to drive. Next time I buy, it's in another state. Not that there'll be a next
time. Market was up, I'd sell everything."

"What can you tell us about her daily
routine?"

"From what I saw she kept to herself,
didn't go out much."

"Except for meals."

"Once in a while she'd walk over to Bijou. I know because I've been there myself, saw her a couple times. Cheap and good, I'd be there more but the wife's into cooking, takes lessons, likes to try stuff out. Now it's French, that's why I'm not skinny like I used to be."

Milo said, "Vita eat anywhere else besides Bijou?"

"Mostly what I saw was takeout," said Belleveaux. "From the boxes she'd throw out in the garbage. I know because she'd miss, I'd have to pick them up. The automated trucks they use nowadays, it's not in the can, it stays there and I don't want rats."

"What kind of takeout?"

"What I saw was pizza boxes. So I guess she liked pizza."

"From where?"

"Where? I don't know—I think Domino's, they're the ones in the blue hats, right? Maybe other places, I don't know. It's not like I was checking out her eating habits through the drapes. The less I had to do with her, the better."

"Did she get pizza delivered last night?"

"Wouldn't know," said Belleveaux. "I was at Staples, watching the Lakers take one from Utah. Went with my boys, they're both master sergeants in the army, had leave the same week, we did a basketball thing and later we went to Philippe's for some grub." He touched his belt buckle. "Overdid it with the French dip, but how many times do you get to go out with your kids, do guy stuff, everyone's being a grown-up? Got home late, slept late till seven, got her message on the machine, why didn't I come yesterday after the first call, the toilet's busted, it's her right to have a functional toilet, all the fixtures are old and cheap and lousy, if I'm not going to replace them the least I can do is repair them in a timely manner, I'd best be there no later than eight a.m. or she's filing a complaint."

Milo said, "What time did she call you?"

"I didn't check."

"Message still on the machine?"

"Nah, I erased it."

"Can you narrow it down?"

"Hmm," said Belleveaux. "Well, I left for the game around four, stopped by at the Soos' apartment to look at an electrical outlet, so it had to be after that."

"What time did you get home?"

"Close to midnight. Drove Anthony and Dmitri to where they parked their rental car in the Union Station lot, Anthony drove Dmitri to the airport then he drove himself to Fort Irwin."

"When you got home were Vita Berlin's lights on?"

"Let's see . . . can't rightly say. She paid her own electric, what she did with her lights was her own business."

"Where can we find the Feldmans?"

"They're good kids, still don't know about this."

"Why's that?"

"Probably at work, they're doctors— resident doctors. He's at Cedars, she's somewhere else, maybe the U., I'm not sure."

"First names?"

"David and Sondra with an *o*. Trust me, they had nothing to do with this."

"Doctors," said Milo. Thinking: *surgical cut.*

Stanleigh Belleveaux said, "Exactly. Respectable."

CHAPTER

4

By the time we left Belleveaux's house a crime lab van was parked outside the tape. Two techs, both young men, were inside the apartment. Their kits rested out on the landing. The body remained in place.

Milo said, "Lance, Kenny."

"Lieutenant," said the taller man. *L. Sakura* on his tag. "This sure is disgusting."

K. Flores didn't react.

Milo said, "Keeps life interesting. Don't let me stop you."

Flores said, "How far do you want us to take this?"

"As far as you need to."

"What I mean, Lieutenant, is there's no sign of disruption in the room, it all seems centered on the body. Obviously we'll print and look for fibers but do you see any reason to luminol?"

Sakura said, "Looks way too clean even for someone doing a mop-up. No bleach smell, either. We'll check the drains, call in a forensic plumber if the fixtures give us a problem, but we don't see much chance for significant blood evidence."

"Other than *her* blood," said Flores. "Which is probably the small spots on the towel. Even there, whoever did this was super-careful. Probably dabbed as he went and took whatever he used with him."

"This is a freak," said Sakura.

Milo said, "C.I. said most of the blood is pooled inside the body. Let's see what you pull up print- and fiber-wise then we'll talk about spraying."

Flores said, "We pulled up one thing so far, probably no big deal."

"What?"

"A note in the bedroom. We left it there."

After donning new gloves and foot coverings, we followed Flores in while Sakura began fiddling with his kit.

Vita Berlin's sleeping chamber was close, dim, spare, with walls also painted apartment-beige and linens of the same characterless hue. Double bed, no head-board or footboard, no personal touches. The books Milo had described were piled high on a white fiberboard night-stand. The surface of a three-door dresser was bare. Two more beehive lamps.

She hadn't indulged others or herself.

Flores pointed to the foot of the bed where a rumpled scrap of white paper rested. "It was underneath, I took a photo of it there, then slid it out."

We kneeled, read. In neat script some-one had written:

Dr. B. Shacker

Below that, a 310 number. A diagonal line slashed the name. At the bottom of the page, a single word in larger, darker caps:

QUACK!!!

Flores said, "There's dust and maybe crumbs down there but nothing weird."

Milo copied down the information. "Thanks, Kenny, bag it."

Back on the landing, he said, "Might as well talk to this doctor." Half smiling. "Maybe he's a surgeon."

He 411'd, got a listing.

"Bernhard Shacker, Ph.D. North Bedford Drive, Beverly Hills. A colleague, Alex: That makes it a bit more interesting, no? Vita obviously had what you guys call issues, maybe she decided to get some help, tried out therapy, changed her mind. What's that phrase you use about screwed-up folk resisting the most?"

"Baloney afraid of the slicer."

"But she got sliced anyway. Maybe Shacker can educate us on her personality. Know him?"

I shook my head.

"Bedford Drive," he said. "That's high-ticket Couch Row, seems a little frou-frou for someone who lived like Vita did." Phoning Shacker's number, he listened, frowned, clicked off.

"Recorded spiel," he said. "I like your way better."

I still use an answering service because talking to human beings is at the core of my job. "You didn't leave a message."

"Didn't want to scare him off, in case he gets all pissy about confidentiality. Also I figured maybe talking to him is something you could do. One mind-prober to another."

"While we're at it, we can figure out transmigration of the soul."

"Wouldn't put it past you, amigo. So you'll do it?"

I smiled.

He said, "Great, let's check out that restaurant."

He left his unmarked at the crime scene and we drove west to Robertson in my Seville. Bijou: A Dining Place was a brown-brick storefront set close enough to the 10 Freeway to harvest soot on its signage. The brick was grimy, too, but a picture window sparkled.

The morning special was blueberry pancakes. Posted hours said *Breakfast and Lunch Only, Closed by Three p.m.*

The restaurant's interior said it was probably a venerable diner remodeled to look even older. From the freshness of the green vinyl seating and the laminate tabletops patterned to look like Formica, a recent upgrade. The kind of movie-star headshots you see in dry cleaners hung on the walls, along with black-and-white shots of pre-freeway L.A.

An old man reading *The Wall Street Journal* sat at the counter, nursing coffee and a sweet roll. Three of seven booths were occupied: Up in front, two young moms tried to chat while tending to bibbed, squirming toddlers in booster chairs. Behind them, a husky apple-faced man in his thirties ate steak and eggs while penciling a puzzle book. At the back, a brown-uniformed parcel driver small enough to be a jockey worked on a mountain of pancakes while

grooving to his iPod. Both men looked
up when we entered, returned to their
recreation. The women were too busy
with their kids to notice.

A waitress, young, blond, shapely,
sleeve-tattooed, had the shift to herself.
A short-order cook with an Incan face
sweated behind the pass-through.

Milo waited until the waitress had re-
filled Wall Street's coffee before approaching.

She said, "Sit anywhere you like,
guys."

Her badge chirped *Hedy!* Milo's badge
ruined her smile. The old man put his
paper aside and eavesdropped.

Hedy said, "Let me get the owner."

Milo said, "Do you know Vita Berlin?"

"She eats here."

"Regularly?"

"Kind of," she said. "Like two times a
week?"

The old man said, "What'd *that* one
do, now?"

Milo faced him. "She died."

Hedy said, "Omigod!"

The old man, unperturbed, said,
"How?"

"Unnaturally."

"What does that mean? Suicide? Accident?" A bushy white eyebrow compressed to the shape of a croquet wicket. "Worse? Yeah, probably worse if the constabulary's bothering to show up."

Hedy said, "Oh, Sam."

The old man regarded her with pity.

Milo turned to him. "You knew Vita."

"Knew enough not to like her. What happened to her—she mouthed off to the wrong guy and he hauled off and bopped her one?"

Hedy said, "Omigod, Sam, this is terrible. Can I go get Ralph, Officers? He's in back."

Milo said, "Ralph's the owner?"

The old man said, "Of this gourmet establishment."

"Sure."

Hedy rushed toward the *Exit* sign.

The old man said, "They've got a thing going. Her and Ralph."

Milo said, "Sam?"

"Samuel Lipschitz, certified actuary," said the old man. "Blessedly retired." He wore a burnt-orange cardigan over a white shirt buttoned to the neck, gray hopsack slacks, argyle socks, cordovan lace-ups.

"What was it about Vita you didn't like, Mr. Lipschitz?"

"So you're verifying she was murdered."

Raising his voice on the last word caused the young mothers to look over. The driver and the puzzle-solver didn't react.

Milo said, "That wouldn't surprise you."

"Yes and no," said Lipschitz. "Yes, because murder's a low-frequency event. No, because, as I said, she had a provocative personality."

"Who'd she provoke?"

"Anyone she felt like. She was an equal-opportunity harridan."

"She was disruptive here?"

"She'd come swaggering in like a man, plop down in a booth, and start glaring, like she was just waiting for someone to do something that would give her the excuse to pull a snit. Everyone was wise to her so we ignored her. She'd sulk, order her food, eat, sulk some more, pay and leave."

Lipschitz chuckled.

"So she really pushed someone too far, ay? How'd they do it? Where'd they do it?"

"I can't get into that, sir."

"Just tell me one thing: Was it around here? I don't live in the neighborhood anymore, moved to Alhambra when I retired. But I come back to this place because I like the pastries, they get 'em from a Danish baker all the way out in Covina. So if there's something I should worry about personal-security-wise, I'd appreciate your telling me. I'm seventy-four, would like to squeeze in a few more years."

"From what we've seen, sir, there's nothing for you to worry about."

"That's ambiguous to the point of being meaningless," said Lipschitz.

"It wasn't a street crime. It doesn't appear connected to gangs or a robbery."

"When did it happen?"

"Sometime last night."

"I come here during the day I should be fine?"

"Mr. Lipschitz, is there anything else you can tell us about Vita?"

"Other than her being abrasive and antisocial? I did hear about something but I didn't witness it firsthand. A confrontation, right here. Four, five days ago, I was in Palm Springs visiting my son. Missed my pastry and all the excitement."

"Who told you about it?"

"Ralph—here he is, let him tell you himself."

Ralph Veronese was no older than thirty, tall and borderline-emaciated with long, thick dark hair, a rock star's cheekbones and slouchy stance. He wore a black bowling shirt, low-slung skinny jeans, work boots, a diamond stud in his left lobe. One arm was brocaded in blue ink.

His hands were rough, his voice soft. He asked if we could speak outside and when Milo assented, voiced his thanks profusely and guided us through the café to a rear alley. A red van occupied the single parking slot.

"Hedy just told me about Vita. I can't believe it."

"You don't see anyone wanting to hurt her?"

"No, it's not that. I mean I'm not saying someone would hurt her, it's just . . . someone you know. She was here a couple of days ago."

"She was a regular?"

"Two, three times a week."

"Big fan of the food."

Veronese didn't answer.

Milo said, "Something must've drawn her here."

"She could walk from her house. That's what she told me once. 'It's not like you're a great chef, I don't have to waste gas.' I said, 'And hopefully we won't give you any.' She didn't laugh. She never laughed."

"Cranky lady."

"Oh, yeah."

"Mr. Lipschitz said she'd had some kind of confrontation here a few days ago."

Veronese rotated his earring. "I'm sure that had nothing to do with what happened to her."

"Why's that, Mr. Veronese?"

"Mr. Veronese was my grandfather,

Ralph's fine . . . yeah, Vita had a tough personality but I just can't see anything that happened here being relevant."

"Tell us about the confrontation, Ralph."

He sighed. "There was no excuse for her behavior but I don't even know the people's names, it was the first time they were here!"

"What happened?"

"These people came in with their kid. Vita was already here, reading the *Times* that she always borrows from us and eating away."

"How many people?"

"Mom, dad, the kid was little—four, five, I'm not good with ages." Veronese tugged at a forelock, positioned it over his left eyebrow. "Bald. The kid. Skinny, these humongous eyes. Like you see on those ads for starving kids?" He tapped the crook of one arm. "Big bandage here. Like she got stuck with a shot, it was a she, a little girl."

I said, "Sounds like a sick little girl."

"Exactly, I figured cancer or something," said Veronese. He sighed. "See something like that, makes you want to cry."

I said, "Vita didn't cry."

"Oh, man." His voice tightened. "I knew she was a pain in the ass but no way I figured something like that would happen. If I had, I'da seated them far from her. I seated them right next to her, make it easy for Hedy, you know?"

"Vita wasn't happy about that?"

"At first she didn't seem to notice them, she's reading and eating, everything's copacetic. Then the kid starts making noises. Not being annoying, like a moan, you know? Like she's hurting, like something hurts. The parents are leaning over, whispering. Trying to comfort her, I guess. It goes on for a while. The moaning. Then the kid quiets down. Then she moans again and Vita puts down her paper, gives her the eye, you know?"

"Angry."

"Angry with sharp eyes," said Veronese. "What do they call it, dagger eyes? Like you can stab someone with them? My grandmother used to say that, 'Don't be shooting me those dagger eyes, you gonna draw my blood.' Vita's doing that, the dagger eyes. Right at the kid. The parents aren't noticing, they're concentrating on the kid. Finally, she quiets down again, Hedy takes their order, offers the kid a donut but the parents say the kid's stomach can't take it. Vita mutters something, the father looks over, Vita glares at him, goes back behind her paper. Then the kid starts moaning again, a little louder. The father walks to the counter and asks me for some ice cream. Like he's figuring that might calm the kid down. I say you bet and fix a double scoop, he goes back, tries to feed the kid the ice cream, she tastes it but then she's not having it. Starts crying *again.* All of a sudden, Vita's out of her booth, like this." He clamped a hand on each hip. "Looking down at them, like they're evil. Then she says something, then the kid's father is up on his feet, too, and they're going at each other."

"Going how?"

"Arguing, I couldn't hear what, 'cause I had gone back to the kitchen, same for Hedy, so all we heard was some kind of commotion. I thought something had happened to the kid, a medical emergency. So I rush back and the father and Vita are in each other's faces and he looks ready to—he's really pissed off but his wife grabs his arm, holds him back. Vita says something that makes him pull his arm free, he raises a fist. Just holds it there. Shaking. All of him is shaking. Then he calms down, swoops up the kid, and they head for the door. Funny thing is, now the kid's calm. Like nothing ever happened."

Another earring-tug. "I rush out, ask if there's something I can do. I felt like shit, a sick kid, you know? It wasn't her fault she didn't feel good. Father looks at me, shakes his head, they drive off. I go back inside, Vita's back in her booth, smiling. Says, 'Some people have no class, I told them why would you people think the rest of the world wants to see your sick little brat, ruin their appetite? Sick people belong in hospitals, not restaurants.'"

Milo said, "Describe these people."

"Thirty-five, forty," said Veronese. "Nicely dressed." Looking away.

I said, "Something else?"

"Black."

"That 'you people' part probably didn't go over well."

"Yeah," said Veronese, "that was evil."

"Did Vita show other signs of racism?"

"Nah, she hated everyone." He frowned. "Would've loved to toss her but she sues people, it's all I can do to keep this place afloat, last thing I need is to be sued."

"Who'd she sue?"

"The place she used to work, some kind of discrimination, they paid her off, that's how she lives."

"Who told you?"

"She did. Bragging."

Milo said, "The people she had a to-do with. Thirty-five to forty, well dressed, and black. What else?"

"They drove a Mercedes. Not a big one, small station wagon." Veronese scratched at his hairline. "Silver. I think. I'm sure they had nothing to do with it."

"Why's that?"

"How would they know who she was, where to find her?"

"Maybe they knew her before."

"Didn't seem that way," said Veronese.

"I mean they didn't use names or any-thing."

"Who else has Vita had words with?"

"Everyone leaves her alone."

"Big tipper, huh?"

"You kidding?—oh, yeah, you are. Her top rate's ten percent and for each thing that pisses her off, she drops a percent. And tells you. Hedy laughs about it, only reason she's here is to do me a favor, her main thing's singing, she sings in a band. I play bass behind her." Smiling. "I like looking at the back of her."

CHAPTER

5

We drove back to the crime scene. The coroner's van had taken the body. Sakura and Flores were still busy at work, scraping, diluting, bagging, tagging.

"Lots of prints," said Sakura, "where you'd expect them to be. Nothing on the doorknob, that's wiped clean. We got a few hairs off the towels, gray, consistent with hers. We did find more blood on the towels—tiny little specks tucked into the nap. Same for the carpet, we'll cut out squares. If he nicked himself operating on her, you could get lucky."

Milo said, "From your mouth to the Evidence God's ears."

Flores said, "The sink drain's kind of tricky, we are going to call in the plumber. Could take a couple of days."

"Whatever it takes, guys. Anything else?"

"I don't want to tell you your business, Lieutenant, but it was me, I'd put in for a tox screen super-stat."

"You think she was doped?"

"This little resistance, maybe the offender used something on her—like an anesthetic. Something that didn't need to be injected, like chloroform or ether, because we didn't find any needle marks. But maybe she medicated herself and that made his job easy. We found booze bottles under her bathroom sink when we were checking out the plumbing. Stashed at the back behind rolls of toilet paper."

Reaching into an evidence bag, he drew out two 177ml Jack Daniel's bottles, one sealed, the other down a third.

I said, "No booze anywhere else?"

"Nowhere."

Sakura said, "Big bottles, she bought in bulk."

I said, "She lived alone but hid her habit."

"Living alone doesn't mean she drank alone," said Milo.

"Then why hide the booze?"

He had no answer for that and it made him frown.

I said, "If she did have a drinking pal, it was someone who wouldn't pry in the bathroom."

"Meaning?"

"No intimacy."

"Behind toilet paper's not the first place anyone would look. And if she was a solitary drinker, why bother to conceal?"

"Hiding a habit from herself," I said. "Someone who needed to think of herself as totally in control. And righteous."

That didn't impress anyone.

Flores said, "What's your take on the broken neck, Lieutenant, some sort of karate move?"

"I should be checking out dojos? Asking if they have anyone likes also to cut people up and play with their guts." He turned to the pizza box. "You guys ready to open it up?"

"Sure," said Sakura. "We already dusted, no prints or anything else. Didn't feel like there was any pizza in there. Or anything else."

"Pop it."

Flores pried open the top.

Empty but on the bottom surface of the box a piece of plain white paper had been Scotch-taped, margins precise, just like the towels beneath the body. In the center of the paper someone had computer-printed in a large bold-faced font:

?

Milo flushed a deeper red than I'd ever seen. A pulse in his neck raced. For a moment I was worried about his health.

Then he grinned and some of the color faded. Like a joke had just been played on him and he was determined to be a good sport.

He said, "What's this, a fucking challenge? Fine. Game on, you bastard." To the techs: "Print every damn surface of this. Look for spots where someone would be likely to screw up and leave a partial. You don't find anything, do it again. You tell me there's nothing, I want it to really *be* nothing."

Flores said, "Yes, sir."

Sakura said, "You bet."

Milo walked me to my car, keeping slightly ahead and making me feel I was being ushered away. He leaned in when I started up the engine.

"Thanks for showing up. I'm gonna be tied up with basics: her bank, her phone records, finding next of kin. I'm also gonna try for a face-to-face with the two doctor neighbors, I get lucky they'll turn out to be Jack the Ripper and his nefarious little Jill. Meanwhile, if you could try that shrink—Shacker."

"I'll call him when I get home."

"Thanks. What you said before, the part about Vita wanting to feel in control, I agree with. Righteous, I'm not so sure. What kind of morally upright person unloads on a little sick kid?"

I said, "Righteous is a broad category. She could've seen herself as the guardian of all that's proper. Restaurants are for eating, hospitals are for sick people, disease is unappetizing, stay away. It's a common feeling. Most people are a lot more subtle but you'd be surprised how often sick people get stigmatized. Back when I worked in oncology, families talked about it all the time."

He shook his head. "However she *felt* about herself, she was a major-league jerk and that means the suspect list just expanded to the entire goddamn universe."

I shifted into Drive.

He said, "Are there diseases other than cancer that can cause baldness?"

"A few," I said, "but cancer would be my guess."

"And if the kid had cancer there's a good chance she'd be treated at your old turf."

Western Pediatric Medical, where I'd trained and worked and learned which questions to ask, which to ignore.

I said, "It's the best place in town."

"Hmm."

I said, "Sorry, no."

"No, what?"

"You're my pal but I'm not going snooping in the oncology files."

He poked his chest. "I would ask for such a thing? Now I know what you *really* think of me."

"I think you're being your usual ace-detective self."

His nostrils flared. "Oh, man, we go too far back to spread the bullshit. Yeah, I'd love for you to dig around. You can't do it, even discreetly?"

"There's no way to do it discreetly. And even if there was, I wouldn't want to be the one pointing a finger at a family that's had more than enough to cope with."

He exhaled. "Yeah, yeah, I'm thinking like a hunter, not a human being."

"You're unlikely to be losing a lead, Big Guy. Like Veronese said, no way for them to know who Vita was and where she lived."

"Unless," he said, "they live in the

neighborhood and happened to spot her and were still pissed and decided to act."

"They go back and carve her up?" I said. "That's one helluva grudge."

"True but dealing with a high level of stress could kick up the frustration level, right? What if the poor little thing passed away shortly after the confrontation? That would jam one helluva memory into Mommy and Daddy's heads. Daddy stewed on it, started eating himself up. Eating his guts out. So to speak. He spots Vita, maybe she even snots off again. He decides to—whatever you guys call it—displace his anger."

"That's what we call it." And I'd seen plenty of it. Families railing against hospital food, a misspoken phrase, anything but the core issue because you can only deal with so much. More than once I'd been called to ease a weapon away from a grieving father. But nothing at the level of the savagery visited upon Vita Berlin and I said so.

Milo said, "So if I wanna go there, I'm on my own."

"Where I'm going is phoning Dr.

Shacker. If he has an opening, I'll priori-
tize a meeting."

"Thanks."

"No problem."

"Oh, there are plenty of problems," he
said. "But they're all mine."

CHAPTER

6

I drove home thinking about the horror, tried to switch off The Unthinkable Channel.

The body floated back into my head.

Switching on the radio, I amped the volume to ear-bruise. Knowing that each thunder-chunk of noise was ripping loose tiny hairs in my auditory canal but figuring a little hearing loss was worth it. But station-surfing fed me a bland stew of passionless jingly crap and nerve-scraping chatter that failed to do the trick, so I pulled over, popped the trunk,

took out a battered black vinyl case I
hadn't touched in a long time.

Audiocassettes.

To anyone under thirty, as relevant as
wax cylinders. The Seville has a different opinion. She's a '79 who rumbled
out of Detroit a few months before Detroit turned her successors into Bloat-
mobiles. Fifteen thousand miles on the
third engine with an enhanced suspension. Regular oil and filter changes keep
her appeased. I retrofitted a CD player
years ago, a hands-off phone system
recently. But I've resisted an MP3 and
kept the original tape deck in place because back when I was a grad student
tapes were a major luxury and I've got
lots of them, purchased secondhand
back when that mattered.

As I got back in the car, the growling
in my head grew thunderous. I've seen
a lot of bad things and I don't get that
way often but I'm pretty sure where the
noise comes from: hiding from my father when he drank too much and decided someone needed to be punished.
Blocking the *bump-bump* of my racing
heart with imaginary white noise.

But now I couldn't turn it off and just as amphetamines quiet a hyperactive mind, my consciousness craved something loud and dark and aggressively competitive.

Thrash metal might've been nice but I'd never bought any. I flipped through tapes, found something promising: ZZ Top. *Eliminator.*

I slipped the tape into the deck, started up the car, resumed the drive home. Covered a block and cranked the music louder.

Minimalistic guitar, truck-engine drum, and ominous synthesizer backup worked pretty well. Then I turned off Sunset and got close to home and the peace and beauty of Beverly Glen, the sinuous silence of the old bridal path leading up to my pretty white house, the prospect of kissing my beautiful girlfriend, patting my adorable dog, feeding the pretty fish in my pond, sparked a sly little voice:

Nice life, huh?

Then: malevolent laughter.

The house was empty and sun-suffused. Wood floors tom-tommed as I trudged to my office and left a collegial message for Dr. Bernhard Shacker. His soft, reassuring, recorded voice promised he'd get back to me as soon as possible. The kind of voice you believed. I made coffee, drank two cups without tasting, went out back and tossed pellets to the koi and tried to appreciate their slurpy gratitude and continued on to the tree-shrouded studio out back.

A saw-buzz sounded through an open window. Beautiful Girlfriend was goggled and masked and brightened by skylights set into the high sloping ceiling as she eased a piece of rosewood through a band saw. Long auburn curls were bunched under a red bandanna. Her hands were coated with purplish dust.

Adorable Dog crouched a few feet away, nibbling on one of the barbecue-sauce-crusted bones Girlfriend prepares for her with customary meticulousness.

Girlfriend smiled, kept her hands working. Dog waddled over and kissed my hand.

The saw rasped as it ate hardwood. Loud, nasty. Good.

◆

I sat with Blanche on my lap until Robin finished working, rubbing a knobby little French bulldog head. Robin switched off the saw, placed the guitar-shaped slab on her worktable, pushed up the goggles, and lowered the mask. She had on red overalls, a black T-shirt, black-and-white Keds.

I placed Blanche on the floor and she followed me to the bench. Robin and I hugged and kissed and she mussed my hair the way I like.

"How'd it go, baby?"

I touched the rosewood. "Nice grain."

"One of those days?" she said.

How much I talk about cases has always been an issue for us. I've progressed from shutting her out completely to parceling the information I think she can handle. Sometimes it works in Milo's favor because Robin is smart and able to bring in an outsider's perspective.

As if I'm an insider. I'm not sure what I am.

I said, "Definitely one of those."

She touched my face. "You're a little pale. Have you eaten?"

"Bagel before."

"Want something now?"

"Maybe later."

"If you change your mind," she said.

"About food?"

"About anything."

"Sure." I kissed her forehead.

She eyed the rosewood. "I guess I should get back to this."

I said, "Dinner will probably work. Maybe a little on the late side."

"Sounds good."

"If you get hungry sooner, I'm flexible."

"You bet," she said.

As I turned to leave, she touched my face. Her almond eyes were soft with compassion. "The bad days, long-term planning doesn't work so well."

I returned to my office. No call-back from Dr. Shacker. I did some paperwork, paid some bills, got on the computer.

A search of *disemboweling* and *murder* pulled up a disquieting mountain of hits: just under a hundred thousand.

Nearly all were irrelevant, resulting from the use of both words in complex sentences, song lyrics by deservedly obscure bands, political hyperbole by blogo-simps who've never lived with anything worse than a paper cut. (*"The current administration is disemboweling civil liberties and committing premeditated murder on personal liberties with the bloody abandon of a serial killer."*)

The literal murders I found were mostly single-victim crimes: stalking outrages fueled by sexual fantasy or long-simmering resentment before building to a starburst of violence that led to mutilation and sometimes cannibalism. The crimes were generally carried out carelessly and solves were quick. In several cases, floridly psychotic suspects turned themselves in. In one instance, an offender dropped a human liver on the desk of a police receptionist and begged to be arrested because he'd done a "bad thing."

The few open cases were of the historical variety, most notably Jack the Ripper.

The scourge of Whitechapel had en-

gaged in abdominal mutilation and organ theft, but differences outweighed
any similarities to the meticulously organized degradation visited upon Vita Berlin.

Vita's abrasive personality said this
could very well be a one-off.

I hoped to God it had nothing to do
with the child she'd humiliated.

I surfed a bit more, trying *abdominal
mutilation, visceral display, intestinal
wounds,* had gotten nowhere when my
service called.

"Dr. Delaware, it's Louise. A Dr. Shacker
just called, returning yours."

"Thanks."

"He's one of you, right? A psychologist."

"Good guess, Louise."

"Actually, it's more than a guess, Dr.
Delaware, it's intuition. I've been doing
this a long time."

"We all sound alike?"

"Actually you kind of do," she said.
"No offense, I mean that in a good way.
You guys tend to be calm and patient.
Surgeons don't sound like that. Anyway,

he seemed like a nice guy. Have a good day, Dr. Delaware."

A pleasant, boyish voice said, "Bern Shacker."

"Alex Delaware, thanks for calling back."

"No problem," he said. "You said this was about Vita. Does that mean you're the lucky guy treating her now?"

"I'm afraid no one's treating her."

"Oh?"

"She's been murdered."

"My God. What happened?"

I gave him the basics.

He said, "That's dreadful, absolutely dreadful. Murdered . . . and you're calling me because . . ."

Because Vita had labeled him a quack. I said, "She had your card in her apartment."

"Did she . . . her apartment? I'm a little—you said you were a psychologist. Why would you be in her apartment? And why, for that matter, are you following up on a murder?"

"I consult to the police and the detective in charge asked me to call you. One shrink to another."

"Shrink," he said. "Unfortunate term . . . well, I don't really—I didn't exactly engage in long-term therapy with Vita—this is a bit complicated. I need to make a call or two before we go any further."

"Death and confidentiality," I said. "The rules change every year."

"True, but it's not only that," said Shacker. "Vita wasn't a typical therapy patient. I'm not trying to be mysterious but I can't say more until I get clearance. If I do, we can chat."

"Appreciate it, Dr. Shacker."

"Murder," he said. "Unbelievable. Where are you located?"

"The Westside."

"I'm in Beverly Hills. If we do talk, would you mind it being face-to-face? So I can document the conversation?"

"That would be fine."

"I'll get back to you."

Forty-three minutes later, he was true to his word. "Alex? This is Bern. The insurance attorneys have cleared me and so did my personal attorney. I've got an opening at six. Does that work for you?"

"Perfectly."

"Perfectly," he echoed. "You sound like a positive person."

As if he'd just uncovered a character flaw.

"I try."

"Try," said Shacker, "is all we can do."

CHAPTER

7

Shacker's building was three stories of lime and brick in the midst of Beverly Hills' business district. Glossy navy carpeting smothered footsteps. Walls were paneled in bleached oak. A pharmacy calling itself a Dispensing Apothecarie and designed to look Victorian took up a quarter of the ground floor. The rest of the tenants were M.D.'s, D.D.S.'s, a few other psychologists.

B. Shacker, Ph.D., Suite 207.

His waiting room was tiny, white, and set up with three friendly chairs and a wall-stack of magazines. Soft new-age music played from somewhere. A two-bulb panel sat to the left of the inner door. Red for *In Session,* green for free. Red was illuminated but moments after I sat down, it went dark.

The door opened. An arm extended. "Alex? Bern Shacker."

The body attached to the arm was five six, thin, narrow-shouldered. The handshake offered was firm, dry, solid.

Shacker looked around fifty. A fine-boned, rosy-cheeked face was topped by thinning chestnut hair laced with silver and styled in a not-too-bad comb-over. Prominent ears and a slightly crooked pug nose gave him an elfin look. His eyes were soft, hazel, vaguely rueful. He wore a gray V-neck sweater over a black shirt, charcoal slacks, black loafers. The sleeves of the sweater were pushed to his elbows. Black shirt-cuffs overlapped the edges.

"Thanks for taking the time, Bern."

"Please, come in."

The treatment room was painted pale aqua, carpeted in a darker variant of the same hue, dimmed by brown silk drapes shielding the window that looked out to

Bedford Drive. Not a trace of street noise; double- or triple-glazed glass. The requisite professional paper adorned the wall behind a modest walnut desk: doctorate, internship, postdoc, license. The only thing mildly interesting was a Ph.D. from the University of Louvain in Belgium.

Shacker said, "My Catholic days," and smiled.

The wall to the left of the desk bore the auxiliary door that had allowed Shacker's patient to exit into the hallway without encountering me. Next to that hung a chrome-framed cubist print of fruit and bread. Two Scandinavian leather chairs sat in front of the desk, facing each other. Shacker motioned me to one, took the other.

He crossed a leg, tugged his trousers up, flashed argyle sock. "Over the phone I mentioned insurance lawyers. They're the ones who sent Vita to me."

"Therapy was part of a settlement?"

"Three years ago she sued her employer. The case dragged on. Finally the employer's coverer was ready to settle but insisted upon a psych evaluation.

Insurance work isn't my usual thing but I'd treated an individual with a connection to the insurer—obviously I can't say more—and was asked to see Vita."

I said, "What was the purpose of the evaluation?"

"To see if she was malingering."

"She was claiming some sort of emotional damage?"

"Supposedly she'd been bullied at work and the company hadn't done enough to ensure a hostility-free work environment."

"What company are we talking about?"

Shacker recrossed his legs. "I'm sorry, I can't give you that, one condition of the settlement was a ban on discussion by both sides. What I can tell you is that it was an insurance company. Health insurance, to be exact. Vita worked for them as a screener."

"She decided who got care and who didn't?"

"The company would call it managing the flow of treatment requests."

"Was she a nurse?"

"She'd had two years of secretarial

school and her employment history consisted of nonmedical clerical positions."

"That qualified her to decide who got
to talk to a doctor?"

"Who got to talk to a *nurse*," he said.
"She was a *pre*-screening screener. It's
called diagnosis-specific utilization management and yes, it's atrocious. Vita
described working at a huge phone-
bank, claimed she'd been provided
scripts to read from. Certain conditions
were to be ignored, for others she'd
suggest an over-the-counter remedy.
She was given a list of various call-back
protocols—a week for this, a month for
that. Acute conditions were to be referred to local emergency rooms, serious diagnoses were put on hold as she
pretended to search for the next available nurse."

I said, "Telemarketing in reverse: Don't
use our product."

Shacker said, "This is what it's come
to. What was different about Vita was
that she loved her job. Getting back at
'weaklings' and 'fakers.'"

I said, "That didn't apply to her post-
traumatic symptoms."

He smiled. "What can I tell you?"

"What kind of bullying are we talking about?"

"No physical intimidation, just pranks and ridicule from some of her co-workers. Vita said she complained repeatedly to her supervisors but was ignored. Her suit was for five million dollars."

"High-priced ridicule. What were her symptoms?"

"Difficulty concentrating, insomnia, appetite loss, stomach problems, aches and pains. Ambiguous things unlikely to show up on a medical exam but impossible to disprove. Since the alleged root cause was emotional trauma, the health insurer's casualty insurer wanted an official opinion as to her psychological status."

"What did you tell them?"

"That her claims couldn't be validated or invalidated and that she came across as a hostile individual. I didn't offer a diagnosis as it wasn't requested. Had I been asked, I suppose I could've dug around the DSM for something that fit, but I'm not one of those therapists who feel bad behavior's a disease."

"What was Vita's bad behavior?"

He folded his arms across his chest. "May I tell you something in utter confidence, Alex? Really, I don't want this entered in any official record."

"Absolutely."

"Thank you." He chewed his lip, played with a sleeve. "Vita was quite possibly the least pleasant person I've ever met. I know we're not supposed to judge, but let's face it, we do. It didn't help that she had no motivation to cooperate and regarded our profession with obvious disdain. Most of our sessions consisted of her complaining that I was wasting her time. That anyone with half a brain could see she'd suffered grievous injury. She just about came out and called me a quack. Now you tell me she's been murdered. Was there evidence of rage? Because I can see her inciting someone's anger past the point of no return."

"I'm also limited in what I can say, Bern."

"I see . . . all right. Then that's really all I can tell you."

"Could we go back to her lawsuit?

What kind of pranks and ridicule did she say she'd experienced?"

"Gluing her desk drawer shut, hiding her headset, making off with her snacks. She claimed she overheard people referring to her as the 'Mad Cow' and 'Grumpy Gertie.'"

"Claimed," I said. "You think she was pouring it on."

"I have no doubt she wasn't popular but all I had to go on was her self-report. The question in my mind was what role did her behavior play in provoking hostility? But figuring that out wasn't my job. I was asked to render an opinion about her faking and couldn't. Apparently that was enough because the settlement went through."

"How much of the five million did she get?"

"I wasn't privy to details but the lawyer said it was considerably less—under a million."

"Pretty nice payoff for having your drawers glued."

Shacker stifled a laugh that pitched his spare frame forward, as if he'd been shoved from behind. "Forgive me, this is a terrible situation. But what you just said—'Having her drawers glued.' I'm no Freudian, but that's some image, no? And you could certainly describe Vita as being sealed up. In every way."

"No sex life?"

"Nonexistent sex life and social life, according to her. She said she preferred it that way. Was that true or merely rationalization? I don't know. In fact, I can't say anything about her with confidence because I never got to see her long enough to break through the resistance. In the end, it didn't matter: She got what she wanted. That's the world we're living in, Alex. Genuinely sick people encounter the likes of Vita who block their treatment and big money's doled out for exaggerated claims because it's cheaper to settle."

"What's the name of the lawyer who represented her?"

"I asked for official documents but never got them, had to work from a case summary provided by the casualty insurers."

"Why all the hush-hush?"

"Their position was I needed to be

viewed as objective in case my conclusions were called into question."

The regretful look in his eyes deepened. "Looking back, sure, I was used. I'll never repeat the experience."

"What kind of personal information did Vita give you?"

"Not much, taking a history was an ordeal," he said. "I did get her to grudgingly admit to a difficult childhood. But once again, can we be sure Vita didn't bring some of that upon herself?"

"Cranky kid."

"I've come to appreciate the importance of temperament. We're all dealt set hands, the key is how we play them. After observing Vita Berlin as a middle-aged woman it's hard to imagine her as a sweet, cheerful child. But I could be wrong. Perhaps something turned her sour."

"Was she ever married?"

"She admitted to an early marriage but refused to talk about it. There was one sibling, a sister, they grew up near Chicago. Vita moved to L.A. ten years ago because she hated the weather in the Midwest. But she hated L.A., too. Everyone was stupid, superficial. Anything else—oh, yes, she never had children, detested kids, called them wastes of sperm and eggs—her phrasing. So how long have you worked for the police?"

"I'm not on payroll, more of an independent contractor."

"Sounds interesting," said Shacker. "Seeing the dark side and all that. Though I'm not sure I could handle it. To tell the truth, I'm really not that curious about horrible things. All those terrible dyssynchronies."

"Me, neither," I lied. "It's the solution that's gratifying."

"My impression is that profiling has turned out to be quite a dud."

"Cookbooking never works. Could I ask you a few more questions about Vita?"

"Such as?"

"Did she have friends or outside interests?"

"My impression is she was somewhat of a homebody."

"Did you pick up any signs of substance abuse?"

"No. Why?"

"The police found a couple of bulk-sized whiskey bottles in her apartment. Hidden."

"Did they? Well, that's humbling, Alex, I never caught that. Not that I could be expected to, given her resistance." He looked at his watch. "If there's nothing else—"

"How many sessions did she have?"

"A few—six, seven."

"Do you have her chart here?"

"The insurance company took possession of all records."

His desk phone rang. He went over and picked it up. "Dr. Shacker . . . oh, hi . . . well, I could squeeze you in today if that would work . . . yes, of course, it's my pleasure, we'll go over all of that once you're here."

Hanging up, he said, "There's one more thing, Alex. I probably shouldn't be telling you, but I will. She mentioned the name of one of the people who'd harassed her. Samantha, no last name. Might that help?"

"It might. Thanks."

"No problem. Now back to doing what we were trained for, eh? Nice to meet you, Alex."

CHAPTER

8

Walking to the Seville, I thought about the question mark in the pizza box. An old case I'd forgotten.

Milo had assumed a taunt but maybe a question really had been posed. I called his office. He said, "You get an appointment with that shrink?"

"Just finished meeting with him." I summed up.

"Post-traumatic hoohah and a bully named Samantha? It's a start, thank you, Doctor."

"Unfortunately, Shacker's bound by a

confidentiality clause, couldn't tell me what company Vita worked for."

He said, "Well-Start Health Management and Assurance. 'Your well-being is where we start.'"

"Oh."

"Found some of her papers tucked in a kitchen cabinet, including five years of tax returns. She spent two of them at Well-Start, did temp office jobs before that, averaged around thirty G a year. Last year she deposited five hundred eighty-three G in a brokerage account, which threw me, but now it makes sense: a fat, onetime settlement. The money's been sitting in preferred stock paying around six percent interest. A little over thirty-three G a year, so she was getting paid more not to work."

I said, "It sounds like a job she could've enjoyed."

He said, "The chance to torment people every day? Fits what we know about her. I'm gonna try and find this Samantha, work my way through everyone Vita accused of harassing her. Meanwhile Reed and Binchy are visiting every damn pizza joint in a ten-mile radius, see if they can find someone who uses those boxes. I put in a call to the manufacturer, maybe they ship to private parties as well and I'll get lucky and they'll find some weirdo put in an order. Any other insights?"

"That question mark," I said. "I'm not sure it was a taunt."

"What then?"

"Maybe our bad guy was referring to himself: *I'm curious.*"

"About what?"

"The mysteries of the human body."

"A do-it-yourself anatomy lesson? Seemed more to me like abusing the victim."

"Could be."

"You really see this as mining for gore?"

"The way everything was ordered, the meticulous cleanup reminded me of a patient I saw years ago, when I was a postdoc. Ten-year-old boy, extremely bright, polite, well behaved. No problems at all other than some pretty freaky cruelty to animals. Sadistic psychopaths often start by torturing small critters but this kid didn't seem to derive any pleasure from dominance or inflicting pain. He'd capture mice and squirrels in humane traps, hold gasoline-soaked rags over their noses till they died, make sure never to bruise them. 'I hold them just hard enough,' he told me. 'I never hurt them, that would be wrong.' Their death throes bothered him. He shuddered when I asked him about it. But he viewed his hobby as a legitimate science experiment. He dissected meticulously, removed every organ, studied, sketched. Both parents worked full-time, had no idea. His babysitter found him conducting surgery behind the garage and freaked out. As did Mom and Dad. The adult reactions frightened him and he refused to talk about anything he'd done so they sent him to Langley Porter and I got the case. Eventually I got him to talk, but it took months. He really didn't understand what the fuss was about. He'd been taught that curiosity was a good thing and he was curious about what made animals 'work.' Dad was a physicist, Mom a microbiologist, science was the family religion, how was he any different from them? The truth was, both parents had odd personalities—what would now be called Asperger spectrum—and Kevin really *wasn't* much different."

"What'd you do with him?"

"I arranged for anatomy lessons from one of the pathology fellows, had his parents buy him books on the subject, and got him to pledge to limit his interest to reading. He agreed reluctantly but let me know that once he was old enough to take biology with a lab he'd be doing the same exact thing and everyone would think he was smart."

"Maybe we should find out what happened to this little genius."

"What happened to him is when he was seventeen he went hiking in the Sierras looking for specimens, fell off a cliff, and died. His mother thought I deserved to know because I was one of the few people Kevin talked about with any positivity."

"So maybe I've got myself a Kevinoid who never got help."

"A grown-up Kevinoid still stuck in a

childhood that could range from eccentric to highly disordered. The urges are durable and now he's got the maturity and the physical strength to pull off a grand expedition. The precision I saw suggests he's done it before, but I haven't been able to find anything similar. So maybe up until this point he's adopted the optimal strategy: hide or get rid of the body."

"Why switch to show-and-tell with Vita?"

"He's bored, needs a bigger thrill. Or the killing had to do with Vita, specifically. If you can find the ex-husband or the sister, they might shed some light on it."

He said, "Sure, but first let's see what mean ol' Samantha has to say for herself."

Armed with the fact that Vita had worked for Well-Start, finding her tormentor was easy.

During the time it took Robin to shower, I pulled up several photos on the company's employee website, including a group shot, from last year's "Quality Control Department" Christmas party.

Twenty-two unremarkable human beings who got paid to make life difficult for sick people. Not a set of horns in sight. No evidence of guilt eroding holiday spirit.

Samantha Pelleter was chairperson of the Celebration Committee and she appeared in three photos.

Short, pudgy, fortyish, blond. Mile-wide grin.

Being elected or appointed chairperson implied she had leadership qualities and that wasn't at odds with her playing a dominant role in any harassment. But no way was she big enough to overpower a woman as substantial as Vita.

Leadership could also mean subordinates.

I called Milo again. He said, "Just found her myself, meeting her tomorrow at eleven. I'm assuming you don't want to miss the fun?"

"Where's it happening?"

"Her place, she's on reduced hours due to budget issues. Sounded scared witless about being contacted by the police but didn't put up a fuss. As to her curiosity level, we'll see. Meanwhile, mine's spiking out of control."

CHAPTER

9

He picked me up the following morning. "Got your earplugs? She lives right near the airport, I'm talking flight-path hell. This is probably why."

He handed me two sheets of paper. The first contained Samantha Pelleter's credit report. Two bankruptcies in the last ten years, a foreclosed house in San Fernando, a slew of confiscated credit cards. The second page bore his handwritten notes: Pelleter had no criminal record, owned no property. County records pulled up a divorce six months prior to losing her home.

"Her title's a mouthful," he said. "Qual-
ification consultant. Looks like that and
chairing the company party supplied
more ego dollars than the real stuff. This
is a lady on the downslide and I'm wondering if that's related to some sort of
serious mental problem."

"I found a picture of her. She's small."

"I know, got her stats. So she's got a
large friend. Maybe someone else at
Well-Start who Vita accused."

"A revenge killing?"

"Talk about a classic motive."

"Maybe."

"You don't think so."

"Don't know enough to think."

He laughed. "Like the engine ever
stops running."

Samantha Pelleter lived in a two-story,
block-wide apartment building within
walking distance of Sepulveda Boulevard. Aging stucco was the color of
freezer-burned chicken. Incoming planes
descended at angles that seemed too
acute, casting terrible shadows, turning
conversation moot. The air smelled of
jet fuel. Not a tree in sight.

Pelleter lived in a ground-floor flat on the west end of the complex. The half-second lapse between buzzer-push and open door said she'd been waiting for us. From the look in her eyes and a freshly gnawed thumbnail, not a relaxed wait.

Milo introduced himself.

She said, "Sure, sure, come in. Please."

The apartment was small, dim, generically furnished, not dissimilar to Vita Berlin's place.

The woman Vita had accused of masterminding harassment was a shrunken figure with a quavering voice and the slumped-shouldered resignation of a child waiting to be slapped. Watery eyes were blue and so was her expression. Blond had mostly ceded to gray. Her haircut was short, ragged, probably a do-it-yourself. She fooled with the hem of a faded red sweatshirt. A misshapen glass pendant hanging from a thin black cord was her sole adornment. The glass was chipped at one end.

Brushing off the seats of the folding chairs she offered us, she hustled to a cluttered kitchenette, returned with a plastic tray bearing a pitcher, two cups, a jar of instant coffee, a pair of tea bags, loose packets of sugar and sweetener.

"Hot water," she said. "So you guys can have coffee or tea whatever. All's I have is decaf, sorry."

"Thanks, Ms. Pelleter," said Milo, but he didn't touch anything on the tray and neither did I.

She said, "Oh, I forgot the cookies," and turned back.

Milo placed a gentle hand atop her forearm. That was enough to freeze her in place. The blue eyes turned huge.

"Not necessary, Ms. Pelleter, but thanks again. Now please sit down so we can chat."

She tugged an index finger as if trying to remove a nonexistent ring. Complied. "Chat about Vita? I don't get it, all that happened last year, it was supposed to be over."

"The lawsuit."

"Not allowed to talk about it, sorry."

I said, "Must've been an ordeal."

"Not for her, she got rich. The rest of us—no, no, I can't talk about it."

"Her accusations were false?"

"Totally, totally, totally. I never did anything to her."

"What about other people at Well-Start?"

"I—they—Vita was the most—I'm sorry, I'm not allowed to discuss it. I'm really not."

I said, "From what we've heard, Vita had trouble getting along with everyone."

"Ain't that the freakin' truth," said Samantha Pelleter. Blushing. "Pardon my language. But she makes me so . . . frustrated."

"Makes you? You're still in contact?"

"Huh? Oh, no, no way. I haven't seen her since. And I *really* can't talk about it. The lawyers said anyone who stepped out of line was finished, it had already cost the company—" She placed a finger over her lips. "I don't know what's wrong with me, I keep going back to it."

"It upset you," I said.

"Yes, but I'm sorry, I can't. I need my job, I need it bad. As is, they cut us back to twenty-five hours a week. So please.

I'm sorry if you wasted your time, but I *can't*."

I said, "How about we talk about Vita apart from the lawsuit?"

"I don't know anything about Vita apart from the lawsuit. What's going on, anyway? Is she claiming something else? Not happy with what she got? That's crazy, she's the only one who came out ahead."

"Was anyone fired because of her?"

Samantha Pelleter shook her head. "The company didn't want more lawsuits. But none of us got bonuses."

"Meanwhile, Vita's rich."

"Bitch," she said. "I still don't get what this is about."

I turned to Milo.

He said, "Vita's gotten herself in trouble."

"Oh," said Samantha Pelleter. "Oh, wow." New, improved brand of smile. She went into the kitchenette, returned with a box of Oreos, picked one out of the box, and nibbled. "You're saying she tried to con someone else with false accusations and got caught? You want me to say she was a con? I'd love to help you guys, but I can't."

"She was a big-time liar, huh?"

"You have no idea."

"What else did she lie about besides the lawsuit?"

"We have scripts, are supposed to stick to them. Did that matter to Vita? Not a chance."

"She improvised."

"Oh, boy did she. Like with a flu-type thing we're supposed to start by having them list all their symptoms. We take our time so if it's not serious just their talking about it will show them it's no big deal and they'll change their mind about wanting an appointment. If they don't, we suggest over-the-counter meds. And drinking fluids, because let's face it, that's enough in most cases. If they get stubborn or call back, we ask if they've got a fever and if they don't, we tell them they're probably getting better, time will heal, but if they really need an appointment we've got one but it's during working hours. After they've been cleared by the nurse. If they want to pursue that, we

put them on the nurse's call-back list.
It's a system, you know?"

"Vita wasn't satisfied with that."

"Vita would throw in her own stuff.
Give them advice. Like try getting your
mind off your problems. Concentrate on
something else, stress is the cause of
most symptoms, take a look at yours.
Once I actually heard her tell someone
to suck it up, colds were no big deal.
That kind of thing."

I said, "How'd people react?"

She said, "They didn't like it. Sometimes Vita would just hang up on them
before they could complain, sometimes
she'd stay on the line and let them complain. Holding the phone like this."
Stretching her arm. "Away from her ear,
you know. You could hear noise coming
out of the phone like *chirp chirp chirp.*
Vita just smiled and let them go on."

"Enjoying herself."

"She's one of the meanest people I
ever met."

"Did policyholders complain about
her?"

"I'm sure they tried but it would be
tough. We never give our names out and

our extensions are switched all the time so no one gets the same consultant twice."

"High level of customer service," I said.

"It's to keep costs down," she said. "So really sick people can get care."

"You saw Vita improvise. Meaning you sat near her."

"Right next to her. If I was smart, I'd have kept my darn mouth shut. But it bothered me, doing her own thing, so I said something to her."

"What'd you say?"

"'You know, Vita, you really shouldn't leave the script.'" She winced.

I said, "She didn't take that well."

"Actually, she ignored me, like I wasn't even there—talk to the hand. But a few days later she looked real mad so she must've found out."

"Found out what?"

Pelleter looked to the side. "I was stupid. Because I cared."

"You talked to someone else."

"Not a supervisor, just one of the other consultants and they must've snitched because Vita got called in to a supervisor and when she got back to her cubicle she had a crazy look in her eyes, boiling mad. Nothing happened until after the first break but then all of a sudden she's all over me, claiming I'm—a bunch of us—are bullies, we've never treated her like a human being, are out to persecute her."

"How'd you react to that?"

"I didn't do anything, I was so freaked out. But no, I can't talk about it. Please. No more questions."

Milo leaned in close. "Samantha, I promise you nothing you say will get back to the lawyers."

"How can I be sure? I never really snitched on Vita but she thought I did and that's what started the whole thing."

He edged within an inch of her knees. "We know how to keep a secret, Samantha."

"Whatever . . . so what kind of con did she try this time?"

"I know you didn't harass her, Samantha, but did she have any particular problems with another consultant?"

"No one likes her, what goes around comes around."

"Any special bad karma with someone else at work?"

"Everyone avoided her," she said. "But no one bullied her. No one. What'd she do that you're so interested?"

"Nothing."

"Nothing? You said she was in trouble."

"She is, Samantha. The worst kind of trouble."

"I don't understand."

"She's dead, Samantha."

"Huh? What? How?"

"Someone killed her."

"What're you *saying*? That's crazy!"

Milo didn't reply.

She made a run for the kitchenette, stared at the fridge, returned, wringing her hands. "Killed? Oh my God oh my God oh my God. *Killed?* Really? Someone *killed* her? Who? When?"

"Who we don't know. When was the night before last, Samantha."

"So then why are you—oh, no, no, *God* no, not that, you can't believe I'd ever—no, it wasn't like that. I mean I don't—didn't like her but that? No no no no no. No uh-uh. *No.*"

"We're talking to everyone in Vita's past."

"I'm not in her past! Please. I can't stand this!"

"Sorry to upset you, Samantha—"

"I am upset. I'm totally upset. That you would *think* that? That you would—"

"Please sit back down, Samantha, so we can clear this up quickly and be out of your way."

He motioned toward the chair she'd vacated. She stared, sank down. "I really can't take any more stress. I'm like at the end of my—my freakin' husband cheated on me with who was supposed to be my freakin' friend. Then he left me with a pile of debt I didn't even know about that lost me my house and screwed up my credit. Do you know what I used to have? A three-bedroom house in Tujunga, I used to have a horse I rode out in Shadow Hills. I used to have a Jeep Wagoneer. Now you're coming here and thinking terrible things about me and if you go to the company and say those things I won't even have my *job*!"

Milo said, "No one suspects you, Samantha, this is routine. Which is why I need to ask you—even though it's a crazy question—where were you the night before last?"

"Where was I? I was here. I don't go anywhere, it takes money to go anywhere. I watched TV. I used to have a fifty-inch flat-screen. Now I have a little computer screen in my bedroom, everything's tiny, my whole freakin' world's tiny."

Covering her mouth with her hands, she wept.

Maybe the closest to mourning Vita Berlin would merit.

Milo fetched her water and when she stopped crying, eased the glass toward her lips while resting a big paw on her forearm.

She drank. Wiped her eyes. "Thank you."

"Thank you for putting up with us, Samantha. Now please give us the names of the other people Vita claimed had harassed her."

I expected resistance but Samantha

Pelleter's mouth set crookedly. This smile was hard to characterize.

"You bet," she said. "I'll write you out a list. Time to look out for myself, I don't care about anyone else's issues."

From a kitchenette drawer, she retrieved a scrap of paper and a pen. Writing quickly, she presented the list to Milo as if it were a school project.

1. Cleve Dawkins
2. Andrew Montoya
3. Candace Baumgartner
4. Zane Banion

"Appreciate it, Samantha. Are any of these people unusually strong?"

"Sure," she said. "Zane is big and strong. He's fat, but he used to play football. And Andrew's into fitness. He bikes to work, says if people took care of themselves they wouldn't get sick in the first place."

"What about Cleve and Candace?"

"They're regular."

"They stick to the script."

"We all do," she said. "That's the point."

◆

Milo drove north on Sepulveda. "Little Miss Sealed Lips, but get her feeling threatened and she rats out her work buddies. Any alarm bells go off?"

"As a psychologist, her fragility bothers me. As your lackey, I don't see her as a serious suspect."

"Lackey? And here I was thinking sage or pundit."

"Well," I said, "once upon a time there was a particularly obnoxious rooster who wouldn't stop hassling the hens in the barnyard. Finally, the farmer was forced to take action. He castrated the rooster and turned him into a pundit."

He laughed. "Sage, then. Unless you've got a story about that."

"Once upon a time, there was an obnoxious rooster . . ."

"Fine form. Anyway, I agree. If anyone lacks the nerve, the physical ability, and the smarts to do what was done to Vita, it's ol' Samantha. But maybe one of the other jokers at Well-Start will turn out to be more interesting."

He called Moe Reed, passed the four

names along, ordered background checks.

Reed said, "Will do. I had no luck with the pizza box so far but Sean's still out there. You got a call from the coroners, labs are back on Berlin."

"Too quick for a tox."

"Guess they prioritized, Loo."

"I'm talking scientifically, Moses."

"Yeah, I guess that's true," said Reed. "Okay, I'll run these jokers through, get back to you if I learn anything."

Clicking off, Milo punched in a preset number.

Dr. Clarice Jernigan said, "Hi, there."

"Labs are back so soon?"

"Who told you that?"

"That was the message I got."

"Wonderful," said Jernigan. "New secretary, she watches too much TV, likes to throw the jargon around. No, sorry to get your hopes up, Milo. Full labs will take weeks. But I *was* calling about your victim's blood alcohol and with that, you might not need the tox. She pulled a level of .26, more than thrice the legal limit. Even being the serious alcoholic her liver says she was, she'd have been pretty vulnerable. So there'd be no need to use anything else to subdue her."

"Drunk," he said.

"As the perennial black-and-white-striped mammal."

"Her liver," he said. "You've done the autopsy?"

"Not yet, but I was able to do a visual on a few organs, courtesy of your killer. Once we got rid of all the congealed blood. Which by my estimate was nearly all she started out with. Meaning your offender was meticulous, barely spilled a drop."

"Someone with medical training?"

"I can't exclude it but no, you wouldn't need anything close to that level of skill."

"What would you need?"

"The strength and confidence to perform two major incisions with a really sharp blade and a strong enough stomach to snip the intestines free. A butcher could do it. A deer hunter could do it. So could anyone with a warped mind and the wrong kind of knowledge. Which you can get off the Internet, if so inclined. In any event, I didn't need to dissect the liver to know it was seriously cirrhotic. Most of the darn thing was fatty and gray, not a pretty thing to behold. But as I said, even with her being a lush, a .26 could've seriously affected her judgment, reaction time, coordination, and strength. A cinch to overpower. Ask Dr. Delaware next time you speak to him. He can probably give you some behavioral parameters."

I said, "I'm here, Clarice."

"Oh, hi. You concur?"

"Completely."

"Great," she said. "It's nice when there's peace in the valley. Milo, I'll do my best to get the autopsy done by tomorrow. I'll be traveling so one of my people will do the actual cutting, but I'll keep an eye on it."

"Thanks."

"That said, don't be expecting any profound conclusions. She died from a broken neck, was well dead before he cut her up."

"How long is well dead?"

"Enough time for the blood to settle, which is minutes, not hours. I'm picturing your creep sitting there, waiting, that was a big part of his fun. What do you think, Alex?"

"Makes sense."

"Oh, if my teenagers could hear this. Mommy's not always wrong. Bye, guys."

CHAPTER

10

For three days, I heard nothing from Milo. On the fourth morning, he came to the house, vinyl attaché in hand, wearing a black poly suit with lapels from two decades ago and a pumpkin-orange tie and muttering, "Yeah, yeah, happy Halloween." He flicked a pocket flap that buttoned. "Vintage. Live long enough, everything comes back."

Hard to read his emotions. He cruised past me into the kitchen, did his usual surveillance. Robin and I had been going out to dinner regularly so the fridge was light on leftovers. He made do with beer, bread, mayo, hot sauce, barbecue sauce, steak sauce, mustard, ground horseradish sauce, and three long-forgotten lamb sausages yanked from the back of the freezer that he microwaved into submission.

After several gulps of haphazard sandwich, he took a long swig of Grolsch. "Good morning, boys and girls, can you spell futility?"

Another long swallow of beer. "No one local uses that type of pizza box and all the alleged Well-Start bullies have alibis. None of them looked good, anyway. The female is pushing sixty, was babysitting her grandkid, the physical fitness guy was on a nighttime mountain bike ride in Griffith Park vouched for by members of his cycling club, the supposedly big strong guy is big but not strong—close to four hundred and uses a cane and an inhaler and the night of the murder he was at his grandmother's birthday party, verified by the waiter who served his table. The last guy wears Coke-bottle glasses and weighs in at maybe a hundred twenty and he was at the E.R. with one of his kids. Some sort of allergic reaction to shrimp, the nurse and the on-call resident say neither he nor his wife ever left the kid's side and she was hospitalized overnight."

He swigged, put the bottle down. "I resisted the temptation to ask if Daddy had pre-screened the kid so she could get treated. They all claimed to be blindsided by the lawsuit, refused to talk about details. I tried to reach someone at Well-Start's corporate headquarters, big surprise, they stonewalled. I put Sean on it 'cause he's got a high tolerance for failure and boredom and dealing with robotic turd-brains."

He constructed another teetering sandwich, polished it off. "Autopsy results came in early this morning. Like Clarice said, no surprises."

He ripped a slice of bread in half, balled it up, consumed. "Where's Robin?"

"Working out back."

"Must be nice to be productive. I located Vita's sister using phone records. Had to go back nearly a month to find an Illinois number, so we're not talking regular contact. The sister—Patricia's her name—lives in Evanston and the call was her phoning Vita on her birthday. Which, she made sure to tell me, Vita would never do for her."

"Was that after she found out Vita was dead or before?"

"After."

"Not exactly sentimental," I said. "How'd she react to the news?"

"She was shocked but it wore off and she got pretty dispassionate. Analytic, like 'Hmm, who would do something so terrible?' And she had a quick answer: 'If I was a betting woman, I'd say Jay, he despised Vita.'"

"The ex-husband?"

"Bingo, that's why everyone calls you Doctor and bows and scrapes when you enter a room. Jay is one Jackson J. Sloat. He and Vita divorced fifteen years ago but Patricia said the financial battle went on long after. Turns out he's got a record with some violence in it, lives here in L.A. Los Feliz, which is at most a forty-minute drive to Vita's place."

I said, "They hated each other, got divorced, but moved to the same city?"

"Funny about that, huh? So maybe it's one of those obsessive, love-hate things. A drop-in on ol' Jay is clearly the next step but if he is our bad guy he could be smart and manipulative and as the ex he could be expecting us. So I figured I'd tap your ample brain for strategy."

"When were you planning on talking to him?"

"Soon as you finish opining. He works in Brentwood, hopefully he's there or home."

"What does he do for a living?"

"Salesman at a high-end clothing store." He retrieved his notepad from the attaché. "Domenico Valli."

I said, "That's why you got spiffed up."

"Just the opposite." He rubbed a lapel, ended up with brittle threads on his fingertips. "I come in like this, he'll feel superior, maybe let his guard down."

I laughed. "What kind of record does Sloat have?"

"Some lightweight vehicular stuff—operating without a license, the requisite DUIs every self-respecting marginal character needs for self-validation. The serious stuff is two ag assaults, one with a crowbar."

"Who was the victim?"

"Guy at a drinking establishment, he and Sloat had words, Sloat followed him outside. Sloat brained him but also received some fairly serious injuries. That enabled him to claim self-defense and maybe there was something to it because charges were dropped. The other case was similar but it happened inside a bar. That time Sloat used his fists. He got pled down, received ninety days at County, served twenty-six."

"Enough violence to be worrisome," I said. "Two incidents in bars could mean he's got a drinking problem—maybe what he and Vita had in common. More important, he'd be familiar with Vita's drinking habits, know she was a night-time boozer, would be vulnerable. And if there was a love-hate relationship, he could've wheedled his way into the apartment."

"Arrives with what looks like a pizza," he said. "'Hi, honey, I miss you. Remember how we used to share an extra-large pepperoni with sausage?'"

He rolled the beer bottle between his hands. "Everything we know about Vita said she was distrustful, maybe border-line-paranoid. You think she'd fall for that?"

"With the help of Jack Daniel's and old-times'-sake?" I said. "Maybe."

"Real old times. My phone subpoena covered eighteen months of her records and his number's not on it."

"What about a different type of contact?" I said. "Vita used the court system at least once and got rewarded."

"She's still dragging him to court? Yeah, that might kick up the anger level."

He called Deputy D.A. John Nguyen, asked for a quick scan of any legal proceedings between Vita Gertrude Berlin and Jackson Junius Sloat.

Nguyen said, "A quick one I can do for the last five years."

"That'll work, John."

"Hold on . . . nope, nothing here. Berlin's your nasty one, right? How's that going?"

"Nothing profound."

"There's been talk in the office, all that weirdness could be the first installment of a whacko serial."

"Thought you were my friend, John."

"I'm not wishing it on you, just repeating what I heard. And the leak didn't start with us. Are there any looser-lipped dudes than cops?"

"Wish I could argue with that," said Milo. "Anything else I should know about?"

"Some of our guys are hoping it will go serial so they can jockey to take it and career-build."

"But if you want it, you'll get it."

Nguyen laughed. "With Bob Ivey retiring I really am the Senior Junior Dude, meaning even if the boss takes it officially I'm doing the real work. So keep me posted."

"Long as you pray for me, John. Little offering to Buddha's fine."

"I'm an atheist."

"I'll take whatever I can get."

CHAPTER

11

While he ate and washed the dishes, I gave him my best guesses about how to approach Jay Sloat: Keep it non-threatening, preface the news of Vita's murder by emphasizing that Sloat was not a suspect, just someone Milo was turning to for valuable information.

However Sloat reacted verbally, his body language would be the thing to watch. Criminal psychopaths operate with lower anxiety levels than the rest of us but it's a myth that they lack emotion. The smartest, coldest antisocials avoid violence completely because violence is a stupid strategy. Look for their smiling faces on election posters. But those a notch lower on the IQ scale often need to prep before indulging their urges with alcohol or dope or by chanting internal rage mantras that provide self-justification.

So if Jay Sloat was anything but the coldest of killers and had carved up his ex, simply bringing up the topic could result in some sort of physical tell: sudden rise in neck pulse, constricted pupils, muscular tension, the merest hint of moisture around the hairline, an increase in blink rate.

Milo said, "I'm the polygraph."

I said, "Isn't that what you do anyway?"

"What if Sloat doesn't respond?"

"Then that tells us something about him."

Nothing he didn't already know but he seemed more relaxed as he drove to Brentwood. Maybe it was the sandwiches.

Domenico Valli Men's Couture was located on 26th Street, just south of San

Vicente, directly across from the Brentwood Country Mart, bordered by a restaurant run by the latest celebrity chef
and another clothing store that hawked
four-figure outfits for trust-fund toddlers.

The haberdashery was paneled in vi-
olin-grain maple and floored in skinny-
plank black oak. Subdued techno pulsed
from the sound system. Light was courtesy of stainless-steel gallery tracks. The
goods were sparingly displayed, like
works of art. A few suits, a smattering
of sport coats, small steel tables that
would've felt comfortable in the morgue
stocked like altars with offerings of cashmere and brocade. A wall rack featured
gleaming handmade shoes and boots,
black velvet slippers with gold crests on
the toes.

No shoppers were availing themselves
of all that chic. A man sat behind a steel
desk, doing paperwork. Big, fiftyish,
with broad shoulders, he had a long
sunlamped face defined by a wide,
meaty nose. A steel-gray Caesar-do
tried but failed to cover a receding hairline. A bushy white soul patch sprouted

under hyphen lips, bristly and stiff as icicles.

He looked up. "Help you guys?"

"We're looking for Jay Sloat."

His eyes narrowed and he stood and stepped around the desk. Just a touch under Milo's six three and nearly as bulky, he wore a faded, untucked blue chambray shirt with pearl buttons, stove-pipe black jeans, gray suede needle-toe boots, a diamond in his left earlobe. Lots of muscle but also some middle-aged padding.

"Don't bother telling me, you're obviously cops. I haven't done anything, so what gives?"

Broad, faintly Slavic midwestern intonation.

"Lieutenant Sturgis, Mr. Sloat." Milo extended his hand. Sloat studied it for a second, endured a brief clasp before retrieving his big paw. "Okay, now we're all BFFs. Could you please tell me what's going on?"

"Sorry if this is upsetting you, Mr. Sloat. It's certainly not our intention."

"It's not upsetting me," said Sloat. "I mean I'm not worried personally because I know I haven't done anything. I just don't get why the cops are here when I'm trying to work." He frowned. "Oh, man, don't tell me it's something to do with George. If it is, I can't help you, I just work for the guy."

Milo didn't answer.

Jay Sloat pressed his palms together prayerfully. "Tell me it ain't so, guys, okay? I need this job."

"It ain't so. George is the owner?"

Sloat relaxed, exhaled. "So it's not about that. Excellent. Okay, then what's up?"

Milo repeated the question.

Sloat said, "Yeah, he's the owner. George Hassan. He's really an okay guy."

"Why would we be looking for him?"

"No reason."

"No reason, but he's the first one you thought of."

Sloat's brown eyes turned piggishly small as they studied Milo, then me, then Milo again. "George is going through a complicated divorce and she keeps claiming he's holding back on her. She's threatening to close down the business if he doesn't open the books. Last week, she sent around a private investigator pretending to be a customer, dude's dressed like a dork, starts asking me if I have more of these nice worsted suits in the back. *Worsted.* What a doofus. I said, 'Hey, Dan Tana, if you actually want to try something on, let's do it, if this is a game, go play it elsewhere.' Guy turned white and got the fuck out."

Sloat grinned and winked. His bronzed face was smoother than when we'd entered; recounting his dominance put him back in his comfort zone.

Milo said, "I hear you. Well, this has nothing to do with George."

"What then?"

"It's about your ex-wife."

Sloat's jaw muscles swelled. His pupils expanded. "Vita? What about her?"

"She's dead."

"Dead," said Sloat. "As in police dead? Oh, man. What happened?"

"Someone murdered her."

"Yeah, I got that. I mean who, how, when?"

Milo ticked his fingers. "Don't know, nasty, five nights ago."

Sloat stroked his soul patch. "Wo-ho," he said, in a soft, almost boyish voice. "Someone finally did the bitch."

We didn't respond.

He said, "I need a cigarette, let's go outside."

Milo said, "Let's."

Grabbing a pack of wheat-colored Nat Shermans from the steel desk, Jay Sloat led us out of the store to the curb, where he positioned himself in front of the display window and lit up with a gold-plated lighter. "Can't smoke inside, George doesn't want odor on the merchandise."

Milo waited until he'd puffed a third of the cigarette before speaking. "Someone did the bitch. So for you it's not bad news."

"Me and Vita broke up a long time ago."

"Fifteen years ago." Milo cited the date of the final decree.

The detail caused Sloat to recoil. "What, you guys are looking into my past?"

"We've researched Vita, Mr. Sloat. Your name came up."

"So you know about my arrests."

"We do."

"Then you also know they were bullshit. Dorks asking for trouble and getting it."

Neither of us argued.

Sloat said, "I watch those shows, I get it, I'm the ex, you think I did it."

"What shows?"

"Crime—true crap, puts me to sleep at night." Sloat grinned. "When I don't have help getting some nighty-night."

"You get help often?"

"Get pussy as often as I can, good for the complexion." He laughed. "Got it every night last week, including five nights ago."

"From who?"

"A chick who rode me like a rodeo horse and righteously blew my mind."

"How about a name?"

"How about she's married."

"We're discreet, Jay."

"Yeah, I bet. On those shows, cops make promises and break them. And anyway, why do I need an alibi? Like

you said, it was fifteen years ago. Whatever Vita did since then was out of my
life."

"Fifteen years ago was the divorce,"
said Milo. "Our research says the war
kept going."

"Okay," said Sloat, "so she kept jerk-
ing me around for another few. But then
it ended. I haven't seen Vita in a long
time."

"How long is 'another few,' Jay?"

"Let's see . . . last time the bitch took
me to court was . . . I'd have to say six,
maybe seven years ago."

That matched Nguyen's failing to
come up with anything for five.

"What'd she want?"

"What do you think? More money."

"She get it?"

"She got some," said Sloat. "It's not
like I had that much to give."

"When's the last time you actually saw
her?"

"Right after. Maybe a month. She
jerks me around in court, then has the
nerve to drop in, middle of the night."

"What for?"

"What do you think? You go to Jay, you want to play."

Milo said, "She sues you then does a booty-call."

"She was crazy," said Sloat. "Also, old habits die hard." He puffed out his chest. "I'm a tough habit to break."

He laughed, smoked greedily. Dry hairline, steady hands, steady lips.

I said, "You're a tough habit to break but for six, seven years Vita managed."

Sloat's face darkened. "She didn't end it, I did. That time she dropped over, I wouldn't let her in, told her she ever did that again I'd get a restraining order and sue her ass so fast she wouldn't know what was reaming her. She knew I meant it, I'm not a guy takes bullshit."

"Like those guys in the bar."

"You got it," said Sloat, "and I ain't embarrassed about it. Back in Chicago I used to work dispatch for a trucking company. They fucked me over, giving the good shifts to some loser who bribed the supervisor, wanting me to work night shift even though I'd been there ten years. I sued and won. Another time one of our *dark*-skinned brothers dented my car, I had this little Benz convertible, gray on gray, sweet drive, this *dusky* fellow isn't looking where he's going, pow. Everyone said don't hassle, those types never have insurance, it's a lost cause. I said screw that, sued his ass, my lawyer found out his mother owned a house, had given the dude a share. We attached Mommy's house, moved to evict her, he paid up."

"You like the court system."

"What I like is protecting my rights. Which I know I got, right now. In terms of talking to you guys, I don't have to say squat. But it's cool, you don't bother me. I had nothing to do with Vita getting killed. Trust me, the way Vita was, she'd have no trouble arranging it all by herself."

"You think she organized her own murder?"

"No, no, what I'm saying is Vita was the biggest bitch this side of . . . I don't know, Cruella Whatshername? From the cartoon? There'd be tons of people she pissed off. All Vita had to do was go on being Vita. Eventually someone was gonna get pissed off."

"Any suggestions as to who?"

"Nah, Vita was out of my life, I don't have a clue who she was hanging with."

"Think back," I said. "When you were still seeing her. Did she have any enemies?"

"Enemies?" said Sloat. "Walk down the street and pick people at random. To know her was to hate the bitch."

"You married her."

"When I married her, I dug her. *Then* I hated her."

"She was different back then."

"Nope," said Sloat. "Only I thought she was. She conned me, you know?"

"Being nice," I said.

"Nah, Vita was never nice. But she hid what a bitch she was by being quiet about it, you know?"

"How?"

"By being cold. Super-frosty, she'd give you this look, this *I'm-a-bitch-but-I'll-still-suck-your-cock* look. And she did. There was a time she had talent, still looked pretty good. Tall and cold with sharp edges, I used to call her Miss Everest. Then she stopped faking it.

Why bother when you can be a total bitch?"

"The attraction wore off."

"I was attracted to her tits," said Sloat. "She had a nice face, too. She took care of herself, plucking the eyebrows, wearing the makeup, doing the platinum-blond hair. Like that actress. Novak, Kim Novak. People old enough to remember said she looked like Kim Novak. I went to see *Vertigo*. Novak was a helluva lot hotter, give me ten Vitas for one Kim Novak, you'll still owe me change. But Vita was cute, I'll grant her that. Good where it counted, also. That part she kept up, even after we broke up. I'll grant her that."

"Sexy," I said.

"Sexy is a chick hungry to do you. Vita was in the mood, she'd pop you quick. Problem is she got old and fat, stopped dyeing the hair, stopped taking care of herself, the drinking got worse." Sticking out his tongue. "Her breath stunk, she was a mess. So even if she wanted to jump your bones, you didn't want those bones jumped. Finally, I said no more. Life's too short, you know?"

Milo said, "We sure do."

"Bet you do," said Sloat. "Listen, I'm not going to stand here and lie and tell you I give a shit when I don't. Vita tried to take everything I owned. Including the Benz I went to all that trouble to get fixed. Including half any money I made until I went totally broke and stopped working long enough to convince her I wasn't worth going after. I haven't seen her in, like I said, seven years. But at the back of my head is always this thought, she's going to come back. Like those guys in the horror movies—the dude in the leather mask. So it's obvious I didn't kill her. Why would I ruin my life for her?"

I said, "One thing you had in common: Vita also liked using the court system?"

"Just against me."

"She never sued anyone else?"

"Nah," said Sloat. "She was a wimp. Like when I went after that black guy, she's yelling at me, what if he's a gang member, the car isn't worth it. Which didn't stop *her* from going after it, years later. Same thing with suing the trucking company. Don't do it, Jay, they could be

Mafia, it's not worth it. I said, to you it's not worth it, to me it is. Rights are rights, that's why we fight wars."

Milo said, "You were in the service?"

"My dad was. Three years in Europe. So can I go back to work?"

Still no anxiety tell. Milo said, "What you're saying makes sense, Jay. On the other hand, you hated her, you're clearly not upset she's dead, and you won't back up your alibi."

"I can back it up but I don't want to."

"Why?"

Sloat looked over his shoulder, through the glass, at the interior of the store.

Milo said, "Don't worry, no customers."

"I know that. There's never any."

I said, "The cowgirl has something to do with the shop."

Rapid constriction of pupil. A carotid pulse sprang into action.

Milo saw it. "Give us a name, Jay, or we're going to develop a chronic interest in menswear."

Sloat blew out acrid tobacco-air. "Aw, man."

Milo said, "We're talking murder, Jay—"

"I know, I know—okay but swear to keep it secret."

"We don't swear, Jay. We don't even promise. But unless there's some reason to go public, we won't."

"What kind of reason? I didn't kill Vita!"

"Then you'll have no problem, Jay."

Sloat sucked down half an inch of cigarette. "Okay, okay, it's Nina. Nina Hassan."

"George's ex."

"He finds out, he'll fire my ass and roast my balls on one of those shish-kebab thingies."

Milo pulled out his pad. "What's her number?"

"You have to write it down?"

"Phone number, Jay."

"You actually have to call her?"

Milo stared him down.

Sloat gave up the number. "Just don't say what I said about her. Being a cow-girl."

"That I can promise you."

"She's hot," said Sloat. "You see her, you'll understand."

"Looking forward to it, Jay."

"I need this job, guys."

"You also need to be cleared as a suspect."

"What suspect, I didn't do squat to Vita."

"Hopefully Nina will confirm that, Jay. Hopefully we'll believe her."

"Why wouldn't you believe her?"

"Maybe she's so crazy about you, she'd lie."

"She digs me," said Sloat. "But she ain't going to lie."

"It's really important, Jay, that you don't call her before we show up. We're gonna check phone records, so we'll know."

"Yeah, yeah sure." His neck pulse hammered away. Shifty eyes said Milo had altered his plans.

I said, "How long were you and Vita married?"

"Six years."

"No kids."

"We didn't want. Both of us."

"Not into kids."

"Kids are a pain," said Sloat. "So when're you seeing Nina?"

Milo said, "When we're ready."

"She'll clear me. She'll impress you, she's a very impressive girl."

"Bye, Jay."

Jay Sloat said, "You absolutely need to talk to her?"

We walked away from him.

Milo looked up Nina Hassan's address, found it on the western edge of Bel Air, a short drive away.

"Vita and Jay," he said, heading east on Sunset. "Thank God those two didn't breed. So what do you think of him?"

I said, "Unless he's Oscar-caliber, I don't see it."

"Me, neither."

Half a mile later: "Screw those D.A. ghouls, this isn't going serial, it's gonna be one of those wrong-time, wrong-place things. Vita finally ticked off the wrong guy. Speaking of which, I did sic Reed on Western Peds, see if he could come up with any oncology parents with bad tempers. Specifically, black parents."

"You're telling me this because . . ."

"I'm telling you in the spirit of openness."

I said, "Do what you need to do."

"No one would tell him anything."

"Good."

"I figured you'd say that."

CHAPTER
12

Nina Hassan's house in the Bel Air hills was sleek, contemporary, gorgeous. Just like her.

She eased open one of the twin brushed-copper double doors, regarded us as if we were salesmen. Late thirties with velvety skin a tad darker than the doors, she sported a mauve top that revealed an inch of hard belly, a pair of sprayed-on white jeans, silver sandals that revealed pampered, lavender-nailed feet. Her face was heart-shaped, topped by a cloud of black waves and curls. A full nose was graced by a cute little up-

ward sweep at the tip. Probably surgical, but well done. Massive white hoops
hung from seashell ears. A long, smooth
neck swooped to a pair of high-end col-
larbones.

Milo flashed the badge.

"Yes? And?" Her eyes were a uniform
black, defying analysis of her pupils.

"We'd like to talk to you about Jay
Sloat."

"Him? He's not okay?" As if inquiring
about the weather.

"Why wouldn't he be okay?"

"My husband," said Nina Hassan.
"He's not human, he's an animal."

"Jay's fine. May we come in, Mrs.
Hassan?"

She didn't budge. "Call me Nina. I'm
getting rid of *that* name as soon as the
divorce is final. What's with Jay?"

"We need to know the last time you
saw him."

"Why?"

"His ex-wife was murdered."

"Ex-wife? Jay was married?"

"A while back, ma'am."

"He said he was never married."

Milo said, "It was a long time ago."

"Doesn't matter," she said. "I don't put up with lies." Her hand slashed air. "What, you think he killed her?"

"No, ma'am. These are what we call routine questions."

"Nina," she said. "I don't like ma'am. Too old. Too . . . ma'am-ish."

A Maserati coupe purred past the house. The woman behind the wheel slowed to study us. Thin, blond, steely as the car. Nina Hassan waved gaily.

Milo said, "It's better if we talk inside."

Hassan's turn to study us. "How do I know you're really the police?"

"Would you like another look at my—"

"Anyone can make a badge."

"Who else would we be?"

"Scumbags hired by George."

"George is your ex?"

"My scumbag ex. He's always sending them around, trying to find something he can use against me. I sleep with Jay? So what? George sleeps with young girls—maybe you should investigate him, he says they're twenty, maybe they're younger."

She tapped a foot. "What am I supposed to do, sit around like his mother and have no fun and tell stories from the old country?"

Milo said, "Sounds like good riddance, Nina, but we're investigating a murder, so if you can remember the last time you were with Jay, that would be helpful."

"Ex-wife," she said. "Liar—was she hot?"

"The way we found her, not in the least. Can you remember?"

"Of course I can remember, I'm not old. The last time was . . . two nights ago." She smiled. "Every night until two nights ago. Then I told him I needed a rest."

"Five nights ago, as well?"

"I just told you: every night."

"What time?"

"Jay comes over after work, five thirty, five forty."

"How long does he stay?"

"Long as I want him to." Her head drew back. She laughed. "That's a cheeky question."

"Pardon?"

"You want to know do we do it all night. Why's that your business?"

"Sorry for any misunderstanding," said Milo. "What I'm after is can Jay's whereabouts be accounted for five nights ago."

"Five nights," said Nina Hassan. "Wait out here."

She returned moments later with a receipt. "Here it is, five nights ago: take-out from Chinois. I keep everything for documentation. So that bastard has to pay what he deserves."

"Takeout from—"

"For two people," she said. "Me and Jay. He tried to get me to eat chicken feet. Yuck."

"He was here all night."

"You bet," said Nina Hassan, winking. "He was too tired to leave."

"Okay, thanks."

"I helped him out, huh? Too bad. I don't like liars." She tossed her hair. "But I tell it like it is, that's how to handle all of you boys. Buh-*bye.*"

Stepping back into her house, she nudged the door shut with a manicured finger.

◆

We drove back to Sunset, passing big houses, small dogs leading maids, gardeners blowing dirt with airguns.

Milo said, "Scratch the ex, why should life be logical? But it's got to be someone else Vita really got to. Too bad she didn't leave an enemy list."

"That's for presidents."

He harrumphed. "Incriminating tapes would be nice, too. Okay, I'll drop you back home, go enjoy your life while we poor civil servants toil. Not that I'm passive-aggressive."

Just as we approached the Glen, his cell played Mahler and he switched to speaker.

Sean Binchy said, "Loot—"

"You found a pizza psycho."

"Unfortunately no, but there is something you're going to want to—"

"What?"

"There's another one."

The man's shirt was folded neatly by his side. His pants and underwear had been lowered to mid-thigh, arranged neatly, no rumpling. He lay on his back, ten feet to the west of a dirt entry road, in a clearing created by a seven-foot gap in a long hedge of oleander.

Toxic plant. For the person who'd snapped the man's neck, perfect cover.

No towels under this body. A blue tarp had been spread neatly.

A few blood specks dotted plastic and dry dirt, a bit more than at Vita Berlin's apartment, but nothing extensive and no castoff, low- or high-velocity. The earth surrounding the tarp had been smoothed free of footprints.

The man's degradation mimicked Vita's. Broken neck, same change-purse incision pattern, identical display of scooped-out viscera.

The kill-spot was off Temescal Canyon in Pacific Palisades, a quarter mile into the grounds of a former summer camp occasionally used for film shoots but for the most part abandoned. An old wire gate spanning pitted asphalt was hinged to a wooden post. A second post had rotted and crumbled and access was as easy as walking in.

The lack of security was a joke with the locals, according to the first uniform on the scene.

"A few of them bitch about it, Lieutenant, but mostly they like it. Because it's like having an extra park and you know the type of people who live here."

Her name was Cheryl Gates. She was tall, blond, square-shouldered, falcon-eyed. Outwardly unaffected by what she'd discovered on routine patrol. By what she and Milo and I were looking at through the gap in the oleander.

Milo said, "Rich folk."

"Rich and entitled and *connected* folk, sir. By that I mean Deputy Chief Salmon's sister lives not far away so my instruction is to drive by every day. Takes up time but it is kind of pretty. And nothing much ever happens. One time I found a boy and a girl, sixteen, went overboard with E and tequila, spent the night next to the barbecues up there, buck naked, totally wasted. Funny thing was, neither family reported them missing. All the parents in Europe or wherever. Sometimes I find bottles, roaches, condoms, food wrappers. But nothing serious."

Outwardly unaffected but talking fast, a bit too loud.

Milo said, "The spot you found my victim, is that part of your routine?"

"Yes, sir. I figure it's a good place for some homeless type to crash and God forbid the locals should be surprised by some wild-eyed whack when they stroll in with their poodles."

"Come across any whacks recently?"

"No, sir. When I find them and it's only once in a while, it's always up there, near those barbecues. They like to cook, fix themselves a hot meal. Which is a risk—fires, and all that. So I warn them and I've never had one come back twice. But I figure better safe than sorry, so yes, I do check it daily. Which is how I found your vic."

"Any particular whack you think I should be looking into?"

"Doubt it, sir," said Gates. "These aren't aggressive guys, just the opposite. Passive, out of it, messed up physically." She eyed the body. "I'm no expert but that looks pretty organized. The way the dirt's kinda been swept up? I mean that's just my impression."

"Makes sense," said Milo. "Thanks for holding the scene."

"Doing what I'm supposed to, sir. Once backup arrived I stayed right here and had Officers Ruiz and Oliphant check the grounds. Looking just for obvious stuff, we didn't want to mess anything up. They found nothing, sir, and there's no exit out of here other than the way you come in. So I'm pretty confident we didn't miss any suspect hiding out."

"Good work."

"So what do you think, sir, was this a sex thing? Those pants down, maybe some gay thing that got crazy?"

"Could be."

"With a sex thing, though," said Gates, "wouldn't you see direct involvement of the genitals, not just . . . that?"

"There are no rules, Officer."

Gates tucked a strand of blond hair behind her ear. "Of course, sir. I'd best be leaving you to go about your business. If there's nothing else."

"We're fine, Officer. Hope tomorrow morning's more pleasant."

Gates stood taller. "Actually, sir, and this is probably an inopportune time to say so but I've been thinking about applying to be a D. Would you recommend that?"

"You're observant, Officer Gates. Go for it and good luck."

"Same to you, sir. On the case, I mean."

◆

Sean Binchy and Moe Reed and three other uniforms remained stationed at the entrance, guarding the road between Sunset and the broken gate. The coroner's investigator hadn't arrived so all we could do was stand at the mouth of the clearing and peer in.

The man was middle-aged—closer to fifty-five than forty-five—with thick curly hair, pewter on top, silver at the sides. So tightly coiled it showed no sign of disarray.

Not so for the head and neck below the hair.

Incompatible with life.

Not a particularly memorable-looking man. Average height, average build, average everything. The pants were cotton, medium beige, pressed, pleated, cuffed. Clean where blood hadn't intruded. The shirt was nut-brown, a polo, folded in a way that obscured any logo. His shoes were white Nikes with well-worn soles. A runner or a serious walker? No car parked near the entrance fit with that.

Blue socks clashed. He hadn't figured on being inspected.

I'd approached the scene expecting to react more strongly than I had to Vita Berlin's corpse. The opposite occurred: Taking in the butchery released an odd, detergent wash of calm that settled my nervous system.

Getting used to it?

Maybe that was the worst part of it.

Milo said, "No pizza box, guess that's not part of the signature. So maybe it's just something the bastard came upon and used for Vita, not tracing it won't be any big deal . . . poor devil, I hope he was a total sonofabitch, Vita's spiritual brother."

A female voice said, "Hi, again. Unfortunately."

The C.I. named Gloria walked between us and gazed into the opening. "Good God." She gloved up and covered her feet with paper booties, stepped in, got to work.

A wallet emerged from the right rear pocket of the man's khakis. A driver's license I.D.'d him as Marlon Quigg, fifty-six, with an address on Sunset, a mile or two east of the campground. A unit number said condo or apartment. We'd passed some nice buildings on the way over, neatly kept places on the south side of the boulevard, some affording ocean views.

Five eight, one sixty-eight, gray hair, brown eyes, needs corrective lenses.

Gloria checked his eyes. "Contacts are still in there. Kind of surprising considering the force it took to snap the neck."

I said, "They could've fallen out and the killer put them back. He's all about order."

She thought about that. Tweezed out the tiny clear disks, bagged and tagged.

Armed with a name, Milo got busy learning about his victim. Quigg's ride was a three-year-old Kia. No wants or warrants or brushes with the criminal justice system.

The wallet held seventy-three dollars in cash and three credit cards. Two snapshots remained in plastic sleeves. One featured Quigg and a smallish, dark-haired woman around his age, the other showed the couple with a pair of brunettes in their early twenties. One girl resembled Quigg, down to the tight, curly hair. The other could've been anyone's progeny but her arm rested on the shoulder of the older woman, so the reasonable guess was Daughter Number Two.

Both shots were studio poses, backdropped by green faux-marble. Everyone dressed up, a little stiff and uncertain, but smiling.

Gloria said, "He's not wearing a watch . . . no pale stripe on his arm, either, so maybe he wasn't a time-bound Type A."

"Or he took off his watch when he walked," said Milo.

I said, "The soles of his shoes say he liked to cover ground."

"They do," said Gloria, "but why come in here? It'd be kind of spooky in the dark, no?"

Milo said, "The locals consider it their private park. He lives close, maybe felt it was safe."

"Okay . . . but maybe he was meeting someone." She shifted uncomfortably. "The way the pants are . . . you know."

"Anything's possible, kid."

"Though I guess with something sexual you'd expect the genitals to be attacked." She looked at me.

I said, "Same answer."

She checked the pants, using a magnifier. "Well, look at this, I've got foreign hairs . . . whole bunch of them . . . long ones . . . blond."

Milo kneeled down beside her, plucked several filaments with latex-sheathed fingers that looked too big and thick for the task. Holding the hairs up to the light, he squinted. Sniffed. "Maybe Marilyn Monroe came back from the grave to do him but they look kinda coarse and I'm picking up doggy odor."

Gloria said, "My nose is stuffed." She tried anyway. "Sorry, I'm not picking up anything but you could be right about the texture." Smiling. "Unless someone's using a real bad conditioner."

She produced an evidence bag. "I

know the techies generally do hair unless we're running drug screens on the
shaft, but we happen to have an intern
from the U. doing DNA analysis on all
kinds of critters. Want me to take it,
maybe I can get you something on spe-
cies and breed?"

"Appreciate it."

Gloria took another look at Quigg.
"Poor guy goes out for his nightly dog-
walk and this happens?" Frowning. "So
where's the canine in question? Maybe
Fido got left at home."

Milo said, "Or maybe our bad guy
took a live trophy."

"Rover stands by and watches his
master get murdered and then goes off
willingly with the perpetrator? Not a protective breed, that's for sure." Catching
her breath. "Or the poor thing's lying
somewhere looking like Mr. Quigg."

"Uniforms checked the immediate
area but we'll go over it again after the
techies arrive."

Gloria scanned the dirt. "Don't see
any prints in here, dog or human."

"Our bad guy cleaned up carefully."

"Just like the first time," she said. "To me that makes it even more repulsive."

I said, "I don't see him cleaning every inch of ground all the way to Sunset."

Milo cell-phoned Reed. "Moses, keep the entire area tight, no one in or out until whoever's on duty helps you examine every inch of dirt between Sunset and the gate for prints. I'm talking tire, foot, paw, anything."

Clicked off without waiting for an answer.

Gloria bent back down and turned out Marlon Quigg's remaining pants pockets. "Empty." Back on her feet, she photographed the scene at multiple angles, ending with close-ups of the folded brown shirt.

She inspected the label. "Macy's generic, size M."

No blood; the garment had been removed prior to the cutting.

She got back down near the body, started rolling it. Stopped and reached under and drew something out.

Piece of paper, folded into a packet, corners perfectly square.

She photographed it closed, then

placed a sterile cloth under it and spread it open.

White, standard letter size. In the center, a simple message:

?

CHAPTER

14

Marlon Quigg's apartment was in one of the nice buildings we'd passed.

A nearby traffic light would've provided easy crossing of Sunset. The walk to Temescal Canyon would've been pleasant.

The complex was designed to resemble an enormous hacienda, tricked out with a too-red tile roof, a false bell tower, and a front loggia that shaded arched entry doors. A tile-roofed carport faced the main structure across a broad, flagstone court.

Eight slots in the port. Quigg's Kia sat

in Number Two. *Quigg, B and M* appeared on Unit Two's mailbox.

Ground-floor unit in the middle of the building. I recognized the woman who answered the door because I'd just seen her photo.

Milo said, "Mrs. Quigg?"

"Yes, yes, I'm Belle. You found them?"

"Them?"

"Marlon and Louie."

"We found Mr. Quigg."

"Not Louie? Marlon went out walking him last night, they never came back. I've been frantic, when I called you people, you said it couldn't be a missing person until—" She stopped, put a hand to her mouth. "Marlon's okay?"

Milo sighed. "I'm sorry, he's not."

"He's hurt?"

"Ma'am, this is hard to—"

Belle Quigg said, "Oh, no, oh *no no no no no.*"

"I'm so sorry, Mrs. Quigg—"

She raised her hands and yanked down, as if tugging clouds from a cruel clear sky. Glared at us. Gasped. Then she began beating Milo on the chest.

◆

Small woman pummeling big man isn't much of an assault. Milo bore it until she ran out of steam and dropped her fists to her side.

"Mrs. Qui—"

Her head flopped to one side, skin blanched to a bad shade of gray. Eyes rolling upward, she rasped once before pitching backward. Both of us lunged; we each caught an arm, eased her inside her home.

She woke up on the way to the nearest armchair. Milo stayed with her while I fetched water.

When I held the glass to her lips, her mouth opened with all the volition of a marionette. I took her pulse. Slow, but steady.

I eased more water into her mouth. She dribbled. Put her head back. The eyes rolled again.

After a few seconds, her pulse normalized and some color returned to her face. She stared up at us. "What?"

Milo held her hand. "I'm Lieutenant Sturgis—"

She said, "Oh. You. So where's Louie?"

♦

It took another few minutes for her to settle into grief-stricken numbness.

Milo sat holding her hand; I worked the water glass. When she said, "No more," I returned the glass to the kitchen.

Spacious sunlit kitchen, shiny granite, stainless steel. The rest of the apartment was done up nicely, too, furnished with timeless furniture, maybe a few real antiques, unremarkable but inoffensive seascapes. A double set of sliding glass doors granted an oblique view of blue swimming pool bleeding to bluer Pacific. The sky was clear, the grass around the pool was clipped, birds flew, a squirrel scampered up a magnificent Canary Island pine.

Marlon Quigg had arrived at a nice place in middle age.

At least one person cared about him. I knew I shouldn't be judging but that made his monstrous end seem even worse than Vita's.

Belle Quigg said, "Oh, God, God, Louie's probably . . . also gone."

"Louie's your dog," said Milo.

"More like Marlon's dog, the two of

them were like . . . we got him as a res-
cue, Louie loved everyone but mostly
he loved Marlon. I loved Marlon. Britt
and Sarah loved Marlon, *everyone* loved
Marlon."

She grabbed Milo's sleeve. "Who
would hurt him—was he robbed?"

"It doesn't look that way, ma'am."

"What, then? What? Who would do
this? Who?"

"We're gonna work real hard to find
out, ma'am. I'm sorry to have to be the
one to deliver such terrible news and I
know this isn't a good time but if I could
ask you some questions?"

"What kind of questions?"

"The more we know about Marlon the
better we can do our job."

"I *love* Marlon. We've been together
twenty-six—oh, God, our anniversary is
next week. I already made reservations.
What am I going to do?"

Two bouts of sobbing later, Milo said,
"What kind of work did Marlon do?"

"Work?" said Belle Quigg. "Yes, he
worked, of course he worked, Marlon
wasn't a bum—why, did one of those
bums kill him?"

"Those bums?"

"They call them homeless, I call them bums because that's what they are. You see them at Sunset and PCH, panhandling, drunk. The light's long, gives them plenty of time to come up and beg. I never give them a dime. Marlon always gave them something."

"Why would you suspect one of them?"

"Because they're bums," said Belle Quigg. "I always told Marlon that. Don't encourage them. He has a soft heart."

"The crime occurred over in Temescal Canyon—"

"The Little Indians Camp! I *told* Marlon not to walk there at night! That just proves what I was saying. Anyone can walk in, what's to stop a bum? You want to find them? Go down to Sunset and PCH."

"We'll definitely check that out, ma'am. Is there anyone else we should be thinking of?"

"What do you mean?"

"Anyone Marlon might've had conflict with, say at work?"

"Never."

"What kind of work did he do?"

"Marlon was an accountant."

"Where?"

"Peterson, Danville and Shapiro in Century City. He handled one major client, the Happy Boy supermarket chain. Marlon did a great job, always got the best performance ratings."

"How long had he been working there?"

"Fifteen years," she said. "Before that he worked for the city—DWP—but only for a year, while he was waiting to take his CPA. Before that, he was a teacher. He worked with disabled children."

"Before he picked up the Happy Boy account did he work with any insurance companies?"

"Happy Boy has been his assignment right from the beginning. They're a huge chain, it's all Marlon can do to keep up with their taxes."

"So no problems at work."

"Why would there be a problem? No, of course not, this had nothing to do with Marlon, Marlon's the best."

"And obviously your personal life is great."

"Better than great," said Belle Quigg. "It's . . . excellent." Her lips parted. Color began leeching again. "I'm going to have to tell Britt and Sar— Oh God, how can I do that—"

"How old are they?"

"Britt's eighteen, Sarah's twenty-two."

"Are they close by?"

Head shake. "Britt's in Colorado, Sarah's in . . . I . . . where is she, that place underneath Colorado . . ." Her face screwed up. "It's on the tip of my . . . that place . . ."

I said, "New Mexico."

"New Mexico. She's in Gallup, it sounds like horses running around, that's how I remember it. She's there because her boyfriend lives in Gallup, so she does, too. She used to drive a car, now she rides a lot of horses, it's a ranch, one of those ranches. Britt's not married, I hope she will be but she's not, she lives in Colorado. Vail. She works as a waitress, gets real busy when it's ski season. She skis, Sarah rides horses. They're beautiful girls—how am I going to *tell* them!"

"If you'd like us to stick around while you call—"

"No, no no, *you* call."

"You're sure, ma'am?"

"It's your job," said Belle Quigg. "Everyone needs to do their job."

She turned silent, almost stuporous, as Milo phoned her daughters. The conversations were brief, terrible, and every second seemed to diminish him. If Belle Quigg had eavesdropped, she showed no signs of reacting.

He sat back down. "Sarah would like to talk to you, Mrs. Quigg."

"Britt, too?"

"Britt will call you back when she composes herself."

"Composes," said Belle Quigg. "Like a composition. She was always good in English."

"Will you speak with Sarah?"

"No, no, no, tell her I'll call back. I need to sleep. I need to sleep forever."

"Is there someone, a friend, a neighbor, that we could call to come over to be with you?"

"Be with me while I sleep?"

"To offer support, ma'am."

"I'm fine, I just want to die in peace."

I returned to the kitchen, looked for an address book, found a cell phone. A scan of recent calls listed a speed-dial number for Letty. I phoned it.

A woman said, "Belle?"

I said, "I'm calling on Belle's behalf."

It took a while to clarify, longer until Letty Pomeroy stopped gasping, but she agreed readily to come over to take care of her friend.

"Are you nearby?"

"Like a five-minute drive."

"We really appreciate it, Mrs. Pomeroy."

"Of course. Marlon's really . . ."

"I'm afraid so."

"That's crazy—do you know who did it?"

"Not yet."

"Where did it happen?

"In Temescal Canyon."

"Where Marlon walked Louie."

"That's common knowledge?"

"Anyone who knows Marlon knows he likes to walk Louie there. Because he didn't need to clean up after Louie, it's so . . . rural. I mean I guess officially he did but . . . was Louie also . . .”

"Louie's missing.”

"Figures,” said Letty Pomeroy. "That he wouldn't protect Marlon.”

"Pushover?”

"Moron.”

"What kind of breed is he?”

"Golden retriever. Or maybe a retriever mix. Mixed-up is more like it, that has to be the dumbest animal I've ever encountered. You could step on him, he'd grin up at you like the village idiot. Kind of like Marlon, I guess. No, that came out wrong, I'm not saying Marlon was stupid, God forbid no, Marlon was smart, he was a bright man, very mathematical.”

"But easygoing,” I said.

"*That's* what I meant. Marlon was the easiest-going guy, I can't believe someone would hurt him. I mean *Marlon,* for God's sake. He was the original bleeding heart. That's how he got Louie, no one wanted to adopt Louie, probably because he's so dim. My husband and I used to call him the Dumb Blond. A breathing, pooping throw rug. Anyone

who'd steal that mutt is a worse idiot . . . sorry, I'm ranting, I still can't believe this. Someone actually hurt *Marlon.* Unbelievable."

"Mrs. Quigg's pretty traumatized, if
you think you're up to coming over right
now—"

"I'll be there in a jif."

Back in the living room, Belle Quigg was
resting her head on Milo's shoulder.
Eyes closed, maybe sleeping, maybe
withdrawing deeper than slumber. She'd
caught him in an awkward position but
he didn't budge.

I told him a friend would be showing
up shortly.

Belle Quigg stirred.

Milo said, "Ma'am?"

"Huh?"

"If you can handle a few more questions."

Her eyes opened. "Whu?"

"Is the name Vita Berlin familiar?"

"Like the city?"

"Yes."

"No."

"Not familiar with Vita Berlin?"

"Sounds like a food supplement."

"What about an insurance company named Well-Start?"

"Huh?"

He repeated the name.

"We use Allstate."

"Allstate's casualty, Well-Start does health insurance."

"We use one of the blue ones, Marlon paid all the bills."

"So neither Vita Berlin or Well-Start rings a bell."

"No." Flash of clarity. She sat up but remained pressed against him. "No. Neither. Why?"

"Just routine questions."

Smiling, the new widow placed a hand on his chest. Snuggling closer, she said, "You're so *big*."

CHAPTER

15

Two women entered the Quigg condo. First through the door was a tall buxom redhead with short, feathered hair, wearing a green sweater over a black unitard and red Chinese slippers. She announced herself as Letty, identified her shorter, sweats-attired companion as "Sally Ritter, she's also a friend."

Belle Quigg didn't react. Her eyes were open but they'd been blank for the last quarter hour. One hand continued to grip Milo's wrist. The other rested on his chest.

Letty Pomeroy said, "Oh, honey!" and surged forward.

Milo manage to extricate himself and stretch.

Sally Ritter said, "So what exactly happened?"

I said, "I've explained to Ms. Pomeroy."

"From what she told me on the way over, that's not much."

Milo said, "We don't know much, that's why we need to investigate. Thanks, ladies." He headed for the door.

Belle Quigg said, "Wait."

Everyone looked at her.

"You've remembered something, ma'am?"

She shook her head. "But *everyone* should stay."

Milo started up the engine before closing the driver's door, sped onto Sunset. Crossing the next intersection on an iffy amber evoked honks and curses. He said, "Sue me," and steered with one finger as he celled Moe Reed.

"Any shoe prints out front?"

Reed's voice came on speaker, grainy

but audible. "A few closer to the gate like you suggested. Techies arrived just after you left and I had them cast. Unfortunately, nothing was clear enough, all they got is an approximation of shoe size."

"Which is?"

"We're talking at least five different sets, ranging from small to big."

"What about tire tracks?"

"I really have to be the one to tell you, huh?"

"That bad?"

"No tracks whatsoever, Loo. Whoever sliced that poor guy up either walked in and out or he parked somewhere in the surrounding neighborhood. Street parking is illegal after eight p.m., any vehicle would've stood out and the locals would've probably complained. I checked with Traffic. No one called in anything and no tickets were issued last night."

"Have the uniforms canvass the entire grounds again."

"Uniforms just finished canvassing a second time. Nothing."

"Do it a third time. You supervise.

Have Sean participate, sometimes he notices things."

"Sean's doing a door-to-door with the nearest neighbors."

"You, then. Make sure it's done right."

"Yes, sir."

"I'm not only talking juicy obvious evidence, Moses. I'm talking random trash, a bottle, a candy wrapper. Anything but the damn trees and shrubs and rocks that God put there."

"Only different thing that came up the second time was a dead snake near an empty garbage can. California king, a baby, pretty little thing, with blue and yellow and red stripes. And I'm not sure you can call that out of place."

"Didn't know you watched Animal Planet, kid. Bring me a cobra and I'll be impressed."

Reed laughed. "Really was a nice snake, poor thing."

Milo ended the call; a second later it beeped Brahms. "Sturgis . . . oh, hi. Thanks for calling back . . . sure . . . actually I understand the whole schedule thing, a good friend of mine's a physician . . . Richard Silverman, he's also at Cedars . . . you do? Yes, he is. So when can I speak to both of you? Sooner's better than later . . . I see. Well, that's fine, just give me your room number. Great, see you in twenty."

He accelerated, zoomed around curves. The unmarked's loose suspension griped. He kept racing, zipping past the tree-shrouded northern border of the U.'s massive campus.

I said, "Vita's downstairs neighbors?"

"The Drs. Feldman. That was the male half. They both just got off call, found out about Vita, and are too freaked out to return home. So they're staying at the Sofitel across from Cedars."

I said, "Freaked out because they know something or just general anxiety?"

"We'll find out soon enough, I'm headed straight there. Any thoughts about poor Mr. Quigg?"

I repeated what Letty Pomeroy had told me.

"Mr. Nice Guy," he growled, as if that

was the gravest personality flaw of all. "Maybe too trusting?"

"Sounds like Louie sure was. No protective instinct at all."

"And now he's probably lying in a ditch with his own guts churned up. What the hell's going on, Alex? One victim's the most hated woman in Southern California, the other's ready to be sainted. There's a rational pattern for you."

I said, "Only thing I can see in common is they were about the same age."

"A psycho who targets aging boomers? Now all I have to do is keep a close watch on a few million potential carvees. Hell, Alex, maybe I sic AARP on the damn case. Here I'd convinced myself this had something to do with Vita specifically. Now I'm picking up that random stench. Or something so crazy it might as well be random. Please tell me I'm wrong."

"Too much planning went into the killings for a random strike. Same goes for the cleanup and sitting by the bodies until they were safely dead before mutilating."

"So something nuts. Wonderful."

"Calculated evil, not insanity. My bet is Vita and Quigg were both stalked. Vita was a stay-at-home who went out to shop and eat. Quigg took the same walk with his dog every night."

"Creatures of habit," he said. "Fine, but what made them targets? Vita pissing off some psycho I can see. But mild-mannered Marlon? So maybe Quigg's not as perfect as his wife made out. You have time to revisit her? Maybe she'll give something up."

"I have time, but she sure seemed to like your big manly chest."

"Hate to deprive her but you'll be an excellent second choice."

A mile later, he said: "The dog bothers me. So he's no pit bull. But standing around while Quigg got butchered?"

I said, "All the killer needed to do was incapacitate Quigg then tie the dog's leash to a branch or pin it under a rock. If Louie did react to seeing his master die horribly, that could've heightened the pleasure."

"A sadist."

"With a captive audience."

"Think the dog's dead or a live tro-phy?"

"Could go either way."

"Either," he said. "God, I hate that word."

CHAPTER
16

Dr. David Feldman sat on the edge of the hotel bed. Dr. Sondra Feldman sat so close the two of them looked glued together. The room was compact, tidy, air-conditioned frigid.

He was thirty or so, tall, thin, and long-limbed as an egret, with wavy black hair and the anxious nobility of a Velasquez prince. His wife, pretty and grave with nervous hands and straight black hair, could've been mistaken for his sib.

They'd insisted that Milo slip I.D. under the door before unlatching. The chain had remained in place while two sets of eyes checked us over through the crack.

After letting us in, Sondra Feldman bolted and rechained and David Feldman double-checked the strength of the hardware. Both Feldmans wore jeans, sneakers, and polo shirts, hers a pink Ralph Lauren Polo, his a sky-blue Lacoste. Their white coats were draped individually over separate chair-backs. A bowl of fruit on a nightstand was untouched. A bottle of Merlot had been touched to half empty.

Sondra Feldman saw me looking at the wine. "We thought it might help but it was all we could do to hold it down."

Milo said, "Thanks for getting back to me."

David Feldman said, "We're hoping you can protect us. Or is that unrealistic?"

"You think you're in danger?"

"A neighbor gets murdered right above us? Wouldn't you consider that danger?"

Sondra said, "There's no alarm system in the apartment. That always bothered me."

"Have you had security problems?"

"No, but we're into prevention not treatment. We talked to Stanleigh—Mr. Belleveaux. He was reluctant to install anything for a one-year lease."

David said, "For lack of contradictory data, we're assuming we're in danger. We'll be moving soon as we find another place but at some point, we'll need to go back to retrieve our stuff. Is there any way we could receive some sort of police escort? I know we're not celebs and the city's tight financially, but we're not asking for anything extensive, maybe one cop."

Milo said, "Until you find a new place, you'll be staying here?"

Sondra frowned. "The cost is crazy and we get what, two hundred square feet?"

David said, "We both have tons of loans. Stanleigh's place seemed like a great deal because he was friendly and honest and it was reasonably close to both our work. But after this? Not a chance."

"You're a resident at Cedars?"

"And Sonny's at the U."

The mention of work seemed to relax them. I said, "What are your specialties?"

"I'm in medicine, want to do a gastro fellowship. Sonny's pediatrics."

Sondra Feldman said, "Can we interpret your not answering the request for an escort as a no?"

Milo said, "Not at all. Once you're ready, get in touch. If I can't accompany you myself, I'll get someone else."

"You'd do that?"

"Sure. I'll be back to the scene several times, anyway."

The Feldmans exchanged quick rabbity looks. Sondra said, "Well, thank you."

Milo said, "Hey, a neighbor murdered is heavy-duty, I don't blame you for being on edge. But is there some specific reason you feel you might be targeted?"

Another exchange of jumpy eye-language.

David said, "We may just be paranoid, but we think we might have seen something."

Sondra said, "Some*one*. The first time

was around three weeks ago. Davey saw him—you tell them, honey."

David nodded. "I can't be sure exactly when this was, given our sleep patterns, time blurs. We get home, take Ambien, collapse. The only reason I noticed him in the first place was the neighborhood's generally quiet, you never see anyone out past five. Not like Philly, we lived in City Center, there was street life all the time."

Sondra said, "The second time was maybe two weeks ago and I was the one who saw him. Davey hadn't told me he saw him so I never mentioned it. It was only after what happened to Vita that we compared notes."

Milo said, "Who's him?"

She said, "Before we get into it, Lieutenant, we need to feel certain we're doing the right thing."

"Believe me, Doctor, you are."

"We don't mean morally, we mean personal-safety-wise. What if it gets back to him that we played a role in his apprehension and he comes after us?"

"Dr. Feldman, we're a long way from that."

"We're just saying," said Sondra. "Once we pass along information we're part of the process. There'll be no way to get *un*involved."

Milo said, "I appreciate your concern but I've been doing this a long time and I've never had someone in your situation harmed."

David said, "Please excuse us for not finding that comforting. There's always a first time."

I said, "You returned Lieutenant Sturgis's call. That wasn't just to ask for a police escort to pick up your stuff."

"That's true," said David. "We wanted to do the right thing. But then we got to discussing it."

"A criminal investigation is a complex process. Before anyone's apprehended, let alone charged and brought to trial, there'll be thousands of bits of data added to the pile. Your contribution won't stand out."

Sondra said, "You sound like my father. He's a psych prof, always dissecting things logically."

"What does your father think you should do?"

"I haven't told him! Neither of us has told anyone."

David said, "If he knew, he'd be here on the next plane. Trying to run things, telling us, See, I was right, you should've stayed in Philly."

She smiled. "Your mom, too."

"In spades. Meddle-city."

They held hands.

I said, "Who'd you both see?"

Sondra said, "If our contribution's so insignificant, you probably don't need us in the first place."

"Not insignificant," I said. "But not conspicuous, either. Isn't medicine like that? You don't always know what will work?"

David said, "We'd like to think medicine can be pretty scientific."

"We'd like to think criminal investigations can be scientific but reality doesn't always cooperate. The information you have may turn out to be irrelevant. But if it narrows things down, it could help."

Sondra said, "Okay, fine."

"Sonny?"

"It's the right thing, Davey. Let's just get it over with."

He inhaled, massaged the little croc-
odile snarling at his left breast. "I was
coming home from work around a month
ago, saw a guy across the street. It was
at night but I could see him, I guess
there were stars out, I really don't know.
My initial impression was he was staring
at our building. Up, at the second story."

I said, "Vita's apartment."

"I can't swear to it but from the way
his neck was tilted that's what it seemed
like. I found that curious because in all
the time we'd been there, we never saw
Vita have a visitor. I suppose it's possible she entertained during the day when
we were gone. But all the times we were
home during the day, we never saw anyone."

"Total loner," said Sondra. "No surprise."

"Why's that?"

"Her personality."

"Abrasive, combative, obnoxious, pick
your adjective," said David. "She's on
top, we're on bottom, if anyone's going
to hear footsteps it's us. But we never
complained and trust me, her steps
were heavy, she wasn't exactly a fash-

ion model. Sometimes, after we'd been on call, it was hell being woken up by her clomping around."

Sondra said, "It seemed to happen a *lot* when we came back from call."

Milo said, "You think she was trying to bug you?"

"We wondered."

David said, "We didn't get into it with her, what's the point? Then she goes and complains to Stanleigh about us."

Sondra said, "How can you hear footsteps from downstairs? Plus we always go barefoot. Plus we're careful. Stanleigh was cool, said he was sorry. Obviously he was paying lip service. After that, anytime we'd see Vita she'd give us the stink eye."

David said, "Anyway, back to the salient issue: She never once had a visitor that we saw and now some guy was looking up at her place."

I said, "From across the street."

"He took off the moment he saw me watching him."

"What did he look like?"

"White, maybe five eleven. What I did find unusual was how he was dressed.

It was a warm day but he was wearing
a coat. No one wears coats in L.A., I
brought one from Philly, it's still in a garment bag."

"What kind of coat?"

"Kind of bulky. Or maybe he was
bulky and filled it out."

Sondra said, "Given the benefit of
hindsight, maybe he chose a bulky garment in order to conceal a gun. Was
she shot?"

Milo said, "She was stabbed."

She gripped her husband's arm. "God,
even if we had been there, it could've
gone on right under our noses and we
might not have heard it. That's *repel-
lent.*"

I said, "What else can you remember
about this person, David?"

"That's it."

"What was his age?"

"I really can't say."

"When he left how did he move?"

He thought. "He didn't limp if that's
what you're getting at . . . didn't move
like an old guy, so probably not too old.
I wasn't close enough to get details. I
was more concerned about what he

was doing there. In fact, I wasn't really worried, more like curious. It's when he got out of there that I started to wonder."

Milo said, "Think he was younger than fifty?"

"Hmm . . . probably."

"Younger than forty?"

"That I can't tell you."

"If you had to guess."

"Twenties or thirties," he said. "And I don't even know why I'm saying that."

"Fair enough." Milo turned to Sondra.

She said, "Three weeks ago—I know that because I was rotating at a clinic in Palmdale, too far to commute so mostly I slept out there but that night I got off early and David was on call and I wanted to clean up the apartment. So that would make it a week or two after Davey saw him. It was also at night, nine-ish, I'd gotten home at eight, eaten, showered, was doing some puttering, it relaxes me. Part of that was emptying the trash baskets into a big garbage bag and taking them out to the alley."

She bit her lip. "In retrospect, it's terrifying."

I said, "Someone was in the alley."

She nodded. "Not near our garbage, near the garbage next door. I must've spooked him because as soon as I got to our garbage, I heard footsteps. Then I saw him running. That freaked me out. Not only had he been there and I was unaware, but the fact that he ran away. Why would you run if you weren't up to no good? He ran fast, west up the alley. Some of the properties have security lights and as he passed under them I could see his form diminishing. Could see his coat billowing. That's why I know—I think—it's the same person Davey saw. It was a warm night, why wear a coat? I can't give you his age, saw him from the distance and from the back. But from the way he moved— more like a bear than a deer—I got the feeling he was kind of husky, the bulk just wasn't the coat. Do you think Vita's murder had to do with her specifically?"

Milo said, "As opposed to?"

"A random psychopath."

David said, "Obviously we'd rather it be something specific and not some sexual predator targeting all women."

Sondra said, "That night, when I went down to the garbage, it really was warm. I had on a tank top and shorts. And I'm not sure I drew all the drapes on our windows."

Her eyes teared up.

Milo said, "We have no evidence he was after anyone at the building other than Vita."

"Okay," she said. Her tone belied any confidence.

David said, "No matter, we're out of there."

I said, "Sonny, when you saw this person running away, what did you do?"

"I hurried back inside."

"The only rational response," said David.

Her eyes shot to the left.

I said, "Did you look around at all before you hurried back?"

David said, "Why would she?"

Sondra said, "Actually . . ."

David stared at her.

"Just for a second, Davey. I was frightened but I was also curious, what would someone be doing there? I wanted to see if he left something. Some kind of evidence. So I'd have something to report to the police if he came back."

"Wow," said David. "Wow-ow."

"It's okay, hon, he was long gone, there was absolutely no danger. I only looked around a bit and then I went right back inside."

I said, "What'd you see?"

"Not much. There was a box on the ground so I assumed he'd been rooting around in the trash. I wondered if he was just a homeless guy scrounging for something to eat. That could explain the coat. When I rotated through Psych they told us schizophrenics sometimes dressed way too heavy."

"What kind of box?"

"A pizza box, empty. I know that because I picked it up and put it in the trash and from the weight you could tell it was empty."

David said, "Ugh, time for Purell."

She shot him a sharp look. "Like I didn't?"

"I'm kidding."

Milo said, "Any markings on the pizza box?"

JONATHAN KELLERMAN

"I didn't notice. Why? Does pizza have something to do with Vita?"

Milo said, "Nope."

"So maybe," said Sondra, "he was just a mentally disturbed homeless guy Dumpster-diving, no big deal."

"Anything else?"

Twin head shakes.

"Okay, thanks, here's my card and when you need that escort, give a ring."

Both Feldmans stood. He was an easy six four, she was four inches shorter. One day they might breed and create a brainy power forward.

As we headed for the door, I said, "Philly as in Penn?"

Sondra said, "Undergrad and med school for me, med school for Davey, he did undergrad at Princeton."

David allowed himself a smile. "We come across as Ivy League twits?"

"You come across as serious thinkers."

"Thanks," he said. "I think."

"Thinking," said his wife, "can be a big pain."

CHAPTER
17

Milo had his phone out before beginning the drive back to the station. He started with Moe Reed, checking again on the campgrounds.

Reed said, "Nothing, but Sean has something for you."

Sean Binchy came on. "A neighbor thinks she saw someone lurking three days ago. White, indeterminate age, wore a coat, which she thought was weird, seeing as it was a warm night."

"What kind of coat?"

"I didn't ask. Is that important?"

"Maybe." He recounted the Feldmans'

sightings, Sondra's theory about a concealed weapon.

"Oh, boy," said Binchy. "I'll go back and requestion her."

"No need," said Milo. "Give me her info."

We sped to Temescal Canyon.

The house was a wood-sided, two-story Craftsman on a generous lot due west and slightly north of the campground entrance, separated from the road by a densely planted berm. Plenty of hiding places among trees and shrubs.

Not ideal for a woman living alone, and that's what the informant turned out to be. Stunning, fortyish, athletically built, she responded to Milo's I.D. with, "Hi, Milo B. Sturgis, I'm Erica A. Vail."

Stepping out onto her lawn, she bent to pluck a dead bud from an azalea bush. She wore a skimpy black top, leggings in a curious shade of green that took on pink highlights when the sun hit the fabric at a certain angle, pink Vans. Her hair was huge, dark, artfully mussed. A diamond chip pierced her left nostril.

"I don't know what I can add to what

I told that young cop. Didn't know you guys could be so hip. Spiky hair, that whole surfer thing, Doc Martens. Someone brought that to me in a script I'd tell them to get authentic. But apparently I need to be more broad-minded."

"You're a director?"

"Producer." She name-dropped a comedy series that had been off the air for five years, added the fact that she had three pilots in development for three separate networks.

"Glad Detective Binchy was helpful," said Milo. "I'm his boss."

Erica Vail flashed blindingly white teeth. "I merit the boss? Flattered. Maybe you'll be a little more forthcoming. Who exactly got killed?"

"A man who lives nearby."

"How nearby?"

"Couple of miles."

"By lives do you mean actually lives, like in a house? Or one of those homeless guys who congregate at PCH?"

"He had a home. His name was Marlon Quigg."

"Never heard of him," she said. "I'd figured it for a homeless guy, once in a while they wander in. But when one of us asks them to leave we've never had a problem—did one of them kill Mr. Quigg?"

"Too early to say, Ms. Vail."

"The guy I saw didn't impress me as homeless. Too healthy-looking. Even a little on the heavy side."

"Tell us about it."

"Sure," said Erica Vail, bright-eyed, cheerful. "Three nights ago, must've been close to ten, I came out and there he was." Pointing to the berm. "I was just about where I am now and I could see him because the moon was fat, it created kind of a halo around him." She smiled. "Almost a special-effects thing, forgive me, I tend to think in terms of movie frames."

Milo said, "You don't seem upset."

"About the murder or seeing him?"

"Either."

"The murder doesn't bother me because it's too abstract and back in a former life I was a surgical nurse, including duty in Afghanistan. So it takes a lot to gross me out. Seeing him didn't bother me because of Bella."

"Who's Bella?"

She jogged back inside her house, returned moments later with a beast in tow.

At least a hundred fifty pounds of defined blue-gray muscle was graced by a massive, blunt-nosed head. Spots of gold accented the brow above the small, watchful eyes, same for the bottoms of the legs. A color-morphed rottweiler. But bigger and leggier than a rottweiler with a tail docked to a stub and ears cropped to pointy remnants. Circling a tree-trunk neck was a stainless-steel pinch collar tethered to a stout leather leash.

"Say hello to the nice policemen, Bella."

The dog's lips drew back, baring lion-sized fangs. A low but thunderous noise—abdominal, menacing—emerged from its maws.

Erica Vail said, "Apart from me, Bella doesn't like people."

As if on cue, the dog lunged at us. Even with a pinch chain, Erica Vail had to labor to hold her at bay.

Erica Vail laughed. "Men, in particular.

She was my present to myself after my divorce."

"What's her breed?" I said.

"Cane Corso. Combination of Roman war dog and some sort of Sicilian hound. Back in the old country they guard Mafia estates and hunt boar."

Bella growled.

"I am woman, hear me roar," said Milo.

Erica Vail laughed. "You can see why Mr. Lurker didn't bother me. Bella smelled him when she was still in the house. That's why I came out, she was getting all restless, whining near the door. Once we got out she went straight for him, would've had him for a snack if I hadn't been able to hold her back."

"How'd he react?"

"That's the funny thing," she said. "Most people see Bella coming, they cross the street. This idiot just stood there. Maybe he was trying to prove how macho he was. But it was stupid, Bella pulls hard enough, I'm not sacrificing my shoulder."

She tossed her hair, loosened her grip on the dog. Bella edged closer. I tried a closed-mouth smile; some dogs view teeth as a threat. She cocked her head, not unlike Blanche when she's thinking. Favored me with a long stare and settled for aloof condescension.

Erica Vail said, "I was about to warn the fool when he finally got smart and split."

Milo said, "Which way did he go?"

"Down the street, that way—south. If he'd disappeared into the berm I'd have called you guys."

"Anything else you remember about him?"

"I figured him for a perv because he was wearing a coat. You know, a yanker, Joe Raincoat."

"Exhibitionist," said Milo.

"Exhibitionists I'm used to," said Vail. "See 'em every day on the set. So what, you think he killed Mr. Quigley?"

"We're just starting to investigate. How big was the guy you saw?"

"Average size." Tapping my shoulder. "More like him than you."

"What about the coat?"

"Knee-length. He wore it open, that's another."

"You could tell it was open because—"

"The shape, too wide to be zipped up. I got the impression of bulk, so nothing like microfiber. Hope you catch whoever killed that poor man. Bella and I are going back inside to read scripts."

The dog had sidled close. I ventured a pet of her head. She purred.

Erica Vail stared at me. "Unbelievable, she never likes guys." Smiling. "You married?"

Milo said, "What kind of scripts does Bella like?"

"She's eclectic," said Vail. "But discerning. If she doesn't whine at a page of dialogue, I give it a second look. The caliber of stuff I'm getting lately, she whines plenty."

CHAPTER

18

Over the next few days, data trickled in.

Neither of Marlon Quigg's daughters had any idea who'd want to harm their father. The same went for family friends Milo and Reed and Binchy interviewed. Belle Quigg, requestioned through a fog of sedation, repeated a mantra: Everyone loved Marlon, this had to be a maniac.

Animal Control reported thirty-three dead canines collected across the county since Quigg's murder. Milo and the young D's took the time to check each one. None was Louie.

Most of the dogs had been abandoned and had died of malnutrition or disease or from being hit by cars. A golden retriever mix discovered on a Canoga Park side street had been shot in the head, execution-style, and Milo took the time to contact its owners. Two college girls had shared Maximilian; both were bereft and guilt-stricken. The ex-boyfriend of one young woman was their prime suspect and a background check revealed a husky thirty-year-old with a misdemeanor record of assaults and disorderly conduct.

Milo grew excited and looked for the man. He turned out to have been on the open sea for seven months, working as a deckhand on a commercial freighter on its way to Japan.

The shelter where Marlon Quigg had adopted Louie employed no one who matched the description of the broadly built white man seen lurking near both murder scenes. With the exception of a Vietnamese American high school student and two octogenarian retirees, the staff was exclusively female.

The woman who'd handled Louie's paperwork recalled Marlon Quigg because he'd been so easy to deal with and opined that he'd seemed the perfect match for Louie: quiet, laid-back, no-fuss kind of guy.

I thought: *Easy victim.*

Binchy and Reed visited other shelters with no better results.

Inspection of Quigg's phone and financial records revealed nothing suspicious. An additional search of the campgrounds and interviews with a score of homeless people congregating near PCH and Sunset were futile, though one of the panhandlers, a wild-eyed, gap-toothed woman named Aggie, was certain Quigg had once driven by and given her fifty dollars.

Milo said, "Big haul."

"Oh, yeah, he was great."

"What kind of car was he driving, Aggie?"

"What else? Big Rolls-Royce. Like I say, some of those rich folk are nice!"

◆

Quigg's autopsy and lab results came in.

A significant bruise where the back of the neck met the skull suggested he'd been subjected to a single hard blow from behind. The C.I. hadn't caught it at the scene because Quigg's thick hair concealed it. Not a fatal blow but hard enough to stun.

No human hairs other than Quigg's had been found on his person but Louie had shed a few more strands onto his master's shirt. Three additional fibers turned out to be synthetic sheepskin.

I said, "Our bad guy wears a bulky coat. Maybe it's a cheap shearling."

"Dressed for the hunt . . . in Montana . . . may-be." Milo scrawled in his pad. "What do you think of that head wound?"

I said, "Classic sneak-attack sucker punch. Vita didn't need to be blitzed because she was reeling drunk and the pizza ruse caught her off guard. If the killer's the guy Erica Vail saw, he was near the scene three days before he did Quigg. Quigg's walks were predictable, it wouldn't have been much of a challenge to pretend to be taking a walk himself. Pass by and smile and wave, maybe even stop to pet Louie."

"Friendly stalking," he said. "Till it's not."

"I'd go back to Belle Quigg and ask if Marlon ever mentioned encountering anyone during his walks."

More writing. "On my list . . . so we have a good idea how each of them was done. But that still begs the big question: What turned them into victims? There's got to be something in common but hell if I can find it. I was hoping it would be Vita's lawsuit but it's not shaping up that way. The suits at Well-Start ended up being a lot more forthcoming than I expected. Not because they're nice guys, because Vita's murder has them worried the original gag order will be rescinded, they'll have to deal with a whole bunch of bad publicity. They actually sent a lawyer over yesterday and she showed me a lot of paper: the prelim motions, all the interviews with the accused co-workers, Shacker's report. Which came across as a lot of shrinky bullshit, no offense. But all in all, nothing new and the mouthpiece swore the company had no connection with Quigg. I didn't take her word for it, emailed Well-Start's CEO's second in command in Hartford, Connecticut. He called me personally, gave me the name of the accounting firm that does their books, greased the skids so they'd talk to me. They'd never hired Quigg nor, to their knowledge, had Quigg ever applied for a job. That was backed up by Mrs. Quigg. Marlon wasn't a 'seeker.' Happy with the status quo and figuring on retiring in a few years. Despite *that,* I got hold of Quigg's boss at the CPA firm and probed about Quigg doing insurance work. The firm does some but not for Well-Start and not for Well-Start's liability carrier. And even if they had, Quigg wouldn't have been assigned to it, he was more than busy with his supermarket account. He described ol' Marlon the way everyone else has: pleasant, compliant, even-tempered. So why were the two of them singled out? Or maybe there is no X factor and this bastard drives around, spots random prey, stalks and studies and sets up the hunt."

Nothing about this kind of murder was ever random but it wasn't the time to say so.

"Meanwhile," he said, "both cases are thawing out fast. Bastard quits right now, he may get away with it."

He needn't have worried about that.

CHAPTER

19

The following day, Milo's mood lifted from subterranean to glum.

Belle Quigg had remembered a "nice young fellow" Marlon had met during his nightly walk.

Louie had "taken" to the man, a clear sign to Quigg that he was a person of sterling character.

Milo hmmphed. "Because we all know dogs are such great judges." He spooned lentils onto a hillock of basmati rice. Sucked-out lobster claws were heaped in front of him, a gruesome display if you thought too much about it.

We were at his usual corner table at Café Moghul, an Indian restaurant around the corner from the station that serves as his second office. Over the years he'd handled a few disruptive psychotics wandering in from Santa Monica Boulevard. The owner, a sweet bespectacled woman who never wears the same sari twice, views him as Lord Protector and feeds him accordingly.

Today it was the lobster, plus tandoori lamb and a farm-plot's worth of slow-cooked vegetables enriched by clarified butter. He'd downed six glasses of iced clove tea.

With nowhere to go on the murders, I figured it for an easy day and was nursing my second Grolsch. "Marlon say anything else about this nice fellow?"

"If he did, Belle doesn't remember. By the way, I talked to a fabric analyst at the lab and the synthetic fleece found on Quigg would definitely be consistent with a low-budget shearling-type lining. Not that it leads me anywhere."

I said, "You heard what David Feldman said: He still hasn't unwrapped his winter coat. The fact that our boy wears his could mean he's originally from a cold climate."

"Or just rummaged at the right thrift shop. But if I come across a dogsled and mittens, I'll go with that. I find the fact that Quigg could've been primed for days hugely creepy. Like those wasps, stroking caterpillars into a stupor before they plunge the stinger."

I said, "Priming could serve an additional purpose: We've got a wasp who enjoys playing with his food."

"Joy of the hunt."

"A shearling might be something a hunter would own."

"Homicidal fore-prey." His laughter was harsh. The woman in the sari glided over. Today's garment was a celebration of turquoise and coral-pink and saffron-yellow. The pink matched her eyeglass frames.

"You are enjoying?"

"As always."

"More lobster?"

Milo patted his paunch. "Couldn't handle another bite. I've already demolished an entire coral reef."

She was confused by the reference,

covered with a smile. "You want more, tell me please, Lieutenant."

"Will do, but honestly, I'm done."

"Not totally done," she said. "Dessert."

"Hmm," he said. "*Gulab jamun* sounds good."

"Very fine." She glided away moving her lips. I caught two words: "My lieutenant."

Milo caught nothing because his phone was vibrating on the table. When he processed the digital readout, his shoulders dropped.

"Sturgis, sir. Oh, hi, Maria . . . oh. Jesu—when? Oh. Okay. Yeah. Right away."

Pushing away from the table, he threw cash down, swiped his chin viciously with a napkin. As I followed his trot for the door, the woman in the sari emerged from the kitchen bearing a platter of dough balls glazed with rosewater syrup and two bowls filled to the brim with rice pudding.

"There's *kir,* too," she said. "For extra sweet."

"Unfortunately, life isn't," said Milo,

shoving the door open and leaving me
to catch it.

He race-walked south on Butler, heading back to the station, flushed and
breathing hard and wiping his face and
grinding his teeth.

I said, "What's up?"

"What do you think?"

"Maria Thomas is a pencil-pusher.
Something mindlessly bureaucratic, like
a meeting you've been avoiding?"

He stopped short, wiped his face so
hard it was almost a slap.

"Our bad boy's back in action and instead of calling me, the watch com-
mander went straight to His Splendifer-
ousness. Who handed off to Maria
because he didn't want to hear the
sound of my voice. Obviously I've been
under the microscope on these murders
and not engendering confidence. I'm
heading over to the scene now. Don't
be surprised if they yank me off."

He resumed his march.

I said, "Who's the victim?"

His jaw was tight; the answer came
out hoarse and strangled.

"Think plural. This time the bastard doubled his fun."

The house was a low, wide ranch on a street of similar structures in a no-name neighborhood of West L.A.

The man had been found in the back-yard, lying on his stomach, wearing a black silk bathrobe. Deep stab wounds concentrated in a tight circle at the center of his chest. A couple of coup de grâce throat slashes had severed the right jugular and carotid and the trachea.

No disembowelment, nothing similar to Vita and Quigg. I watched as Milo examined the body.

The man's hair was long, dark, and wavy. His mustache was clipped precisely. Thirty to forty, good-sized, well muscled.

No effort to clean up the blood; the grass beneath the body was glazed a slick, unpleasant brown. No shredded lawn or damaged shrubs or other sign of struggle.

No blow from behind; this time, the C.I. had probed under the hair immediately, found no swelling or bruising.

The killer had taken on a serious foe face-to-face, dispatched him easily.

Maybe darkness had been his ally.

Milo circled the body for the fourth time.

The crime scene techs had finished their initial work and were waiting for him before leaving. Deputy Chief Maria Thomas had taken her time calling him to the scene.

Out in front of the house, the coroner's van was waiting to transport.

Nice, sunny day on the Westside. The yard where the man in the robe lay dead was ringed with high block walls laced with trumpet vine. In Missouri, where I'd grown up, no one bothered with fences and a kid could pretend he owned the world. Behind our rattrap house was a dense black forest that yielded an occasional dead animal and two human corpses. The first had been a hunter, shot accidentally by a buddy. The second had been a little girl, five years old, my age at the time. I supposed freedom could be the stuff of bad dreams but right now this boxy, confined space felt oppressive. Why was I thinking about that?

Because I had nothing constructive to offer.

Milo completed another circle before heading for Maria Thomas.

The D.C. had positioned herself mid-way up the blue house's driveway, on the near side of two parked vehicles. Sheltered from the ugliness, she made love to her cell phone.

Blond-coiffed and trim with a prefer-ence for tailored suits, Maria had been a captain when I'd met her a couple of years ago. Well spoken, cautious, deco-rous, she was the ideal corporate cog. The only time I'd seen her in action, she'd screwed up big-time by usurping a detective's role, leading to the death of a suspect in an interview room.

Somehow that disaster had earned her a promotion.

She kept Milo waiting as she talked, finally pointed to the house's rear door but didn't end the conversation.

Milo and I made our way through the bright, neatly kept house. The laundry room and the kitchen and the living room appeared untouched, no blood from the yard tracked in.

The kitchen smelled of cinnamon.

Everything neat and clean and normal.

The master bedroom was another story.

The woman lay on her back atop a queen-size bed. Her hair was short and wavy, a careful blend of several shades of subdued caramel. Her left hand was tethered to a brass headboard with a blue necktie. The tie's label was visible. Gucci.

No towels or tarp had been spread underneath her naked body. A few ruby specks dotted pale blue sheets, but no arterial explosion or castoff or significant leakage.

Waiting until every organ system had shut down before doing his thing.

The exact same thing he'd done to Vita Berlin and Marlon Quigg.

This woman's eyes were wide open, maybe positioned that way postmortem or perhaps they'd opened spasmodically and stayed that way.

Big and gray and artfully shadowed, the lashes enriched with mascara.

Disturbingly lifelike despite the impossible angle of her broken neck and putrid guts piled up in grotesque decoration.

On the carpet next to the bed was a filmy, pink negligee. The woman's nails were silver nacre, her toes, claret.

Just beneath the baby toe of her left foot was a sheet of white paper.

?

Milo growled. "You're getting boring, asshole."

The uniform by the door said, "Pardon?"

Milo ignored him and took in the room.

I was already scanning the space for the second time, concentrating on the left-hand nightstand where a pair of frilly pink panties draped a lamp shade. Spread across the stand was a careless array: a tube of Love Jam apricot-flavored lubricant, a package of ribbed condoms, an unopened bottle of Sauvignon Blanc, a corkscrew, two wine-glasses.

A similar lamp graced the other stand, minus the undergarment. The only object it housed besides the lamp was a silver-framed photo.

Good-looking couple. Tux and wedding dress, big smiles as they cut into a four-tiered cake festooned with yellow sugar roses.

No younger than they appeared now. Newlyweds?

A ceiling lamp glowed faint orange. A dimmer switch near the bed was set on low.

Romantic lighting.

The scene shot into my head, as surely as if I'd scripted it.

The two of them retire for bed, counting on a night of romance.

One or both of them hears something out back.

They ignore it because you can't go check on every little leaf-rustle and imagined intrusion.

They hear it again.

Someone—some*thing*—out in the yard?

No big deal, at worst a raccoon or a possum or a skunk. Or just a stray cat or dog, that had happened before.

They hear it again.

A faint scratching. Rustling of foliage. Again.

Too enduring to be ignored.

Is there really something out there, honey?

No prob, I'll check.

Be careful.

I'm sure it's nothing.

He throws on his robe, goes to check it out. Because that's what husbands do.

She waits, thinking it's nice to be married, have someone to squish bugs and play Protector.

Lying back, she relaxes, anticipating deliciousness.

He doesn't return quickly the way he usually does.

The moments pile up.

She begins to wonder.

Don't be silly, maybe he really did encounter a critter and had to deal with it.

Hopefully not a raccoon, they carry rabies. And get mean when cornered.

But no sound of struggle, so maybe he's just being careful.

The notion of her darling and a critter makes her smile. So . . . primal. He'll be careful, he always is, and it'll turn out to be one of those funny stories they'll tell their grandchildren.

But it *is* taking a long time . . .

More time passes.

She calls his name.

Silence.

Then, the door closes. Good. Everything's fine, maybe he'll come in with one of his yummy surprises. Last time it was Godiva chocolate.

This time it could be another treat. Food or otherwise . . .

She closes her eyes, arranges herself the way he likes. The comforting sound of male footsteps grows louder.

She loves that sound.

She coos his name.

Silence.

Or perhaps a vague masculine grunt.

Baby's playing Caveman. Excellent, this is going to be one of *those* nights.

Something *not* to tell the grandchildren.

She smiles. Purrs.

Positions herself a little racier than usual, creating sublime invitation.

He's in the room, now. She hears his breathing intensify.

"Baby," she says.

Silence.

Fine, *that* game.

He's right next to her, she senses him, feels his heat. But . . .

Something different.

She opens her eyes.

Everything changes.

Papers in the desk of the home office next to the bedroom conformed to DMV info.

Barron and Glenda Parnell.

He'd lived just over two months past his thirty-sixth birthday. She'd made it thirteen months longer.

A picture I.D. badge from North Hollywood Day Hospital tagged her as *G. A. Usfel-Parnell, M.D. Nuclear Medicine.* In the picture, she was grave, still pretty, wearing big, rimless glasses. Milo found them in a nightstand drawer.

I wondered about the extent of Dr.

Glenda Parnell's visual impairment. What had she actually seen when she'd opened her eyes?

Had she ever really focused?

Trembled at the horror but composed herself sufficiently to bargain?

Fear about her husband's fate would have shaken her, but perhaps she'd been able to put that aside, sufficiently adrenalized to concentrate on her own survival.

Had the killer pretended to go along as he had her tie her own arm to the bedpost? Or had he relied, at the outset, on terror and intimidation?

Had she sensed it was futile the moment he'd breached the door? Complied out of self-preservation as well as love for Barron, hoping cooperation would spare both of them?

If so, she'd spoken a completely different language from the killer. To him, Barron was nothing more than an obstacle to overcome.

He'd pulled the prelim off perfectly, drawing the guy into his trap.

Now the fun part.

◆

Once prints had been taken, Milo gloved up and gave the office desk a thorough search. Glenda Parnell's malpractice insurance was paid up, as were her subscriptions to several medical journals. Mail addressed to Barron Parnell appended CFP to his name. A mailer from a brokerage house expanded that to Certified Financial Planner.

So did a letter from an attorney representing the Cameron Family Trust that specified malfeasance and "incautious" investing.

The date was nineteen months ago. Milo copied down the particulars.

Further excavation of the desk drawers indicated Parnell worked out of the home with no apparent clients other than himself and his wife. He'd done well, amassing just over a million dollars in a stock account, two hundred thousand more in a corporate bond account, just under ten thousand in a joint savings-checking account.

The two vehicles parked in the driveway were a three-year-old yellow Porsche Cayman registered to Barron and a gray Infiniti QX registered to

Glenda. Both had been recently washed and appeared undisturbed.

Also unmolested was a pricey bank of computers in the office, some serious jewelry in a leather box barely concealed behind blankets in the linen closet, a case of sparkling Christofle silverware in the pantry, a home entertainment system in the living room that included a sixty-inch plasma TV.

We returned to the bedroom. In Barron's sock drawer, Milo found a silver-framed glamour shot of Glenda. Fuzzy focus, the suggestion of nudity, cornucopia of cleavage, glistening teeth.

To Barry Boo from Sweet Gee. Love 4ever. Happy anniversary. XXXX

The inscribed date was forty-two days ago.

Maria Thomas stuck her head in the room. "Anything?"

Milo shook his head.

"Got a sec?"

"Yeah." He might've been agreeing to do-it-yourself root canal.

The three of us powwowed in the Parnells' spotless kitchen. Someone had put money into the décor: matte-black Euro cabinets trimmed in chrome, white marble counters that appeared unused, copper pots hanging from a cast-iron ceiling rack, everything else brushed steel.

Maria Thomas plinked a counter with a fingernail. "Marble's good for rolling pastry dough, not cooking. No one did serious food, here."

"Didn't know you were into the culinary arts, Maria."

"I'm not, my daughter is. That translates to she's the one gets addicted to *Top Chef,* I'm the one pays tuition at some overpriced institute in New York. Now she wants to spend next summer in France, learning how to properly slice onions. This is a kid who survived the first four years of her life on hot dogs and chocolate milk."

She fingered a crisp tweed lapel. Her hair was sprayed in place. Not helmet-stiff, a higher level of fixative that lent the illusion of softness. An expensive-looking phone dangled from her other hand. "Some mess, huh?"

Milo said, "It's a step up."

"From what?"

"Not from, for," he said. "The offender. He took risks with the husband in order to get to the wife. Earned himself a two-fer, kicked up the thrill level. But you know that, already. Seeing as you've been here for a while."

She stared at him. "Someone's touchy."

He turned his back on her. Interesting move; she outranked him significantly. He'd been there when she'd screwed up, had never exploited it. Maybe Maria figured that gave him a certain power. Maybe that would eventually work against him.

"Okay," she said, "let's clear the air right now so we can go about our respective businesses?"

"Thought we were in the same business."

Thomas's gray eyes turned to pond pebbles. "I'm here because the chief has been following this since the second one, Mister"—consulting her phone—"Quigg. The reason the chief was informed early is someone thought a serial pattern might be forming and that the details were sufficiently out of the ordinary for the chief to need to be apprised. Don't ask who informed him, that's irrelevant."

"I couldn't care less about any of that, Maria, all I want to do is clear four murders."

"That's what we all want. Think there's a remote chance of your accomplishing it anytime in the near future?"

"You betcha, boss," he said. "Everything will be gift-wrapped and presented for your approval by"—reading his Timex—"nine forty-three tonight. Give or take a nanosecond. Also on the schedule is the capture of Osama's entire organization but in the meantime be sure to warn His Amazingness to treat any packages from Pakistan with caution."

"Hey—"

"Is there a remote chance? What kind of *question* is that, Maria? You think this is writing traffic tickets?"

"Ah, the temper." She winked. "The classic *Irish* temper and I can say that because half my family traces back to County Derry."

"Whoopee for genealogy, Maria. Is there a point to this conversation?"

Thomas caressed marble, ran a finger under the counter rim. "Indulge yourself, Milo, keep venting. Get all the bad feeling out so we can both do our jobs like grown-ups."

She turned to me, seeking confirmation of something.

I kept studying the double-wide refrigerator. No magnets, no memos or photos. Nothing like a blank panel of steel to keep one fascinated.

Maria Thomas turned back to Milo. "You bet it's a reasonable question. When's the last time you dealt with a serial remotely similar to this, Milo? A necktie of guts? Jesus, it's beyond disgusting."

He didn't answer.

She said, "I can't see any common thread among the victims other than they're all white. Can you?"

"Not yet."

"Not yet," she repeated. To me: "*You* ever see anything like this? A sexual psychopath who throws such a wide net?"

Milo said, "It's not necessarily sexual."

"Then what?"

"Some kind of grudge. The first victim was engaged in a big-time lawsuit and I just found a financial complaint in Mr. Parnell's desk."

"I saw that," she said. "You can't seriously think a money thing led to *that.* And what about Mr. Quigg? He sue anyone or vice versa?"

"Nothing's come up yet."

"You should've checked his financials."

"I have."

"And you haven't found anything. So the answer's no, not 'nothing's come up.' Meaning there's no common thread. Meaning a money thing's less than unlikely. You go along with his theory, Dr. Delaware? You don't see this as a sexual psychopath?"

"Can't say."

"Can't or won't?"

"I don't see the point of guessing."

"So far I've heard nothing but guessing—all right, enough of this pleasantry. I'm expected to go back to the boss and report something. What do *you* suggest, Milo?"

Milo said, "Tell him each time the killer strikes he increases the possibility of a lead. In the meantime, I'll be concentrating on the Parnells."

"Each time," she said. "Maybe by the time we get ten, eleven victims, we'll be in great shape. Very reassuring."

Milo grinned in that lupine way: teeth bared in anticipation of ripping flesh.

Maria Thomas said, "You always see humor when no one else does. When were you planning to go to the public?"

"His Perfectness thinks I should?"

"Word to the wise, Milo: You really need to stop with the obnoxious nicknames, one day it'll get back to him."

"He doesn't like being perfect?"

"The *public. When?*"

"I hadn't thought about it."

"No? That's too bad because the chief thinks it might be useful." She looked over her shoulder, in the direction of the bedroom. "Given the steadily rising corpse count. And something tells me he won't find your lassitude reassuring."

Milo walked away from her again. Her

face tensed with anger but before she could speak, he circled back. "Okay, here's something to tell him: If this *was* a confirmed sexually motivated psychopath, some rapist who escalated to murder, I'd have been talking to Public Affairs as soon as the second one surfaced, hoping an earlier, live victim would come forth. The same goes for a serial asshole targeting a specific victim population— hookers, convenience clerks, whatever. In that case there'd be a moral as well as a practical benefit: letting high-risk targets know so they can protect themselves. But what do we go public on, here, Maria? A bogeyman stalking and butchering random citizens? That risks setting off a panic with very little upside."

"What's your alternative?" she said. "A nice collection of murder books?"

"I haven't even started working these two victims. Maybe I'll learn something that will change everything. If you let me do the damn job."

"*I'm* holding you back?"

"Wasting time explaining myself is holding me back."

"Oh, so you're different from anyone else?" Back to me: "What's with the question mark on these two, Doctor?"

I said, "The same thing was left with the first two victims."

She blinked. "Yes, of course. So what does it mean?"

"Could be a taunt," I said.

Milo smiled. "Or our bad boy's expressing his curiosity."

"About what?" said Thomas.

"The mysteries of the human body."

"That's grotesque. You know what *I* thought when I saw it? Some weird mystical symbolism, like the Zodiac used to send. You look into any witchcraft angles?"

"I'm open to anything, Maria."

"Meaning you haven't. And you're opposed to going public. How many bodies will it take to get you flexible?"

"If nothing on these two—"

"Good," she said. "You're openminded when forced to be. He'll be happy to hear it. He respects you, you know."

"I'm touched."

"You really should be. Get back to me

if you learn something. Sooner rather than later."

"You're the glove," said Milo.

"Pardon."

"He doesn't want to dirty his hands so he gloves up."

Maria Thomas examined her spotless, manicured digits. "You have a way with words. Sure, view me as a glove. And bear in mind that finger-poking can be painful."

CHAPTER

20

Thomas left the scene scolding her phone. Drove off in a sparkling blue city sedan.

Milo said, "Before she stuck her nose in, I was thinking about going public at some point. But right now I don't see what it'll accomplish and the panic thing's an issue."

I said, "If you release any data, I'd choose the question marks. They're unique to our bad guy, might jog someone's memory."

He shuffled over to the Parnells' cars, looked inside. "I don't make some kind of progress soon, the decision won't be mine. You got the point of Thomas showing up."

"Behave or else."

"More than that. The chief smells a big-time loser in these cases so he's keeping his distance." He flipped his pad open. "Where's that lawyer who threatened Barron Parnell . . . here we go, 'William Leventhal, Esquire, representing the Cameron Family Trust.' Sounds like a big money deal, let's see if this legal eagle earned his cut."

William B. Leventhal ran a one-man practice on Olympic near Sepulveda.

On the way over, Milo said, "Booze and surprise for Vita, sucker punch for Marlon. Now he does two young healthy ones."

I said, "Same basic technique: surprise supplemented this time by darkness. Barron was the serious threat so he was drawn outside, blitzed, and stabbed to death. But no surgery, not even later when our bad guy had a chance. That says Glenda was the primary target and with Barron unlocking the door, she was easy prey. Also, her glasses were off because the two of them were planning a romantic evening and the room was dim, leading to a loss of focus. Before she had time to figure out what was going on, he was in charge. We know he stalked his first two victims, so he probably did the same with her."

"You don't see it as a two-fer? Doubling his pleasure?"

"Upping the body count was a bonus, but I think Barron was a hurdle to jump so he could get to Glenda."

"So I'm wasting my time with Leventhal."

"Only one way to find out," I said.

The lawyer's front office staff was a woman in her seventies at a hundred-year-old desk. A brass nameplate said *Miss Dorothy Band, Exec. Secy. to Mr. Wm. B. Leventhal.* An IBM Selectric took up half her desk. Near the machine sat a precisely cornered stack of elegant beige stationery, a shorter pile of carbon paper, and a Bakelite intercom box

that predated the Truman administration.

Unflustered by our drop-in, Miss Dorothy Band pressed a button on the box.
"Mr. L, police to see you."

The machine barked back: "I paid
those tickets."

"They say it's about the Cameron
case."

"What about it?"

"They say they need to talk to you directly."

"That's a civil case, none of their business."

"Sir . . ."

"Fine. See-*yend* them in."

The trek to Leventhal's inner sanctum
took us past a vast law library. A man
was there to greet us, a good ten years
older than Dorothy Band. Short, thick,
and broad-shouldered, William Leventhal had bright, burnt-chocolate eyes,
white hair still tinged rusty in spots. An
uncannily deep voice said, "Police. Heh.
C'mon in."

Leventhal's office was vast, wood-
paneled, shag-carpeted in the precise

green of pimiento olives, redolent of dill pickles and old paper and musky after-shave. Heat streamed from a floor vent, creating a tropical ambience. William B. Leventhal wore a three-piece English-cut herringbone suit of heavy tweed, a starched white shirt, and a bolo tie held in place by a mammoth nugget of amethyst.

Not a trace of sweat on his plump face. A tweedy leprechaun, he lowered himself into a tufted leather chair commodious enough to harbor a panda. "The girl informs me this is about Cameron."

Milo started to explain.

Leventhal said, "Murder? You won't find the solution here. Never met Parnell, never even deposed him. Heh."

"You sent him a letter—"

"He was named along with everyone else in that firm. The case settled. *Finis.* Good-bye."

"What firm is that, sir?"

"'Sir,'" said Leventhal. "A kid with manners, I like that. If you must know, the miscreants in question are Lakewood, Parriser and DiBono, alleged money managers. Parnell worked there as a fixed-income specialist. In plain terms, boys, he bought bonds for rich people."

"The Cameron Trust is—"

"An inspired creation that has allowed two generations of not-too-bright Camerons to avoid gainful employment."

"Parnell's investments didn't do well?"

"They did fine," said Leventhal. "Though a trained parakeet could've handled the task. We're talking triple-A conservative investments, you read a daily list and pick. Or peck, if you're a parakeet. Heh."

"Then why did you—"

"In order to proceed optimally against the *primary* scoundrels, I was required to name everyone through whose hands Cameron money had passed." He rubbed chubby palms together. "I got to sue their office manager, their Human Resources person, their bookkeepers. The cleaning crew's fortunate they weren't named. Heh."

"The scoundrels were—"

"Lakewood." Leventhal ticked a finger. "DiBono. Parriser. Not necessarily in that order."

"What I'm getting at," said Milo, "is the nature of their scam—"

"No scam," said Leventhal. "I never said scam, no, no, no, no-*ooow*. A clear case of deceit would've been easy to ferret out. No, these geniuses were subtle. Promising verbally to invest in secure products but engaging in all sorts of risky nonsense. Commodity futures, derivatives, inadequately secured real estate loans. The veneer of solidity but once you looked closely, a house of cards." He winked. "I sued their outside accountant. Brought the lot of them to their knees."

"So the Camerons never lost money."

"Preventive medicine, boys. The rascals tried to claim that the original terms of the trust gave them lifetime control. I put the lie to that notion."

The left side of Leventhal's mouth rose. "And now the Camerons remain free to avoid honest labor."

"Congratulations," said Milo.

"Virtue is its own reward, young man. No, actually a fat contingency commission is far better recompense. So. Who murdered poor Mr. Parnell? Whom I've never met."

"That's what we're trying to find out."

"Well, you won't find out here. Was the wife involved?"

"Why do you ask that?"

"Because she was a battle-ax. I say that because when we served Parnell, she was abusive to the server. He described her with the B word but I'll stick with 'battle-ax' because memories of my mother washing my mouth out with soap still linger."

"The process server told you this?"

"He's my great-grandson, of course he told me."

"We'd like to speak with him."

"Suit yourselves," said Leventhal, rattling off an international number. "That's England, Brian's international cell phone. Brian Cohn, no e. Cambridge University, he's on fellowship. International relations, whatever that is. Jesus College. Brian Cohn at Jesus College. Heh. Tell him he owes me ten hours of work. You're thinking the wife was involved?"

"She was definitely involved," said Milo. "She's also dead."

"I see . . . did her death occur within the same approximate time frame as Mr. Parnell's?"

"Yes, sir."

"Both bodies at the scene?"

"Sir—"

"I'll take that as a yes," said Leventhal. "Wouldn't the obvious answer be murder-suicide?"

"Why would you think that, sir?"

"Because when a couple expires in a near-simultaneous manner, we always zeroed in on the murder-suicide angle and we were almost invariably correct. I'm referring to back in the day. When I did criminal prosecution at the Brooklyn D.A. Two bodies, weapon on the scene, first thing we'd look for was one party going berserk and victimizing the alleged loved one. You could put money on it. Sometimes we did. Office pools and such."

"That didn't happen here, Mr. Leventhal."

"You're certain."

"We are."

"Okay, hmm . . . did the wife have a boyfriend? Did *he* have a *girl*friend? Was

money taken? Jewelry, other valuables?
Do acquaintances imply loss of mental
control for one of the parties—some
sort of personality disintegration? How
were the two of them dispatched? Gun?
Knife? Blunt object? None of the above?"

Milo said, "Sorry, we can't—"

"Of course you can't," said Leventhal.
"Because if you could you might stum-
ble upon someone with half a brain,
sixty-two years of legal experience, one-
third of that prosecutorial. But why make
your life easier?"

He sprang up and waved us to the
door. "Despite your reticence, I'll reiter-
ate some sage advice, boys: Check out
the wife. Even without a murder-suicide
angle, we always hurt the one we love.
And someone as short-tempered as her
was bound to evoke hostility. Take a
close look to see if she'd engaged in
any sort of emotional dustup recently. If
you find out she had a boyfriend to boot,
we're talking emotional TNT."

"Thanks for the tip, sir."

"No problem," said Leventhal. "I won't
even bill you."

◆

Milo called Cambridge from the car. Brian Cohn picked up, sounding hungover. "Yuh?"

Milo explained.

Cohn said, "This is England, man, you know what time it is?" He coughed, cleared his throat. Phlegm-laden laughter. "Oh, man, there he goes again."

"Who?"

"Wild Bill. Aka Greatest-Grandpa. *He* gets up at four a.m. so we all have to."

"He's quite a guy. Says you owe him—"

"Ten hours of work, yada yada yada. By his calculation. Which was probably done on an abacus." Cohn laughed again. A female voice sounded in the background. "One sec, babe." Yawn. "Okay, I'm quasi-awake, what do you need to know about that crazy shrew?"

"Tell us about your encounter."

"Why?"

"She's dead."

"Oh. That's too bad. Even for someone like that."

Milo said, "Like what?"

"Hostile. No one likes to be served

but the worst you usually get is a sneer, some cursing. She came to the door wearing her white coat; I figured, good, a doctor, someone rational. Because plenty of times you're dealing with Neanderthals. This was one of those deals where I didn't need to hand it to Parnell personally, just ascertain his primary residence and verify that someone had accepted it. I used the flower ruse, bought some cheap ones at the supermarket. She came to the door, said, 'Is this from Barry? Hold on, I'll get you a tip.' I said not necessary, handed her the papers, informed her she'd just accepted service, and split. She came after me, running into the street, screaming I'm a lowlife. Then she grabbed me by the shoulder, tried to force the paper back on me. First time anyone ever got physical other than one drunk guy and that time I was prepared, took a friend who played halfback at the U. From a woman, let alone a doctor, I wasn't ready for it, I'm trying to peel her off me, her nails are digging in my arm, the papers are flying all over the place. Finally, I free myself and get the hell out of there. So what, she pissed someone off and they killed her?"

"Don't know, yet."

"Well," said Brian Cohn. "I'd sure look into that possibility."

As we drove away from Leventhal's building, Milo said, "Another tough personality, shades of Vita. Without Quigg stuck between the two of them I'd say we had ourselves a nice little pattern: women with short fuses."

"Be interesting to see if Glenda's co-workers saw her that way."

"Interesting would be okay," he said. "Intriguing would be better."

CHAPTER
21

North Hollywood Day Hospital was an off-white sugar cube on a marginal block of Lankershim Boulevard. Windows were barred. A bearish uniformed guard lurked near the front door, smoking.

Bordering the building were storefront offices catering to personal injury lawyers, physicians and chiropractors specializing in "Industrial Rehabilitation," and medical equipment suppliers. The largest concern, double-wide and neon-lit, advertised walk-in occupational and physical therapy.

Welcome to Slip-and-Fall Heaven.

Milo said, "Lordy, my sacroiliac is a-throbbin'," as he pulled into a loading zone and left a long-expired crime scene parking card on the dash.

The guard studied our approach above a smog-burst of tobacco. When we got close, he stepped in front of the door and folded his arms across his chest.

Milo said, "You're kidding."

"Huh?"

"A pro like you can't sniff out a big clue?"

"Wuh clue?"

"We ain't selling catheters, Marshal Dillon." Out came the badge. The guard shifted just wide enough to clear the entry.

"Fast learner," said Milo and we strode past him.

The waiting area was bright, stuffy, standing room only. Despair vied with boredom for the dominant emotion. Wheelchairs, walkers, oxygen tanks abounded. Anyone who seemed physically okay looked psychologically stricken. All the joy of death row.

The queue at the reception window was a dozen deep. Milo pushed past and rapped his knuckles on the glass. The woman on the other side kept clicking computer keys.

He rapped again.

Her eyes remained on her keyboard.

Third time's the charm. She snapped, "Just hold on!" A speaker box transformed her voice into something metallic and unwelcoming. Or maybe that was just her.

Milo banged hard enough to vibrate the glass and the receptionist wheeled, teeth bared, ready to confront. The badge silenced her and she took it out on a button under her desktop, stabbing viciously. A door on the far side of the waiting room gave off a loud *click.*

Someone said, "How come he gets to jump?"

Milo said, "Because I'm handsome."

Another large but soft guard waited on the other side. Behind him was a beige corridor lined with doors the same color.

Identical hue, also, for the vinyl flooring and the plastic signs directing the infirm toward Exam 1, Exam 2 . . . Ecru faces on the patients, as well. Welcome to Planet Bread Dough.

"Police, what for?" said the guard.

"I need to talk to Dr. Glenda Usfel-Parnell's boss."

The guard's lips moved as he tried to get his mouth around the hyphenation.

Milo said, "Get me the head of nuclear medicine."

The guard reached into his pocket and drew out a wilted piece of paper. "Um . . . that's . . . Usfel, G."

"Not anymore. Who's her boss?"

"I dunno."

"How long you been working here?"

"Three weeks tomorrow."

"You know Dr. Usfel?"

"You don't hardly see the doctors, they go in and out through there." Pointing to a door at the end of the hallway.

"Who's the big boss?"

"That would be Mr. Ostrovine."

"That would be who you go find."

◆

The man who burst through the rear door wore a too-snug gray suit of ambiguous cloth, a blue shirt with a high, stiff collar, and a pink paisley tie that had never gone near a silkworm. With better fabrics, the result would've been foppish. This screamed *Trying Too Hard.*

The same went for fruity aftershave, a scary tan, and a toupee that landed well short of possible. "Mick Ostrovine. How can I help you?"

"We're here about Dr. Usfel."

"What about her?"

"She's deceased."

Ostrovine's spray tan drained to the ambient beige. "Glenda? She worked a double shift yesterday, she was fine, what happened?"

"Someone broke into her home and killed her."

"Oh my God, that's insane. Her home? Some kind of home invasion?"

"We're sorting things out, Mr. Ostrovine."

A nearby door opened, silent as the gill-slit on a shark. A heavy woman in scrubs pushed a wheelchair toward us. Her passenger was an ancient man wrapped in a blanket, hairless, blue-veined, slumped, barely conscious.

"Hey, Mr. O," she said. "Got all them tests run, taking him to the physical therapy for that exercise."

"Sure, sure," said Ostrovine.

His abruptness made her blink. As the chair rolled past, another exam room disgorged a burly man brandishing a crutch. The implement was tucked under one arm. He took a couple of unaided steps, saw us, placed his weight on the device, and assumed an exaggerated limp.

"Mr. O," he said. "Gonna get myself some hydrotherapy."

"Good, good," said Ostrovine.

When a third door opened and a twenty-year-old girl came skipping out waving a shiny chromium cane like a cheerleader's baton, Milo said, "Could we go somewhere to talk?" Nudging me. *You know hospitals, handle this.*

Ostrovine's office was a beige rectangle that faced the parking lot. The rest of the hospital's rear section housed orthopedics, nuclear medicine, physical medicine, anesthesiology, radiology.

Not a bed in sight.

I said, "You do outpatient care."

"We're adjunctive," said Ostrovine, settling behind a desk, bare but for a laptop. The room looked unused.

"Meaning . . ."

"We fill a niche."

"What's that?"

Ostrovine sighed. "We're better equipped than a clinic and more efficiently specialized than a larger institution. We don't do E.R. so that frees us up for other modes of delivery. Our primary specialty is aftercare: pain management, disability evaluation, lifestyle readjustment."

"What was Dr. Usfel's specialty?"

"Glenda ran nuke med. That's cutting-edge technology assessing how parts of the body are actually working. As opposed to conventional radiology, which is primarily static, nuke uses dyes, radio-isotopes to capture ongoing function."

He shook his head and the toupee shifted downward. He nudged it back in place without a trace of self-consciousness. "Glenda was terrific. This is horrible."

I said, "How'd she get along with patients and staff?"

"Everyone here gets along."

"Did she have an easygoing personality?"

Ostrovine's jaw rotated, settled slightly left of center. "What are you getting at?"

"We've heard she could display a bit of temper."

"I don't know what you heard but it doesn't apply to her performance here."

"So anyone we talk to here is going to tell us she was easygoing."

He unbuttoned his suit jacket, let out an inch of abdomen, sucked it back in, refastened. "Glenda was businesslike."

"Efficient but not touchy-feely."

"She never had a problem with anyone."

I said, "You can't think of anyone who'd resent her."

"I cannot."

"Who are her friends here?"

He thought. "I suppose she didn't socialize much on the job. We're task-oriented, anyway. A lot of our employees are floats."

"Who'd she work with most closely?"

"That would be her technicians."

"We'd like to talk to them."

Ostrovine opened the laptop, typed. "The tech on duty today is Cheryl Wannamaker. She's fairly new, I doubt she can tell you much."

"We'll give her a try, anyway. And please give us the names of the others."

"What makes you think Glenda's work had anything to do with what happened to her?"

"We need to look at everything."

"I suppose," said Ostrovine, "but in this case you'd be best off looking outside the workplace. We're low on drama, run a business, not a production company."

"Insurance business?"

"The business of wellness often involves third-party payment."

"Do you deal a lot with Well-Start?"

"We deal with everyone."

"If I give you some names could you check if they've been your patients?"

"Impossible," said Ostrovine. "Confidentiality's our first commandment."

"How about checking and if the names aren't there we won't have to come back with subpoenas."

"I'm afraid I can't do that."

"I understand. As I'm sure you will when we show up with the appropriate paperwork and all those tasks you're oriented toward come to a grinding halt."

Ostrovine flashed oversized dental caps. "Is this really necessary, guys? I'm sure Glenda's . . . tragedy had nothing to do with work."

Milo said, "Maybe you should switch careers and become a detective."

"Fine, give me those names. But if they are here, I can't give you details."

"Vita Berlin."

Keyboard arpeggio. Sigh of relief. "No. Next."

"Marlon Quigg."

"No, again. Now, if there's nothing more—"

"Dr. Usfel's techs."

"Oh," said Ostrovine. "That. Fine. I'll call Cheryl for you."

◆

Cheryl Wannamaker was young, stoic, dreadlocked, with a Jamaican lilt to her speech. We talked to her in the parking lot, near a black Mercedes parked in *M. Ostrovine*'s spot.

The news of Glenda Usfel-Parnell's death seemed not to impact her immediately. Then her eyes got wet and her chin shook. "Another one."

"Ma'am?" said Milo.

"Lost my nephew," she said. "Two weeks ago. Hit by a drunk driver."

"I'm so sorry."

"DeJon was twelve." She wiped her eyes. "Now Dr. U. This world. Dear God."

"How long did you work with Dr. U?"

"Five weeks."

"Anyone have a beef with her?"

"Not that I saw."

"What kind of person was she?"

"She was an okay person," said Cheryl Wannamaker.

"Friendly?"

"Sure." She smiled. "Actually, not so much. She was all about let's get the work done and go home."

"Not a lot of chitchat."

"No chitchat at all, sir."

"That create tension?"

"Not for me," said Wannamaker. "I don't like wasting time."

"What about others?"

"Everything seemed okay."

"We've heard she had a temper."

"Well," said Wannamaker, "she kind of did."

"Who'd she get mad at?"

"Not mad, more like . . . grumpy. When things got backed up, when people didn't do what she wanted."

"How'd she show her grumpiness?"

"She'd get all quiet." Cheryl Wannamaker licked her lips. "Too quiet, like a kettle gonna overflow."

"What happened when she overflowed?"

"She never did. She just got that heavy quiet thing going. You'd talk to her, she wouldn't answer, even though you knew she heard you. So you just guessed what she wanted and hoped it *was* what she wanted."

"You never saw her go off on anyone?"

"Never," she said. "But I heard someone went off on her."

"Who?"

"Some patient," said Wannamaker. "Before my time, I just heard about it."

"What'd you hear?"

"Someone lost it in the scan room."

"Who told you?"

"Margaret," she said. "Margaret Wheeling, she's on when I'm off."

"How long before you arrived did this happen?"

"I couldn't say."

"But people were still talking about it when you began work."

"No, just Margaret. To educate me."

"About?"

"Dr. U, what she was like. How she could be tough. When the patient went off on her, she didn't back down, stood right up to him and said, 'Calm down or leave right now.' And he did. Margaret was saying we all needed to be assertive like that because you never know what's going to walk in."

"Did that patient ever show up again?"

"Couldn't tell you, sir."

"Margaret tell you anything else about Dr. Usfel?"

"She said when Doctor gets quiet, give her space."

"Where can we find Margaret?"

"Right here," said Cheryl Wannamaker, producing a cell phone. "I have her number."

Margaret Wheeling lived a quarter hour from her job, in a town house on Laurel Canyon just north of Riverside. She opened the door holding a glass of ice water. Milo gave her the news gently.

She said, "Oh my God."

"I'm sorry to have to tell you."

"Dr. U," she said. "Glenda . . . come in."

Rawboned and ruddy with curly gray hair and unadorned yellow-gray eyes, she led us to a living room heavy on golden maple furniture and needlepoint pillows. Toby mugs filled a glass-front cabinet. Another was chocked with souvenir ashtrays with an emphasis on national parks and Nevada casinos. A jowly man sat drowsing on a sofa, sports pages spread on his lap.

"My husband," said Margaret Wheeling, sounding proud of the fact. She kissed his forehead lightly. "Don, they're here."

Don Wheeling blinked, stood, shook our hands. She told him about Glenda Usfel. He said, "You're kidding."

"Oh, Don, isn't that horrid?"

He cupped the bottom of her chin. "You be okay, Meg?"

"I'll be fine. Go use the bedroom, take a real nap."

"You need me, you know where to find me, Meg."

When he was gone, she said, "Don was in law enforcement, rode a motorcycle for Tulsa PD for a year, back when he was right out of the service. By the time I met him he was already in asphalt and concrete. Please sit. Some cookies? Coffee, tea, soda?"

"No, thanks," said Milo.

Margaret Wheeling said, "Dr. U murdered. I still can't believe it. You have any idea who did it?"

"Unfortunately, we don't. Cheryl Wannamaker told us about a patient who gave Dr. U a hassle."

"That small thing? Why would anyone kill over something like that?"

"Tell us about it."

"It was stupid," said Wheeling. "One of those stupid things. Dr. U keeps the temp low in the scan room. For the machines. This idiot got all huffy because we didn't have blankets. Because the linen service hadn't delivered that morning, not our fault. I tried to explain to him but he got abusive."

"Abusive, how?"

"Cursing me out, saying I was stupid. Like it's my fault the service screwed up."

"What'd you do?"

"Called Dr. U," she said. "She makes decisions, I just follow directions."

"Then what happened?"

"He started in with her. I'm cold, you should have a blanket. A grown man but he acted like a spoiled kid. She told him to calm down, it's not the end of the world, we'll do the procedure quickly and get you out of here. He called her the same names he called me. That was it for Dr. U. She went up to him, told him off. Not loud, but firm."

"What'd she say?"

"That his behavior was out of line and he needed to leave. *Now.*"

I said, "No second chance."

"He had his chance," said Wheeling. "We had a waiting room full of scans, who needed him? The idiot probably thought her being a woman he could intimidate her. It was a little chilly, sure, but it's not like he didn't have insulation."

"What do you mean?"

"Plenty of body fat. And obviously he wasn't screwed on too tight because he came in wearing a heavy coat and it wasn't cold outside, just the opposite. Not that at first he looked like a weirdo. That being the case I'd have called security from the beginning. He seemed okay. Real quiet. Then it was just like he . . . came apart."

"Do you call security a lot?"

"When I need to. We get all types."

"But this guy set off no warning bells."

"I guess I should've noticed that crazy coat, but I'm not looking at them, I'm checking the machines."

"He came apart."

"Went from normal to ticked off like *that*." Snapping her fingers.

"Scary," I said. "But Dr. Usfel handled it."

"She's tough, went to med school in Guadalajara, Mexico, told me she saw things there you wouldn't see in the States. You don't really think that guy had anything to do with it? I mean how would he find her? And this was like two months ago. And he never came back."

I said, "What else can you tell us about him?"

"Just what I told you. White, normal-looking, thirty, thirty-five."

"Clean-shaven?"

"Yup."

"Hair?"

"Brown. Short. Pretty neat appearance, actually. Except for that crazy coat, we're talking heavy-duty winter wear, one of those shearlings."

"What color?"

"Some kind of brown. I think."

"Any distinguishing marks? Like scars, tattoos, unusual features?"

She thought. "No, he looked like a regular person."

"To get scanned he'd need paper-work. Did you see his?"

"We don't see paperwork, the front desk handles all that. They come in with a day-chart that has an I.D. number, not even a name."

I said, "What procedure was he sent for?"

"Who remembers?"

I gave her time.

She shook her head. "I'm not sure I even looked."

Milo said, "How about you sit down with an artist and help produce a draw-ing?"

"You're saying it *was* him?"

"No, ma'am, but we've got to nail down every detail we can if we're gonna solve Dr. Usfel's murder."

"My name wouldn't be on it, right?" she said. "The drawing?"

"Of course not."

"Really, you'd be wasting your time. All I'd tell an artist is what I just told you."

"Would you be willing to give it a try? To help us out?"

"I can totally keep myself out of it?"

"Absolutely."

She crossed a leg, scratched a bare ankle. "You really think it's important?"

"Honestly, Ms. Wheeling, we don't know. But unless you can tell us of some other person Dr. U had problems with, we've got to follow up."

"What kind of person would go kill someone over a small thing?"

"Not a normal person."

"That's for sure . . . an artist? I don't know."

Milo said, "Back when Don was in law enforcement, I'll bet he appreciated any help he could get."

"I suppose," said Margaret Wheeling. "Okay, I'll try. But you're wasting your time, he just looked like a regular person."

CHAPTER
22

Wheeling's door closed behind us and we headed for the unmarked.

Milo said, "Heavyset guy in a shearling. Usfel pissed him off royally, no doubt Vita did, too." He frowned. "And somehow nice Mr. Quigg managed to get on his bad side."

I said, "His confrontation with Usfel was a brief onetimer that took on huge proportions in his mind only. So his brushes with the others wouldn't need to be dramatic."

"Touchy fellow."

"Leading to increased element of surprise." We got in the car. I said, "One thing different about Usfel is he tied her up. Maybe because he'd seen her in action, knew she was tough enough to be a threat."

"Not so tough that she didn't give in easily, Alex. There was no sign of struggle in that bedroom."

"He could have controlled her with a gun. She probably expected to be raped, figured on negotiating her life, had no idea what he was really after."

"If he used a gun on Usfel, he could've done the same for the others. Knock knock, pizza delivery, here's my little steel friend. Vita being drunk would have made his job easier. And a guy like Quigg wouldn't have fought back. Okay, let's put a face on this choirboy."

He called Alex Shimoff, a Hollenbeck detective with serious artistic talent whom he'd used before. When Shimoff's cell and home lines didn't pick up, he left a message and tried Petra Connor at Hollywood Division. Same story.

He turned on the engine. "I don't get my blankie, I gut you. There's a reasonable motive."

I said, "That place is an insurance mill and Vita was involved in a lawsuit. Maybe she and Shearling met there or at a place like it. Though Vita's alleged damages were emotional; she wouldn't have needed any scans and I can't see Well-Start paying for them."

"Maybe her lawyer had a deal with Ostrovine or someone like him. Problem is I can't find out who handled the suit. Well-Start won't say and because it settled early, nothing was filed. I'll try them again."

He headed for the station. A few miles later, I thought of something. "Wanting a blanket even though he's overdressed could be a psychiatric issue. But it could also mean his temperature regulation really is off. And that could be due to a physical condition."

"Such as?"

"The first thing that comes to mind is low thyroid function. Nothing severe enough to incapacitate him but just enough to make him put on a few pounds and feel chilly. And hypothyroidism can also increase irritability."

"Perfect," he said. "He ever gets

caught, some lawyer claims diminished capacity due to bad glands. I like the other thing you said: He and Vita crossed paths during some medical procedure. A waiting room spat. Given Vita's level of tact, I can see her dissing his damn coat and that being enough."

"Was there anything in the paper Well-Start showed you that said she got medically evaluated?"

"Nope, but who knows? Hell, given the fact that this guy's obviously unbalanced, maybe he and Vita ran into each other at Shacker's office."

"Shacker's got a separate exit so patients don't cross paths, but anything's possible."

"Why don't you call him, see if he knows Shearling."

"He wasn't that comfortable talking about Vita and asking him to identify a patient would be off the table, ethically, unless you could show imminent danger to a specific person."

"The specific person's his next damn victim . . . yeah, you're right but bug him anyway. I need to do *something*."

I made the call, left a message on Shacker's voicemail.

He said, "Thanks. Any other ideas?"

I said, "Ostrovine buckled when we threatened to shut him down for a day. If he was lying about Vita, maybe he'll eventually give up the info."

"Let's go back there," he said, hanging a U. "He balks, I'll grab that stupid rug on his head and hold it for ransom."

This time, Ostrovine kept us waiting for twenty minutes.

When we entered his office, there were papers on the desk. Columns of numbers, probably financial spreadsheets. He put down a gold Cross pen and said, "What now, Lieutenant?"

Milo told him.

"You're kidding."

"Nothing funny about Dr. Usfel's murder, sir."

"Of course not," said Ostrovine. "But I can't help you. First of all, I've never heard about any confrontation between Glenda and any patient. Second, I still don't believe Glenda's death had anything to do with her work here. And third, like I told you, I have no knowledge of anyone named Vita Berlin."

"We know a confrontation occurred," said Milo. "How come there wasn't a report?"

"Obviously, Dr. Usfel never informed security of the need for one because she viewed it as insignificant." Ostrovine laid his hands flat on the desk. Milo had pulled his chair close. The wig was in reach of his long arm. "And frankly, so do I."

"Who referred this guy to you?"

"How can I tell you that when I don't even know his name?"

"Check the patient list for that day."

"He wouldn't be on there because incompletes aren't recorded."

"Not even their referrals?"

"Not anything," said Ostrovine. "Why would we pile up extraneous data? As is, we've got storage issues."

"What if the patient was referred for another procedure that was completed?"

"You're asking me to examine my entire patient database."

"Just white males seen two months ago, give or take two weeks either way."

"That's huge," said Ostrovine. "And what will I be looking for? Inappropriate clothing? We don't list attire in our charts."

"Just tease out white males in a particular age range and we'll take it from there."

"No can do, Lieutenant. Even if we had the manpower for that kind of scavenger hunt, we're legally forbidden."

"In terms of manpower, I can send you a couple of detectives."

"That's generous of you," said Ostrovine, "but it doesn't solve the main problem: Rooting around in patient records without clear justification is illegal."

Milo waited.

Ostrovine fiddled with his pen, placed his hand on his toupee, as if anticipating attack. "Look, guys, Glenda was one of ours, her death is a tragedy and if I could help you, I'd jump at the opportunity. But I can't. You have to understand."

"Then we'll have to go the subpoena route, sir. Which would cause all those delays we discussed before."

Ostrovine clicked his tongue. "We didn't discuss anything, Lieutenant Sturgis. You threatened me. I understand that you've got an important job to do. But further intimidation is not going to work. I've talked to our attorneys and they say it'll never get that far."

Milo stood. "Guess we'll just have to see."

"We won't see anything, Lieutenant. The rules are clear. I'm sorry, I really am. But what took place in the scan room was just one of those things."

"Business as usual."

"People as usual," said Ostrovine. "Put enough of them together and heads will bump. That's a far cry from murder."

"Human nature," said Milo. "You learn about it from all those insurance scams you do?"

Ostrovine's smile sped toward sincere, screeched to a halt just short of the goal. "I learned about it from reality."

On the way back to the station, Dr. Bern Shacker returned my call.

Ten to the hour; catching up between patients.

I thanked him. He said, "The police have caught someone?"

"They may have a lead." I described the man in the shearling.

Silence.

"Doctor—"

"But no one's been caught. So you're telling me this because . . ."

"We're wondering if Vita crossed paths with him. Perhaps during an evaluation. I don't want to put you in a bind but it could be a *Tarasoff* situation."

"Imminent danger?" he said. "To whom?"

"He's killed two other people."

"That's horrible but obviously they're no longer in danger."

"It's a tough situation, Bern."

"I know, I know. Dreadful. Well, fortunately he isn't a patient of mine. No one in my practice dresses like that."

"Okay, thanks."

"Self-swaddling," he said. "That smells a bit like schizophrenia, no?"

"Or a medical problem."

"Such as?"

"Hypothyroidism."

"Hmm . . . interesting. Yes, I suppose so. But I'd still lean toward the psychological. In view of what he's done. And it sounds as if he's reacting to threat. At the core, psychotics are helpless, no? Fear biters, not attack dogs."

"True."

"What a mess," said Shacker. "Poor Vita. All the others, as well."

Just before we turned onto Butler, Alex Shimoff called back.

"You need another masterpiece, Lieutenant?"

"You're the man, Detective."

"Last time was easy," said Shimoff. "Dr. Delaware's girlfriend had a good eye for detail, she gave me a lot to work with."

"Nothing like a challenge," said Milo.

"I'm married with children, I know about challenge. Sure, what's your schedule?"

"I'll get back to you with a time and place."

"Tomorrow would be good," said Shimoff. "Got a day off, my wife wants me to take her shopping, you can help me get out of it."

Back at his desk, Milo phoned D.C. Maria Thomas, told her of his intention to release a suspect drawing and the question marks to the media, asked her to facilitate with Public Affairs.

She said, "Cart before horse, Milo."

"Pardon?"

"Go get your rendering but nothing gets facilitated until the basic decision is reified. That's a fancy word for it turns real. That means the chief clears it."

"His orders?"

"Do anyone else's matter?"

She hung up. Milo cursed and called Margaret Wheeling. She'd had enough time to retreat from the offer to cooperate, claimed she really hadn't seen the man in the shearling well enough to be useful. He worked with her for a while to get her to agree to the sit-down with Shimoff.

He was reaching for a panatela when his phone rang. "Homicide, Sturgis."

"Better be," said a raspy, Brooklyn-tinged voice. "This is *your* fucking extension."

"Afternoon, sir."

The chief said, "When all else fails go the artistic route?"

"Whatever works, sir."

"You have enough to turn out a decent enough drawing? 'Cause we probably won't get more than one bite of the apple and I don't want to waste it on some ambiguous bullshit."

"Me neither, sir, but at this point—"

"Nothing else has worked, you're stuck, you're freaking out about more victims popping up. I *get* it, Sturgis. Which is why I swallowed my pride and put in a call to a guy I know at the Bureau who is a lard-ass pencil-pusher but used to be a behavioral sciences honcho at Quantico. Not that I think their bullshit profiles are more than a carny show, which is why I called him personally, said forget your stupid questionnaire and just give me something off the top of your head about a loony who snaps necks then cuts out guts and plays with them. He gave me big-time Ph.D. wisdom, so now you're going to hear it: white male, twenty-five to fifty, probably a loner, probably doesn't have a happy domestic life, probably going to be living in a weird home situation, probably jacks off when he thinks about what he did. That any worse than what Delaware's given you so far? So what does this suspect whose image you want to foist on a neurotic public look like?"

"White, thirty to forty."

"There you go," said the chief. "Science."

Milo said, "He wears a heavy coat in all sorts of weather."

"Big deal, he's concealing a weapon."

"That could be part of it, sir, but Dr. Delaware says it could be a sign of mental illness."

"Does he?" The chief laughed. "Big fucking genius. I'd say ripping people's intestines out covers that base pretty well."

I said, "It sure does."

Silence.

"I figured you were there, Doctor. How's life treating you?"

"Fine."

"That makes one of us. Charlie sends his regards."

Charlie was his son and the regards part was a lie. A brilliant, alienated kid, he'd asked me to write a college recommendation, emailed me a couple of times a month from the seminary he was using to defer college.

He hated, loved, feared his father, would never use him for a messenger.

I said, "Hope he's doing well."

"He's being Charlie. By the way, the department still owes you some consult money on the last one."

"True."

"You haven't bugged my office about it."

"Would it have helped?"

Dead air. "Your loyalty in the face of our bureaucratic ineptitude is laudable, Doc. So you concur that broadcasting this lunatic's face is a good idea?"

"I think if we keep the information tight it's got potential."

"What does tight mean?"

"Limit it to the artist rendering and the question marks and don't let on that anyone could theoretically be a victim."

"Yeah, that would set off some skivvy-soiling panic, wouldn't it? Speaking of those question marks, what the hell do they mean? The FBI guy said he'd never seen that before. Checked his files and there was nothing. Only similar gutting was Jack the Ripper and there were enough differences between our boy and Jack to make that avenue a dead end."

"Don't know."

"Don't know what?"

"What the question marks mean."

"So much for higher education ... what do you think about releasing details on the coat? Could jog some citizen's memory."

"It might also cause the bad guy to ditch the coat and you'd lose potential evidence."

Silence. "Yeah, there could be spatter on the fucking thing, gut juice, whatever. Okay, keep it tight. But you could still be screwed—I'm talking to you, Sturgis. He sees himself on the six o'clock, he rabbits."

"There's always that chance, sir."

Another silence, longer.

The chief said, "Doctor, what's your take on another victim coming up sooner rather than later?"

"Hard to say."

"That all you do? Sidestep questions?"

"That's a poser, Chief."

"Shrink humor," he said. "I wouldn't count on getting a sitcom anytime in the near future. You still awake, Sturgis?"

"Wide awake."

"Stay that way."

"God forbid I should sleep, sir."

"More to the point," said the chief. "*I* forbid."

CHAPTER
23

Alex Shimoff delivered his rendering to Milo's office the following afternoon.

"Don't tell anyone who did this," he said. "This is garbage."

The last time he'd sat down to draw for Milo, Shimoff had produced a stunningly accurate re-creation of a girl whose face had been blown off. What he presented this time was an ambiguous pale disk filled with bland, male features.

Color it yellow you'd have Mr. Happy Face's noncommittal brother.

And yet, it twanged a memory synapse deep in my brain.

Had I seen him before? Mental scouring produced nothing.

Milo told Shimoff, "Thanks, kid."

"Don't thank me for doing crap, El Tee. That Wheeling lady couldn't come up with anything useful. I hate the computer Identi-Kit but after she gave me nothing I tried it. She said it confused her more, too many choices. She couldn't even respond to my questions. Wider, longer, rounder, nothing. She claimed she barely saw the guy."

"Did she seem scared?" I said.

"Maybe," said Shimoff. "Or she's just stupid and can't process visually."

Milo studied the likeness. "It's better than what we had before."

Shimoff looked ready to vomit. "It's any pie-faced white guy."

"Hey, kiddo, maybe this is what he actually looks like. Like that cartoon, the kid brings in a stick figure drawing of his family, on parent-teacher day stick figures show up?"

Shimoff wasn't amused.

I tried again to figure out why the crude drawing gnawed at me.

Blank mental screen.

Shimoff said, "At art school I could get away sometimes with jokes. Real life? It sucks to turn out garbage. Top of that, I still have to take my wife shopping tonight."

Clenching his fists, he left.

Milo murmured, "Creative types," and took the photo to the big detective room where he told Moe Reed to scan and email it to Maria Thomas.

That evening at six the rendering was featured on the news, along with a sketchy tale of a Westside home invader who broke his victims' necks and left behind a **?** calling card. Ambiguity made the story more frightening and the phones began ringing seconds after the ensuing commercial.

By six fifteen, Milo had commandeered Moe Reed and Sean Binchy to help work the lines. He moved out of his office and took a desk in the big D-room left unoccupied by a daywatch detective on sick leave. Manipulating three separate lines himself, pushing buttons like a concertina player, he kept the conversations brief, took a few notes, the most frequent notation being "B.S." followed by "schizo," "ESP," and "prank." Reed's dominant notation was "neg.," Binchy's, "t.n.g." When Sean saw me trying to figure that out, he cupped his hand over the receiver, smiled, and said, "Totally no good."

I heard Reed say, "Yes, I understand, ma'am, but you live in Bakersfield, there's no reason to be worried."

Binchy: "Absolutely, sir. There's no indication he has anything against Samoans."

Milo: "I know about the Chance cards in Monopoly. No, there wasn't one."

Slipping out of the room, I drove home thinking about victims.

Robin said, "No blanket? Doesn't take much to set this maniac off."

We sat near the pond, tossing pellets at the fish, Blanche wedged between us, snoring lightly. I'd finished a couple ounces of Chivas, was nursing the ice. Robin hadn't made much headway with a glass of Riesling. The night smelled of ozone and jasmine. The sky was char-coal felt stretched tight. A few stars peeked through like ice-pick wounds.

She said, "She kicks him out of the clinic and he comes back to get her months later?"

I said, "Maybe he took his time be-cause planning was part of the fun. For all I know, he set up the confrontation."

"To give himself an excuse?"

"Even psychopaths need to self-jus-tify and I don't think his real motive is avenging insult. It's got to be rooted in fantasies he's had since childhood but he frames his victims as bad people so he can feel righteous. Glenda Usfel maintained control by being the alpha female only this time it backfired. The same probably went for Berlin. Spread-ing bad cheer was her hobby but she tried it with the wrong guy. What doesn't fit is brutalizing Marlon Quigg, who's described by everyone as the mildest man on the planet."

"Maybe he wasn't always that way."

"Reformed crank?"

"People can change." She smiled.

"Someone once told me that. What did Quigg do for a living?"

"Accountant."

"Not an IRS auditor by any chance?"

"Not even close, just a cog in a big firm, sat at his desk and number-crunched for a big grocery chain."

"Someone didn't like the tomatoes, they wouldn't take it out on him. Did he have any outside interests?"

"No one's mentioned any. Family man, walked his dog, led a quiet life. Before that he taught disabled kids. We're talking a softie, Rob. Totally different from the other two victims."

"Interesting switch," she said.

"What is?"

"Trading a job where you're constantly dealing with people for one where you stare at ledgers all day."

"His wife said the money wasn't there so he took the CPA exam."

"I'm sure that's it."

"You have your doubts?"

"It just seems like a radical shift, Alex, but money is important."

I thought about that. "Something happened when Quigg was teaching that pushed him in a totally different direction?"

"You just said the killer's motive goes back to childhood. 'Disabled kids' covers a lot of territory."

"A student with serious psychiatric issues," I said. "Revenge on the teacher? Oh, man."

She said, "What if Quigg left teaching because he encountered a student who scared him out of the profession? I know it's far-fetched but you just said this guy loves the thrill of the hunt. What if now that he's an adult, he's decided to revisit old enemies?"

The sky seemed to darken and drop, stars receding. Robin tried to flex her fingers and I realized I was squeezing her hand and let go.

"I'm just tossing stuff out," she said, raising the wineglass to her lips. Good vintage but tonight it evoked a frown and she put it aside. "Let's change the subject."

I said, "Mind if I make a call?"

Belle Quigg said, "*Who* is this?"

I repeated my name. "I was at your

home the other day, and also with Lieutenant Sturgis."

"Oh. You're the other one. Has something happened about Marlon?"

"I have a few more questions, Mrs. Quigg. How long ago did Marlon teach school?"

"A long time. Why?"

"We're being thorough."

"I don't understand."

I said, "The more we know about Marlon, the better our chances of catching whoever did that to him."

"Did that," she said. "You can say killed. *I* say it. I *think* it. I think it all the time."

I didn't answer.

She said, "I don't see what his teaching has to do with it. That was years ago. This is a madman who killed Marlon and Louie, and it had nothing to do with anything Marlon did or said."

"I'm sure you're right, ma'am, but if you could—"

"Marlon didn't teach at a school, he taught at a hospital. Ventura State."

Once the largest psychiatric facility in

the state, long-shuttered. "How long ago?"

"This was before we got married, I'd just met him and he told me he used to be a teacher, so . . . at least twenty-four years ago."

"What kind of disabled children did he teach?"

"He just said disabled," she said. "He didn't talk much about it and I wasn't that curious, that kind of thing's not for me. Marlon said the reason he quit was the pay was awful, that's why he was doing bookkeeping for the city, studying for his CPA. Also he found out the hospital was closing down, told me years later that's the real reason he quit, he didn't want to be left stranded."

"How'd he feel about the closure?"

"It bothered him. Because of the kids. He said, 'Where will they go, Belle?' That was Marlon. He *cared.*"

CHAPTER

24

Nice-guy Marlon Quigg had lied to his wife.

There had been no plans to close Ventura State back when he worked there.

I knew that because I'd been there weeks before the hospital had emptied, hired by a law firm representing two wards of wheelchair-bound, minimally functioning children facing a terrifyingly ambiguous future. I evaluated each patient and made detailed recommendations for the aftercare promised by the state. Some of what I advised was put into effect. Mostly the state reneged.

Several years before that, well after Quigg had already quit, I'd rotated through as an intern, augmenting my training at Langley Porter with a month of observation at the largest mental hospital west of the Mississippi.

That spring, I'd set out from San Francisco at sundown, slept on the beach in San Simeon and watched elephant seals lolling, ended up in Camarillo by mid-morning where I showered and dressed in the restroom of a public beach, checked my map, and got back on the freeway.

A poorly marked road slanting east of the 101 had guided me inland over a dry creek, past empty fields, copses of native sycamore and oak, and Australian eucalyptus that had long made themselves comfortable in Southern California. For the next few miles nothing hinted at the hospital's presence. Then a twenty-foot gate of heavy-duty iron painted red snapped into view just around a severe bend and forced me to brake hard.

A watchful guard checked my I.D., frowned, pointed to a *Five MPH* sign, and buzzed me through. Snailing through more twisting, shaded road, I came to a stop at the mouth of a stadium-worthy parking lot full of cars. Rising behind the auto glare were buildings sheathed in dun stucco and prettied by moldings, medallions, pediments, and arched loggias. Most of the windows were grilled in that same rusty red.

City of the Sad.

Decades before, Ventura State had gained infamy as a place where anything went if a doctor said so. A host of horrors had taken place behind its walls until World War II drew the doctors to Europe and the Pacific, and the Holocaust got people thinking harder about degradation of personal liberty: lobotomies and other untested surgeries, crude versions of shock and insulin therapy, forced commitment of those labeled a nuisance, forced sterilizations of those deemed unfit to breed. Reforms had been drastic and thorough and the hospital had gained a reputation for enlightenment and humanism; I was eager to experience a new clinical setting and to be back in Southern California.

I spent my first two days in orientation sessions delivered by a nursing supervisor, accompanied by freshly minted psychiatric residents, other psychology interns, new-hire nurses and orderlies. Once educated, we were free to explore the grounds, with the exception of the easternmost end where a compound marked *Specialized Care* sat. An orderly asked the training nurse what specialized meant. She said, "Unique situations, it varies," and went on to the next topic.

With hours to go before my first assignment, I wandered the campus staggered by the dimensions and ambitions of the place. The near-worshipful silence of the other rookies as they explored told me I wasn't alone in my reaction.

Built in the twenties as the California State Mental Hygiene Sanitarium at Ventura, the place that had come to be known as V-State was graced by a combination of Old World craftsmanship and New Deal optimism that had created some of the finest public buildings in the state. In the case of the hospital, that meant twenty-eight buildings on over two hundred fifty acres. Pink flagstone pathways slinked through the grounds like rosy streams, flower beds were riotous with color, shrubs appeared trimmed by nail scissors. The entire property sat in a shallow valley graced by fog-capped mountains on three sides.

Auxiliary structures on the west end kept the hospital self-sufficient: refrigeration house, butcher, dairy, vegetable and fruit gardens, bowling alley, two movie theaters and a concert stage, employee dorms, on-site police and fire departments. Self-sufficiency was partly the product of noble rehabilitative intentions. It also shielded the rest of Ventura County from neighbors locked up by reason of insanity, deficiency, and "unique situations."

I spent my entire month with children more advanced than the unfortunates I evaluated years later but still too impaired to handle school. More often than not an organic factor was at play: seizure disorders, post-encephalitic brain injury, genetic syndromes, and puzzling groups of symptoms that, decades later, would be labeled autism-spectrum disorder but were classified back then by a variety of terms. The one I remembered was "idiopathic neurosocial irregularity."

I spent sixty hours a week honing my observational skills, doing some testing, and receiving solid training in child psychopathology, play therapy, cognitive restructuring, and applied behavioral analysis. Most important, I learned humility and the value of reserving judgment. V-State was no place for those craving heroism; when improvement occurred it was gradual and minuscule. I learned to fuel each day with a mantra: **Keep your goals specific and realistic, be happy when anything goes well.**

At first glance, the hospital was a pastoral retreat from reality but I came to learn that turgid silence could be shattered without warning by screams and mewls and the crack of what sounded like wood on flesh from the easternmost tip of the campus.

Specialized Care was a hospital within

a hospital, a cluster of low, mean structures nudging up against an eastern butte of granite, sectioned by the ever-present red iron fencing topped by razor wire. The bars were stouter, the windows skimpier. Behind the fence, uniformed guards patrolled irregularly. Mostly, the surrounding yard was unoccupied. Never once did I spot a patient.

One day I asked my supervisor what went on there.

An elegant, gray-haired psychologist, Gertrude Vanderveul was American but British-trained at the Maudsley Hospital, fond of beautifully tailored suits and inexpensive, sensible shoes, passionate about Mahler but otherwise dismissive of post-Bach music, a former research assistant to Anna Freud during the London years. (*"Lovely woman but far too attached to Daddy to acquire a conventional social life."*)

The day I posed the question, Gertrude was supervising me outdoors because the weather was perfect. We walked the hospital grounds under a cloudless sky, the air fragrant as fresh laundry, drinking coffee and reviewing my cases. That done, she shifted the focus to a discussion of the limitations of Piaget's methodology, encouraging me to give my opinions.

"Excellent," she said. "Your insights are acute."

"Thanks," I said. "Could I ask you about Specialized Care?"

She didn't answer.

Thinking she hadn't heard, I began to repeat myself. She held up a silencing finger and we continued our stroll.

A few moments later she said, "That place isn't for you, dear boy."

"I'm too green?"

"There's that," she said. "Also, I like you."

When I didn't reply, she said, "Trust me on this, Alex."

Had Marlon Quigg learned the same thing through direct experience?

Interesting career switch.

Smart girl, Robin.

I went out back to tell her she might be onto something but she'd left the pond and her studio windows were lit and I could hear the whir of a saw. I returned to my office and phoned Milo.

"Quigg didn't teach at a school, he worked at Ventura State Hospital."

"Okay." Distracted.

I said, "He may have given his wife a phony reason for changing careers and that makes me wonder if something—or someone—at V-State scared him."

I recounted the unsettling sounds I'd heard from Specialized Care, Gertrude's protectiveness. "That could be Quigg's connection."

He said, "Patient with an old grudge? How long ago are we talking, Alex?"

"Quigg was out of there twenty-four years ago but our guy could have a long memory."

"Twenty-four years and something sets him off?"

"Killing sets him off," I said. "He got into the swing, thought back to his bad old days at V-State."

"Kill Teach. So Quigg wasn't such a softie back then?"

"Not necessarily. For someone with paranoid tendencies it could've been a wrong look, anything."

"Wonderful . . . but other than you think Quigg fibbed, there's no proof he actually worked that special ward."

"Not yet, but I'll keep digging."

"Fine. Let's talk after I get back."

"Where you going?"

"To meet Victim Number Five."

"Oh, no. When?"

"Body just turned up. This time it was Hollywood Division that got lucky. Petra caught it. She's a tough girl but she sounded pretty shaken. I'm on my way over now."

"What's the address."

"Don't bother," he said. "It's already a circus and you know what you're gonna see."

"Okay."

He exhaled. "Look, I'm not sure I'm gonna be kept on, word is His Grandiloquence is 'reassessing.' So there's no sense you ruining your night. Top of that, I'm fielding a pile of useless tips and I have a sit-down with Usfel's and Parnell's families at an airport hotel first thing tomorrow morning. Both sets of parents, this is gonna be rollicking."

◆

A murder so soon after the media play felt like a taunt and I reassessed my theory about the question marks, figured Milo had been right. I went to my office, sat at the computer, and shuffled varying combinations of *ventura state hospital criminally insane child murderer young disembowel question mark.* When that pulled up nothing useful, I spent some time wondering if Shimoff's drawing had stimulated my memory because, years ago, I'd seen a younger version of the round-faced man on the grounds of V-State.

A patient I'd worked with? Or just passed in the wards? A dangerous kid who'd eluded Specialized Care because he'd been smooth enough to fool the staff and remain on an open ward?

Hospital teachers spent more time with patients than anyone. Had Marlon Quigg noticed something about a deeply disturbed boy that everyone else had missed? Had he spoken up and convinced the doctors about the need for extreme confinement?

Motive for a major-league grudge.

But Milo's question remained: Why wait so long to wreak vengeance?

Because the dangerous kid had turned into a truly frightening adult and had been locked up all these years.

Now released, he sets about righting wrongs. Locating Quigg, stalking him, grooming him with cordial greetings during Quigg's dog-walk in the park.

Recognizing Quigg but no reason for Quigg to associate a child with a grown man in a shearling.

?

Guess why I'm doing this.

Ha ha ha.

Gertrude Vanderveul had known enough about what went on at Specialized Care to keep me away.

Trust me on this, Alex.

Maybe now she'd agree to tell me why.

I looked for her in cyberspace, starting with the APA directory and the state psychology board website and fanning out from there.

She wasn't listed anywhere, but a

Magnus Vanderveul, M.D., practiced ophthalmology in Seattle. Maybe kin, maybe not, and too late in the day to find out. I played with the computer some more, hit nothing but sour notes, was feeling cranky when Robin and Blanche returned to the house, worked hard at faking pleasant.

Blanche sensed my true mood right away but she licked my hand and nuzzled my leg, a cobby little wrinkly bundle of empathy.

Robin was there a second later. "What's the matter?"

I told her about Quigg's lie. "You might have put it together, Lady Sherlock."

She said, "What kind of things did the scariest kids do?"

"Don't know because I never saw them." I described Specialized Care, Gertrude's protectiveness. "Couldn't get her to explain. I'm trying to locate her, maybe she'll be more open."

"Work on her maternal instincts."

"How so?"

"Tell her all you've accomplished. Make her proud. And confident."

◆

Milo hadn't gotten in touch by ten the following morning. Nothing about the latest victim appeared in the news and I figured the chief had kept things tight.

I tried Dr. Magnus Vanderveul's office in Seattle. A woman answered, "LASIK by Design."

Doctor was busy with procedures all day but if I wanted information about myopia or presbyopia she'd be happy to transfer me to an educational recording.

"Appreciate that but I need to speak to Dr. Vanderveul personally."

"Regarding?"

"His mother and I are old friends and I'm trying to get in touch with her."

"I'm afraid that's impossible," said the receptionist. "She passed last year. Doctor flew to the funeral."

"I'm sorry," I said, feeling that on multiple levels. "Where was the funeral?"

A second of silence. "Sir, I'll give him your message. Bye, now."

I found the death certificate. Palm Beach, Florida. Downloaded the obituary from the archives of a local paper.

Professor Gertrude Vanderveul had succumbed to a brief illness. Her tenure at V-State was noted, as was a subsequent move to Connecticut to teach at the university level. She'd published a book on child psychotherapy and served as a consultant to a White House commission on foster care. Ten years ago, she'd relocated to Florida where she'd advised various welfare agencies and pursued a lifelong interest in lily cultivation. Predeceased decades ago by an orchestra conductor husband, she was survived by a son, Dr. Magnus Vanderveul, of Redmond, Washington, daughters Dr. Trude Prosser of Glendale, California, and Dr. Ava McClatchey of Vero Beach, and eight grandchildren.

Contributions to the Florida Foundation for Child Development were requested in lieu of flowers.

Trude Prosser practiced clinical neuropsychology from a Brand Boulevard office. A voicemail greeting recited by an automated voice greeted me. Same deal at Ava McClatchey's obstetrics group.

Having left messages for all three of Gertrude's erudite progeny, I went for a run, wondering if any of them would bother to call.

By the time I returned, all three had.

Keeping it local, I started with Trude. This time she picked up, announcing "Dr. Prosser" in a sweet girlish voice.

"This is Alex Delaware. Thanks for getting back."

"You were one of Mother's students." Statement, not a question.

"She supervised me during an internship rotation. She was a wonderful teacher."

"Yes, she was," said Trude Prosser. "How can I help you?"

I started to explain.

She said, "Did Mother ever talk about a murderous little monster? No, she never talked about *any* of her patients. And I should tell you that while I don't know you, I know *about* you through Mother. She found what you do now quite fascinating. The investigative work."

"I had no idea she was aware of it."

"Quite aware. She read about some case in the paper and remembered you. We were having lunch and she pointed to your name. Quite tickled, really. 'This was one of my trainees, Trude. Bright boy, very inquisitive. I kept him away from the nasty stuff but apparently I only whetted his appetite.'"

"Any idea what she was protecting me from?" I said.

"I assumed the dangerous patients."

"In Specialized Care."

"Mother felt they were untreatable. That nothing psychology or psychiatry had to offer could put a dent in personality issues of that severity."

"Did she herself ever work with patients there?"

"If she did, she never shared that," said Trude Prosser. "Not only was she ethical, she avoided talking to us about work, in general. But she was at V-State for years, so it's possible she circulated there. How much time did you spend with her, Alex?"

"A memorable month," I said.

"She was a wonderful mother. Father died when we were young and she raised us by herself. One of my brother's teachers once asked her what the secret was to raising such well-behaved kids, did she have some kind of psychological formula?"

She laughed. "The truth is, at home we were wild animals but we knew enough to fake it on the outside. Mother nodded gravely and told the woman, 'It's very simple. I lock them in a root cellar and feed them crusts and stagnant water.' The poor thing nearly fell over before she realized Mother was having her on. Anyway, sorry I can't help more."

"This is going to sound strange, but did the issue of question marks ever come up?"

"Pardon?"

"A child who drew question marks. Did your mother ever allude to something like that?"

"No," she said. "Really, Mother's patients never came up, period. She was ironclad about confidentiality."

"Did she ever mention a teacher named Marlon Quigg?"

"Marlon," she said. "Like the fish. Now, that I can say yes to. I remember the name because it became a bit of family entertainment. Mag—my brother—

was home from college and had quickly regressed to being a loudmouthed oaf. So when Mother announced that someone named Marlon was coming over, could we please make ourselves scarce and not intrude, it was an obvious cue for Mag to get obnoxious. Insisting to Mother we should ply Mr. Fish with tuna salad and watch him wax cannibalistic. Of course Ava—my sister—and I thought that was hilarious, though we were old enough not to act like blithering idiots. But Mag brought that out in us, when he was home, we all regressed. And of course that spurred Mag on and he began making more terrible puns—Marlon had no sole, Marlon was getting crabby, what a shrimp. Et cetera. When Mother stopped laughing, she demanded that we not show our faces until the poor boy left because he was a teacher at V-State going through a rough patch and needed some bucking up."

"She called Quigg a boy?"

"Hmm," said Trude Prosser. "It was long ago, but I believe I'm recalling accurately. He wasn't of course, he must've been a man. Being a teacher. But perhaps his vulnerability made her think of him as a child. Anyway, we knew better than to mess with Mother when she was waxing clinically protective, so we went to a movie and by the time we got back, it was just Mother in the house."

"Did Quigg ever show up again?"

"If he did, I'm unaware. You're wondering if something happened back then that ties in to his murder? Some homicidal patient killed him after all these years?"

"Right now the investigation's pretty much dead-ended so we're looking at everything. Is there anyone else I might talk to who'd remember those days at V-State?"

"Mother's boss was a psychiatrist named Emil Cahane. I think he was the assistant director of the hospital, or something along those lines." She spelled the name. "I met him a couple of times—Christmas parties, that kind of thing. He came for dinner a few times. He was older than Mother, would be well into his eighties by now."

"Did you know any of her other students?"

"She never brought students home. Or talked about them. Until she pointed out that article in the paper, I'd never heard of you."

"So no staff person ever visited other than Marlon Quigg and Dr. Cahane?"

"Dr. Cahane coming for dinner was more social," she said. "Besides that, nothing."

"She told you Quigg was having a rough patch."

"That could mean anything, I suppose. But now that I think about it, for Mother to bend her rules it must've been serious. So perhaps you're onto something. But someone bearing a grudge that long? Goodness, that's grisly."

I said, "Your brother and sister also called me back. Think they might have something to add?"

"Mag's a bit older so perhaps his perspective would be different, but by then he really wasn't around very much. Ava's the youngest, I doubt she'd know anything I don't but give her a try."

"I appreciate your taking the time."

"I appreciate your getting me to talk about Mother."

◆

Dr. Ava McClatchey said, "Trude just called me. At first I didn't even remember the guy's visit. Once Trude reminded me of Mag's stupid fish puns, I got a vague memory but nothing Trude didn't already tell you. Got a C-section to do. Good luck."

Dr. Magnus Vanderveul said, "Nope, we went to the movies before the fellow came over and he was gone when we came back. I did start to torment Mother with more fish puns—was he gone because she was into catch and release." He chuckled. "The look on her face told me to cool it."

"Upset?"

"Bothered," he said. "Now that I think about it, that was odd. Mother was Superwoman, it took a lot to bother her."

CHAPTER

25

I'd never met Dr. Emil Cahane. No reason for the hospital's deputy director to have contact with a floating intern.

If I got lucky, that would change soon.

Cahane wasn't listed in any public directories nor was he a member of the American Psychiatric Association, any psychoanalytic institutes, or scientific interest groups. No active medical license in California; same for the neighboring states. I checked East Coast locales with high concentrations of psychiatrists. Nothing in New England, New

York, Pennsylvania, Illinois, New Jersey. Florida, where Gertrude had ended up.

Nothing.

Well into his eighties. The worst-case scenario loomed.

Then a search using Cahane's name pulled up a career achievement award he'd received from the L.A. Mental Health Commission eighteen months ago.

An accompanying photo revealed a thin, hawkish white-haired man with a crooked smile and a listing physique that suggested a stroke or other injury.

Cahane's listed accomplishments included his years at V-State, two decades of volunteer work with abused children, foster families, and the offspring of military veterans. He'd researched post-traumatic stress disorder, closed head injuries, and integrated methods of pain control, had endowed a study of the emotional effects of prolonged parental separation at the med school cross-town where he held a clinical professorship.

The same med school had graced me with an identical title.

Twenty years of volunteer work said he'd left V-State a few years after Marlon Quigg.

I phoned the med school, got a receptionist who knew me, and asked for a current address and number for Cahane.

"Here you go, Doctor."

Ventura Boulevard address in Encino. That had to be office space.

No active license but working? At what?

A woman answered crisply: "Cahane and Geraldo, how may I help you?"

"This is Dr. Delaware calling Dr. Cahane?"

"This is the office of *Mister* Michael Cahane."

"He's a lawyer?"

"Business manager."

"I got this number from the medical school."

"The medical school—oh," she said. "Mr. Cahane's uncle uses us as a mail-drop."

"Dr. Emil Cahane."

"What is it exactly that you want?"

"I trained under Dr. Cahane at Ventura State Hospital and was looking to get in touch."

"I couldn't give out his personal information."

"Could I speak with Mr. Cahane?"

"In a meeting."

"When will he be free?"

"How about I give him your number." Statement, no question.

"Thanks. Please let Dr. Cahane know that another staffer from the hospital passed away and I thought he might want to know. Marlon Quigg."

"How sad," she said, without emotion. "You get to an age and your friends start dropping off."

The phone rang nine minutes later. I picked it up, ready with my sales pitch for Dr. Cahane.

Milo said, "Petra and I are having a skull session, feel free."

"When and where?"

"In an hour, the usual place."

Café Moghul was empty but for two slumping detectives.

Milo's Everest of tandoori lamb was

untouched. Ditto, Petra Connor's sea-food salad.

His greeting was a choppy wave that could be misinterpreted as apathy. Petra managed a half smile. I sat down.

Petra's a young, bright homicide D working Hollywood Division, a former commercial artist with an especially keen eye and a quiet, thoughtful manner that some mistake for iciness.

She's got the kind of slender, angular good looks that, rightly or wrongly, imply confidence and imperturbability. Thick, straight black hair cut in a functional wedge is never mussed. Her makeup's minimal but artful, her eyes clear and dark. She dresses in tailored black or navy pantsuits and moves with economy. Listens more than she talks. All in all, she comes across as the girl everyone looked up to in high school. Over the years, she'd let out enough personal details to tell me it hadn't been that easy.

Today her lips were pallid and parched, her eyes red-rimmed. Every hair remained in place but her hands clasped each other with enough force to blanch fine-boned knuckles. One cuticle was raw.

She looked as if she'd been on a long, harrowing journey.

Seeing it.

She loosened her hands, placed them flat on the table. Milo rubbed the side of his nose. A bespectacled woman came over in a swoosh of red sari silk and asked what she could get me. I ordered iced tea. Petra ate a lettuce leaf and checked a cell phone that didn't need checking.

Milo dared to fork some lamb into his mouth, grimaced as if he'd just swallowed vomit. He shoved the platter away, ran a finger under his belt, pushed his chair back a few inches, distancing himself from the notion of eating.

He looked at Petra.

She said, "Go ahead."

He said, "Number Five is a poor soul named Lemuel Eccles, male Cauc, sixty-seven. Homeless street person, crashed in various alleys, one of which served as his final resting place. East Hollywood, specifically: just north of the Boulevard, just shy of Western, behind an auto parts store."

I said, "Who found him?"

"Private garbage service. Eccles was left next to a Dumpster."

"Same technique?"

Petra flinched and muttered "Dear God" before looking away. "Patrol knew Eccles, he's got an extensive record. Aggressive panhandling, shoplifting, drunk and disorderly, creating a disturbance for shoving a tourist, he was in and out of County."

"Your basic revolving-door juicehead nuisance," said Milo.

She said, "Obviously, someone thought he was more than a nuisance. To do *that* to him."

"Not necessarily," I said.

Both of them stared at me.

"Things we'd consider petty could loom huge in our boy's mind. Righting wrongs, real or imaginary, gives him justification to act out his body-exploration fantasies."

Petra said, "People irk him so he *guts* them? Insane."

Milo patted my shoulder. "Ergo *his* presence."

She closed her eyes, massaged the lids, exhaled long and slow.

I said, "Glenda Usfel kicked him out of the clinic. Vita Berlin was constitutionally nasty, it's not hard to imagine her getting in his face. And Mr. Eccles's tendency to beg with a heavy hand and become rowdy while drunk would fit, too. Most people would walk away. Shearling took another approach. That section of Hollywood's commercial and industrial. Meaning at night there wouldn't be a lot of people around. An elderly wino snoozing in the alley would've been easy prey. Were there any other wounds besides the abdominal incisions?"

Petra said, "Black-and-blue mark on his upper lip, right under the nose."

"A cold-cock, like Marlon Quigg, but from the front because Eccles was probably inebriated. Or sleeping in the alley."

"Could be, but Eccles's entire body was full of bruises and most of them looked old. Maybe bleeding issues due to alcohol, or he bumped into things."

Milo said, "To me the lip bruise looked fresher, I'm betting on a cold-cock while he was out of it."

"Or," said Petra, "Eccles heard the bad guy approaching, stirred, and got sent back to slumberland."

"Fine," said Milo, "once again we're getting a notion of how but the why's still far from clear. Not that I don't buy your theory about overreacting to small slights, Alex. Giving himself an excuse to do what he loves to do. But Marlon Quigg doesn't fit any of that. Unless you found out he taught Shearling when Shearling was a tyke, rapped his knuckles with a steel ruler or something."

"Not there yet, but I'm getting closer." I told them what I'd learned from the Vanderveul children.

Milo said, "Quigg pays her a visit for moral support? That could mean anything."

"Not in Gertrude's case," I said. "She was adamant about separating work from her home life, had never entertained anyone else from the hospital in that manner. So whatever Quigg had on his mind was serious. And she made sure her kids weren't around to hear it."

"Heavy-duty therapy."

"Maybe heavy-duty advice," I said. "Like telling Quigg to quit the hospital. And shortly after, he did. Left teaching completely and took up a whole new profession and lied to his wife about his reason."

Petra said, "Something happened at work that freaked him out."

"What if he came upon a patient committing acts that alarmed him and warned the staff about it? If he was ignored that could've been extremely upsetting. If he wasn't, it could've gotten the patient a transfer to Specialized Care and earned Quigg a serious enemy."

I described the layout of the ward behind the fence. Curdled silence broken by the occasional ragged noise.

"If Quigg succeeded in having a child moved there, it would've brought about a profound shift in quality of life, trading an open therapeutic environment for what was essentially a prison. Possibly for years."

"The main hospital was that cushy?" said Milo.

"There were a few locked wards but they were used for the patients' safety, profoundly delayed individuals who'd hurt themselves if allowed to wander. Specialized Care was designed with everyone *else's* safety in mind."

"Shackles and rubber rooms?"

"I never found out what went on there because Gertrude wouldn't let me near the place. Because she liked me."

"They have teachers there?"

"Same answer. I couldn't say."

Petra said, "Well, something bothered Quigg enough to get him out of that place. How old of a scary kid would we be talking about?"

"The few descriptions we have of our suspect are a man in his thirties and Quigg left V-State twenty-four years ago, so probably a preteen or an early adolescent. The hospital closed down ten years ago. If he was kept there until the end, we're talking a disturbed, angry man in his twenties possibly released to the streets. Or it took him this long to act out because he wasn't released, he

was transferred to Atascadero or Starkweather before finally earning his freedom."

"Or," said Milo, "he's been out for a
while and these aren't his only murders."

Petra said, "Other surgeries," and
shook her head. "No one including the
Feebies has seen anything like his pattern."

"Not every murder gets discovered,
kid."

"For ten years he's careful and con-
ceals his handiwork, then all of a sudden he goes public?"

"It happens," said Milo. "They get
confident."

"Or," I said, "they start to get bored
and need more stimulation."

Milo pulled out his phone. "Let's find
this psychiatrist—Cahane." He called in
a real estate search. Negative.

Petra said, "He's in his eighties, could
be in some kind of assisted living."

Milo said, "Hopefully he's not too se-
nile to help us."

I said, "If he doesn't pan out, there
are others who might know—someone
who actually worked in Specialized."

Petra said, "We could look for old hospital personnel records." Producing a tube of MAC lipstick from her purse, she refreshed. Smiled. "Being de-*tec*-tives and all."

As we left the restaurant, both their phones went off simultaneously. Not coincidence; two minions from the chief's office were ordering them downtown immediately for a "planning session."

As we headed for the West L.A. parking lot, Petra's cell chirped again. This time the call was from her partner, Raul Biro, back at his desk in Hollywood Division.

He'd located Lemuel Eccles's son, an attorney from San Diego. Because of the distance, Biro had done a telephonic notification. But Lem Jr. had business in San Gabriel tomorrow and would stop in L.A. for a face-to-face.

Petra said, "We can do the interview together, Big Guy, or if you're tied up, I'll handle it. Assuming we don't get 'planned' off the case."

"Assuming," said Milo. They walked off wordlessly, a bear and a gazelle.

Five paces later, Petra stopped and looked back. "Thanks for the ideas, Alex."

Without breaking step, Milo bellowed, "I second the motion."

CHAPTER
26

I got home prepared to examine Ventura State Hospital's history, seeking out anyone who could tell me about the patients in Specialized Care.

One curious boy, in particular.

If that failed, I'd press Emil Cahane's nephew to gain access to the psychiatrist. As I settled in my chair, my service called in. "I have a Dr. Angel on the line, she says it's important."

Donna Angel and I go way back, to my first job fresh out of training, working the cancer ward at Western Pediatric. Donna had been an oncology fellow, one of the best, and the department had asked her to stay on as a faculty member. After I went into private practice, she referred occasional patients, always with insight and wisdom.

Picking up a new patient right now would be a distraction but sick kids never lost their priority. I said, "Put her through."

"Good to talk to you, Alex." Donna's Tallulah voice was even huskier than usual. When I'd met her, she smoked, a habit picked up in college. It had taken years for her to quit; I hoped the vocal change meant nothing.

She coughed. "Darn cold, kids are like petri dishes for viruses."

I said, "Heal up. What's new?"

"I've got someone you should meet."

"Sure."

"Not a referral," she said. "This time I'm helping you."

She told me about it.

I said, "When?"

"Right now, if you can swing it. There's some . . . eagerness at play."

◆

I made the drive to Sunset and Vermont in a little under an hour. Western Pediatric Medical Center was in its usual state of demolition and construction: another gleaming building rising from a rebar-lined maw, new marble on the façade, chronic deficits be damned.

The campus was a vein of noble intention in the drab bedrock that was East Hollywood. Half a mile to the north, Lemuel Eccles had been savaged and dumped. No time to ponder coincidence or karma or metaphysics.

I parked in the doctors' lot, rode to the fifth floor of a glass-fronted structure named after a long-dead benefactor, smiled my way past the hem-onc receptionist, and knocked on Donna's door.

She opened before my knuckles left the wood, hugged me and guided me inside.

Her desk was the usual clutter. A man stood next to one of two visitors' chairs.

"Dr. Delaware, this is Mr. Banforth."

"John," said the man, extending a hand.

"Thanks for seeing me."

"Maybe I should be thanking you."

Banforth waited for me to sit before lowering himself into the chair.

Thirty-five or so, he was six feet tall, solidly built, black, with close-cropped hair graying early and tortoiseshell eyeglasses resting on a small, straight nose. He wore a brown cashmere crewneck, mocha slacks, mahogany suede running shoes. A golf-ball pin was fastened to the left breast of the sweater. A thin gold chain around his neck held two tiny figurines. Outlines of a boy and a girl.

Donna said, "I'll leave you two to talk," and headed for the door.

When it closed, John Banforth said, "This has been weighing on me." He crossed his legs, frowned as if anything close to relaxation felt wrong, and planted both feet on the floor.

"Okay," he said, "here goes." Inhaling. "As Dr. Angel told you, my daughter Cerise is her patient. She's five years old, her diagnosis is Wilms' tumor, she was diagnosed at Stage Three, one of her kidneys had to be removed, and we thought we were going to lose her. But she's doing great now, really responding to treatment and we firmly believe, all of us, including Dr. Angel, that she's going to live to a ripe old age."

"That's fantastic."

"I can't say enough about Dr. Angel. If anyone fits their name, it's her . . . but it's still an ordeal. Cerise's treatment. Her body's sensitive, she reacts to everything. A few weeks ago, she finished another course, had to be hospitalized until her labs stabilized. Finally, we were able to take her home. We live in Playa Del Rey and were on the freeway when Cerise started crying, she was hungry. I got off at the next exit, which was Robertson, mostly fast-food places then this café—Bijou—that looked nice. If Cerise was going to eat, we wanted it to be good quality. Also, to be honest, it was lunchtime, my wife and I figured we'd eat, too. Madeleine's a dance instructor, I'm a golf pro, we try to keep in shape."

"Makes sense."

"So we went in and ordered some food and everything was going okay, then Cerise got cranky. I guess we should've taken her home right then and there but her labs were really good . . . your

kid goes through hell, she wants something, you give it to her, right?"

"Of course."

"Still," said Banforth. "We should've
known, because sometimes after treatment, Cerise overestimates her strength."
His eyes watered. "She's been through
hell but she's always trying to be strong."

Fishing out a wallet, he showed me
photos. A chubby-cheeked little girl
sporting a mass of brass-colored ring-
lets, then the same child barely older,
bald, paler, *why-me* eyes rendered huge
by the shrinkage of the surrounding
face.

I said, "She's adorable," was surprised
by the catch in my voice.

"You see what I mean, it tugs at your
heart, you say yes maybe when you
shouldn't."

"Of course."

"So that's what we did and everything
was okay for a while, then Cerise started
to get super-cranky. Moaning, at first
we thought she was in pain, but when
we asked she said no but she couldn't
tell us what was bothering her, sometimes I think she really doesn't know.

Then all of a sudden she said what would make her happy was ice cream. Normally she gets ice cream once she's finished her dinner, but . . ."

He made another attempt to cross his legs. Same discomfort and reversal. "Yes, we spoil her. Jared—our son, he's ten—complains about it all the time. But with everything Cerise has gone through . . . anyway, we ordered ice cream but when it arrived Cerise changed her mind, started making noise again, the waitress came over and asked if she wanted a fresh donut, she said yes."

Banforth's forehead had slicked. He dabbed with a linen handkerchief. "Sure, she manipulates us. We figure it's the only power she has, when she's out of the woods, we'll start to . . . anyway, at this point we're thinking we definitely need to pay and leave but before I get my wallet out, the woman in the next booth shoots up like she's been bitten in the butt, stamps over and glares down at Cerise. Like she hates her. Cerise is sensitive, she freaks out, starts wailing. A normal person would realize and back off. Not this one, she actually glares *harder.* Like she's trying to break Cerise's spirit, just break her in two, you know?"

"Unbelievable," I said.

"My wife and I are too shocked to react. This woman evil-eyes me. I say, 'What's the problem?' She says, 'You people are. Sick people eat in hospitals not restaurants.' I'm tongue-tied, I mean I can't believe what I just heard, but Madeleine, she's always rational, she starts to explain and this crazy woman, this *terrible* woman, waves her off and says, '*You* people. What makes you think it's okay to inflict your brat on the rest of us?' And I just lost it, I mean I really lost it."

Banforth looked at the floor. "I should've known better. I was in the military, trained to withstand pressure. But this was my *kid.* Calling Cerise a *brat.* It was like she was mixing up some explosive to make me blow and I *understood* that but still I *lost* it. Didn't touch her, that crazy I'm not but I jumped up, got in her face, I tell you, Doctor, I was *this* close to doing something stupid but fortunately my army training helped. Also Madeleine's got hold of my hand and she's begging me to back off. So I did and the bitch went back to her booth but she kept on smirking at us. Like she won. We got the hell out of there, all three of us are real quiet. Including Cerise. But when we got home, she said, 'I make everything bad.' And oh, man, Madeleine and I just lost it in a whole different way. After Cerise went down for a nap we collapsed and bawled like babies."

"I'm so sorry you had to go through that."

"Yeah, it sucked. But we're okay, now. And you know what, the next day, Cerise was fine, like it never happened." He shrugged. "We roll with the punches. Cerise shows us the way."

He fingered the chain, found the child figurines and touched each one.

"So why," he said, "did I tell Dr. Angel I wanted to talk to you? Actually, it was her idea after I told her another part of the story, how it was weighing on me. She said she knew a doctor used to work here now works with that particular detective—I'm getting ahead of my-self."

A third leg-crossing endured but Banforth still looked as if he'd been forced into a painful contortion. "Here's the part that's going to sound weird. I went back there, Doc."

"To Bijou."

"A couple days later. I know it sounds crazy but I'd composed myself, thought maybe I'd go back and if by some chance she was there, I'd try to talk to her rationally. Educate her, you know? About sick kids, how you need to be flexible. I wanted to make it right—to be rational with her no matter how she behaved. So I could prove to myself I had it together."

He looked to the side. "It was stupid, what can I say? Anyway, I went in and the owner—a long-haired guy with an earring—recognized me and was real nice, saying my family was welcome back anytime, he felt awful about what happened. I thanked him and then I asked if that woman ever came back, maybe one day I could explain to her about sick kids—keeping it friendly. And he got this weird expression and said, 'Vita? She was murdered.' I said, 'Oh, crap, when?' He said a few days after you were here. I'm speechless. I leave. But later, driving to work, I remember something that happened the day this Vita started up with us. I put it aside, for sure it's nothing. But it stays in my head and I can't stop thinking about it and finally I tell Dr. Angel."

I waited.

John Banforth said, "When we left and reached our car a guy came out behind us. At first he walked the other way. Then he turned and walked toward us, I'm thinking oh no, another nutcase, so I hustle to get Cerise and Madeleine into the car. He comes closer and he's smiling but I don't know if it's a friendly smile or a crazy smile, sometimes you can't tell. I must've tensed up because he stops a few feet away and does this."

He held both palms frontward. "Like *I come in peace.* I stay on my guard anyway and he winks and smiles. Friendly but also weird, I can't tell you why I felt that, he just creeped me out. Then he winks again and gives the V-sign for victory and he walks away. It confused me and creeped me out but my mind was on getting home and settling Cerise. But when I found out this Vita got murdered, I start wondering but I'm like no way, he was just reassuring us, being a nice guy. But the V-sign didn't fit that, it was like he was saying we were on the same team and we'd won. And that didn't make sense. So it started bothering me, what if he thought he was doing us a favor? It's probably nothing, I tend to dwell on stuff. I actually called the police and asked who's handling the murder of a woman named Vita. It took them a while but finally they said Detective Sturgis, we'll put you through. I hung up, figured they'd trace me, I'd get a callback. But it never happened."

"Police lines don't have caller I.D.," I said. "So people won't be inhibited about giving tips."

"Oh . . . makes sense. Anyway, I couldn't stop wondering if he actually *did* it, some crazy sonofabitch who thought we were on the same side. Finally, I told Dr. Angel and she said funny thing, you worked with that exact detective and I said, whoa, karma, I definitely need to get this off my chest."

Shrugging. "So here we are, Doc."

"Thanks for getting in touch. What did the guy look like?"

"So it *is* relevant," said Banforth. "Damn."

"Not necessarily, John. At this point, the cops look at everything."

"They don't have a suspect?"

"They've got various bits of information that may or may not be important. What did he look like?"

"White guy," he said. "Around thirty-five, forty. Heavyset, kind of a round face, that's about it."

"Hair color?"

"Brown—short, like it was growing back from a buzz."

"Eye color?"

"Couldn't tell you."

"He never spoke."

"Nope, just the wink and the V-sign. It's not like evidence, that's why I tried to put it aside."

"Your first impression was something about him seemed off."

"But I can't tell you why, sorry."

I gave him time. He shook his head.

"How was he dressed?"

"In a coat. Like a winter coat, even though it was a warm day—*that's* different, I guess. Maybe that's what seemed off?"

"What kind of coat?"

"One of those fleece-lined things," said Banforth. "Brown on the outside, maybe suede, maybe cloth, I wasn't paying attention. Oh, yeah, something else: He was carrying a book. Like students do but he didn't look like a student."

"What kind of book?"

"Not a hardcover—more like a magazine, actually. Maybe some sort of puzzle magazine because it had a big question mark on the cover?"

My heart raced. Now I knew why Alex Shimoff's sketch had tweaked my brain.

The morning after the murder, when Milo and I had visited Bijou, an apple-faced man had been there.

Sitting in a booth behind the soccer moms and their toddlers.

Eating steak and eggs, a book in front of him, penciling a puzzle.

Enjoying a hearty breakfast hours after he'd gutted Vita.

John Banforth said, "Doc?"

"You did the right thing."

"He's the guy? Oh, man."

"Not necessarily but it's a lead and Detective Sturgis needs anything he can get."

"Well okay, then, I feel better not wasting anyone's time."

"Would you mind sitting with a police sketch artist? So we can get a clearer image?"

"They still do that? Thought everything was computers."

"They still do."

"An artist, huh? Would my name have to be on it?"

"No."

"Then guess so," he said. "If you can fit it to my schedule. And if Madeleine doesn't know, she has no idea about any of this, including the fact that I'm here."

"We'll do it at your convenience."

"All right, here's my business card, call the top number, it's my reservation line for lessons."

"Thanks very much."

"Just doing what I had to."

We headed for the door. He got there first, stopped. "She was a nasty one. That Vita. Madeleine and I took to calling her the Evil One. As in wonder who the Evil One's tormenting now. We turned it into a joke. To ease what happened. But I guess no one deserves to be murdered."

His voice wavered on "guess."

27

On the way home, I detoured and drove through Vita Berlin's neighborhood, rolling through sunlit streets and shadowed alleys, searching for a man dressed too heavily for the weather. When four circuits produced nothing, I headed to Bijou.

It was just past the three o'clock closing time. The storefront window afforded a view of Ralph Veronese sweeping up, his long hair bunched in a topknot that was part girlie, part Samurai warrior. I rapped on the glass. Without breaking rhythm, he pointed to the *Closed* sign. I rapped harder and he looked up.

He cracked the door halfway, propped his broom against the jamb. "Hey."

"I'm doing follow-up on Vita."

"You caught the guy?"

"Not yet. I want to ask you about a customer I noticed the first time I was here." I described Shearling.

"Nope, doesn't ring a bell."

"He's been here at least twice."

"Twice doesn't make him a regular. Half the time I'm in back."

"He sat in that corner booth, eating steak and eggs, worked on a puzzle book."

Veronese said, "Oh."

"You remember him."

"Not so much him, I remember the book. Thinking here's another camper, going to use us as the public library. But then he ordered. Campers just like to stretch out a coffee, bring their laptops, gripe when they find out we don't have wireless."

"Has he been here any other times?"

"Not that I know of."

"How about checking your receipts for both the days we know he was here?"

"Receipts are with my bookkeeper, I send paperwork to her every Friday."

"Then please call her."

He dialed a preset number, spoke to someone named Amy, hung up.

"She says it's already in the storage bin, she can try to find it but it'll take time."

"Sooner's better than later, Ralph."

"She charges me by the hour."

"Send me the bill."

"You're serious?"

"You bet."

He texted Amy.

I said, "You're in the back but Hedy's always out front. Please get her on the line for me and if you can't reach her, give me her number."

"Her number's my number," said Veronese. "We're thinking of getting married."

"Congratulations."

I pointed to his phone. He reached Hedy, explained, passed it over.

She said, "The guy with the puzzle book? Sure, I remember him. But I have to tell you, he paid cash. I know for sure because it was all singles and a lot of coins. Like he busted open his piggy bank."

"What else can you say about him?"

"Um . . . he cleaned his plate . . . didn't talk except to order . . . had kind of a girlie voice—high-pitched, didn't fit his body, he's kind of a football-player type, you know?"

"Not much for conversation."

"Kept his head in that book even when he was eating."

"What kind of puzzles was he working on?"

"Couldn't tell you. You're thinking he's the one who killed Vita?"

"He's someone we want to talk to."

"Because he's a little off?"

"Off how?"

"You know, mentally."

"He impressed you that way?"

"I'm no shrink," she said, "but he just wasn't . . . like he never made eye contact. Kind of mumbled. In that high voice. Like he was trying to whisper—to like stay in the background."

"Not sociable."

"Exactly. Just the opposite. Like *I want to be in my own world.* So I respected that, my job you have to be a shrink."

"Anything else about him strike you as odd?"

"His clothes. It's pretty warm inside Bijou, we don't have the best A.C. and he's wearing this fleece-lined shearling. I've got one of those in my closet from when I lived in Pittsburgh, haven't used it once since I moved to L.A."

"Was he sweating?"

"Hmm . . . I don't think so—oh, yeah, one more thing, he had a scar. In the front of his neck, like at the bottom. Nothing gross, like a white line running across his neck."

"Across the Adam's apple?"

"Lower, in the soft part. Like someone cut him a long time ago but it healed up pretty good."

"Any other marks?"

"Not that I saw."

"Tattoos?"

"If he has 'em, they were covered up. *He* was pretty much covered up."

"What else was he wearing besides the shearling?"

"You think he's the one?" she said. "That kind of freaks me out. What if he comes in again?"

"No reason to worry, but if that happens just call this number." I recited Milo's extension.

Hedy said, "Got it. What else was he wearing? I guess he had a shirt on underneath but I wasn't paying attention. Sorry, the shearling's all I noticed. Because it was out of place. Mostly I was concentrating on getting the orders right. You want to know exactly what his order was, I can tell you: steak and scramble with onions and mushrooms, steak medium, no instructions on the scramble. He left like a ten percent tip, all coins, but I didn't mind. Because it wasn't like he was trying to be a jerk, you know."

"More like he didn't know better," I said.

"Exactly," she said. "A little out of it. You feel sorry for those people."

◆

I drove a mile north to a newspaper stand I knew on Robertson near Pico. The primary merchandise was a mix of fan mags and porn. Small selection of puzzle books in a corner.

Nothing with a question mark on the cover. I flashed my dubious consultant's I.D. to the Sikh proprietor and described Shearling.

He said, "No, sir, I don't know him."

I gave him Milo's card, anyway, asked him to call if Shearling showed up. "He might buy a puzzle book."

He smiled as if it was a perfectly reasonable request. "Certainly, sir, anything to help."

Good attitude, so I spent ten bucks on a glossy design magazine. Robin likes looking at dream houses.

I tried Milo again from the car, then Petra, and when she was also out I switched to Raul Biro. His voicemail answered but I left no message.

Was Shearling's presence at Bijou evidence of long-term stalking, or had he happened upon the café, seen Vita torment Cerise Banforth, and decided she merited execution? If the latter, maybe he lived nearby. Reversing direction on Robertson, I gave Vita's neighborhood another try, starting with her street.

Stanleigh Belleveaux was outside, watering his shrubs. A *For Lease* sign was staked on the lawn of the duplex. Two vacant units. I drove slowly enough for Belleveaux to notice but he didn't look up and I continued south.

No sign of a man in a shearling and other than a young woman wheeling a baby in a stroller, all the activity was automotive: people pulling in and out of driveways. A door opened and a beanpole kid came out with a basketball, began shooting hoops.

Everything back to normal. People need to believe in normal.

It was close to eleven p.m. when Milo called.

"Still on the case and so is Petra."

"Congratulations."

"Or condolences. His Magnanimousness made it painfully clear I didn't deserve it but starting from scratch ran the risk of 'butt-fucking this one into oblivion.'"

I said, "Next Christmas, he'll be Santa at the office party."

He laughed. "Petra and I know the real reason he's not shifting gears to Robbery-Homicide. Any hotshots who aren't already on long-termers are being flown to Arizona courtesy the taxpayers for a confab on Mexican drug cartels, gonna be PowerPoint galore. What's up?"

I told him about John Banforth, Shearling's presence at Bijou hours after Vita's murder, Hedy's description.

"A nutcase with a taste for steak."

"Plus the way he ate—fixed on his food—smacks of an institutional background. Thirty-five to forty means that back when Quigg was working at V-State, he'd have been eleven to sixteen."

"A kid," he said. "But scary enough to be transferred to Specialized Care."

"I'm also convinced of the thyroid angle. The waitress noticed a neck scar. So maybe a thyroid scan's what brought him to North Hollywood Day. The most common reason for a thyroidectomy is cancer. There are also immune disorders that can justify it, like Hashimoto's disease. Whatever the reason, he'd need to take a daily pill to regulate his metabolism. Sometimes dosages can be tricky and if he's a street guy, he may not be getting optimal care. That could explain feeling cold and putting on a few pounds."

"Cancer?" he said. "Now I'm dealing with a psycho with serious sympathy issues?"

"Thyroid cancer's one of the most curable malignancies. He'd have the potential to live to a ripe old age."

"Except his chemistry's off."

"Which would explain the scan. He needs his prescription renewed, would have to see a doctor at some point. A physician who picked up on his symptoms and found out he hadn't been followed up regularly might want comprehensive data before adjusting his dosage. North Hollywood Day is an insurance mill but no doubt they see lots of Medi-Cal patients, so a referral there makes sense."

"He comes in to get nuked, gets on Glenda Usfel's bad side, she boots his ass out."

"Wrong guy to boot."

"'Ladies and gentlemen of the jury, yes my client's a bit touchy but not only is he certifiably loony, his glands are out of whack and he endured the big C.'"

"Cart before the horse, Big Guy."

"Yeah, yeah, find him first. Before someone *else* gets on his bad side. So where do I go with this thyroid stuff, Alex? Call every endocrinologist in town?"

"They're unlikely to talk to you but the general public won't have those compunctions. Have John Banforth sit down with Shimoff and work up a better likeness. If Banforth can't give enough details, I'll try to fill them in because I got a decent look at the guy. That and the scar, the coat, and the puzzle book could tweak someone's memory. Even if he's underground, he's got to surface occasionally. Assuming he's got an institutional background, I'd also check health clinics, welfare offices, halfway houses, and aftercare facilities near each of the murder sites. He paid for his meal with coins, I doubt that's interest from a brokerage account."

"On the dole," he said. "Or he panhandles. Like Eccles. Hell, maybe that's why he *did* Eccles: The two of them got into a competitive thing and Shearling decided to engage in unfair business practices . . . okay, I'll get Banforth and Shimoff together. This is helpful, amigo."

"One more thing," I said. "Check out newsstands, see if anyone sells a puzzle book with a question mark on the cover. The one near Vita's scene doesn't but there are plenty of others."

"There's a big one off Hollywood Boulevard, not that far from where Lem Eccles got it. Speaking of which, Jernigan called on Eccles's autopsy. The bruise on Eccles's lip was from a hard blow or a kick, most likely a kick from a blunt-toed shoe. Not severe enough to be lethal but it could've stunned him. Other than that, the details are like the others. Eccles's son's trip to L.A. is tomorrow. Want to be there?"

"Wouldn't miss it."

CHAPTER
28

Lemuel Eccles Jr., aka "Lee," was thirty-eight and rock-jawed, with meaty shoulders, blue eyes that tended to wander, and longish light brown hair lightened to blond at the tips.

Your basic aging surfer. This one sported a manicure, a two-thousand-dollar charcoal chalk-stripe suit, a purple Hermès tie, a canary-and-violet pocket square.

His card said he was an attorney specializing in real estate.

Milo said, "Leases and mortgages?"

Eccles said, "Used to be, now it's

evictions and foreclosures. Basically I'm a vulture." His smile was practiced and pretty, but lacked staying power. We'd been in the interview room for less than a minute. Eccles had spent most of that time sneaking glances at Petra Connor.

Easy to see why, especially given the competition. Her lips had moistened since yesterday, her eyes were clear, her skin tone had warmed. She wore a simple gold chain and diamond-chip earstuds. The drape of her black pantsuit was even better than that of Lee Eccles's suit.

The first few times she caught Eccles checking her out, she pretended not to notice. Finally, she smiled at him and edged closer.

She's in a committed relationship with a former detective named Eric Stahl, but you use what you have.

Milo sniffed the chemistry early on and let her take the interview.

"Lee," she said, as if savoring the word, "we're so sorry about your dad."

"Thanks. Appreciate it." Eccles loosened a jacket button. "I guess I shouldn't be totally surprised because he led what you guys would call a high-risk life. But still . . ."

"You can never be prepared for something like this, Lee."

Eccles's eyes filmed a bit. A tissue box sat nearby. Petra didn't offer it. No sense highlighting vulnerability.

Eccles used his pocket square to swipe quickly, took the time to refold and put the handkerchief back with four points showing. "What exactly happened?"

Petra said, "Your dad was murdered and we're determined to catch the bad guy. Anything you can tell us will be a big help."

"The first thing you need to know," said Eccles, "is he was crazy. I mean that literally. Paranoid schizophrenic, he was diagnosed years ago, not long after I was born. He and my mom divorced when I was four and I rarely saw him. After I got out of law school, he found me somehow and dropped in at my office. I was foolish enough to bring him home. It didn't take long for things to get hairy. Right from the beginning he scared Tracy—my wife. He ended up scaring me, too."

"In what way, Lee?"

"He wasn't actually violent but the threat of violence always seemed to hover around him and in a sense that was even worse. The look in his eyes, the way he'd suddenly go silent in the midst of a conversation. Then one time, we let him sleep over and he punched holes in the wall. Woke us up in the middle of the night, we were terrified. When I went in to see what was wrong, he was sitting on the floor, huddled in a corner, claimed he'd fended off an intruder. But the alarm was still on, no one had gotten in. I finally calmed him down and left. Later, I heard him crying in bed."

"What an ordeal," said Petra.

"I learned that it kicked in when he drank. Problem is, that was often. Eventually, Tracy and I agreed: No more visits, we really needed to cut him off. The next time he showed up we told him and he got pissed off and cussed us out. I offered to rent him a motel for as long as he needed and we could still see each other during the day. That pissed him off even more, he stormed off. A few weeks later he showed up and tried to force himself inside the house— pushed the door as I held it. That's when I decided to have him committed. I tried three separate times. For his sake as much as for ours, he needed to be cared for in a supervised setting, not drift around on the street. Each time I showed up in court, some do-gooder Legal Aid type was there to block me. Some ass-hole who'd never met him but claimed to be defending his rights. Apparently they scan the dockets and even when someone's only requesting a seventy-two-hour hold, they come to make trouble."

"Oh, man," said Petra.

Lee Eccles said, "I'm talking publicly funded wienies who know all the angles and brain-dead judges they probably take out to lunch. I'm an attorney and I still couldn't get it done. After the third time, I talked to a buddy who does health law and he said don't waste your time and money, until he actually as-saults—which means drawing blood—

or makes a suicide attempt, it's not going to happen. Even then, all they're going to do is warehouse him for a couple of days and turn him loose."

"Not enough imminent danger," said Petra.

"What a crock. The mere fact he was living on the street put him in imminent danger. *Obviously.*" His strong jaw shifted to the side. Settled back in place. "You know what I'd like to do? Haul one of those wienies over to the morgue and show them what their meddling accomplished."

He tugged at his tie knot. "Do you have any idea who did this to him?"

Him. He. No Dad, Pops, Father, the Old Man.

"Unfortunately not yet, Lee. Do you?"

"I wish. Where was he killed?"

"In an alley near Hollywood and Western."

"Oh, Jesus," said Eccles. "That's right where I dropped him off when I bailed him out of jail."

"When was that, Lee?"

"About a month ago, he'd gotten busted for pushing someone while panhandling. He used his call to beg me to get him out. I figured he'd get out anyway, be pissed if I didn't help him so I paid the bail and picked him up and dropped him where he wanted to be dropped. Where he *instructed* me to drop him. Like I'm his limo driver. So that's where it happened?"

Petra said, "Did you observe where he went after you dropped him off?"

"No, I just booked out of there as fast as I could."

"Did you notice him making any contact with someone?"

"No. But something just occurred to me, it's probably psychotic delusion but I might as well tell you. On the ride from the jail he got on one of his rants about some guy hassling him, he was scared. Then he got all paranoid with me, I was a goddamn lawyer, lawyers ran the system, why couldn't I help him? I said if he was scared I could find him somewhere to stay. He went ballistic, accused me of wanting to lock him up in some 'loony bin' and throw away the key, I was like all lawyers, a scumbag. I said, 'You're the one complaining someone's after you, I'm just trying to help.' That made him clam up, ignore me totally. When I reached where he wanted, he said, 'Stop here,' and he got out, didn't bother to look back."

Petra said, "Who'd he say was he scared of?"

"Trust me, it was delusional. An old delusion."

"What do you mean?"

"This guy he complained about didn't exist. He's been bitching about it my whole life. According to my mother since he actually *was* locked up in a mental hospital."

"Where's that?" said Petra.

"A place that no longer exists," said Lee Eccles. "Ventura State Hospital, he got committed for an indefinite term but was out in pretty short time according to my mother. Back then it was easier to commit someone, a judge put him in after he busted some guy's jaw in a bar, got on the stand and claimed the guy was implanting radio speakers in his head."

"How long ago was this, Lee?"

"Let's see, I was thirteen . . . no, fourteen, I was playing baseball, which means I was in high school. So twenty-three years ago. I remember the baseball part because I was always worried he'd show up at a game and embarrass me."

"So what's the old delusion?"

"While he was locked up, one of the guards supposedly killed his wife. Not my mother, not even a real wife, some woman he'd been living with, a barfly like him."

"Where was he living before he was committed?"

"Oxnard. We were in Santa Monica, which sounds far enough but the things Mom told me, I was always worried he'd show up. So was she, she moved us down to O.C., trying to put some distance between us."

"This woman who was allegedly murdered," said Petra. "Did your mom mention her name?"

"I think Mom said Rosetta. Or Rosita, I don't know. But don't waste your time, Detective. The story was insane. Like a guard could poison someone? Or want to? I'm not sure the woman even existed. Or if she did, that what happened to her is what he told Mom."

"What's that?"

"Rosita comes to visit him, leaves, drops dead in the parking lot. He knows this guard did it to get back at him. Why I can't tell you. Anyway, now it's the same person who's bothering him in Hollywood and I'm supposed to do something about it because I'm a lawyer."

"This imaginary person has a name."

"Petty," he said. "Or maybe it was Pitty. My father was originally from Oklahoma, had a twang that got worse when he was agitated. His story was the guy's popping up on the street, following him, giving him quote unquote X-ray eyes. It was a ridiculous story all those years ago and didn't get better in the retelling but I figure you should know everything."

"Appreciate it, Lee," said Petra. "Would you mind if we talked to your mother? Just to fill in details?"

"I'd love if you'd talk to her because that would mean she's alive. Unfortunately, Parkinson's disease had other ideas."

"I'm so sorry."

"So am I, Detective. They say you don't grow up until you lose your parents. Frankly, I'd prefer to be immature."

Petra's mother had died giving birth to her. Her father had succumbed a few years back. She said, "I've heard that."

Eccles stood, checked the folds of his hankie.

"I guess," he said, "I'm responsible for the body."

A uniformed officer saw Lee Eccles out.

Petra said, "He has no idea what he just gave us. Marlon Quigg worked at that hospital at the same time Lem Eccles was committed there. Looks like you were right about some sort of ancient history, Alex."

I said, "Maybe for those two but I can't see Vita and Glenda Usfel connected to V-State that long ago. Usfel was a young child and Vita grew up in Chicago."

"Fine," said Milo. "So their problems with Mr. Shearling were more recent, he's an equal-opportunity disemboweler."

Petra said, "Eccles Junior is one angry man, that boy did not like his daddy. Can't say that I blame him but he's lucky Daddy's murder is part of a serial because if I picked it up as a one-shot I'd be looking at him as my prime. And if Eccles alienated his own offspring that thoroughly, imagine what he could evoke in a homicidal maniac. Especially if the two of them went way back to V-State."

Milo said, "Mr. Crazy, meet Mr. Curious. Where do we go with this Pitty-Patty-Petty dude? If any of it's true, we've got complications because Shearling's too young to have worked as a guard twenty-three years ago."

I said, "The story could be partially true. Eccles knew someone named Pitty years ago, convinced himself the guy was after him. He notices someone stalking him and resurrects his old personal bogeyman."

"You believe the stalking part?" said Petra.

"Eccles was murdered."

Milo said, "The bumper sticker."

"What?"

"Even paranoids have enemies."

She laughed.

Milo said, "Even if Pitty did exist, Alex is probably right and he's irrelevant. Eccles was schizo, had a fixation, flashed back to it. Or Pitty's a squid in a three-piece suit or some other figment. In any event, we've got multiple sightings of Shearling."

Petra said, "If Shearling was a patient at V-State, we might be able to find some known associates, family, anything that could lead us to him. Any word back from that psychiatrist, Alex?"

"No."

Milo said, "Got his address just before Eccles Junior showed up. Social Security records, don't ask."

She said, "Excellent. Let's pay him a visit, Big Guy."

"I don't know. He's under no obligation to let us past the door let alone cough up patient info. We get heavy-handed, he invokes the doctor confidentiality thing. So my vote's for having Alex try first, shrink-to-shrink."

Petra looked at me.

I said, "He could refuse me, too, but sure."

Milo fished out a scrap of paper and handed it over. Van Nuys address, 818 landline.

"Meanwhile, we can have Shimoff do a better drawing with Banforth and push to get it on the media along with the new info. I've got Sean and Moe checking out newsstands and bookstores, see if anyone remembers an asshole buying puzzle books."

Petra said, "Raul's been talking to street people but so far no one had a special beef with Eccles, basically everyone thought he was a general pain." Smiling. "I'll tell him to look for a cephalopod in a suit."

I said, "Eccles's last arrest, the one his son bailed him out for, was for shoving a tourist. Have you looked at the arrest report?"

"I read the summary. Your basic citizen versus nutcase."

"Citizen have a name?"

"I didn't make note of it. Why?"

"Maybe it's worthwhile. On the off chance that it was Shearling."

"Nutcase versus nutcase?" said Milo.

"Flagrant psychotic versus someone

able to maintain outward control," I said. "What was the exact nature of the charge?"

Petra said, "Eccles tried to get money from a tourist, the tourist resisted, Eccles did some screaming and pushing and shoving."

"Did the tourist phone in the complaint?"

"No, someone on the street did and a car was a block away."

I said, "Think what the officers would've found: a he said–he said between a quiet young man and an angry alcoholic with a record for aggressive panhandling whom they knew as a neighborhood nuisance."

Milo said, "Shearling's able to fake normal."

"Five murders without a trace of physical evidence says he's organized, meticulous, able to slip in and out without setting off alarms. He impressed Hedy the waitress as eccentric but didn't scare her. John Banforth thought his behavior was odd but it didn't trouble him too much until he learned of Vita's murder. So we're talking someone who's not overwhelmingly threatening. When contrasted with Eccles's ravings, there's no doubt who the cops would've seen as the offender."

"Monster trumps maniac," she said. "Okay, I'll check the complete report. And as long as we're dotting *i*'s, I'm going to call Oxnard PD and see if I can dig up something about this Rosetta woman." Winking. "The bumper sticker and all that."

The three of us headed for the exit.

"Crazy," said Milo. "The only time I like it is when Patsy Cline's singing about it."

CHAPTER
29

Caught in a traffic jam on Wilshire and Westwood, I phoned my service.

Three calls, none of them from Emil Cahane.

I tried the Valley number Milo had given me. No answer.

When I got home, I began working the computer, searching for staff lists at V-State and finally coming upon an old one that listed Cahane as deputy director with one person above him, Dr. Saul Landesberg.

A search using Landesberg's name pulled up a four-year-old obituary.

Him, Gertrude, I wasn't even sure if Cahane was coherent.

Ancient history. But not to a man in a fleece-lined coat.

Robin was working out back. I dropped in, kissed her, petted Blanche, engaged in a brief discussion of dinner. Yes, Japanese sounded fine, maybe we'd splurge on Matsuhisa.

When I returned to my office, the phone was ringing.

Milo said, "Guess what, we actually learned some stuff. A clerk at a stand on San Vicente in Brentwood told Reed he sold an armload of puzzle books to someone about a week ago. Unfortunately, he remembers the books, not the purchaser. Who cleaned him out. And paid with small bills and coins."

I said, "Go west from that location, hook north to Sunset and keep going, you'll reach Quigg's apartment. Couple of miles farther, you're at Temescal Canyon."

"Stocking up on reading material for a thorough surveillance? Interesting . . . The second thing is Petra found out from Oxnard that there really was a Rosetta who died in the parking lot at V-State, last name Macomber. She lived in a public housing project, had coke and booze issues. So Eccles had at least some reality testing, but there was no evidence it was murder, more likely a heart attack."

"Not a scratch on her," I said. "That's why Eccles thought she'd been poisoned. Was she visiting him?"

"The cop Petra talked to didn't know, only reason he remembered was he'd patrolled near the hospital, was called to the scene by their on-site security. Thought it was ironic for someone to walk out of a hospital and keel over. Even though it wasn't *that* kind of hospital. The last bit of news is Shimoff's second drawing is much more detailed than the one he did with Wheeling, I'm working on getting it to the media. So thanks for directing us to Mr. Banforth. Anything from Cahane?"

"Not yet."

"He gets back to you, fine. He doesn't, we'll figure out what to do. Sayonara."

◆

I returned to the list of V-State senior staffers, tried the next name, the head social worker, a Helen Barofsky. Her personal data had managed to elude me for nearly an hour by the time my service rang in.

"A Dr. Cahane called," said the operator. "He said it wasn't an emergency."

Depends on your definition.

The number she gave me matched the one I'd received from Milo. I waited seven rings before a soft voice said, "Yes?"

"Dr. Cahane? This is Alex Delaware returning—"

"Dr. Delaware." Soft, wispy voice, tremulous at the tail end of each word, like an amp set on slow vibrato. "I'm afraid your name isn't familiar."

"No reason it should be," I said. "I floated through V-State years ago as an intern. Gertrude Vanderveul was my supervisor. Years later, when the hospital closed down, I did some consulting on getting the patients in E Ward some decent aftercare."

"Aftercare," he said. "Promises were made, weren't they?" Sigh. "I was gone by then. Gertrude . . . have you been in contact with her?"

"Unfortunately, she passed away."

"Oh. How terrible, she was young." A beat. "Relatively . . . my nephew's secretary said something about a Mr. Quib passing but I can't say I know who that is, either."

"Marlon Quigg." I spelled it.

"No, sorry, doesn't ring a bell."

Yet he'd returned my call.

As if reading my mind, he said, "I responded to your message because at my age any bit of novelty is welcome. In any event, sorry I couldn't be more helpful."

"Marlon Quigg worked as a teacher at V-State during your tenure."

"We employed many teachers," said Cahane. "At the height of our glory, we were quite the enlightened institution."

"This teacher was murdered and the police have reason to believe his death relates to his work at the hospital."

Silence.

"Dr. Cahane?"

"This is a bit to digest, Dr. Delaware.

The police have reason to believe, yet they're not calling me, you are."

"I work with them."

"In what capacity?"

"A consultant."

"Meaning?"

"Sometimes they think psychology has something to offer. Could you spare a few minutes to meet?"

"Hmm," he said. "And if I phoned the police, Alex, they'd confirm that you're a consultant?"

I rattled off Milo's name, rank, and private number. "He'd be more than happy to speak to you, Doctor. He's the one who asked me to get in contact with you."

"Why is that?"

"You were the deputy director at V-State when Marlon Quigg worked there, had access to information."

"Patient information?"

"Specifically dangerous patients."

"That, as I'm sure you know, raises all kinds of issues."

"The situation," I said, "is way beyond *Tarasoff.* We're not talking imminent danger, we're talking empirical brutality with a significant risk of more."

"That sounds rather dramatic."

"I saw the body, Dr. Cahane."

Silence.

He said, "What exactly are you looking for?"

"The identity of a child Quigg was teaching whose behavior frightened him, perhaps to the point of suggesting a transfer to Specialized Care."

"And this person killed him?" said Cahane. "All these years later?"

"It's possible."

"You're supposing, you really don't know."

"If I knew I wouldn't need to speak to you, Dr. Cahane."

"Specialized Care," he said. "Did you ever rotate through there?"

"Gertrude felt I shouldn't."

"Why was that?"

"She said it was because she liked me."

"I see . . . well, there are always judgments to make and for the most part Gertrude made sound ones. But Special-C wasn't a hellhole, far from it.

Whatever steps were taken to control patients were taken judiciously."

"This isn't about hospital procedure, Dr. Cahane. It's about a particularly calculating, vicious murderer acting out years of resentment and fantasy."

"Why exactly do the police believe Mr. Quigg's death had something to do with a patient at V-State?"

Because I told them so.

I said, "It's complex. Could we meet face-to-face?"

"You want a prolonged opportunity to convince me."

"I don't think you'll need much convincing."

"Why's that?"

"Something was left on Mr. Quigg's body," I said. "A piece of paper upon which the killer had printed a question mark."

I could hear Cahane's breathing, rapid and shallow.

Finally, he said, "I don't drive anymore. You'd need to come to me."

The address Milo gave me matched an apartment building a few miles east of

Cahane's nephew's office in Encino, a plain-faced, two-story rhombus stuccoed the color of raspberry yogurt and planted with yuccas, palms, and enough agave to cook up a year's worth of margaritas.

The freeway passed within a couple of blocks, its roar the awakening yawn of an especially cranky ogre. The building's front door was closed but unlocked. The center-spine hallway was freshly painted and immaculately maintained.

Five units above, five below. Cahane's flat was ground floor rear. As I approached the door, the ogre's growl muted to a disgruntled hum. I knocked.

"Open."

Cahane sat ten feet away in a scarred leather easy chair that faced the door. His body tilted to the left. His face was even thinner than in the tribute photo, white hair longer and shaggier, a couple days' worth of stubble snowing chin and cheeks. He had long legs and arms, not much upper body, was dressed in a clean white shirt and pressed navy slacks under a fuzzy plaid bathrobe.

Black suede slippers that had once been expensive fit over white socks that hadn't been. A mahogany piecrust table held a cup of still-steaming tea and a book. Evelyn Waugh's hilarious take on travel.

Extending a quivering hand, he said, "Forgive me for not rising but the joints aren't cooperating today."

His palm was cool and waxy, his grip surprisingly strong but contact was as brief as he could manage without being rude. He shook his head. "Can't say I remember you."

"No reason—"

"Sometimes images register anyway. Would you care for something to drink?" Pointing to a kitchen behind the front room. "I've got soda and juice and the kettle's still warm. Even bourbon, if you'd like."

"I'm fine."

"Then please sit."

No puzzle about where to settle. The sole option was a blue brocade sofa pushed to the wall opposite Cahane's chair. Like the slippers, it looked pricey but worn. Same for the piecrust table and the Persian rug that stretched unevenly atop soot-colored wall-to-wall. Disparate bookcases covered every inch of wall space save for doorways into the kitchen and the bedroom. Every case was full and some shelves were double-stacked.

A quick scan of the titles showed Cahane's reading taste to be unclassifiable: history, geography, religion, photography, physics, gardening, cooking, a wide range of fiction, political satire. Two shelves directly behind his chair held volumes on psychology and psychiatry. Basic stuff and not much of it, considering.

Chair, beverage, robe and slippers, reading material. He had enough money to endow a program, had pruned to the basics.

He kept studying my face, as if trying to retrieve a memory. Or just reverting to what he'd learned in school.

When in doubt, do nothing.

I half expected to be presented a Rorschach card.

I said, "Doctor—"

"Tell me about Marlon Quigg's end."

I described the murder, giving him the

level of detail I figured Milo would approve. Wanting to communicate the horror without divulging too much and making sure not to mention the other victims lest Cahane interpret that as pointing away from V-State.

He said, "That is beyond brutal."

"Does the question mark mean anything to you, Dr. Cahane?"

His lips folded inward. He rubbed chin stubble. "How about fetching that bourbon? Bring two glasses."

The kitchen was as spare as the front room, clean but shabby. The glasses were cut crystal, the bourbon was Knob Creek.

Cahane said, "A finger and a half for me, calibrate your own dosage."

I allotted myself a thin amber stripe. We clinked crystal. No one toasted.

I sat down and watched him drain his glass in two swallows. He rubbed his stubble again. "You're wondering why I live this way."

"It wasn't the first thing on my mind."

"But you are curious."

I didn't argue.

He said, "Like most people, I spent quite a bit of my adult life accumulating things. After my wife died I began to feel smothered by things so I gave most of them away. I'm not stupid or impulsive, nor am I ruled by neurotic anhedonia. I held on to enough passive income to ensure freedom from worry. It was an experiment, really. To see how it felt to cleanse oneself of the rococo trim we think we crave. Sometimes I miss my big house, my cars, my art. Mostly, I do not."

Long monologue. Probably a stall. I had no choice but to listen.

Cahane said, "You've put me in a difficult position. You've come to me with nothing more than hypotheses. Granted, hypotheses are often based on logic but the problem is you don't have facts and now you're asking me to break confidentiality."

"Your position at V-State wouldn't necessarily obligate you to confidentiality," I said.

His eyebrows dipped. "What do you mean?"

"A case can be made that administrators aren't bound the way clinicians are. Of course, if you did treat the person in question, that assertion might be challenged."

He lifted his empty glass. "Would you mind fetching the bottle?"

I complied and he poured himself another two fingers, finished half. His eyes had grown restless. He closed them. His hands had begun to shake. Then they stilled and he didn't move.

I waited.

For a moment I thought he'd fallen asleep.

The eyes opened. He looked at me sadly and I braced myself for refusal.

"There was a boy," he said. "A curious boy."

CHAPTER

30

Emil Cahane poured another half inch of bourbon. Studying the liquid as if it held both promise and threat, he took a tentative sip then swigged like a sot.

His head tilted up at the ceiling. His eyes closed. His breathing grew rapid.

"All right," he said. But he spent another half minute sitting there. Then: "This child, this . . . unusual boy was sent to us from another state. No sense specifying, it doesn't matter. They had no idea how to deal with him and we were considered among the best. He arrived in a pale green sedan . . . a

Ford . . . he was accompanied by two state troopers. Large men, it emphasized how small he was. I tried to interview him but he wouldn't talk. I placed him in G Building. Perhaps you remember it."

I'd spent most of my time there. "An open ward rather than Specialized Care."

"There were no youngsters in Specialized Care," said Cahane. "I felt it would've been barbaric to subject someone of that age to the offenders housed there. We're talking murderers, rapists, necrophiles, cannibals. Psychotics judged too disturbed for the prison system and sheltered from the outside world for their sake and ours." He massaged his empty glass. "This was a *child.*"

"How old was he?"

He shifted in his chair. "Young."

"Pre-adolescent?"

"Eleven," he said. "You can see how we were faced with a unique set of circumstances. He had his own room in G with an atmosphere that emphasized treatment, not confinement. You remember the array of services we offered. He made good use of our programs, caused no trouble whatsoever."

I said, "His crime justified Specialized Care but his age complicated matters."

He shot me a sharp look. "You're trying to draw out details I'm not sure I'm willing to offer."

"I appreciate your talking with me, Dr. Cahane, but without details—"

"If I'm not performing to your satisfaction, feel free to walk through that door."

I sat there.

"I apologize," he said. "I'm having a difficult time with this."

"I can understand that."

"With all due respect, Dr. Delaware, you really can't understand. You're assuming I'm waffling because of medicolegal constraints but that's not it."

He poured yet more bourbon, tossed it back. Tamped white hair, succeeded only in mussing the long, brittle strands. His eyes had pinkened. His lips vibrated. He looked like an old, wild man.

"I'm too old to care about the medico-legal system. My reservations are selfish: covering my geriatric buttocks."

"You think you screwed up."

"I don't think. I know, Dr. Delaware."

"With patients like that, it's often im-possible to know—"

He waved me quiet. "Thanks for the attempt at empathy but you can't know. That place was a city. The director was a do-nothing ass and that left me the mayor. The buck stopped at me."

Tears filled his eyes.

I said, "Still—"

"Please. Stop." The soft voice, the sympathetic look. "Even if you are being sincere and not using rapport to crack me open, sympathy without context churns my bowels."

I said, "Let's talk about him. What did he do at eleven that his home state couldn't handle?"

"Eleven," he said, "and every bit a child. A small, soft, prepubescent boy with a soft voice and soft little hands and soft, outwardly innocent eyes. I held his hand as I led him to the room that would be his new home. He clutched me with fear. Sweaty. 'When can I go back?' I had no comforting answer but I never lie so I did what we mind-science types do when we're flummoxed. I veered into bland reassurances—he'd be comfortable, we'd take good care of him. Then I used another tactic: peppered him with questions so I wouldn't have to provide answers. What did he like to eat? What did he do for fun? He turned silent, and slumped as if he'd given up. But he marched on like a good little soldier, sat on his bed and picked up one of the books we provided and began reading. I stuck around but he ignored me. Finally, I asked if there was anything he needed and he looked up and smiled and said, 'No, thank you, sir, I'm fine.'"

Cahane winced. "After that, I resorted to cowardice. Inquiring periodically about his progress but having no direct contact with him. The official reason was it wasn't part of my job description, by that time I was essentially an administrator, saw no patients whatsoever. The real reason, of course, is I had nothing to offer him, didn't want to be reminded of that."

"He confused you."

Instead of responding to that, he said,

"I did keep tabs on him. The consensus was that he was doing better than expected. No problems at all, really."

Bracing his hands on the arms of his chair, he tried to get up, fell back and gave a sick smile. When I moved to help him, he said, "I'm fine," and struggled to his feet. "Bathroom." Tottering, he trudged through the doorway that bisected his bookshelves.

Ten minutes passed before a toilet flushed and sink-water burbled. When he returned, his color had deepened and his hands were trembling.

Settling back down, he said, "So he was doing fine. Then he wasn't. Or so I was told."

"By Marlon Quigg."

"By a senior staff member who'd been informed by an intern who'd been informed by a teacher." He sighed. "Yes, your Mr. Quigg, one of those breathlessly idealistic young men who thought he'd found a calling."

"What did he report?"

"Regression," said Cahane. "Severe behavioral regression."

"Back to what brought the boy to you."

"Dear God," said Cahane. He laughed oddly.

I said, "Anatomical curiosity?"

His hands pressed together. He mumbled.

I said, "What was his original crime?"

Cahane shook a finger at me. I expected reproach. The finger curled, arced back toward him, hooked in an ear. He sat back. "He killed his mother. Shot her in the back of the head as she watched television. No one missed her at the farm where she cleaned barns because it was the weekend. She didn't socialize much, it was just her and him, their home in Kan— They lived in a trailer at the edge of the farm."

"He stayed with her corpse."

Nod.

I went on, "Once he was sure she was dead he used a knife."

"Knives," said Cahane. "From the kitchen. Carving tools, as well, a Christmas gift from her. So he could whittle. He used a whetstone she'd employed when she slaughtered chickens that she brought home for their dinner. She used to slaughter the birds in front of him, wasted nothing, reserved the blood for sausage. When the police finally found her, the stench was overpowering. But he didn't seem to mind, displayed no emotion at all. The police were stunned, didn't know where to take him and ended up using a locked room at a local clinic. Because the jail was filled with adult criminals, no one knew what would happen to him in that environment. He didn't protest. He was a polite boy. Later, when one of the nurses asked him why he'd stayed with the body he said he'd been trying to know her better."

I described the wounds Shearling had left on Quigg.

He said, "The troopers who brought him also brought crime scene photos from the trailer. When I'm feeling remorseful about something, I dial those images up and make myself downright miserable. The home was a sty, utter disorder. But not his room, his room was neat. He'd decorated the walls. Anatomical charts. Hanging everywhere. Where a child that age would obtain such things baffled me. The police hadn't been interested enough to ask but I pressed them and they made inquiries. A physician, a general practitioner to whom the boy had been taken far too infrequently, had befriended him. Because he seemed like such a *good* little boy with his interest in biology. Might very well make a *splendid* doctor, one day."

"What do you know about his mother?"

"Reclusive, hardworking. She'd moved to town from parts unknown with a two-year-old, got the job cleaning barns and kept it. The trailer she lived in was at the far end of a wheat field. Owned by the farmer and she was allowed to live there gratis."

"Was there evidence of premeditation?"

"He shot her while she was watching her favorite TV show. Apart from that, I couldn't say."

"Any remorse?"

"No."

"How was she discovered?"

"On Monday she didn't show up for

work. The first time she'd ever missed, she was dependable, you could set your clock by her. She had no phone so a farmhand went to check, smelled the stench, and cracked the door and saw her. The boy was sitting next to her. Exploring. He'd fixed himself a sandwich. Peanut butter but no jelly." He smiled. "The details policemen put in their reports. They found a few smudges on the charts in his room, didn't know what to make of that. My guess is he was looking for confirmation. Between what was on the chart and what he'd . . . palpated. Her intestines, in particular, seemed . . . of interest."

I said, "Homeschooling himself in biology. Kansas couldn't deal so you got him."

"Several institutions were solicited and refused. We accepted him because I was arrogant. I'm sure you're familiar with V-State's history, all those terrible things carried out in the name of medicine. By the time I got there—the reason I went there—all that had been expunged and we had a well-justified reputation for being humane." He studied me. "When you were there did you find indications to the contrary?"

"Not at all. I got great training."

"Glad to hear you say that. Glad and proud . . . there was the notion that he wouldn't be safe in Kansas. Too much notoriety."

"What caused Marlon Quigg to be concerned?"

"I'm sure you recall the beauty of our grounds."

Apparent non sequitur. I nodded.

He said, "*Pastoral* was a term I heard bandied about quite often. Abundant flora *and* fauna."

I said, "Animals. He trapped them. Resumed exploring."

"Small animals," said Cahane. "Analysis of the bones identified squirrels, mice, lizards. A garter snake. A stray cat. Birds, as well, we never figured out how he caught them. Caught any of them. He was clever enough to conceal his handiwork for months. Found a quiet spot behind a remote storage shed, conducted his experiments, buried the remains and tidied the ground. He'd been allowed to leave the ward for two hours a day, once in the morning, once before dinner. From the body count, we estimated he worked with one creature a day."

Tidying. I thought of the clean dirt at Marlon Quigg's kill-site. "How was he discovered?"

"Young Mr. Quigg had grown suspicious and chose to follow him one evening. The chosen creature was a baby mole."

"What made Quigg suspicious?"

"The boy had grown uncommunicative, even surly. Should someone else have noticed? Perhaps. What can I tell you?"

"Teachers and nurses spend a lot more time with patients than we do."

"They do . . . In any event, faced with a new set of facts, we needed to shift our paradigm but we weren't sure how. Some of the staff, most vocally Marlon Quigg, agitated for an immediate transfer to Specialized Care. Others disagreed."

Cahane's eyes shifted to the right. "I listened to everyone, said I'd take some time and decide. As if I was being deliberative. The truth was I was unable to make a decision. Not only because he posed problems I was ill prepared for. My own life was in shambles. My father had just died, I'd applied for positions at Harvard and UC San Francisco, had been turned down at both places. My marriage was falling apart. There had always been issues but I'd brought them to a head by straying with another woman, a beautiful, brilliant woman but, of course, that doesn't excuse it. In a pathetic attempt to reconcile with my wife, I booked a cruise through the Panama Canal. Even under the guise of sensitivity I was being selfish, because sailing through the canal was something I'd always wanted."

He picked up his glass, changed his mind, put it down hard. "Twenty-four days on a ship, preceded by several weeks on the Outer Banks of North Carolina because Eleanor hailed from there. I was away from the hospital for forty-three days and during my absence, someone took it upon himself to deal with the boy. The psychologist who'd come to me with Quigg's original complaint. He agreed with Quigg, viewed the boy as untreatable and tainted. His term. He was a foolish, authoritarian man, too confident in his own meager abilities. I'd long had my reservations about him but his credentials, though foreign, were excellent. As a state employee he had all sorts of contractual protection, had never made an error that would jeopardize that."

Cahane's shaky fingers entangled in his hair. "Then, he did. And now *this* moment has arrived."

His eyes lost focus. "There I was, on a beautiful ship, dining, dancing. Marveling at the canal." He poured bourbon, spilled some, studied the droplets on his sleeve. "Dear God."

I said, "The boy was sent to Specialized Care."

"If only that was all of it," said Cahane. "That man, that overconfident *ass,* decided—on his own, with no evidence or prior discussion—that the boy's problems were primarily hormonal. *Glandular irregularity* was the way he termed it. Like something out of a Victorian medical book. He prepared papers, had the boy transported to a clinic in Camarillo where he was operated on by a surgeon who lacked the judgment to question the request."

"Thyroidectomy," I said.

Cahane's head jerked back. "You already know?"

"A witness described a scar across the front of his neck."

He gripped his glass with both hands, hurled it awkwardly across the room. It landed on the carpet, rolled. "A complete thyroidectomy for absolutely no reason at all. After a week's recuperation, the boy was transferred to Specialized Care. The quack claimed he was looking out for the boy—trying to *regulate* his behavior because clearly nothing else had worked. But I always suspected there was an element of base, vicious revenge."

"You like to operate, Sonny? See how it feels?"

"One of the animals the boy had chosen to explore had been the fool's unofficial pet. A stray cat that he fed from time to time. Of course he denied that this was all about *helping* the lad. I returned from my cruise, learned what had happened, was horrified, livid at my staff for not intervening. Everyone claimed they'd been unaware. I sat the bastard down, had a long talk with him, told him he was retiring and that if he ever applied for a position at another state hospital, I'd write a letter. He protested, switched to sniveling, tried to bargain, ended up making a pathetic threat: Anything he'd done had been under my supervision so I wouldn't escape scrutiny. I called his bluff and he deflated. He was over the hill, anyway. Pushing eighty."

He smiled. "Younger than I am today. Some of us rot more quickly than others."

"Foreign credentials," I said. "From where?"

"Belgium."

My chest tightened. "University of Louvain?"

Cahane nodded. "A fussy little twit with a fussy, comical Teutonic accent who wore ridiculous bow ties and slicked his hair and strutted around as if he'd kissed Freud's ring."

"What was his name?"

Unnecessary request.

Cahane said, "Why the hell not? His name was Shacker. *Buhrrrn*-hard Shacker. Don't waste your time looking for him, he's quite dead. Suffered a heart attack the day after I fired him, collapsed right in the hospital parking lot. No doubt stress was a factor but those sandwiches he brought to staff lunches couldn't have helped. Fatty pork and the like, slathered with butter."

"What happened to the boy?"

"Did I remove him from Special-C?" said Cahane. "That didn't seem advisable, given signs of impending puberty and the enormity of what had been done to him. Instead, I created a custom environment for him within the walls of Special. Kept him out of a barred cell and put him in a locked room that been used for storage but had a window and a nice view of the mountains. We painted it a cheerful blue, moved in a proper bed not a cot, installed wall-to-wall carpeting, a television, a radio, a stereo, audiotapes. It was a nice room."

"You kept him in Special-C because you expected him to grow increasingly violent."

"And he defied my expectations, Dr. Delaware. Developed into a pleasant, compliant adolescent who spent his days reading. At that point, I was a good deal more hands-on, visiting him, making sure everything was going well. I brought in an endocrinologist to monitor his Synthroid dosage. He responded well to T4 maintenance."

"Did he receive any psychiatric treatment?"

"He didn't want any and he wasn't displaying symptoms. After what he'd been through, the last thing I wanted to do was coerce. Which isn't to say he wasn't monitored thoroughly. Every effort was made to ensure that he didn't regress."

"No access to animals."

"His recreational time was supervised and confined to the Special-C yard. He shot hoops, did calisthenics, walked around. He ate well, groomed himself just fine, denied any delusions or hallucinations."

"Who supervised him?"

"Guards."

"Any guard in particular?"

"No."

"Do you recall a guard named Pitty or Petty?"

"I didn't know any of their names. Why?"

"The name came up."

"With regard to?"

"A murder."

"Quigg's?"

"Yes," I lied.

Cahane stared. "A murderous *team*?"

"It's possible."

"Pitty Petty," he said. "No, that name isn't familiar to me."

"What happened to the boy after the hospital closed down?"

"I was gone by then."

"You have no idea?"

"I was living in another city."

"Miami?"

He reached for his glass, realized he'd tossed it. Clamped his eyes shut as if in pain, opened them and stared into mine. "Why would you suggest that?"

I said, "Gertrude moved to Miami and men have been known to follow beautiful, brilliant women."

"Gertrude," he said. "Did she ever speak of me?"

"Not by name. She did imply she was in love again."

Another lie, blatant, manipulative. Use what you have.

Emil Cahane sighed. "No, I moved down here, to L.A. It wasn't until years later that I showed up at her doorstep in Miami. Unannounced, hoping she was still single. I emptied my heart. She let me down easy. Said that what we'd had was wonderful but that was ancient history, there was no looking back. I was utterly crushed but pretended to be valiant, got on the next plane back here. Unable to settle myself, I moved to Colorado, took a job that proved lucrative but unsatisfying, quit, and did the exact same thing. It took four job changes before I realized I was little more than a prescribing robot. I decided to live off my pension and give away most of what I owned. My charity has extended to the point where I need to budget. Ergo, my mansion."

He laughed. "Ever the narcissist, I can't refrain from boasting."

I said, "Where would you guess the boy went after V-State shut down?"

"Many of the Specialized patients were transferred to other institutions."

"Which ones?"

"Atascadero, Starkweather. No doubt some of them ended up in prison. That's our system, we're all about punishment."

"Help me understand the timeline," I said. "What year did the boy arrive at V-State?"

"Just over twenty-five years ago."

"Eleven years old."

"A few months shy of twelve."

"How long did he stay on the open ward?"

"A year and some months."

"So he was thirteen when he got operated on and transferred." Right around the time Marlon Quigg had left the hospital and abandoned a teaching career.

Had the switch been due to horror at what he'd witnessed behind the shed, or remorse over what his suspicions had led to?

Either way, he'd been called to pay.

I said, "What's the boy's name?"

Cahane turned away.

"Doctor, I need a name before other people die."

"People such as myself?"

Ever the narcissist.

"It's possible."

"Don't worry about me, Dr. Delaware. If you're correct that he killed Quigg out of revenge, I can't imagine any personal danger to myself. Because Quigg got the ball rolling, without Quigg none of the rest of it would've ensued. I, on the other hand, did my utmost to help the boy and he recognized that."

"Providing a nice room."

"A protective environment that provided security vis-à-vis the other patients."

"You know he appreciated that because—"

"He thanked me."

"When?"

"When I told him I was leaving."

"How old was he, then?"

"Fifteen."

"Two years in Specialized."

"In Specialized *technically*," he said. "But for all purposes, he had his own private ward. He *thanked* me, Dr. Delaware. He'd have no reason to harm me."

"That assumes rationality on his part."

"Do you have some concrete evidence that I'm in peril, Dr. Delaware?"

"We're talking about a highly disturbed—"

He smirked. "You're trying to fish out information."

"This isn't about you," I said. "He needs to be stopped. Give me a name."

I'd raised my voice, put some steel into it. For no obvious reason Cahane brightened. "Alex, would you be so kind as to check my bathroom? I believe I've left my glasses there and I'd like to spend a pleasant afternoon with Spinoza and Leibniz. Rationality and all that."

"First tell me—"

"Young man," he said. "I don't like being out of focus. Help restore some visual coherence and perhaps we'll chat further."

I passed through the doorway to the lav. The space was cramped, white tiles crisscrossed by grubby grout. A threadbare gray towel hung from a pebbled glass shower door. The smell was bay rum, cheap soap, faulty plumbing.

No eyeglasses anywhere.

Something white and peaked sat atop the toilet tank.

Piece of paper folded, origami-style, the folds uneven, the flaps wrinkled by unsteady hands. Some sort of small squat animal.

Serrated edges said the paper had been ripped from a spiral notebook. I spotted the book in a ragged wicker basket to the left of the commode, along with a tract on philosophy and several old copies of *Smithsonian*.

Every page of the notebook was blank.

I unfolded. Black ballpoint block printing centered the page, made ragged by several hesitation breaks.

GRANT HUGGLER
(The Curious Boy)

I hurried back to Cahane's living room, note in hand. The big leather chair was empty. Cahane was nowhere in sight.

To the left of the bathroom was a closed door.

I knocked.

No answer.

"Dr. Cahane?"

"I need to sleep."

I turned the knob. Locked. "Is there anything else you can tell me?"

"I need to sleep."

"Thank you."

"I need to sleep."

CHAPTER
31

Alex Shimoff's second drawing aired on the six o'clock news. A bored talking-head noted the suspect's "winter coat" and a possible history of "thyroid issues." Total broadcast time: thirty-two seconds.

I froze the frame. This sketch was lifelike, the broad face impassive.

This was the man I'd seen huddled in a corner booth at Bijou, inches from a group of moms and tots.

Robin said, "He looks blank. Like something's missing. Or maybe Shimoff didn't have enough to work with."

"He did."

She looked at me. I'd already told her some of what Cahane had related. Took it no further.

Blanche studied each of us. We sat there.

Robin said, "Eleven years old," and walked out of the room.

Milo'd been off the radar all day but he phoned about an hour after the broadcast. My searches using Grant Huggler's name had proved fruitless.

He said, "Catch it? Big improvement, no? His Exaltedness pulled strings because 'shit needs turning over so it won't stink worse than it already is.' Anyway, we've got a piece of fine art, even Shimoff's satisfied. The tip lines just started to light up, so far it's fewer than we got the first time, maybe Joe Public's played out. But Moe caught one worth looking into. Anonymous female caller says a guy fitting Shearling's description received his thyroid prescription at a clinic in Hollywood, she hung up when Reed asked her which one. A place in Hollywood fits a guy on the streets and puts him in proximity to Lem Eccles. All the clinics Petra called are closed until tomorrow, she'll follow up and if God's feeling generous we'll get a name."

"God loves you," I said. "His name's Grant Huggler."

"What?"

I recapped the meeting with Cahane.

He said, "He leaves it for you to find in the damn bathroom? What was that, pretending he wasn't actually a snitch?"

"He left it folded like origami. Setting up a little production but distancing himself from it. He's a complicated guy, spends a lot of energy on self-justification."

"Is he a reliable guy?"

"I believe what he told me."

"Grant Huggler," he said. "Eleven years old a quarter century ago makes him thirty-six, which fits our witness reports. Can't be too many with that name, I'm plugging him in now—well looky here, male Cauc, six feet, two thirty-six, picked up five years ago in Morro Bay for trespassing, possible intent to commit burglary . . . a doctor's office, that probably means they nabbed him just as he broke in to score dope . . . which fits with a street guy with psych issues . . . no prison sentence, he got pled down to jail time served . . . here's the mug shot. Long hair, scruffy beard but the face behind all that pelt looks kinda chubby . . . talk about weird eyes. Dead, like he's staring into the Great Abyss."

"No busts before then?"

"Nope, that's it. Not much of a criminal history for someone who's now a serial gutter."

I said, "Morro Bay's not far from Atascadero, which is one of the places dangerous patients were transferred when V-State shut down. A first offense five years ago could mean he was locked up until then. If so, he's been incarcerated for twenty years."

"Plenty of time to stew."

"And to fantasize."

"He'd be treated with meds, right?"

"Possibly."

"I'm asking that because if it was dope he was after, maybe he got hooked on something, tried to boost from a doctor's office. Though once he got out, wouldn't he be sent to some kind of outpatient facility where he could score legally?"

"That assumes he'd show up," I said. "And few patients crave psychotropics, something recreational would be more likely. I'm betting he was noncompliant about aftercare, if for no other reason than he'd want to avoid waiting rooms."

"Little medical phobia, huh? Yeah, getting your neck sliced for no reason can do that to you—so maybe he was trying to swipe *thyroid* meds because he hated waiting rooms."

"Anxiety about medical settings could explain being so tense in Glenda Usfel's scan room. Toss in some hormonal irritability, add Usfel's aggressive nature, and you'd have a volatile situation. But he didn't react impulsively, just the opposite. He bided his time, planned, stalked her, took action. I suppose spending most of your life in a highly structured environment could instill patience and an interesting sense of focus."

"Losing an organ he didn't have to lose," he said. "Doing that to a kid. Barbaric. Now he's out, practicing his own brand of surgery."

"Avenging old wrongs and some new ones," I said. "I'd like to know the name of the surgeon who operated on him. All Cahane remembered was that the office was in Camarillo."

"Another victim before he got to L.A.? No similars have shown up anywhere."

"One person who did meet an interesting end was the psychologist who orchestrated the thyroidectomy. When Cahane got back, he lost no time firing him and the following day he dropped dead in the hospital parking lot. Apparent heart attack. Sound familiar?"

"Lem Eccles's wife—Rosetta. Oh, Jesus. Eccles was nuts but not wrong?"

"There's more, Big Guy. The psychologist's name was Bernhard Shacker."

"Same as the guy who analyzed Vita for Well-Start? What the hell's going on? Some sort of identity theft?"

"Has to be," I said. "The man I spoke to was in his late forties and the real Shacker was nearly eighty when he keeled over. The real Shacker was Belgian and the diploma I saw in that office was from a university in Belgium. When Shacker—the guy calling himself Shacker—saw me looking at it, he said something about his Catholic phase. Photoshopping fancy-looking paper isn't any big deal."

"A scamster making it in B.H.?"

"I'm wondering if his transgressions go beyond practicing without a license. Because pulling off the murders would be a lot easier with two people involved."

"Where'd *that* come from?"

"Eccles's fear of a guard at V-State. Huggler may be your prototypical odd loner but that doesn't preclude someone from gaining his trust. Someone he met while at V-State."

"Another lunatic?" he said. "Working as a guard? Now he's palming himself off as a shrink? Good Lord."

"Faking it would be a lot easier for someone who'd worked on psych wards long enough to soak up the terminology. Eccles was confined at V-State the same time as Huggler. Maybe in Specialized Care because he'd gotten overly aggressive with a judge. There's no reason to think he didn't continue being his usual combative, obnoxious self. That got him on a guard's bad side. But the guard was too clever to face off against Eccles, took it out on Eccles's only visitor. The woman Eccles considered his wife. She really was poisoned and when he got away with it, he did the same to Bernhard Shacker."

"Get on my bad side, you die," he said. "Another touchy one?"

"Common ground for a relationship. Cahane described Huggler as cooperative, compliant. Even so, his recreational time was supervised. For *his* safety. That meant being supervised by a guard whenever he left his room. What if it was the same guard each time and a bond developed? The man passing himself off as Shacker would've been in his twenties back then, perfect age to be a mentor to an isolated adolescent. The bond was solidified forever when he eliminated the man who'd robbed Huggler of a vital organ. And the bond could've remained strong enough for the mentor to travel with Huggler—seeking out a job at Atascadero when Huggler got transferred there."

"And now they're traveling together."

"For at least five years," I said. "If that's the case, Huggler's not crashing on the street. He's living securely with his self-appointed guardian. Who's making a nice living in a Beverly Hills office. And who could be sending Huggler to inflict his particular brand of curiosity upon those who've gotten on *his* nerves. Case in point, Vita. Huggler witnessed her tormenting the Banforth family but I don't see him as out for truth and justice. More likely he was already at Bijou because he'd been stalking Vita for a while. And the reason for that was Vita had offended Fake Dr. Shacker. I know that because he told me she'd just about come out and called him a quack, no one had ever treated him that way. He was bothered. It was the only time he dropped his professional guard."

"Doing her mean thing," he said. "No pity from Pitty. Hold on." *Click click.* "No Shacker or Pitty in the files . . . not at DMV, either . . . all I'm finding is the office address on Bedford."

I said, "Let's work out a plan tonight, bop over there tomorrow."

"Analyze the analyst," he said. "He's that dangerous, we should bring an army."

"I figured I'd talk to him, you'd be there for backup."

"What's your angle?"

"Does he remember anything else about Vita? If it feels right, I'll probe deeper about the quack issue. If not, I'll bring up additional victims, did he have any theories? Get people talking, they make mistakes."

"Let me call Petra, see what she thinks."

Six minutes later:

"Poor kid was having some face-time with her lovey-dove at L'Oise in Brentwood. Not far from your place, you mind hosting us in say an hour?"

"No prob."

"Check with Robin."

"She'll be fine with it."

"How do you know?"

"She loves you."

"Rare lapse of taste on her part," he said. "An hour."

CHAPTER

32

Petra rang the bell, white paper bag in hand. She had on a sleeveless navy silk sheath, red sandals with heels, strategic pearls, darker-than-usual lipstick. First time I'd seen her in a dress.

Robin said, "Date night interrupted?"

"Woman plans, God laughs."

Petra bent to pet Blanche. Blanche rolled on her back, earned a massage.

Petra said, "We made it through the first course, I took dessert to go."

I said, "Want some coffee?"

"Strong, if you don't mind."

I brewed Kenyan, kicking up the octane. Robin and Petra settled at the table and Petra pulled plastic-topped boxes out of the bag. Assortment of cookies, four slabs of chocolate cake.

Robin said, "That's more like catering."

"I brought for everyone, seeing as you guys are donating home and hearth to the dark side."

A heavy hand pounded the door.

Milo trudged in bearing a brown bag, greasy, flecked with powdered sugar. He scowled. "Who mugged a pastry chef?"

Robin sniffed the air. "This Magi brings churros?"

"It seemed like a good idea." His eyes fixed on the chocolate cake.

"Flourless," said Petra.

"Got nothing against flour, but why not?"

He put the churros aside, was ingesting cake before his haunches met his chair. Blanche waddled over and nuzzled his ankle. He said, "Yeah, yeah," and conceded a rub behind her ear. She purred like a cat. "Yeah, yeah, again."

Robin took her cup and headed for

the back door. Blanche followed. "Good luck."

No one invited her to stay. They like her.

Petra said, "This fake psychologist is Huggler's confederate, as well as the Pitty character Eccles claimed was stalking him?"

Milo said, "Working assumption, kid, but it feels right. He steals one identity, why not another? Can't find any 'Pitty' in the file, so maybe it's a nickname. Or Eccles was totally delusional and we're wrong."

She turned to me. "How did fake-o come across when you talked to him?"

"Pleasant, professional, the right paper on the wall. The only time he stepped out of the role was when he complained that Vita had implied he was a quack. At the time, I took it as collegial banter."

"Looks like she was right. Sometimes I wonder if those nasty people don't have special insights. Maybe because they see everyone as a threat."

Milo said, "But look what happens after they get elected."

"Good point." She turned to me. "You see Vita insulting him as the reason she got killed?"

I nodded. "His trigger, Huggler's fun. We have two people working in concert, with layers of pathology building on each other. I'm not sure either of *them* understands it fully. At the base is Huggler's fascination with human plumbing and no, I can't tell you how that developed. It's normal for children to wonder how their bodies work and kids who hold on to that curiosity sometimes channel it professionally—become mechanics, engineers, anatomists, surgeons. For a few, interest grows to obsession and gets tangled up with sexuality in a really bad way."

She said, "Dahmer, Nilsen, Gein."

"All of whom were described as odd children but none of whom had especially horrific childhoods," I said. "Huggler killing his mother at eleven suggests a less-than-optimal upbringing, but it doesn't come close to explaining the act. Whatever the reason, something short-circuited in his brain and he began pairing sexual gratification with plunging his hands into visceral muck. Being locked up for most of his life made him a prime target for observation and I'm betting one of his sharpest and most frequent observers wasn't a doctor. It was a young man working a low-status job. Someone who'd never be invited to staff meetings but craved authority and had the time to pick up all sorts of interesting things."

"Doctors come and go," she said, "but guards stay on the ward for eight-hour shifts."

"And this guard's ability to sniff out depravity could've been fine-tuned because he could relate to it on a personal level."

"His own kinks."

Milo said, "Psychopath pheromones. One beast smells another."

I said, "Pitty, or whatever his name really is, studied Huggler long enough to become a Huggler scholar. He befriended the boy and a mentor-trainee relationship developed. The boy had finally met someone who appreciated his urges instead of condemning them.

Maybe it was Pitty who caught small animals for Huggler to play with."

"What was the payoff for him?"

"Adulation, subservience, or maybe just having someone like himself to relate to. Given Huggler's age and his apparent adjustment, there was a good chance he'd get out when he became an adult. Then Marlon Quigg ruined everything by exercising his own powers of observation, Huggler was subjected to unnecessary surgery and got put in Specialized Care. If I'm right about his only being out for five or so years, he was shipped off to another hospital, probably Atascadero, and got thoroughly institutionalized. A relationship with someone who claimed to care about him would've been his only link to reality."

"Pitty moves with him, Pitty's reality becomes his?" said Petra. She shook her head. "That surgery, talk about institutional abuse. I guess you could see a tit-for-tat: They cut his neck, he breaks other people's necks. But then why haven't we seen any throat-slashing?

Wouldn't that be a more direct symbolic revenge?"

"I could theorize for you all day—maybe he chose to avoid slashing because it cut too close to home. So to speak. The truth is we may never know what's been stoking Huggler's engine."

Milo said, "V-State closes, mentor follows mentee, mentee finally gets out, mentor turns him into a lethal weapon. That's your layer two?"

I nodded. "A weapon aimed at people who anger each or both of them. Pitty might not want to soil his own hands but if he's the brittle, power-craving narcissist I think he is, he'd crave payback for slights the rest of us would shrug off."

Petra said, "Are we talking something sexual between the two of them?"

"Maybe but not necessarily. It's possible neither of them has anything close to a conventional sex life."

"People irk me," Milo said, "I sic Lil Buddy at them and they become anatomy projects."

I said, "And Lil Buddy loves the assignment. That's layer three: a perfect partnership that satisfies both of their needs. Let's start with Vita Berlin: obnoxious, combative, spreading misery wherever she went. Like most bullies she had a keen sense about who'd make a safe victim and the man she knew as Dr. Shacker seemed perfect: physically unprepossessing, outwardly mild, and a psychologist—we're expected to be patient, nonjudgmental. Think of the movies you've seen about therapists: Most show them as absentminded wimps. Vita may have been forced into sessions with the little wuss in order to collect her insurance settlement but she was damn sure going to have fun along the way. Right from the start she resisted, needled him, finally came out and let him know she thought he was a charlatan. Unfortunately for her, he's anything but nonjudgmental. I wouldn't be surprised if the death sentence was passed the moment the words left her mouth."

"Call in Huggler," said Milo. "Easy hit because fake-o-Shacker had her address, phone number, knew what she looked like."

I said, "And despite her resistance

she might've given out some personal details during the evaluation that also made stalking her easier. Huggler was spotted lurking near her garbage cans. My guess is he went through them, found her empties, knew she was a serious solitary drinker. If he found pizza boxes, that would also have helped set up the kill. In general, her routine was easy to learn because she rarely went out except for shopping and occasional meals at Bijou."

"Think Pitty was in on the kill?"

"It's possible he held a gun on the victims, served as a lookout. Two actors would explain no sign of struggle, even from someone as aggressive as Vita."

Petra said, "The pizza box ruse was still a gamble, given Vita's temper. What if she was sober enough to make a ruckus?"

I said, "'Oops, gee sorry, ma'am, wrong address.' Huggler leaves and they wait for a second chance."

Milo said, "Eccles snoozing in the alley would've been a piece of cake. Same for Quigg."

Petra said, "If we're right about Quigg,

he'd have been *the* major target—the person to blame for everything bad that happened to Huggler. With that kind of rage, why wait five years to get him?"

"Maybe there were other targets just as important—like Shacker—and they're going down a list."

Milo said, "Like the doc who actually did the throat-cutting."

"Oh," I said.

They looked at me.

"Huggler was busted for trespassing behind a medical office. The police assumed he was about to break in and steal dope. But what if Huggler had a more personal connection to the doctor?"

Milo said, "Stalking the surgeon. Problem with that is the arrest was in Morro Bay and Huggler's surgery took place a hundred miles away in Camarillo."

"People move."

"The same surgeon just happened to live near two hospitals where Huggler was confined?"

I thought about that. "Maybe Huggler was taken to that particular surgeon because of an arrangement with V-State—

some sort of consultancy. When V-State closed the guy went for the same thing at Atascadero."

Petra said, "A guy who couldn't make it in private practice. Maybe he had his own issues."

I said, "Obviously, he had ethical issues."

"Going for government dole," said Milo. "I guess anything's possible."

She produced her iPhone, poked and scrolled.

Milo said, "What's on that?"

"My notes."

"You're totally digital?"

"I copy stuff from the murder book so I can follow up at home . . . here we go. Huggler was busted at Bayview Surgical Group of San Luis Obispo County. It's the right specialty, isn't it?"

We shifted to my office and I ran a search on Bayview, found no current listings. But a four-year-old item from a San Luis Obispo TV station featured the disappearance of "local surgeon Dr. Louis Wainright, staff member of Bayview Surgical Group. Wainright, 54, was last seen hiking in the foothills above San Luis Obispo with his dog 11 days ago. The doctor's SUV was found in a park service lot but neither he nor his German shorthaired pointer Ned has been seen since."

Additional hits on the disappearance described futile searches conducted by law enforcement and a cadre of Eagle Scouts. A picture of Wainright showed him grim, gray-haired, and bearded with a strong jaw and outdoor skin.

"Dr. Hemingway," said Petra. "Walking with his dog, just like Quigg. And our boy has a thing for animals."

Milo said, "Let's make sure Wainright didn't eventually show up."

He phoned the Morro Bay Police Department. A desk officer named Lucchese remembered Wainright because the surgeon had once removed a fatty tumor from his back.

"Good surgeon?"

"Not really," said Lucchese. "Left me a lump scar. No bedside manner, either, just get in there and slice. Only reason I used him is he had a contract with the union."

"Any theories about what happened to him?"

"That was some pretty rough terrain he was climbing. Best guess is he broke a leg or fainted or had a heart attack or a stroke or whatever, lay there without anyone noticing and either died outright or from dehydration or hypothermia. Eventually he probably got taken care of by mountain lions or kye-oats or both."

"Human suspects were never on the radar?"

"No reason for them to be. Why's this interest you, Lieutenant?"

"A former patient of Wainright's is a suspect in a killing down here."

"That so. Who?"

"Former inmate at Ventura State in Camarillo, back when Wainright worked there."

"A nutter? We got plenty of those over at Atascadero and I guess one of them could've known Wainright from there. But those guys never get out, they're the least of our problems." He chuckled. "Best therapy: Lock 'em up and toss the key."

"Wainright worked at Atascadero?"

"Part-time," said Lucchese. "Guess he had a contract there, too. But there were no escapes around the time he went missing, no alerts, nothing. I'll ask around for you but I won't learn anything."

Milo thanked him and clicked off.

Petra said, "Oh, my."

I said, "Shacker was first, then as soon as Huggler got out, they went after Wainright. The trespassing bust delayed but didn't deter them. A year later, Wainright was dispatched."

"Easy to stalk the guy while he hiked," said Milo. "Why would he fear a vengeful patient from almost twenty years before?"

"Even Huggler's arrest wouldn't have alerted him. If he even remembered—or knew—Huggler's name. Morro Bay PD figured Huggler for an addict out to score, no reason to I.D. him to Wainright after they picked him up. Even if they had, why would Wainright connect a grown man to a kid he'd operated on years before?"

"Surgeon becomes patient," said Petra. "God, how many others are out there?"

Milo said, "If Huggler and his mentor could wait to handle Wainright and Quigg and whoever else they might've done in between, why'd Shacker have to go right away?"

I said, "Shacker was a solo act by Pitty so Pitty could prove himself to Huggler and cement their bond. For that, he needed a quick, dramatic result."

"Look what I did for you, Little Buddy," said Petra.

"There was also time pressure: Shacker was elderly and he'd just been fired, meaning he would've left town. So Pitty reverted to something that had worked for him a few months before."

"Poisoning, as in Eccles's lady friend," said Petra. "Two people drop dead within moments of leaving the hospital. What kind of poison could be calibrated that precisely?"

I said, "It wouldn't have to be poison, per se. With a man of Shacker's age and dietary habits, a huge dose of a strong heart stimulant could do the trick.

As an alcoholic and a cocaine abuser, Eccles's wife would also be vulnerable to cardiac insult."

Milo said, "No poison, per se, means nothing on the tox screen."

He got up, paced, tugged an earlobe. "Everything you're saying makes sense, Alex, but unless one of these two monsters confesses, I don't see Men*tor* going down for anything other than I.D. theft and practicing without a license. And Men*tee* could get away clean. He's left no trace evidence and all we have on him are ambiguous sightings and a V-sign he shot to John Banforth that could be interpreted any number of ways."

I said, "Find them and separate them. Huggler could be crackable."

"Your mouth FedExed to God's ears," said Petra. "I've got another timing issue: If Pitty got slimed one too many times by Eccles and took it out on Eccles's wife, why wait all these years to get the slimer himself?"

"Maybe he figured he'd get more immediate pleasure from watching Eccles suffer than from dispatching him. From having Eccles know what had happened and being powerless to do anything about it."

Milo said, "Who the hell's gonna pay attention to some lunatic's ravings?"

I said, "Pitty could've planned to do Eccles after Eccles was discharged but Eccles went underground and Pitty couldn't find him. As to why didn't Eccles try to get back at Pitty, maybe his mental illness got in the way—too disturbed and scattered to devise a plan."

"Or," said Petra, "he was scared and got the heck out of Dodge."

Milo said, "Then Pitty just happens to spot Eccles years later in Hollyweird?"

I said, "It's not that big a coincidence. You've got a tip placing Huggler at a Hollywood clinic. The neighborhood's a magnet for drifters and short-term residents. With Shacker renting a Beverly Hills office, I've been figuring him for a nice crib. But maybe he economizes in order to afford that office and he and Huggler are bunking in some pay-by-the-week."

"On my turf," said Petra. "Thrilling."

Milo said, "We could write screenplays all night but at this point we don't even know if Huggler was actually transferred to Atascadero, let alone Pitty or whatever his name is moving to be with him. So let's stake out this fake shrink, nab him on I.D. theft, and see what shakes out. B.H. business district is small, we'll need to be subtle, meaning more sets of eyes, extra-low profile. I'm gonna have Moe and Sean with me and whoever B.H. wants to send, assuming they cooperate. Wouldn't mind Raul, either, if it's okay with you."

Petra made the call. "Done."

I said, "Did you manage to get hold of Eccles's last arrest report?"

"Sure did and the complainant wasn't named Pitty or close. Something Stewart."

"What'd he list for an address?"

"You really think he could be Pitty?"

"Something about him got Eccles hyped up."

Back to her iPhone. "Mr. Loyal Steward. With a *d*." She read off a phone number and a street address and her eyes got tight. "Main Street, City of Ventura. That's commercial, isn't it?"

"It's also two towns north of Ca-marillo."

Her aerial GPS confirmed it. "Big old parking lot, guys."

She checked the phone number Loyal Steward had given to the arresting offi-cers. Inactive, and a call to the phone company revealed it had never been in use.

"Loyal Steward," said Milo. "That's gotta be phony."

I said, "It's not a name. It's how he sees himself."

CHAPTER

33

Milo played database piano on my computer with the grim concentration of a lonely kid at an arcade.

No residential listings, driver's license, or criminal record for Loyal Steward.

He said, "Big surprise," and called Deputy Chief Maria Thomas. She was miffed about being interrupted at home and balked at disturbing the chief. Milo began with tact, eased into bland persistence, ended up with barely veiled menace. Like a lot of bureaucrats, she had a weak will when confronted with dedication.

Within minutes, the chief had phoned Milo and Milo was doing a lot of blank-faced listening. Soon after, a senior Beverly Hills detective named Eaton rang in.

Milo started to explain.

Eaton said, "It came straight from my boss, like I'm gonna say no?"

When Milo hung up, Petra said, "Maybe one day *I* can be a *loo*-tenant."

"That's like wishing for wrinkles, kid."

Six the following morning found eight people surveilling the office building on Bedford Drive where a yet-to-be-identified man pretended to be Dr. Bernhard Shacker. Downtown Beverly Hills was yawning itself awake, vanilla swirls of daylight scratching their way through a gray-satin sky. A few delivery trucks rumbled by. But for a scatter of joggers and put-upon citizens ruled by the intestinal tracts of fluffy dogs, the sidewalks were bare.

BHPD knew the building, couldn't recall a problem there since three years ago when a plastic surgeon and his wife had been hauled off for mutual domestic violence.

"They start whaling on each other in the waiting room," said B.H. detective Roland Munoz. "Anorexic women with stitched-up faces are sitting there, freaking out."

An hour into the watch, a custodian unlocked the building's brass front doors. Tenants had keys and the alarm code and could come and go 24/7 but none had appeared after nine the night before when Munoz and Detective Richard Eaton had earned overtime watching the last trickle of weary health-care providers, none of them Shacker, exiting. Between nine and this morning, hourly drive-bys by B.H. patrol cars had spotted no activity in or around the structure. Not an ironclad assurance, but confidence was high that the identity thief had yet to appear.

The rear alley door was also key-operated and Sean Binchy watched it from the front seat of a borrowed Con Edison van, accompanied by Munoz, a jovial man whose mood was even rosier because he'd rather be doing this than responding to false intruder calls phoned in by hysterical rich people. Lost cats, too; last week a woman on North Linden Drive had 911'd on "Melissa." Making her sound like a human in jeopardy, not an Angora up a tree.

The building offered no on-site parking but doctors and their staffs got a discount at the private pay facility two doors south that opened at six thirty. This early, plenty of metered street parking remained available but only seven vehicles had seized the opportunity. Milo ran the tags. Nothing interesting.

He and I were stationed on the east side of Bedford Drive, twenty yards north of the brass doors, in a silver, black-windowed Mercedes 500 that he'd borrowed from the LAPD confiscation lot. The former owner was an Ecstasy dealer from Torrance. The interior was spotless black calfskin, the brightwork polished steel, the white bunny-rabbit headliner and matching carpeting sucked free of lint. A strong shampoo fragrance lingered, mixed in with the smell of honey-roasted peanuts.

Milo had told me to "dress B.H."

"Meaning?"

"Knock yourself out so you blend in with the hoohahs."

The best I could come up with was jeans and a gray wool pullover emblazoned with an Italian designer's surname. The sweater was a ten-year-old gift from the sister I never saw. Other people's names on my clothing make me feel like an impostor; this was the first time I'd worn it.

Milo's costume consisted of a royal-blue velour tracksuit piped with thick strands of silver lamé resembling rivulets of mercury. Oversized designer logo on the sleeves and on one thigh, some sort of hip-hop artiste I'd never heard of. The outfit managed to be too large for him, settled in folds, tucks, and wrinkles a shar-pei would covet.

I'd controlled myself but now I said, "Congrats."

"For what?"

"High-bidding on Suge Knight's storage bin."

"Hmmph. Got it at the Barneys sale. VIP night, if you will. In case you find that relevant."

"My job, everything's relevant. How'd you get vipped?"

"Store manager was in a car crash, Rick saved his nose."

A slim, dark figure zipped past us, heading north.

Petra dressed in black bicycle pants and pullover neared completion of her second square-block jog. The role Milo had assigned her was a variant of her normal morning routine and she ran like she meant it.

Up near Wilshire, a grubby homeless person in shapeless gray-brown tatters shuffled, bobbed his ski-capped head, gazed up at the morning sun, jaywalked east.

Moe Reed had volunteered for that part.

Milo'd said, "Clean-cut kid like you?"

"I did it last year, El Tee. Checking out a bad guy in Hollywood."

Petra had said, "He was convincing, trust me."

"Fine," said Milo. "We'll get you some bum duds."

"No need," said Reed. "Still have the threads from last year."

"Wash 'em?"

"Sure."

"Then you won't be authentic, but hey, go for it."

Observers Seven and Eight were two female B.H. officers patrolling in a black-and-white on a ten-minute circuit. Shimoff's second drawing of Grant "Shearling" Huggler was taped to their dashboard along with a description of faux-Dr.-Shacker that I'd supplied. Nothing unusual about a conspicuous police presence in Beverly Hills. Response time was three minutes and citizens liked seeing their protectors.

By six thirty, the pay lot had opened and cars trickled in. Thirteen more street spots had been taken. Every tag checked out clean except for a woman with an address on South Doheny Drive who owed over six hundred bucks in parking tickets. This morning, her Lexus was being driven by an Asian woman in a white housekeeper's uniform doing a pickup at the deli on the corner.

No sign of either suspect and that remained the status by eight a.m. when patients began showing up at the brass doors.

Same for nine a.m., ten, ten thirty.

Milo yawned, turned to me. "When you were in practice when did you start work?"

"Depended," I said.

"On what?"

"The patient load, emergencies, court. Maybe all he does is insurance work. That could mean easy hours."

"Insurance companies hire a murderous fraud." He smiled. "Maybe he put that on his application."

He got out, loped to the deli, ordered something, and scanned the three customers at the counter. A few minutes later, he returned with bagels and overboiled coffee. We ate and drank and lapsed into silence.

At eleven a.m., he stretched and yawned again and said, "Enough." Radioing Reed, he instructed the young detective to alter his bum-shamble from Wilshire to Bedford where he could keep an eye on the building's entrance. Then he informed everyone else that he was going inside to have a look.

I said, "I'll go, too. I can point him out to you."

He thought about that. "Doubt he's in there but sure."

As we walked through the blue-carpeted, oak-paneled hallway, his oversized tracksuit flapped, eliciting a few amused looks.

My designer sweater didn't seem overly humorous but two young women in nurses' uniforms smiled at me then broke into muted giggles as I passed.

Just a coupla wannabe clowns providing comic relief.

We took the stairs to the second floor where Milo cracked the door and scanned the corridor.

Suite 207 was just a few feet away.

The nameplate on Shacker's door was gone.

He went and had a close look, waved me over. The glue outlines surrounding the sign were visible. Recent removal.

"Shimoff's too good an artist," he said. "Bastard saw his prodigy's face on TV, burrowed straight underground."

He radioed the detail, told them the

suspects were unlikely to show but to stay in place, anyway. We took the stairs back down, searched the directory for the building's manager, found no listing. A clerk at the ground-floor *Dispensing Apothecarie* had a business card on file.

Nourzadeh Realty, headquartered in a building on Camden Drive, right around the corner. The name on the card was the managing partner, Ali Nourzadeh. He wasn't in and Milo spoke to a secretary.

Ten minutes later, a young woman in a red cowl-neck cashmere sweater studded with rhinestones at neck and cuffs, black tights, and three-inch heels arrived with a ring of keys big enough to burglarize a suburb.

"I'm Donna Nourzadeh. What seems to be the problem?"

Milo flashed his card, pointed to the glue-frame. "Unless your signs tend to fall off, looks like your tenant cut out."

"Darn," she said. "You're sure?"

"No, but let's have a look inside."

"I don't know if I can do that."

"Why not?"

"The tenant has rights."

"Not if he abandoned the office."

"We don't know that."

"We will once we go in."

"Hmm."

"Donna, how long has Dr. Shacker been renting?"

"Seven months."

Shortly before he'd screened Vita Berlin using fake credentials. Maybe he'd offered Well-Start a bargain fee that got them slavering.

Milo said, "Was he a good tenant?"

Donna Nourzadeh thought about that. "We never heard any complaints from him and he paid six months up front."

"How much was that?"

"Twenty-four thousand."

Milo eyed the keys.

Donna Nourzadeh said, "He did something?"

"Quite likely."

"You don't need a warrant?"

"Like I said, if Dr. Shacker left prematurely, you control the premises and all I need is your permission."

"Hmm."

"Call your boss," said Milo. "Please."

She complied, spoke in Farsi, selected a key, and moved toward the lock. Milo stilled her with a big index finger atop a small wrist. "Better I do it."

"What do I do in the meantime?"

"Other business."

He took the key. She hurried away.

The tiny white waiting room was unchanged from the time I'd seen it. Same trio of chairs, identical magazines.

Same new-age music, some sort of digitalized harp solo streaming at low volume.

The red light on the two-bulb panel was lit. In session.

Milo freed his 9mm, approached the door to the inner office and knocked.

No answer. He rapped again, tried the doorknob. It rotated with a squeal.

Stepping to the left of the door, he called out, "Doctor?"

No answer.

Louder: "Dr. Shacker?"

The music switched to flute, a nasal arpeggio, vibrating with the subtlety of a human voice.

An unhappy human, keening, whining.

Milo nudged the door another inch with his toe. Waited. Afforded himself another half inch and peeked through.

Cherry-sized lumps sprouted along his jawline. His teeth clicked as he holstered his gun.

He motioned me to follow him in.

CHAPTER

34

Drapes were drawn on the window overlooking Bedford Drive. Low-voltage light from a desk lamp turned the pale aqua walls grayish blue.

The walnut desk was bare. The same diplomas remained affixed to the walls.

He had no further need for them, had moved on to another role.

In reduced light, the cubist print of fruit and bread looked drab and cheap. The Scandinavian chairs had been nudged closer together, set for an intimate chat.

One chair was bare.

Something occupied its mate.

Milo flicked on the ceiling light and we had a look.

A mason jar filled with clear, greasy liquid was propped against the chair-back.

Floating inside were two grayish round things.

Milo gloved up, kneeled, lifted the jar. One of the orbs shifted, exposing additional color: pale blue dot centered by a black sphere. Pinkish strands streamed like tiny worms from the other side.

He shifted the jar again and the second orb bounced and turned, showed the same decoration, the same fuzzy pink filaments.

A pair of eyeballs. Human. Oversized pearl onions bobbing in a horrific cocktail.

Milo put the jar where it had originally sat, called for a crime scene crew, priority.

As he radioed the others, I noticed a discordant detail across the room.

The largest diploma, placed dead center behind the desk chair, had been altered. When I'd seen it, it had verified

Bernhard Shacker's doctorate from the University of Louvain.

Now a sheet of white paper blocked that boast.

I walked over.

Glue marks were evident at the periphery of the glass, bubbling the underside of the sheet.

Blank, white rectangle, but for a single message:

?

CHAPTER
35

A coroner's investigator named Rubenfeld took possession of the jar.

"Never seen that before," he said. "Always a first time."

Milo said, "Any way to tell how long they've been in there?"

Rubenfeld squinted. "If the fluid was real old I'd expect more discoloration, but can't really say." He bobbled the jar gently. "The severed ends are a little faded out—that's small blood vessels you're seeing, look like feathers . . . the eyes themselves seem a little rubbery, no? That could mean they've been pre-

served for a while, could be lab specimens."

"They're specimens all right," said
Milo, "but not from a lab."

Rubenfeld licked his lips. "Giving time
estimates of body parts really isn't my
pay grade, Lieutenant. Maybe Dr. Jernigan will be able to tell you." He glanced
back at the chair. "One thing you can be
pretty sure of. That blue in the irises,
your victim's probably Caucasian."

"Thanks for the tip," said Milo. Well
before the crime scene crew arrived,
he'd obtained a readout of Dr. Louis
Wainright's last recorded California driver's license. Blue eyes, no need for corrective lenses.

Rubenfeld swung the carrier gently.
"Least I don't need a gurney."

Milo got the cleaning schedule from
Donna Nourzadeh. The suites were
tended to weekly by a crew of five, but
this week there'd been a delay and no
office had been touched for three nights.

"Scheduling issues," she said. "Now,
if you don't need me . . ."

Milo let her go, turned to me. "Sometime during the last seventy-two hours, the bastard planted the jar."

I thought: He'd displayed the eyes, expecting to be discovered. Left the question mark behind to confirm his connection to the murders.

Boasting. Unworried; because he was on to a new phase?

Whatever his intentions, the man who called himself Shacker had cleaned up with care, vacuuming the rugs so thoroughly that the crime scene techs pulled up only a few crumbs. Hard surfaces had been wiped free of prints, including in places where you'd expect to find them.

The crime scene crew began to lose energy as it went through the final motions.

Then one of the techs said, "Hey!" and brandished a tape she'd pulled off the glass fronting one of the diplomas.

Shacker's date-altered psychology license, positioned to the left of the papered-over diploma, Photoshopped on good-quality paper. Even up close, the forgery was convincing.

The tech held the tape up to the light.

Nice clear pattern of ridges and swirls lifted from the upper right-hand corner of the pane.

"Looks like a thumb and a finger," said the tech. "Like someone leaned on it."

I pointed to the page with the question mark. "Maybe to catch his balance while gluing that."

"Or it's just from the cleaning crew," said Milo.

"Aw c'mon, Lieutenant," the tech said. "Think positive."

"Okay," he said. "How's this: I've got a pension plan, might live long enough to use some of it."

The AFIS match to the latent came back at seven thirteen p.m. Hand-delivered by Sean Binchy to Milo as he presided over a tableful of food at Café Moghul. Petra, Moe Reed, Raul Biro, and I sat around the table. Everyone was hungry in a frustrated, miserably compulsive way, putting away lamb and rice and lentils and vegetables without tasting much.

Milo read the report, bared his teeth, passed it on.

James Pittson Harrie, male Caucasian, forty-six, had been fingerprinted upon joining the staff of Ventura State Hospital a little over twenty-five years ago.

Harrie's five-year-old DMV shot featured the smiling visage of the elfin-faced, rosy-cheeked man I'd met. Slightly longer hair made for a less artful comb-over. Five six, one forty.

One of the few who didn't bother to fib about his stats. Honor among fiends?

Harrie's listed address was a P.O.B. in Oxnard.

Sean said, "Already checked and it's a parcel shipping outlet in a strip mall. They're still in business but they haven't had boxes for five years, well before Harrie used it. I'm thinking he lived in or around that general area, lied to stay off the grid."

I said, "Oxnard's one town north of Camarillo and one below Ventura, where he also lied about living as Loyal Steward."

Biro said, "Everything's revolving

around the beach towns. Returning to roost?"

I nodded.

Sean said, "His last registered ride is a fifteen-year-old blue Acura but he hasn't paid his regs for years, got his license suspended. Want me to put a BOLO on the tags anyway?"

"You bet," said Milo. "Good work, kid. Wanna join us for some grub?"

"Thanks but I'd rather be working." Binchy blushed. "Not that you guys aren't working."

Milo said, "Go be productive, Sean," and Binchy hurried out of the restaurant.

Petra studied James Pittson Harrie's photo. "Aka Pitty. Finally we have a face and a name. Don't imagine driving illegally weighs on someone like that, but if he was stupid enough to hold on to his old wheels and keep expired tags on, that BOLO could be exactly what we need."

Milo cracked his knuckles. "Where the hell are the two of them *crashing*?"

"Like Raul said, the beach towns keep popping up, but that wouldn't stop them from drifting down here to do their dirty work and sticking around for a while."

I said, "If Harrie moved to Atascadero after Huggler got transferred there, maybe he listed a forwarding when he left."

A call to the hospital was fruitless, two records clerks and a supervisor claiming old personnel records couldn't be accessed until business hours began the following morning.

"Even with that, don't get your hopes up," said the supervisor. "We've got major storage issues, don't hold on to everything."

A second intrusion into Maria Thomas's domestic life resulted in a call from Atascadero's deputy director of Human Resources who'd somehow managed to pull Harrie's employment application during non-business hours.

Milo got the restaurant's fax number from the woman in the sari and told him to send everything he had. He asked a few more questions, scrawled unreadable notes, thanked the man and hung up and began reciting.

On his Atascadero application, James

Pittson Harrie had claimed a B.A. in psychology from the University of Oregon in Eugene. For one year after graduation, he'd worked as a veterinary technician at a local animal hospital, then moved to Camarillo where he applied to be a psychiatry tech at V-State.

"From four legs to two legs," said Petra. "Maybe Harrie's the one who likes dogs, that's why they take them."

Reed said, "The question is likes them for what?"

"Ugh."

Milo read on. "He didn't receive a tech job but they did hire him as a janitor. Looks like he did that for thirteen, fourteen months, got promoted to custodial officer, level one. Custodial as in guard, not as in sweeping up . . . that seems to be as high as he got there, but then he moved to Atascadero as part of a compensation program: Staffers who'd lost their jobs at V-State were given priority at other state facilities. And Atascadero granted his wish, he came on as a psychiatric technician, level one. The HR guy insisted they have no records of which specific wards he worked but he must've performed okay because he got promoted to level three and left voluntarily a little over five years ago. Which happens to be shortly before Grant Huggler was discharged. And guess who stayed on? Dr. Louis Wainright. Guy had a half-time consultancy with Atascadero, doing outpatient surgical procedures. Received the same transfer courtesy."

I said, "How long after Harrie resigned was Huggler arrested behind Wainright's office?"

Milo squinted to decipher his own shorthand. "Looks like . . . three days. Guess they got right to work."

Reed said, "Anyone want to lay odds on who bailed Huggler out?"

Petra said, "That leaves four years until they did Vita. Way too long for there to be no one else."

Reed said, "Maybe another doctor was involved in Huggler's surgery. An anesthesiologist or a nurse?"

I said, "Bodies never showed up because at that point Huggler and Harrie were still concealing their handiwork. I'd concentrate on disappearances between Morro Bay and Camarillo, anyone with a health-care job."

Milo said, "Wainright gave up whatever private practice he had in Camarillo to keep working for the state. Unbeknownst to him, he made Harrie and Huggler's job easy."

"But Harrie and Huggler still waited until Huggler got out to do him," said Petra. "Fifteen years of waiting?"

I said, "The key, at that point, was for Huggler to be directly involved. Think of it as therapy."

Biro toyed with his food. "Wonder if those eyes are Wainright's."

Petra said, "Anyone here want to volunteer approaching Wainright's family and explaining why we want their DNA?"

"Even worse," said Reed, "we do it and the eyes turn out not to be Wainright's."

Milo said, "Enough banter, kiddies. Still hungry, Raul?"

Biro looked at his plate. "Nah, I'm finished."

"Then how about starting with the calls, from Morro south, anyone with a medical background disappearing between Wainright's final hike and Vita Berlin's murder."

"You bet." He walked to a corner of the restaurant.

The woman in the sari came over with a silver tray. "Faxes for you, Lieutenant."

"Nothing like dessert." Milo scanned the material, handed it to Petra, who did the same and passed it on.

James Pittson Harrie's Atascadero personnel photo portrayed a young man with long, thick, straight hair draping his brow from hairline to eye-ridge. Much of the remaining facial space was taken up by a dense beard.

Hippie in a uniform.

Grant Huggler's patient I.D. showed him with even longer hair and a patchy beard long enough to conceal his top shirt button.

Moe Reed said, "Wainright was last seen in the mountains and these two look like mountain men. Maybe they camped up there, were ready for him."

Milo compared the photo with Harrie's driver's license. "He cleaned up well enough to fake being a B.H. shrink, got himself insurance gigs. But he had to be doing well before he rented that office because he anted up twenty-four G in cash. So maybe he practiced somewhere else. Or had another scam going."

I said, "Or he collects monthly pension checks. As a state employee for over two decades, he'd have a generous payout, maybe a bonus for leaving early. And Huggler would qualify for all sorts of welfare. If the two of them have lived prudently, they could've saved up plenty. And if they are living off the state, the checks get mailed somewhere."

Milo tried Maria Thomas again, sat there for a while, tapping his fingers on the table. "Dammit, answer."

Unanswered prayer; he tried another number. Same result.

Petra said, "Who was your second choice?"

"His Voluminousness."

"You have his personal line?"

"I've got a line he sometimes answers." A 411 got him the pension board's main office in Sacramento. Closed until working hours tomorrow morning.

He cursed, shoveled food.

Biro returned to the table. "Got an interesting hit in Camarillo, woman named Joanne Morton, eighteen months ago. Went hiking in the foothills, not that far from where V-State used to be and hasn't been seen since. It was initially worked as a low-priority MP then they started considering suicide because Morton had a history of depression and her third divorce had really knocked her low. It was the ex who reported her missing but he didn't stay a suspect for long. Lives in Reno and could account for his whereabouts."

"Why'd he call?" said Petra.

"Concerned about her. They broke up but it was friendly. He told them Joanne had 'issues,' he was worried she might hurt herself. And yes, she was a surgical nurse, freelanced around town."

Reed said, "If I helped Wainright mutilate kids I might have issues."

Milo said, "Was she hiking with a dog?"

"If she was," said Biro, "it's not in the report."

Petra said, "A pet's not a prereq for

getting carved up, it's just a perk for the bad guys. Eighteen months ago. They *are* going down a list."

"Eighteen months ago," said Reed, "leaves plenty of time for someone between Wainright and Morton, or after her and before Berlin."

I said, "Or they started off gradually, picked up the pace. Because it's no longer just about revenge."

"What's it about?" said Milo.

"Recreation."

No one spoke for several seconds.

Milo said, "Moe, you and Sean and whoever else you can get who's competent, do a total and comprehensive recanvass of all the murder neighborhoods using the drawing of Huggler and Harrie's DMV photo. Petra, how about you and Raul try to find the clinic where the tipster claimed Huggler got his thyroid meds. That doesn't work out, go back to North Hollywood Day and lean on Mick Ostrovine to produce medical records for Grant Huggler. We know he was there and I'm not buying Ostrovine's hear-no-evil. I'll contact the pension board first thing tomorrow, find out if checks are being mailed to one or both of our creep-os. If I get an address, we reconvene and map out an assault, probably with SWAT. I'll also talk to Jernigan, see if those eyeballs can be DNA'd and if they can, I'll approach Wainright's family."

He snatched up his phone, called in a DMV on Wainright's nurse, Joanne Morton. "Brown eyes, so they're not hers. Any questions?"

Without waiting for an answer, he stood, brushed off his trousers, threw money on the table.

When the others reached into their wallets, he said, "Not a chance."

Reed said, "You're always footing the bill, El Tee."

"Pay me back with good deeds."

CHAPTER
36

Petra and Raul Biro divided the assignments. He'd look for free clinics where Grant Huggler might've gotten his prescription, she'd have a go at Mick Ostrovine. Figuring a soft touch might work better with the administrator than another dose of male cop.

Ostrovine sighed a lot, said, "Here we go again," paid lip service to patient confidentiality. But sooner than Petra expected he said, "Oh, all right, come around and look for yourself."

She crossed to his side of the desk as he opened up some files.

"See?" said Ostrovine, nudging closer and favoring her with a burnt-whiskey whiff of some terrible cologne.

Alphabetized patient records; no Huggler.

"How about James Harrie, with an *i-e,* maybe middle initial *P.*"

Long, theatrical sigh. Ostrovine pecked.

"See? Nothing. It's like I told those first officers, we're not connected to any of this."

Petra said, "I'm sure you're right, Mick. But Mr. Huggler was definitely here for a thyroid scan."

"I explained the first time: He never *received* the scan so there'd be no record."

Petra flashed him her best wholesome smile. "Just to be sure, Mick, I'd like to show Mr. Harrie's photograph and this drawing of Mr. Huggler to your staff."

"Oh, no. We're swamped."

The horde she'd seen in the waiting room said the mope wasn't lying. "I know you are, Mick, but I'd *really* appreciate it."

She showed Ostrovine the images

first. The drawing elicited nothing but he blinked at the photo.

Giving him a chance to fill in the blank, she sat back down.

"What?" he said, irritated. Maybe her feminine touch had lost its mojo.

"Never seen him?"

"Not in this world or any other."

No one on staff recognized either man.

Even Margaret Wheeling, about to prep a sleepy-looking homeless type for a no-doubt-pricey MRI, had seemed confused when shown Alex Shimoff's second drawing.

"Guess so."

Petra said, "When you spoke to Lieutenant Sturgis, you were sure you'd met him."

"Well . . . my drawing was different."

Like *she* was the artist. Petra said, "This one doesn't resemble the man who confronted Dr. Usfel?"

Wheeling squinted. "I'd need to put on my glasses."

You don't need to see accurately when you're magnetizing someone?

"Go right ahead, Ms. Wheeling."

Wheeling let out a long exhalation followed by an eye roll. Another dramatic type; this place was like one of those summer camps for histrionic kids obsessed with musical theater.

Glasses in place, the fool continued to just stand there.

"Ms. Wheeling?"

"I think it's him. Maybe. That's the best I can do. It was a long time ago."

"What about this man? He's a friend of Huggler's."

Emphatic head shake. "That I can tell you. Never."

Petra reported to Milo.

He said, "Good work, onward, kid."

She frowned at the unearned praise.

At Biro's third clinic, the Hollywood Benevolent Health Center, he got as far as a volunteer receptionist. The place was makeshift, set up with rolling partitions and what looked to be pretty tired medical equipment in the basement of a church on Selma just west of Vine. Big old beautiful Catholic church with intricate plaster details and an oak door that had to weigh a ton. Smaller than but not unlike St. Catherine in Riverside where Biro's parents had taken him for Mass when he was a kid.

All that grace and style ended in the basement. The space was dank, windowless, patchily lit by bare bulbs suspended from extension cords stapled to the ceiling. The wires drooped, some of the bulbs were dead. Where the walls weren't chipped white plaster they were rough gray block. Wilting posters about STDs and immunizations and nutrition were taped randomly. Everything in Federal Government Spanish.

The waiting room wasn't a room at all, just a clearing surrounded on three sides by stacks of long, wooden, folded tables. Half of the lawn chairs provided were occupied, all by Latino women who kept their eyes down and pretended not to notice Biro.

As he approached the desk, his spotless beige suit, white shirt, and olive paisley silk tie drew some admiring glances. Then he flashed his badge and someone's breath caught and all eyes shot downward.

Had to be one of those sanctuary deals for undocumenteds. Biro felt like shouting he wasn't La Migra.

One thing in his favor: an Anglo male like Huggler would stand out, maybe this would lead somewhere.

The receptionist was also Hispanic, a well-groomed, dyed blonde in her late twenties, a little extra-curvy in places where that was okay.

No name tag, no welcoming smile.

Raul grinned at her anyway, explained what he needed.

Her face closed up. "All our doctors are volunteers, they come in and out so I don't know who you'd talk to."

Raul said, "The doctor who treated Grant Huggler."

"I don't know who that is."

"The doctor or Huggler?"

"Both," said the receptionist. "Either."

"Could you please check your files?"

"We don't have files."

"What do you mean?"

"Just that. We don't have files."

"How can you run a clinic without records?"

"There are records," she said. "The doctors take them when they leave."

"Why?"

"The patients are theirs, not ours."

Biro said, "Aw c'mon."

"That's the way we do it," she said. "That's the way we've always done it. We're not an official health-care provider."

"What are you then?"

"A space."

"A space?"

"The church merely provides access for providers to provide."

Merely and *access* and *providers* gave that the sound of a prepared speech. This place was definitely set up for illegals. Scared people coming in with God-knows-what diseases, afraid to broach the county system even though no one there asked questions. He glanced at the women in the lawn chairs. They continued to pretend he didn't exist. No one appeared especially sick but you never knew. His mother had just told him about one of her friends visiting relatives in Guadalajara and coming back with tuberculosis.

Telling it, the way she always did, as if Raul had the power to prevent such disasters.

He said, "No charts here at all?"

The receptionist said, "Not a one."

"That sounds a little disorganized, Miss—"

"Actually it's super-organized," she said, not offering a name. "So we can multitask."

"Multitask how?"

"When the church needs to use the space for something else, we wheel everything out of the way."

"How often do doctors come in and use the space?"

"Most every day."

"So you don't do much wheeling."

Shrug.

Raul leaned in and half whispered, "You've got people waiting but I don't see any doctors."

"Dr. Keefer's due in."

"When?"

"Soon. But he can't help you."

"Why's that?"

"He's new. Yesterday was his first day, so he wouldn't know your Mr. Whatever."

"Huggler."

"Funny name."

Biro looked at her.

She said, "I don't know him."

He gave her a look at his business card.

She said, "You already showed me your badge, I believe that you're police."

"See what this says?"

Moment's hesitation. "Okay."

"Homicide," said Biro. "That's all I care about, solving murders."

"Okay."

"Grant Huggler may have a funny name but he's suspected of committing several really nasty murders. He needs to be stopped before he does more damage."

He glanced back at the waiting women, trying to imply that they could turn up as victims.

The receptionist blinked.

He showed her the drawing.

She shook her head. "Don't know him. We don't want murderers here. If I knew him, I'd tell you."

"Are you the only receptionist here—what *is* your name?"

"Leticia. No, I'm not. A bunch of us volunteer."

"How many is a bunch?"

"I don't know."

He pulled out an enlargement of James Pittson Harrie's lapsed driver's license. "How about him?"

To Biro's surprise, she went pale.

"What's the matter?"

"He's a doctor."

"What kind?"

"Mental health," she said. "A therapist. He came in to ask questions but he never came back."

"What kind of questions?"

"Did we do insurance work. He said he had a lot of experience with it, could help if someone needed help with an accident or an injury. I told him we didn't do that here. He gave me his card but I threw it out. I didn't even read his name."

"But you remember him."

"We don't usually get doctors walking in to drum up business."

"What was his attitude?"

"Like a doctor."

"Meaning?"

"Businesslike. He didn't seem like one of *those* but I guess he was."

"One of those what?"

"Slip-and-fall scammers. Those we get from time to time. Scouts working for lawyers."

"Trying to exploit your patients."

Nod. No attempt to claim they're not *our* patients.

"So Mr. Harrie told you he was a psychologist."

"Or a psychiatrist, I forget. He's not?"

"Nope."

"Oh."

"How'd he react when you turned him down?"

"Just said thanks and gave me the card."

"How long ago did this happen?"

"A while back," said Leticia. "Months."

"How many?"

"I don't know—six, five?"

"That long ago but you remember him."

"Like I told you, it was unusual," she said. "Also, he was Anglo. We don't get too many white guys, period, except for

homeless who come in from the boulevard."

Unzipping his file case, Raul showed
her a mug shot of Lemuel Eccles. "Like
him?"

"Sure, that's Lem, he comes in once
in a while."

"For what?"

"You'd have to ask his doctor."

"Who's that?"

"Dr. Mendes."

"First name?"

"Anna Mendes."

Raul kept the photo in her face. She
turned to the side.

He said, "So Lem comes in but this
white guy"—switching back to the drawing of Huggler—"you don't know about?"

"Correct. Do these guys know each
other or something?"

"You could say that."

"The other one, too? The psychologist?"

"What else can you tell me about
Lem?"

"Just that he comes in," she said. "He
can be difficult but mostly he's okay."

"Difficult, how?"

"Nervous, kind of wired. Talks to himself. Like he's crazy."

"Like?" said Biro.

"We don't judge."

"Do you have a list of the other receptionists?"

"I don't keep any lists and I don't know who they are 'cause when I'm here, they're not."

"And you all volunteer."

"Yeah."

"Through what agency?"

"No agency, I do it for community service."

She was too old for a high school student, didn't look like an ex-con, any kind of troublemaker. "What kind of community service are you doing?"

"It's for a class. Urban issues, I'm a senior at Cal State L.A."

"You think maybe upstairs in the church office they'd have a list?"

"Could be."

Biro said, "Okay, I'm going to leave you my card the way Mr. Harrie did, but please don't throw it out."

She hesitated.

"Take it, Leticia. Good people need to

be good even when they're not volunteering."

Her mouth dropped open. Raul began climbing the steps to the church's ground-floor lobby. One of the women in the lawn chairs said something in Spanish. Too soft for Biro to make out the words, but the emotion was obvious.

Relief.

As he headed for the church office a young man in a white coat and carrying a box crossed his path. M. Keefer, M.D. Resident in medicine at County General.

Ninety-hour work weeks but he had time to volunteer.

Raul said, "Hi, there, Doctor. Ever seen this guy?"

M. Keefer said, "No, sorry," and bounced down the stairs.

The church office was locked, the magnificent marble sanctuary unoccupied. Raul returned to his car and got a number for an Anna Q. Mendes, M.D., in Boyle Heights.

This receptionist answered in Spanish and maybe it was Biro responding in kind, maybe not, but she said, "Of course," and a moment later a warm female voice said, "Dr. Mendes, how can I help you?"

She listened to Biro's explanation, said, "The thyroid case. Sure, I referred him for the scan. He came in for a refill of his Synthroid but his medical history was patchy. He looked a little under-dosed to me and he was well overdue for a good look at his neck. He was reluctant but his therapist helped me convince him."

"His therapist?"

"Some psychologist came with him, I thought that level of care was pretty impressive. Especially because the psychologist's office was in Beverly Hills and Huggler clearly wasn't a paying private patient."

The ease with which she tossed out facts surprised Biro. Not even an attempt at resistance and he wondered if she'd been the anonymous tipster.

He said, "Did the psychologist give his name?"

"He did but I can't recall."

"Dr. Shacker?"

"You know, I think that's it," said Anna Mendes. "He readily agreed that in order to optimize the dosage we'd need better data. In the meantime, I upped Mr. Huggler's dosage a tiny bit and wrote a scrip for three months' worth."

"Anything else you can tell me about Huggler?"

"You said you were in Homicide," said Mendes. "So obviously he killed someone."

Biro hadn't mentioned Homicide. And *obviously* Huggler could've been a victim as easily as an offender.

Definitely the tipster.

"Looks like that, Doctor."

"My brother was murdered six years ago," she said. "Stupid wrong-address drive-by, the imbeciles shot him with an AK while he slept in his bed."

"I'm so sorry."

"They never caught the bastards who did it. That's why I'm talking to you. Someone kills someone, they should get what they deserve. But no, that's really all I can tell you about Huggler."

"What was his attitude?"

"Quiet, passive, didn't say much,

didn't make eye contact. In fact, he was so quiet that even before the therapist— Shacker—came in, I'd started wondering about some sort of mental illness."

"Could that be because of his thyroid?"

"No way," she said. "If he was a bit hypothyroid like I suspected he might slow down a tad, maybe lose some energy, gain some weight, but nothing significant. He might also feel cold, which is the first thing that tipped me off. He was overdressed for the weather, big heavy fleece-lined coat. I never confirmed my hypothesis, though, because he never came back with any lab results."

"Could we expect him to get sicker?"

"Not if he takes his meds. Even with his old dosage this was no weakling, just the opposite. I checked him out and his muscle tone was really good. Excellent, actually. He had huge muscles. In clothes you couldn't tell, he looked almost pudgy."

"Overdressed because he felt cold."

"Or maybe it was a symptom of mental illness, you see that from time to time."

Biro said, "Speaking of mental patients, they told me at the clinic that Lem Eccles was your patient."

"Was? Something happened to him?"

"Afraid so," said Biro. "He's dead."

A beat. "And that's connected to Huggler?"

"Could be."

"Oh, wow," said Mendes. "Well, if you're going to ask me did I see them together, I didn't."

"Could you check your records and see if they happened to be at the clinic on the same day?"

"I could, if I was at my other office in Montebello where I keep all the clinic records."

"Kind of a strange system," said Biro. "Doctors taking the paperwork with them."

"Big pain," said Mendes, "but they insist upon it. That way they're not an official clinic, just donate space."

"In case La Migra asks."

Mendes laughed. "It's not very subtle,

is it? I don't get involved in any of that. I treat patients, politics isn't my thing."

"You work there on a volunteer basis."

She laughed harder. "Did it look like there was any serious money to be made there? Yes, I volunteer. I was a scholarship student at Immaculate Heart and the archdiocese helped with my med school tuition. They ask for a favor, I say sure. So what did this Huggler actually do?"

"It's nasty," said Biro.

"Then forget I asked, Detective, I trained at County, saw more than enough nasty. I certainly hope you catch him and if I ever see him again, you'll be the first to know."

"Couple more things," said Raul. "You said Dr. Shacker showed up after Huggler. So Huggler came in by himself?"

"Technically I guess he did," said Mendes. "A few minutes later, Shacker showed up, said he'd been parking the car. I got the clear impression they'd arrived together. Now if you don't mind, I've got patients waiting."

Parking the car. Small point to her but Raul's brain was screaming *A Vehicle. Ripe for a BOLO.*

He said, "One more question. How come you referred Huggler to North Hollywood Day?"

"Because Dr. Shacker recommended it. You should get the details from him, he really seemed to care about Huggler. Then again, he'd probably have confidentiality issues. So do I, but murder's different."

Biro filled Petra in.

She said, "It's a good bet Shacker spotted Eccles at that clinic. I'll go back to the uniforms who busted Eccles, see if there's anything else they remember about Loyal Steward. And seeing as Harrie directed the doctor to North Hollywood Day and he's an insurance whore and they're an insurance mill, it's obvious my charm didn't work as well with Ostrovine as I thought and he's still holding back. You up for bad-copping him?"

"More than up," said Raul. "Raring to go."

◆

On the way to the Valley, he phoned in and reported to Milo.

Milo said, "Good work, Raul. Onward."

I'd just stepped into his office. He wheeled his chair back. "See how supportive I am with the young'uns?"

"Admirable."

"Not that anything they've learned adds up to a warm bucket of spit until we locate these freakoids."

He summarized.

I'd been up late, trying to answer some questions of my own. Mentally reviewing my brief talk with James Harrie to see if I'd missed something.

Understanding why someone like Huggler would welcome Harrie's caretaking but not getting what was in it for Harrie, because if a man that calculated was able to exact his own brand of vengeance, why raise the risk of discovery by collaborating with someone so deeply disturbed?

Engaging in twenty-plus years of what was effectively foster-parenting.

What was in it for the parent?

The small questions had resolved quickly but the big picture remained clouded and I couldn't shake the feeling that I'd made several wrong turns.

I said, "The pension angle didn't work out?"

"The pension board is absolutely certain that no checks are mailed from any government agency to James P. Harrie, same for the welfare office regarding assistance payments to Grant Huggler. I tried out a whole bunch of spelling variations because paperwork gets messed up. Even checked under Shacker's name, because he'd also been a state employee, maybe Harrie had stolen his benefits as well as his identity. No such luck, those checks are sent to a cousin in Brussels. So maybe we're dealing with free-enterprise criminals, intent on making it the old-fashioned way."

I said, "How much money are we talking about?"

"Best estimate I could get was someone in Harrie's situation could pull a pension of three to four grand a month, depending if he claimed stress or disability. No way to know exactly what Huggler's qualified for, there's an alphabet soup of welfare goodies for someone who knows how to work the system. Top estimate was two or so a month."

"The two of them pool their funds, they can rake in as much as sixty, seventy thousand a year, tax-free. I don't see them forgoing that, Big Guy, even with Harrie making money as a fake psychologist. He put up serious money for that office, must've started with some sort of stash. So the checks are going somewhere. What if Harrie stole I.D.'s other than Shacker's? For himself and for Huggler?"

"Someone cross-checks Social Security numbers, they'd get found out."

"Big if," I said. "But okay, what if they went the legal route and changed their names in court? Any switch for Huggler would have to be within the last four years because he was still using his real name when he got arrested behind Wainright's office."

"Send the check to Jack the Ripper and his lil pal the Zodiac? Some computer obliges without a squawk? Wonderful."

He called a Superior Court clerk he'd

befriended years ago, hung up looking deflated.

"Guess what? Court orders are no longer required for name changes. All you have to do now is use your new moniker consistently while conducting official business and eventually the new data's 'integrated' into the county data bank."

He yanked a drawer open, snatched a panatela, rolled it, still wrapped, between his fingers. "But you're right, no way they'd pass up that much easy dough."

His cell phone played Erik Satie. He barked, "Sturgis!" Then, in an even louder voice: *"What!"*

He turned scarlet. "Back *up,* Sean, give me the details."

He listened for a long time, scrawled notes so angrily the paper tore twice. When he clicked off he was breathing fast.

I said, "What?"

He shook his head. Attacked the phone with both thumbs.

◆

The image appeared moments later, a grainy gray peep show on the phone's tiny screen.

Tagged at the top with rolling digital time and the I.D. number of a Malibu Sheriff cruiser's dash-cam.

Six thirteen a.m. Malibu. Pacific Coast Highway. Mountains to the east, so north of the Colony where the beach city turns rural.

The deputy, Aaron Sanchez, justifying the stop on the fifteen-year-old Acura.

Not because of the BOLO; the tags matched a recent theft from the Cross Creek shopping center.

Felony stop. Extreme caution.

Six fourteen a.m.: Deputy Sanchez calls for backup. Then (on loudspeaker): "Exit the vehicle, now, sir, and place your hands on your head."

No response.

Deputy Sanchez: "Exit the vehicle immediately, sir, and place—"

Driver's door opens.

A man, small, thin, wearing a sweatshirt and jeans, emerges, places his hands on his head.

Flash of bald spot. Bad comb-over.

Deputy Sanchez exits his own vehicle, gun out, aimed at the driver.

"Walk toward me slowly."

The man complies.

"Stop."

The man complies.

"Lie down on the ground."

The man appears to comply then whips around, pulling something out of his waistband. Crouching, he points.

Deputy Sanchez fires five times.

The man's small frame absorbs each impact, billowing like a sail.

He falls.

Sirens in the distance gain volume.

Backup, no longer needed.

The whole thing has taken less than a minute.

Milo said, "Bastard. They ran the car, found the BOLO, contacted Binchy because his name was on the request."

"Was the thing in his hand for real?"

"Nine-millimeter," he said. "Unloaded."

I said, "Suicide by cop."

"Whack-job suicide by cop was the Sheriff's initial assumption because Harrie getting that hard-core to avoid a license plate theft rap made no sense. And initially, they saw nothing in Harrie's car to make him squirrelly, just fruits and vegetables and beef jerky and bottled water, probably from one of those stands on the highway. Then they popped the trunk and found a bunch more firearms, ammo, duct tape, rope, handcuffs, knives."

I said, "Rape-murder kit."

"And stains on the carpet presumptive for blood. What they *didn't* find was any sign Harrie was running with an accomplice."

I said, "Because Huggler's waiting back home for Harrie to return from his grocery run. Somewhere north of where Harrie was pulled over."

"That's a lot of territory. What does a kit say to you?"

"None of our victims showed evidence of restraint and none of the females was assaulted or posed sexually. I'd bet on a separate victim pool."

"Games Harrie played solo."

"More likely with backup by Huggler."

"Jesus."

"It fills in a missing piece," I said.

"Harrie taking Huggler under his wing because of altruism never made sense. He was attracted to a disturbed child because of a shared fascination with dominance and violence. Think of their relationship as Huggler's alternative therapy: The entire time the staffs at V-State and Atascadero were struggling to devise a treatment plan for him, Harrie was sabotaging them by nurturing Huggler's drives. And coaching Huggler in concealing his bad behavior. When Huggler got transferred, Harrie moved with him. When Huggler finally gained his freedom, he and Harrie embarked on a new life together."

"Foundation for a wholesome relationship," he said. "Too bad Harrie bit it before the two of them could be booked on the talk-show circuit."

CHAPTER

37

Sean Binchy's second call pinpointed the coordinates of the shooting.

James Pittson Harrie had died 3.28 miles above the Colony, leaving 15 or so miles of the beach city and anywhere beyond for a hide-spot.

Milo said, "Don't see them scoring a pad on the sand or an ocean-view ranch in the hills. But if they're still doing the mountain man bit, they could be squatting in some remote place up in the hills."

I said, "I'm certain they're cashing government checks, at some point one or both of them ventures out to get cash. So someone's seen them. My mind keeps fixing on the beach cities above Malibu. Harrie's used two phony addresses we know about, the parking lot on Main Street in Ventura when he told the Hollywood cops he was Loyal Steward and the dead mail-drop in Oxnard for his driver's license. Something in the region attracts him."

"What attracts me is nailing Huggler before he does more damage. Once the media latch onto Harrie's death—and they will, a cop shooting's always a story—he's bound to rabbit."

"That assumes Huggler's wired into the media."

"Why wouldn't he be?"

"Harrie could've made himself Huggler's sole link to the outside world."

"No MTV for ol' Grant, huh?" he said. "Keeps his nose buried in puzzle books until Harrie tells him it's time to balance the scales with an anatomy lesson? Even so, Alex, when Harrie doesn't return, Huggler's gonna get antsy. If fear overtakes him, he might reveal himself and get taken down easy. But if he goes the rage-route, more people are gonna die. And those guns in Harrie's trunk might not be the total stash. All I need is a lunatic loaded with heavy-duty firepower."

Balance the scales.

Unbalanced.

My mind raced. Braked hard.

A warm wave of clarity washed over me. The tickle at the back of my brain, finally gone.

He said, "You just floated off somewhere."

"What you just said about balancing the scales reminded me of something Harrie mentioned when I met with him. He asked me about my work with the police then claimed to have no interest in the darker aspects of life. Called them 'terrible dyssynchronies.' Obviously, he was lying and I think he was playing with me by alluding precisely to what's framed the murders from the onset: achieving equilibrium by symbolically undoing the past. And that might help focus the search for Huggler: Start where it all began."

"V-State," he said. "They'd go back there?"

"They would if it was part of Harrie's treatment plan for Huggler."

"You just said his treatment was encouraging Huggler's gut-games."

"I did but I was missing something. Harrie really came to see himself as a therapist. Like most psychopaths, he had an inflated belief in his own abilities. No need to actually earn a degree, he was already smarter than the shrinks. So all he had to do was learn enough jargon to impersonate convincingly. And when he went into practice, he started right at the top: high-rent Couch Row. He zeroed in on insurance evaluations because they were lucrative, thin on oversight, and, most important, short term with no clinical demands: Patients wouldn't spend enough time with him to get suspicious and he wouldn't be required to actually help anyone."

"Vita got suspicious."

"Maybe she sensed something," I said. "Or she was just being Vita. Overall, Harrie got away with it and that had to be a massive ego trip. And that led

him to see himself as a *master* therapist. With a single long-term patient.
Yes, the past five years have been about
bloodlust and revenge, but they've also
been part of a regimen Harrie devised
for Huggler: achieving synchrony by
working through old traumas. And what
better way to achieve that than by returning triumphant to the place where
control was ripped away?"

"Neck-snapping and gut-squishing in
the name of self-actualization," he said.
"The hospital closed down years ago.
What's there now?"

"Let's find out."

Milo typed away. Moments later, we had
a capsule history, courtesy of a historical preservation group: The original plan
had been to maintain the hospital buildings and convert them to a college campus. Shortage of funds caused that to
languish until six years ago when a
group of private developers had purchased the site in a sweetheart deal and
put up a planned community called
SeaBird Estates.

He found the website. "Luxury living

for the discerning? Doesn't sound like our boys would fit in."

I scrolled. "It also says 'nestled in sylvan surroundings.' Enough woodland and our boys could've found refuge."

He shot to his feet, flung his office door open, paced the corridor a few times, returned.

Using both hands to sketch an imaginary window, he peered through, an artless mime.

"Looks like nice weather for a drive, let's go."

CHAPTER

38

Fifty minutes to Camarillo, courtesy Milo's leaden foot.

The same exit off the 101, the same winding road through old, dense trees.

The same feeling of arriving at a strange place, untested, unsure, ready to be surprised.

What had once been an open field of wildflowers was planted with lemon trees, hundreds of them arranged in rows, the ground cleared of stray fruit. The logo of a citrus collective graced several signs on the borders of the grove. The sky was a perfect, improbable, crayon blue.

Milo sped past the grove. I peered through each row, looking for errant human presence.

Just a tractor, unmanned, at the far end. The next sign appeared half a mile later, lettered in aqua and topped by a rendering of three intense-looking gulls.

SEABIRD ESTATES
A Planned Community

A few yards up, shoulder-high blue gates were hinged to cream-colored stucco posts. Superficially reassuring but a whole different level of security from V-State's twenty-foot blood-red barrier.

Keeping them out was different from keeping them in.

A guard inside a tiny booth was texting. Milo tooted his horn. The guard looked over but his fingers kept working. He slid a window open. Milo's badge pretzeled the guard's lips. "We didn't call in no problem."

"No, you didn't. Can we come in, please?"

The guard pondered that. Resuming texting, he stabbed at a button on a built-in console, missed the first time, got it right on the second. The gates swung open.

The main street was Sea Bird Lane. It snaked up a slope that picked up as it climbed. Condos appeared on both sides of the road. Landscaping consisted of predictably placed date palms, red-leaf plum trees, beds of low-maintenance succulents that clung to each curve like green cashmere.

Every building was styled identically: neo-Spanish, cream like the gateposts, red composite roofs trying to pass themselves off as genuine tile.

Superficial resemblance to the old V-State buildings. No bars on these windows. No foot traffic to speak of. During the hospital's tenure, staff and low-risk patients had strolled freely, creating an easy energy. Strangely enough, SeaBird Estates felt more custodial.

Milo drove fifty yards in with a light

foot before I spotted an original structure: the mammoth reception hall where I'd been oriented. A sign staked near the entry read *Sea Horse Club House.* As we continued to explore, other hospital structures appeared. *Sea Breeze Card Room. Sea Foam: A Meeting Place.* Former wards and treatment centers and who-knew-what coexisting with new construction. Transplanted smoothly, a wonder of cosmetic surgery.

Finally, a few people showed themselves: white-haired couples, strolling, casually dressed, tan, relaxed. I was wondering if they had any idea of their neighborhood's origins when a red-haired man in a blue poly blazer one size too large, baggy khakis, and ripple-soled shoes stepped into the middle of the road and blocked our progress.

Milo braked. Blazer examined us, then came around to the driver's side. "Rudy Borchard, head of security. What can I do for you?"

"Milo Sturgis, LAPD. Please to meet you, Rudy."

Mutual badge-flashes. Borchard's was significantly larger than Milo's, a gold-plated star that evoked the OK Corral. Probably larger than anything Earp had worn because why offer a generous target?

"So," said Borchard. Tentative, as if he'd only memorized the script this far. He placed a protective finger on the knot of his clip-on tie. His hair was too long in places, too short in others, dyed the color of overcooked pumpkin. A one-week mustache was a sprinkle of cayenne on a puffy upper lip. "L.A. police, huh? This ain't L.A."

"Neither is it Kansas," said Milo.

Borchard's eyes tilted in confusion. He puffed his chest to compensate. "We didn't call in any problem."

"We know, but—"

"It's like this," Borchard cut in. "Residents' privacy is real important. I'm talking affluent senior retirees, they want to feel private and safe."

"Safety's our goal, too, Rudy. That's why we're inquiring about a suspect who might be in the area."

"A suspect? Here? I don't think so, guys."

"Hope you're right."

"*In* the area or just close to the area?"

"Could go either way."

"Naw, I don't think so," said Borchard. "No one gets in here without my say-so."

Our easy entry put the lie to that. Milo said, "That's excellent, but we'd still like to have a look."

Borchard said, "Who's this suspect?"

Milo showed him the drawing of Huggler.

Borchard said, "Nope, not here, never been here."

Milo kept the drawing in Borchard's face. Borchard stepped back. "I'm telling you nope. Looks like your basic lowlife. Wouldn't last two seconds, here. Do me a favor and put that away, okay? I don't want some resident getting their undies all scrunched."

"Keep it, Rudy. Should you want to post it, that would be fine."

Borchard took the drawing, folded, slipped it into his pocket. "What exactly this lowlife do?"

"Killed a bunch of people."

The red dots atop Borchard's lip bounced as he chewed air. "You kidding? No way I'm posting that picture.

The residents hear *killed,* someone'll have a heart attack for sure."

"Rudy," said Milo, "if Grant Huggler gets in here, it's gonna be a lot worse than a heart attack."

"Trust me, he won't."

"You guys keep it that tight?"

"Tighter than a virgin's—real tight, trust me on that."

"How many ways are there to get in here?"

"You just saw it."

"The front gate is all?"

"Basically."

"Basically but not completely?"

"There's a service entry around the back," said Borchard, hooking a thumb eastward. "But that's just deliveries and it's locked twenty-four seven and it's monitored by c-circuit and we know exactly who ingresses and egresses."

"What comes in that way?"

"Deliveries. Large-scale. Small-scale come through the front, every parcel is checked out before it's delivered."

"Checked out how?"

"The residents give us authorization to sign for UPS and FedEx and we verify addresses and hand-deliver. That way no one gets bothered, it's all part of the service."

A honk from behind made us turn. Elderly couple in a white Mercedes itching to proceed. The woman was stoic but the man's mouth worked.

"You better move over," said Borchard.

Milo pulled to the curb and we got out. The Mercedes passed and Borchard favored the occupants with a wide wave. They ignored him, tooled to the next street, turned left. Sea Cloud Road.

Rudy Borchard said, "Have a nice day, guys."

Milo said, "What constitutes large-scale deliveries?"

"You know, bulk stuff. We're like a town, supplies for the clubhouse and the restaurants—we got two, the formal and the informal—come in all the time. We got nearly eight hundred residents."

I said, "The clubhouse is back there. So there's a way for the trucks to approach it from the back and drive straight to the loading dock."

" 'Zactly," said Borchard. "We can't

have semis rumbling through, messing up the pavement, creating a ruckus."

"Where does the service road connect from?"

"Cuts through the middle."

"Of what?"

"The rest of the property."

"There's a section that's not developed?"

" 'Zactly. Phase Two."

"When's it going to be developed?"

Borchard shrugged.

Milo said, "How do you get to the service road without driving through here?"

"You probably took Lewis off the freeway, right? Next time, get off one exit before, then you travel a few streets and go on some farm roads. But trust me, no one's gonna get in that way. And even if they did—and they didn't—there'd be nowhere to hide. Plus the residents have panic buttons in their condos and they can pay extra for portable ones to carry around. We got no problems here. Never."

Milo said, "So the delivery road cuts through the back and ends up at a loading dock."

"Not one dock, a bunch, and there's always people around. Trust me, your lowlife wouldn't last a minute. What even makes you think he's anywhere near here?"

"Because he used to live here?"

"In Camarillo? It's a big place."

"Not the city, Rudy. Here."

"Huh? Oh. He was one of those."

"One of who?"

"A nutter. From when this was a nuthouse."

I said, "Do the residents know about that?"

Borchard smiled. "It's not on the brochure but sure, some of them would have to. But no one gives two rats. Because that was a long time ago and now everything's normal and safe. Why would a nutter come back to where he was locked up, anyway? That's not logical. Psychologically speaking."

Milo suppressed a smile. "Maybe so, Rudy. How many guys on your security staff?"

"Five. Including me. It's enough, trust me. Nothing happens here. The whole

nut thing's a joke to us. Like when something gets dug up."

"Dug up?"

"When they're doing landscaping,"
said Borchard. "Someone's turning the
dirt for plants, whatever, something pops
up."

"Like what?"

"Oh, no, don't go thinking criminal.
I'm talking spoons, forks, cups. With the
hospital brand on it, this big *VS*. One
time some buckles and a strap got dug
up, probably from one of those strait-
jackets."

"What do you do with all that when
you find it?"

"I don't find it, the landscaping crew
does. They give it to me and I throw it
out, what do you think? It's junk." Borchard checked his watch. "Your maniac
ain't here but if he shows up I'll take
care of it."

Unbuttoning the oversized jacket, he
gave us a view of a holstered Glock.

"Nice piece," said Milo.

"And I know how to use it."

"You were in the military?"

Borchard flushed. "I go to the range. Have a nice day, guys."

Milo said, "How about showing us that service road?"

"You're kidding."

"Just so we can tell the boss we've been careful."

"Bosses," said Borchard. "Yeah, I hear that. Fine, I'll show you, but it's clear on the other end, you don't wanna walk."

"So we'll drive."

Borchard eyed the unmarked. "I'm not getting in the back of that, looks bad to the residents, you know?"

"I promise not to cuff you, Rudy."

"I like your jokes. Not." He touched the spot beneath his jacket where the gun was positioned. "You really need to be doing this?"

"We drove all the way from L.A."

"So go get a fish taco in town and say you looked."

Milo smiled.

"Okay, okay, hold on." A man with a cane was approaching and Borchard hurried to intercept him. Borchard smiled and talked. The man walked away, midsentence, muttering. Borchard shot us an *I-told-you-so* look, disappeared around a leafy turn, and emerged several minutes later driving a canvas-topped golf cart.

"Hop in for the E Ride."

Milo sat next to him, I took the rear bench. The plastic seat was aqua blue patterned with green herons.

"Guys, I'm only doing this cop-to-cop, trust me your nutter didn't stow away in some eighteen-wheeler. Everything comes from recognized vendors, we log every ingress and egress. Now, if the tunnels were still open, I might consider you have a point, but they're not so you don't."

"What tunnels?"

"Ha, knew I'd get you with that," said Borchard, chuckling. "I'm messing with you, trust me, it's nothing."

"No tunnels."

"Not anymore and they're all filled with concrete."

"None, but they're filled."

"You know what I mean, you can't go in 'em."

Milo looked back at me. I shook my head.

Borchard said, "What it was, back in the day there were these underground passages between some of the hospital buildings. For moving supplies, I guess." He laughed harder. "Or maybe they ran the nutters down there for exercise, punishment, whatever. Anyway, when the developers bought the property the county made them fill them all with concrete because of earthquakes. You want to see?"

"Why not?" said Milo, casually.

"Giving you the full tour, gonna be a surcharge." Laughing and flooring the cart's accelerator, Borchard swung a quick U-turn and headed up the road at five mph. Moments later, he stopped at a side street that led to a clump of condos. Sea Wave Road. Motioning us out, he squatted, parted some bushes. Inlaid in the dirt was a metal disk around six feet in diameter. Painted brown, unmarked, like an oversized manhole cover with two metal eyelets.

"Watch, this is cool." Looping a finger around one of the eyelets, Borchard tried to lift. The lid didn't budge. He strained. "Must be stuck or something."

"Want some help?" said Milo.

"No, no, no." Borchard used two hands, turned scarlet. The lid lifted an inch and Borchard let go and some sort of pneumatic mechanism kicked in. The lid rose until it was perpendicular with the ground.

Underneath was a circle of concrete. Borchard stood on top of it, jumped like a kid on a trampoline. "Solid, all the way through. Rebar and concrete, extra-strong to handle the big one."

"How many openings like this are there, Rudy?"

"Who knows? Most of them are buried over, they run under the condos. It's only when they're in landscaped areas that we find them. I've seen four of those and trust me, they're all solid, like this one." He jumped twice more. "Nutter skulking through a tunnel would be a good movie. Unfortunately, this is reality, guys. You really don't want to bother seeing the back fence, do you?"

Milo shrugged. "What can I tell you, Rudy?"

"Knew you'd say that."

◆

We put-putted along Sea Bird Lane, switched to Sea Star Drive, reached the rear of the development. The service road was a single lane of asphalt that passed through a high chain-link gate. A closed-circuit camera was bolted to the right-hand post. Through the links a slice of blue sky and brown field and mauve mountains was visible but the broad view afforded only sky above twenty-plus feet of ficus hedge. The trees had been densely planted on both sides of the fence, creating an impenetrable wall of green.

I strained to catch a lateral glimpse but Borchard swung the cart away and drove along the development's south rim, parallel to the hedge. The road continued for several minutes before branching to a three-tine fork.

"Okay? Satisfied?"

Milo said, "Where do these roads go?"

"They're not roads, they're driveways. That one's to the clubhouse, that's to the recreation center—basically for towels from the linen service—and that one goes to La Mer, which is the formal, open for dinner only, and also to Café

Seabird, which is right next door and does three meals a day and also has a tearoom for snacks—what the hell, I'll show you."

Three loading docks, all of them bolted shut. Not a truck in sight. Despite Borchard's boast of observers everywhere, no workers.

"Quiet day," said Milo.

"It's always quiet," said Borchard, as if he regretted the fact. Reversing the car, he headed back toward the front. As we passed the chain-link gate, Milo said, "Stop for a sec," and hopped out and peered through.

He came back stoic.

"What'd you see?" said Borchard. "Empty land, right? No nutters in sight. Can I go on?"

"You keep the disks from that CC camera?"

"Knew you'd ask that. The disk erases itself every twenty-four and we recycle. 'Cause there's never nothing on it. Now I'm taking you back, I already got too many curious residents wanting to know what's up."

I said, "What are you going to tell them?"

"That you guys are from the county. Making sure we're earthquake-safe. Which we are. Totally."

Back at the unmarked, Milo asked Borchard for detailed directions to the undeveloped land.

"Just what I told you."

"How about if we don't want to get back on the freeway?"

Borchard scratched his head. "I guess you could, as you get out of here, turn left, then left again. But it's way longer, you're making a big square. Then you have to drive a ways till you see an artichoke field. At least now it's artichokes, sometimes they plant it with something else—when it's onions, trust me you'll smell it. You get to the artichokes, you still keep going and then you'll see a whole bunch of nothing, like you just saw through the back gate."

He scraped a tooth with a fingernail. "That's how you'll know you're there. It's a whole lot more nothing than anywhere else around here."

CHAPTER
39

After several wrong turns, we found the artichoke field.

The crop was ample but not ready for picking. A solitary man stood sentry near the south edge of the acreage, positioned on a dirt road above a drainage ditch drinking amber-colored soda. Small and dark-skinned, he wore gray work clothes and a broad-brimmed straw hat. When Milo pulled the unmarked within a yard of his feet, he didn't budge.

Human scarecrow. Effective; not a bird in sight.

We got out and he finally turned. The soda was Jarritos Tamarindo. His work-shirt had two flap pockets. One was empty, the other sagged under the weight of a cellophane-wrapped half sandwich. Some kind of lunch meat, Spanish writing on the pack.

"Hola, amigo," said Milo.

"Hola."

"Ever see this person?"

The drawing of Huggler evoked a head shake.

Same for the photo of the late James Pittson Harrie.

"Ever see anyone around here?"

"No."

"Never?"

"No."

"Okay, gracias."

The man tipped his hat and returned to his post, repositioning himself with his back to the car.

Milo consulted the notes he'd taken from Borchard's sketchy directions, drove another quarter mile, made a turn, came to a stop. "Guess ol' Rudy was right."

Humming first seven bars of "Plenty of Nuthin'," he knuckled an eye.

A vast field stretched west to the twenty-foot ficus hedge and SeaBird's rear gate, thousands of square feet of brambles and weeds, much of it tall as a man. Drought-friendly wildflowers with pinched gray foliage alternated with coarse grass bleached to hay. Ragged bare spots were occupied by shards of rusted metal and tan stucco fragments edged with the snipped ends of chicken wire.

At the far end, a second ficus hedge stood, untrimmed and taller than Sea-Bird's rear border by a good ten feet. The east end, where Specialized Care had once stood. Behind the wall of green, the foothills sprouted like massive tubers.

We sat in the car, dispirited. The failure of my theory meant Huggler could be anywhere.

Milo said, "What the hell, we tried." He lit up a wood-tipped panatela, exhaled acrid smoke through the driver's window and called in for messages, starting with Petra.

The officers who'd arrested Lemuel Eccles thought Complainant Loyal Steward might be James Harrie but they couldn't be positive, they'd been concentrating on the offender not the victim.

Raul Biro had pressured Mick Ostrovine into giving up the truth: Yes, "Dr. Shacker" had sent insurance cases to North Hollywood Day. No, there'd been no kickback, he was just another referral source.

Well-Start Insurance was through returning calls.

Biro said, "There had to be kickbacks. I found out who owns the place, bunch of Russians headquartered in Arcadia and they're billing Medi-Cal gazillions. But I don't see pursuing that unless there's an organized crime aspect to our cases."

"God forbid," said Milo.

"That's what I thought. Can't think of anywhere else to go with this, El Tee."

"Take your girlfriend out to dinner."

"Don't have one," said Biro. "Not this month."

"Then find one," said Milo. "Meal's on me."

"Why?"

" 'Cause you do your job and don't bitch."

"Haven't done much on this one, El Tee."

"So run a tab."

Biro laughed and hung up and Milo called the coroner. Dr. Jernigan was out but she'd authorized her investigator to summarize James Pittson Harrie's autopsy for Milo. Harrie's heart and lungs and brain had been perforated by five bullets fired from the service gun of Sheriff's Deputy Aaron Sanchez, any of which could've proved fatal. No I.D. had been found on Harrie's person but his fingerprints matched some from twenty-five years ago when he'd begun work as a janitor at V-State.

The human blood in the Acura's trunk came from three separate samples, two type A's, one type O. DNA swabs would take a while to analyze but a sex screen had come back female.

Milo hung up and gazed at weed-choked acreage. "A tunnel would've been nice. When you were here, you never heard of that?"

"No," I said.

"Why'd you end up here, anyway?"

"To learn."

"About kids like Huggler?"

"The patients I saw weren't danger-ous, not even close."

"They get better?"

"We made their lives better."

He said, "Uh-huh." His eyes closed. He stretched his long legs, rested his head on the seat-back. Stayed that way for a while. Except for the occasional puff on the cigar, he appeared to be sleeping.

I thought about an unusual child, liv-ing in a special room.

Milo shook himself like a wet dog, stubbed the cigar in the ashtray the city officially forbade him from using. "Let's drive around Camarillo, check out mail-box outlets, shitty motels, and other po-tential squats. Afterward we'll celebrate nothing with a nice fish dinner at Andrea in Ventura. Been there?"

"Robin and I went whale-watching last year, it's right near the launch."

"Rick and I went whale-watching last year, too. Closest we got was when I caught a glimpse of myself in the mirror."

I was expected to chuckle so I did.

He spit a tobacco shred out the window.

Just as he started up the car, something moved.

CHAPTER

40

Blurred movement.

A flickering dot bobbing somewhere past the midpoint of the field's length. Clear of the rear ficus wall but at this distance no way to gauge how far in front.

We watched as the shape bounced above the lower grass, was obscured by taller vegetation.

Up and down, in and out. Sunlight caught the outer edges, limned them gold.

The gold endured. A golden shape. Some sort of animal.

Too large and not furtive enough to be a coyote.

The shape got closer. Lumbering.

A dog. Oblivious to our presence, making its way through the weeds.

Milo and I got out of the car, walked along the border of the field. Got close enough to make out more details.

Sizable dog, obvious golden retriever heritage but too long and narrow in the snout for a purebred. One ear perked, the other flopped.

It stopped to pee. No leg-raising, a brief, submissive squat. Lowering its head, it continued. Stopping, starting, sniffing with no obvious goal. Maybe harking back to some ancient hunting dog imperative.

We kept walking.

The dog looked up, sniffed the air. Turned.

Soft eyes, grizzled muzzle. Not a trace of anxiety.

I said, "Nice to meet you, Louie."

We stood on the roadside as Louie peed again. Squatting longer, he strained to defecate, finally succeeded and pawed the ground before continuing through the field.

A second shape appeared off to his right.

Materializing from nowhere, just as Louie had.

The second dog looked ancient, limping and hobbling as it struggled to catch up with Louie. Tenuous steps alternated with shaky halts. A few seconds of that led to what appeared to be convulsive loss of control that plunged the animal to the ground.

It struggled, moaned, got to its feet, trembling.

Louie turned. Ambled over.

The other dog remained rooted, chest heaving. Louie licked its face. The other dog seemed to revive, managed a few more steps.

Louie and his pal entered a low patch that gave us a clear view. We edged into the field, saw the too-pronounced rib cages of both animals. Louie was underweight, the older dog emaciated with a belly tucked tighter than a greyhound's.

Not the abdomen intended for this breed. What had once been a muscular body was white skin speckled with brown stretched over spindly bones. The head remained noble: brown, with floppy ears, solid bone structure, eyes that appeared vacant but continued to dart around intelligently. A single brown patch ran along a spinal ridge corrugated by age and malnutrition.

German shorthaired pointer.

I said, "Dr. Wainright's hiking buddy, Ned. All these years."

Milo said, "They cut up animals but save these two?"

"Boys and their pets."

Ned paused again, breathing hard, fighting for balance. Louie nuzzled him, sidled up and kept his own body close to that of the pointer, helping the older dog maintain equilibrium. They explored some more, Ned stumbling, Louie there to brace him. Each time the pointer marshaled its energies, Louie rewarded with a lick.

Canine behavior therapist.

For the next quarter hour, we watched both dogs zigzag through the field. If they noticed the unmarked parked off to the side, they gave no indication. One time Louie lifted his head and did seem to be looking at us again, but matter-of-factly, with no alarm.

A trusting creature.

Milo said, "They've been starved . . . if they're here, he's got to be." He scanned the horizon, fingers meandering toward his holster. "C'mon, you sick bastard. Show yourself or I'll sic PETA on you."

The dogs wandered around a bit more for no apparent reason. Then the pointer squatted, took an interminable time to do its business while Louie stood by patiently.

Louie led Ned along what seemed to be an agonizing trek. Both dogs entered a patch of high grass and faded from view.

Twenty minutes later, they hadn't reappeared.

Milo motioned me forward and we stepped into high grass, focusing on the spot where we'd last seen the dogs. Muting noise by parting handfuls of brush before passing through.

Stopping every ten paces to make sure we weren't being watched.

No sign of the dogs, no sign of any other creature.

A few hundred feet in, the vegetation died and we faced a clearing.

Irregular patch of dirt, twenty or so yards in front of the ficus wall. Smooth, brown, swept clean. Just like Marlon Quigg's kill-spot.

Crossing the patch were two sets of paw prints. Milo kneeled and pointed to the left of the dog tracks. A human shoe print. Several, mostly obscured by the dogs.

I made out the shape of a heel. A boomerang-shaped arc of sole.

Feet facing the road. Someone had left this place.

The dogs' trail ended at a hole in the ground. Not irregular, a perfect circle. Six or so feet in diameter, rimmed with rusty metal.

Yawning mouth, flush to the ground. With the slope of the field and the high foliage, you had to get close to see it.

A tunnel entry, identical to the one Borchard had showed us. In place of a pneumatic lid, this one was wide open.

Milo motioned me back, took out his

gun, crept to the opening, and hazarded a look.

His gun-arm grew rigid.

Louie's head sprouted from the opening. He panted, grinned goofily. Unimpressed by Milo's Glock.

Milo waved and Louie emerged, tail wagging. Padding up to Milo, he flipped onto his back in a grand display of surrender.

With his free hand, Milo rubbed Louie's tummy. Louie's eyes clamped shut in ecstasy.

No genius but once a handsome fellow. Now his pelt was gray-tipped and mangy.

Milo motioned for Louie to sit. Louie sat.

Milo tiptoed back to the mouth of the opening.

A sound burst from inside the tunnel, wheezy and wet and amplified by the subterranean tube.

Louie's upright ear stiffened but he remained on his haunches.

Heavy breathing. Scraping.

Ned the pointer stuck his head out.

He studied Milo. Me. Louie.

Louie's composure must have convinced his buddy. The old dog sank down and rested his chin along the rim of the hole.

Milo motioned me over, handed me the keys to the unmarked, gave me my assignment.

The man guarding the artichoke field hadn't budged. I allowed him ten paces of warning before coming up behind him and saying, " 'Scuse me."

He turned as if he'd expected me. Tipped the broad-brimmed hat.

The soda bottle was still in his hand but now it was empty. The sandwich in his pocket was untouched. I showed him the twenty-dollar bill, pointed to the sandwich.

His eyebrows arched. *"¿Veinte para esto?"*

"Sí."

He handed me the sandwich.

"Gracias." I tried to give him the twenty. He shook his head.

I said, *"Por favor,"* dropped the bill in his pocket.

He shrugged and went back to watching the artichokes.

Using the sandwich, Milo coaxed both dogs away from the tunnel hole. He took hold of Louie and I placed my hand on Ned's scruff. Skin and bones was an overstatement. He'd probably once weighed close to seventy pounds, was lucky if he was half of that now. I lifted him gently. Like hoisting a bale of twigs. As I carried him to the car, his head swiveled toward me and I saw that one of his eyes was a gray-blue film stretched over a sunken orbit.

I said, "You're doing great, guy."

He moaned, licked my face with a dry, fetid tongue.

Milo was able to guide Louie with the slightest prod of finger behind ear. We put both dogs in the rear of the unmarked, cracked the windows for air. The sandwich wasn't much, just a scanty portion of lunch meat between slices of white bread. But neither pooch griped when Milo broke off small bites and fed them equal amounts.

Louie chewed pretty well but the

pointer didn't have too many teeth left and was forced to gum. Unneutered male but well past the point where testosterone made a difference.

We gave them both water from bottles we'd brought for ourselves, made sure they lapped slowly.

Ned rolled onto his back, curled up against the car door. Louie placed his paw on his pal's haunch. They both slipped into sleep, snoring in tandem, a comical waltz-like cadence.

We got out of the car and Milo locked up and turned back to the field of weeds. Homing in on the spot, invisible once more, where the tunnel mouth sat.

"Only one set of shoe prints," he said. "Assuming that's Harrie, what're the odds on Huggler still being down there?"

I said, "Good to excellent. He's getting anxious that Harrie hasn't returned with the groceries but has nowhere to go."

"So we'll assume he's down there. Problem is there's no way to know where the tunnel leads. What if Borchard's wrong and not all of SeaBird's tunnels are sealed and Huggler's able to get in there?"

"Trust me, I'm head of security and it couldn't happen."

He laughed. Turned serious. "You were right. It's all about synchrony." He looked back at the snoozing dogs. "Maybe they've got the right idea. Follow your ignorance, reach your bliss."

We returned to the car and pushed it nose-first into the grass. If Grant Huggler headed for the road he'd eventually spot us. But if he remained near his hideaway, the same geography that blocked the tunnel from view would work in our favor.

If I'd guessed wrong and he'd already wandered away and chose to return from any direction, we'd be a clear target.

We stood next to the car. Milo said, "Once we get going, mind looking back every so often so I can concentrate on what's ahead?"

"No prob."

"Lots of probs, but we're solvers." A bird flew. Seagull soaring westward before passing out of view.

Then nothing.

Milo said, "Damn oil painting."

I said, "The tunnel is where Specialized Care used to stand."

"Home sweet home." He gazed through the window crack. "These two geezers are gonna need medical care."

A long, sonorous tone issued from the car. Louie farting in B minor.

"Couldn't agree more, pal," said Milo. "Unfortunately, Animal Control will have to wait its turn."

I said, "Time to call in the human cops?"

"That would be proper procedure, wouldn't it?" He bared his gums. "The question is what constitutes optimal backup in a situation like this? If I call Camarillo PD and explain the situation, they might be cooperative. Or they might figure since it's their jurisdiction they don't need to listen and end up doing something heavy-handed."

"Like bringing in SWAT?"

"And/or one of those hostage negotiators who reads from a script, half the time it turns out bad, because let's face it you can't stop someone if they're intent on checking out. And with a loon like Huggler—if he's even in there, God I hope he is—no crash-course in sweet-talk's gonna help, right?"

"Right."

"They wanna go all military, I can't stop them and then we're stuck with one of those long-term standoffs and Huggler ends up biting it just like Harrie did. Maybe a bunch of cops, too, if he's got firepower down there. With only one way into the tunnel, it's a nightmare. Tear gas could help if it's a short passage but if he's got lots of room to back into, it could get complicated."

He rubbed his face. "I couldn't give an iota of rat-shit about Huggler personally but I need to talk to him, find out what Harrie needed a rape kit for, how many DBs haven't we found. Who belonged to those damn eyeballs."

He phoned Petra again, updated her on the tunnel, told her to clue the other detectives in then make the hour drive to Camarillo with Reed or Binchy or Biro, whoever was closest.

"But don't come out here, stay in town, I'll let you know if I need you."

"Where exactly are you?" she said.

He told her.

"I know a place not far," she said. "Decent pizza, Eric and I go there when we shop the outlets."

"Eric shops?"

"I shop, he pretends not to hate it. Okay, I'll get there soon as I can, good luck."

Just as he clicked off, Louie broke wind again.

"What the hell was in that sandwich?"

"Looked like some variant of baloney," I said.

"We're stuck here long enough, I'm gonna regret sharing."

CHAPTER

41

The first hour slogged by. The second sloth-crawled.

The dogs alternated among sleep, flatulence, and a mellow, glassy-eyed torpor that evoked a weed-fragrant college dorm room.

Milo said, "Someone's thinking right," and closed his eyes.

I was wide awake and I was the one who saw.

Same place, different shape.

Taller than the dogs. Upright. Wearing something brown with a pale collar.

Moving forward. Stopping. Moving again. Stopping.

Facing away from us. So far, so good.

I nudged.

Milo roused, stared. Took hold of his gun, got out of the car, shut the driver's door just shy of latching. Walked forward silently.

He stood, mostly concealed by weeds, as the man in the brown jacket trudged through the field. The man's head stayed canted toward the ground. His pace was deliberate but jerky, broken by frequent stops that seemed to serve no function.

Like a poorly oiled machine.

Milo kept the Glock in his right hand and used his left to part the grass, crouched until he was as high as an average man, and stepped in.

I waited before lowering the car windows a bit more. Not enough for the dogs to get their heads stuck, but sufficient for good ventilation.

They remained drowsy.

I got out.

Backtracking, I mapped out a trajectory that would keep me perpendicular to

Milo's hunter's prowl, aiming to cross the field in a way that kept me to the rear of the man in the brown coat, placing him at the apex of a human triangle.

As we converged on the target, Milo pushed forward, unaware of my presence. Then he saw me and froze. Shot me a long stare but made no attempt to wave me back.

Knowing it wouldn't work.

The two of us maintained the same pace. The man in the brown coat kept trudging without an apparent goal. Head down, weaving, lost in some private world. His head was bare, pale, shiny. Shaved recently.

Milo and I got thirty yards behind him, then twenty. I stopped parting the grass and muting the scratchy sound. Making no attempt at quiet.

The man in brown kept pausing, searching the horizon to the north. Maybe because he was looking for the dogs and that's where they usually headed.

Or he had his own incomprehensible navigational logic.

I picked up my speed, outpaced Milo.

Milo saw it and stiffened and that gave me another few seconds of advantage.

I used them to rush behind the man in brown.

He continued to plod, thick shoulders rounded, hands jammed in his coat pockets. I kept coming, trotting now.

He stopped, raised the back of the coat, and scratched his rear.

Still not hearing me.

Then a patch of particularly brittle grass caught on my pant leg and when I pulled away the *zzzip* was audible.

The man in the brown coat turned.

Saw me.

He didn't move.

I waved flamboyantly, as if meeting an old friend by chance.

The man in brown gaped. His flabby face quivered like uncooked haggis.

I moved in on him, waving, grinning. "Hey, Grant! Long time!"

His jowls tightened. Widening his stance, he planted his legs, flailed the air randomly.

Pudding-faced, snub-featured, un-lined by contemplation, problematic ab-

straction, or any of the mean little demands imposed by sanity.

Terrified.

This was the bogeyman, the nightmare apparition, the cruel messenger in
the dark who'd wreaked so much chaos
and misery.

Now he was too scared to budge, remained frozen in his too-heavy shearling,
fleece collar unraveling, brown suede
greasy, mangy as the dogs, a misshapen
tent of a garment that drooped over a
white shirt and filthy jeans.

I got within arm's reach. "Grant, my
name is Alex."

Windmilling air with both hands, he
stumbled back.

"I'm not out to hurt you, Grant."

His mouth opened. Formed an O. No
sound came out. Then a squeak. The
same sound mice made, mired in sticky
traps, as my father's boot rose above
them.

Turning his back on me, he ran.

Straight into the arms of a big man
with a gun.

◆

Milo used his free hand to spin Huggler so that he was facing me again, twisted Huggler's left arm behind his thick torso, got a handcuff around it. He'd linked two sets of cuffs together, standard procedure for a broad suspect.

Huggler sniffed. Began crying.

His right arm remained at his side. Milo, one hand on his weapon, struggled to bend the uncooperative limb.

"Behind your back, Grant."

Huggler's body sagged, as if ready to comply, but the arm stayed rigid.

I stepped forward.

Milo warned me back with a head shake, repeated the command.

Tears flowed down Huggler's cheeks. His right arm was steel.

Milo holstered the Glock, clamped both hands on Huggler's left wrist, twisted viciously.

Huggler's left arm finally relented, twisting back and up. Milo tried to affix the second cuff but Huggler's width and the bulk of the coat brought him a couple of inches short of the goal.

He pushed Huggler's right hand toward its mate.

Huggler cried out in pain.

"It's okay, Grant," said Milo, lying the way detectives do.

Huggler said, "Really?" in a soft, high, boyish voice.

"Just a little more, son, here we go."

Huggler's right hand was a millimeter from capture when his shoulders shook like those of a rhino rudely awakened. The movement caught Milo off guard, caused his foot to catch.

For a second, his concentration shifted to maintaining his balance.

All at once, Huggler was facing him, had gripped the sides of Milo's head with huge, soft, hairless hands.

Expressionless, he began twisting. Clockwise.

Milo's optimal move might've been a quick grab of his gun but when vise-grip hands take hold of your head and try to rotate it and instincts tell you it won't take much to sever your spine and drain your brain of life-maintaining, thought-engendering nectar, you go for those hands.

Anything to stop the process.

Milo's fingers dug into the tops of

Huggler's hands, straining, clawing, drawing blood.

Huggler remained impassive, kept twisting.

Patient, dry-eyed.

Comfort of the familiar.

Well-practiced routine with predictable results: one way, then the other, feel the body grow limp.

Lay it down gently. Sit and wait.

Explore.

Milo strained to free himself. His eyes bugged. His face was scarlet.

His struggle had twisted his body just enough to put the Glock out of my visual range.

Could I get hold of it fast enough, find a safe way to shoot . . .

My own instincts kicked in and I threw myself behind Huggler, kicked him hard behind the knee.

It's a blow that can reduce strong men to blithering cripples.

Huggler stood there, impassive, managed to move Milo's head a fraction of an inch. Enough to make Milo gasp.

I kicked Huggler's other knee. Like butting an oak stump.

Hooking my hands over the fleece collar, I got them around his massive neck, tried to compress his carotids.

His flesh was sweat-slick. I failed to get purchase.

He moved Milo's neck another tiny fraction of the fatal arc.

I found his Adam's apple, lowered my thumbs to the front of his neck where he'd been incised years ago and robbed of a healthy gland.

I squeezed.

He screamed. His hands flew to the side.

He fell back, tottered, clutching his neck.

I punched him beneath his rib cage, got one foot behind his left heel and hooked him forward as I shoved his chest backward with all the strength I could muster.

Still clutching his neck, he fell back, spine thudding hard on dirt.

He lay there. Helpless.

Synchrony.

Milo, panting, green eyes aflame with fear that wasn't fading quickly enough, fumbled for his Glock, two-handing the weapon, aiming it at Huggler's prone bulk.

His hands were shaking too hard for one to suffice.

Huggler saw the gun. His hands left his neck. His throat was rosy, swollen.

He coughed.

Smiled.

Sat up and lunged.

Milo fired into his left shoe.

Huggler looked down. A small, almost delicate mouth dropped open.

The toe of one grubby sneaker began seeping red.

Huggler's cuffed left hand jangled as he shuddered. He watched the blood stream from the spot where his big toe had once been.

Entranced.

Mystery of the body.

Milo rolled him over roughly, yanked Huggler's right hand hard enough to dislocate, finally got both limbs cuffed.

Huggler lay on his belly. The surrounding earth turned purple as his foot continued to bleed.

No spurt, venous seepage.

Huggler said something. The dirt muf-
fled his words and he turned his head
to the side.

Milo sucked in air. He touched the
side of his face, grimaced.

Not looking at me.

He walked several steps away.

Another gull soared overhead. Or
maybe the same bird, curious.

Grant Huggler said, "Wow."

I said, "Wow, what?"

"My foot. Can I see it, please?"

CHAPTER

42

Petra's pizza had just arrived when Milo called her. She left it behind, arrived nine minutes later. Taking care of business during the drive: calling for an ambulance, making contact with Camarillo PD, and using charm and calm and just enough facts to keep the locals from screaming.

She studied Huggler sitting on the dirt, cuffed, ankles bound, wounded foot wrapped in one of the clean rags Milo keeps in the trunk.

All those years with bodies, it pays to have something for the gore.

Huggler's neck had swelled and was starting to purple. He coughed a lot but was breathing okay. The finger marks on Milo's face had faded to ambiguous splotches. Petra knew something was up and I watched her eyes dance as her brain tried to figure it out.

She said nothing, too smart to ask.

Huggler didn't react to her arrival. Hadn't reacted to much of anything.

Now he looked at Milo. "Um? Mister?" Plaintive.

Please, sir, may I have more gruel?

"What?"

Huggler glanced at the bloody rag. "Could you take this off?"

"Too tight?"

"Um . . ."

"What's the problem?"

"I want to see."

"See what?"

"The inside."

"Of what?"

Huggler pouted. "Me."

Milo said, "Sorry, you need to keep it wrapped."

Apologizing to the man who'd nearly sheared his spine.

Huggler said, "Um, okay." His face settled back into smooth, serene immobility.

I thought about his victims.

The broad, pale disk that had been the final image searing so many people's retinas before the lights went out for good.

Petra was good at maintaining composure but Huggler's request had startled her and she frowned and turned her back on all of us and looked up at the gorgeous sky. Pulling some gum from her purse, she chewed hard. Extended an arm in my direction and offered me a stick.

I took it. When I beared down to masticate, my entire face exploded in pain.

Every muscle and nerve on full-fire, it had been a while since they'd relaxed.

Milo looked at his watch, then at Huggler's shoe. The rag had bloodied some more but Huggler's color was decent, no sign of shock.

"Feel okay?"

Huggler nodded. "Your hands are strong."

"Had to be to deal with you, Grant."

"It's always worked before," said Huggler, puzzled. "Oh, well."

Camarillo EMTs strapped him onto a full-restraint gurney. The local detective was a white-haired man named Ramos who told the driver to wait as he approached Milo. He slid from distrust to professional curiosity to camaraderie as Milo explained the situation.

"Guess you did us a favor. How many victims we talking about?"

"At least six, probably more."

"A situation," said Ramos. "Been doing this thirty years, never had anything like it."

"You don't have to have it now," said Milo. "Unless you've got some masochistic urge to complicate your life."

"You want to handle all of it."

"We started it, we're ready to finish. Paperwork alone's gonna be a full-time job."

Ramos grinned and pulled out a hardpack of Winstons. Milo accepted the offer of a cigarette and the two of them smoked.

"You're making a point," said Ramos.

"So what, we patch him up and ship him back to you in a Brink's truck?"

"A cage would be better." Milo touched the right side of his face. We still hadn't made eye contact and I'd stayed a few inches behind him so as not to push the issue.

Ramos said, "I'll check with my boss but he's a lazy type, can't see there being any problem."

"Whatever works," said Milo. "The legal eagles are gonna be on this, our people will call your people."

"We'll do lunch," said Ramos. "Half a dozen bodies, huh? I'm figuring I should send someone in the ambulance with the asshole. Just be careful." He glanced at the ambulance. "First impression, he looks like a nerd. The kid who never got chose for baseball."

"Part of his charm."

"He's charming, huh?"

"Not in the least."

Ramos chuckled. "Now I got a new worst thing. Before this, it was a case I picked up thirty-nine months ago. Woman shot her kid in the head because he was mouthing off. Just picked up a gun and drilled him, I'm talking a twelve-year-old. She looked like a schoolteacher." He glanced at the ambulance. "This is a whole different thing. You're doing me a favor."

He waved a paramedic over.

Ramos said, "I'm coming with you." Beckoning a tall, husky cop. "Officer Baakeland, too."

"Tight fit," said the EMT.

"We'll survive," said Ramos. "That's the point. Hey, who's that?"

"Animal Control," said Milo.

Ramos looked over at the still-sleeping dogs. "Oh, yeah, for them. Too bad they can't talk."

Gaining access to the tunnel proved tricky. With no evidence any crime had been committed on the premises, John Nguyen said a warrant was probably required.

Milo said, "Probably?"

"Gray area. With something like this you err on the side of caution."

"John—"

"Your only alternative is to contact

whoever owns the property and get consent."

"That's a development firm."

"Then that's who you contact."

Sea Line Development was joint-head-quartered in Newport Beach and Coral Gables, Florida. No one answered at ei-ther office, same for an 888 "emergency" number. Milo left a message, walked over to the mouth of the tunnel opening, squatted and stuck his head in, and got back on his feet. "Too dark, can't see a thing."

I said, "They removed the hatch but there's got to be an inner door not too far down."

He phoned Nguyen again. "Can't reach the owners. Got a recommenda-tion for a judge?"

"The usual suspects."

No answers at four usually coopera-tive jurists. A fifth said, "Camarillo? Get someone local."

"Anyone in particular?"

"What?" said the judge. "I look like a referral agency?"

Milo took out Rudy Borchard's card,

punched the number. Cursed viciously and clicked off. "No one answers their own damn phones anymore. Next week robots are scheduled to wipe our asses."

Talking in my presence but not to me.

Petra said, "It'll work out."

"Easy for you to say, you're cute and thin."

He trudged to the car, got back in. When I slipped into the passenger seat he pretended to sleep. His phone rang and he waited a while to answer.

"Yes, Maria . . . yes, that's true. Yes, I've talked to them and it's all ours . . . why? Because it is . . . whatever, Maria."

He ended the conversation. The phone rang again. He turned it off. Went back to fake-sleep.

I got out of the car.

Petra came over, stuck her head in, sniffed. "Smells like a kennel."

Milo opened his eyes. "Next time I'll use a better deodorant."

She said, "Speaking of scent, that dirt clearing looks awfully clean. What do you think about bringing in a cadaver pooch?"

"Soon as we get the damn warrant."

She turned to me. "This feels weird. A huge one gets closed and we end up sitting around."

"Let's do something, then—put up some tape."

"Around the hole or the entire clearing?"

"How much tape do you have?"

"Not enough."

Milo's phone played Mendelssohn. He said, "Damn pencil-pushers," and switched to conference. "What now?"

A deep male voice said, "Pardon?"

"Who's this?"

"My name is Norm Pettigrew and I'm returning Lieutenant Sturgis's call."

"Sturgis here. You're with Sea Line?"

"Vice president and coordinator of operations. What can I do for you?"

Milo told him.

Pettigrew said, "Incredible. We had no idea anyone was squatting. Or that there was even a tunnel. We thought we had all of those sealed."

"Looks like the grass was cleared to gain access."

"How would anyone know to do that, Lieutenant? And why?"

"Good question," said Milo, lying easily.

Pettigrew said, "Well, by all means go down there, do whatever you need to do."

"Thank you, sir."

"Obviously, Lieutenant, we'd prefer if Sea Line wasn't linked to any of this."

"I'll do my best, sir."

"Let me be more specific," said Pettigrew. "Any encumbrances that can be avoided would be highly appreciated. Have you ever been to Laguna Beach?"

"A while back, sir."

"We've got a project there. High-end condos with ocean views. A couple of the demos are fully furnished and livable and suitable for short-term usage. In your case, being a devoted public servant capable of providing security, I'm sure we can reach an agreement. You and the missus for a weekend. If you enjoy yourselves, two weekends. We've got a great Italian restaurant about to open."

"Sounds great."

"Sea Shore Villas," said Pettigrew. "That's the name of the project. Call me personally, I'll set it up."

"Thank you, sir. And thanks for permission to search."

"Oh, sure. I mean it, about Laguna. Come and enjoy the ocean on us."

The line went dead.

Petra said, "Last thing anyone offered me was a hit of crank if I didn't bust him."

"You like the beach?"

"You don't?"

"Too damn peaceful . . . okay, kids, let's spelunk."

CHAPTER

43

Inches below the hole was a steel ladder that descended ten feet and planted us on a square of concrete with barely enough space for the three of us to stand. A bulb in a wire cage was screwed into the ceiling. The tunnel continued to the left, a cement-lined tube barely taller than Milo. A circular steel hatch like the one Borchard had showed us blocked further exploration. This one responded to the slightest tug before hissing open.

We passed through another twenty feet of vacant passage. No obvious ventilation but the tunnel was cool, dry, surprisingly pleasant. No smell of death, not much odor at all but for occasional wisps of mold and raw rock and, as we kept going, burgeoning human perspiration.

Milo and Petra both had their flashlights in hand but didn't need to turn them on; caged bulbs were set every five steps, bathing the tunnel in hard yellow light from hospital days, old wires forgotten, but still active. The floor was free of debris, swept clean like the clearing. Another circular hatch appeared, left wide open.

A room appeared to the right, fifteen or so square feet.

An old porcelain sign lettered in Gothic was bolted into the stone wall. *Hospital Storage, Non-Perishables Only. Stack Neatly.*

On the floor were two futons, rolled up precisely. Between them sat twin dressers still stickered with IKEA labels. The chest on the left bore a battery-op digital clock, two pairs of cheap reading glasses, a tube of lubricant, a box of tissues, three hardcover books: *Introduction to Psychology, Abnormal Psy-*

chology, Consultations in Forensic Psy-chology. Three drawers contained a modest assortment of men's clothing, size S. Laundry tickets were pinned to several items. A cedar freshener had been placed in each compartment.

The stand on the right was piled high with softcover books, four stacks, at least twenty per pile. Crosswords, ana-grams, sudoku, sum doku, word search, brain-teasers, kakuro, anacrostics. Draw-ers below contained sweats, T-shirts, boxers, and tube socks, size XL.

An adjoining room, smaller, colder, contained two chemical porta-toilets, one clean, the other reeking. Gallon wa-ter bottles were lined up against a wall. A card table was piled with folded white towels. Bulk rolls of toilet paper still in cellophane sat nearby. Off to the side, two cardboard cartons of cookies, bread, cereal, beef jerky, canned spa-ghetti and chili shared space with three bags of generic dry dog food.

"Keeping house," said Petra. "Cozy."

I noticed something behind the tallest stack of provisions, pointed it out.

Milo drew out a brown cardboard

pizza delivery box. Pristine, unopened, printed with the image of a portly, gleeful mustachioed chef.

Lotta taste.

Ooh la la.

Three identical cartons were pinioned against the wall by cans and cases.

We returned to the tunnel, passed through a third hatch. The passageway ended at a final room. A Gothic sign said *No Further Entry.*

Petra tapped the rear stone wall to which the message had been bolted. "Kind of redundant."

Milo said, "Some sign contractor probably greased palms."

"My Lieutenant," she said, though he wasn't, "sage but so cynical."

Milo stepped into the final room, approached the sole piece of furniture. Bare-topped desk, stickered like the end tables.

Muttering, "Doing what they could for the Swedish economy," he slid the top drawer open.

Inside was paper. A detective's treasure.

Check stubs documented a variety of

welfare and disabilities payments from the State of California, Santa Barbara and Ventura Counties, mailed regularly to a Malibu post office box near Carbon Beach and cashed promptly at a nearby Bank of America. Totals varied from twelve hundred to nearly twice that amount.

The recipient: *Lewisohn Clark.*

Petra said, "Some moniker. Sounds like the millionaire on Gilligan."

"Say it out loud," I said.

She did. "Oh."

Milo said, "Lewis and Clark."

I said, "Master explorers."

A separate collection of stubs revealed monthly payments of $3,800.14 sent to the same P.O.B. A recent letter from the state pension board announced that an automatic cost-of-living increase would add just under a hundred eighty bucks to next month's installment.

The recipient: *Sven Galley.*

Milo checked his pad. "Harrie used his own damn Social Security number."

Petra said, "Guess not everyone's curious."

She inspected a stub. "Svengali." Her jawline sharpened. "I'm glad he's dead."

A dark green simulated alligator box beneath the receipts told a new story.

Faded Polaroids of women, young, trussed, terrified. The same terrible sequence for each: rope around neck, fear-frozen eyes, lifeless eyes, gaping mouth.

Underneath the photos were articles printed off the Internet. Missing girls, eight of them, the cases arranged chronologically.

The first victim, a college student at UC Santa Cruz, had vanished ten years ago during a Carmel vacation. The most recent, a sixteen-year-old runaway from New Hampshire, had been last seen five months ago, hitchhiking on Ocean Avenue not far from the Santa Monica Pier.

It didn't take long to match the photos.

Milo opened the bottom drawer.

Another case, this one larger and covered in soiled gray shagreen, sat atop yet more paper. The press of a button-latch revealed an array of surgical tools resting in green velvet, each instrument snuggled in form-fitted compartments. Tiny gold lettering on the inside of the lid spelled out *Chiron, Tutlingen.*

The paper beneath the case was blank. Milo removed a sheet anyway. On the underside, centered perfectly, was the inevitable message.

?

Milo said, "Not anymore, asshole. Let's get out of here."

Petra said, "Good idea, I need a breather, too."

"It's not that, kid." He brandished his cell phone. "Not getting reception."

As we made our way out, I let Petra pass in front of me, advanced closer to Milo, and stared until he made eye contact.

He nodded. Moved on.

By the time the black Lab and the springer spaniel arrived, darkness had settled over the field and field lamps faciliated by Detective Arthur Ramos had been propped.

The handler, a civilian from Oxnard named Judy Kantor who also bred and showed both breeds, said, "They love the dark, less distraction. What's the area?"

Milo said, "That clearance."

"That's it?" said Kantor. "No trees or brush or water? Piece of cake, there's something down there, they'll find it." She clapped her hands. "C'mon Hansel, c'mon Gretel, do your sniffy thing."

Judy Kantor led the dogs around the perimeter, then she let them explore. Within moments, each animal was sitting. Ten feet apart. Judy Kantor marked the spots, signaled for them to resume.

Two more tells. This time, the dogs stayed seated.

She said, "That's it, Lieutenant."

Milo said, "We suspect as many as eight victims."

"If there was another grave nearby, they'd tell you," she said. "Unless it's super-deep—hey, maybe you've got stacked bodies."

Milo thanked her, she gave the dogs treats, the three of them departed with obvious joy.

No stacking.

A quartet of intact skeletons, interred barely three feet below the surface.

Petra said, "They're all pretty petite. Don't need to be an anthropologist to know they're girls."

CHAPTER
44

It did take an anthropologist to make sense of the bones. Moe Reed's girlfriend, Dr. Liz Wilkinson, had the report on Milo's desk nine days later. The skeletons were consistent with the four most recent victims depicted in James Harrie's photo stash. Dental records for two victims solidified the I.D.'s and the remaining two girls were differentiated using femur length.

Wilkinson opined that two of the victims had probably given birth, a fact that didn't emerge during interviews with their parents.

No reason to bring that up. Milo helped facilitate delivery of the bones and has attended every funeral.

A wider, deeper excavation of the field has produced no other bodies, no evidence of any kind.

The burial sites of Dr. Louis Wainright and Nurse Joanne Morton remain unknown.

The eyes left behind in "Bern Shacker's" Beverly Hills office were too degraded by formaldehyde for DNA analysis. Dr. Clarice Jernigan has opined that they may not belong to any victim, could very well be anatomy specimens sold commercially to optometrists and ophthalmologists.

She's a tough-minded expert pathologist with a wealth of experience.

Then again, everyone engages in wishful thinking.

The pizza boxes found in the tunnel match those used by only one restaurant between Santa Barbara and Malibu, a stand in Oxnard just off Highway 1, catering to the motor trade. No one working there is aware of any pilferage. A teenage girl on-site during weekend evenings is almost certain a pleasant man resembling James Harrie was an occasional customer.

An A-student taking a full load of advanced placement courses, she's nearly as confident about his order.

Same thing each time: small plain cheese pie, large pepperoni and mushrooms.

Grant Huggler awaits trial at Starkweather State Hospital for the Criminally Insane. He is a model patient and has defied easy diagnosis. His public defender and deputy D.A. John Nguyen have separately indicated their intention to call me as an expert witness should the case go to trial. I've communicated my reluctance to both of them. They haven't pushed. But they're lawyers, haven't backed off, either.

I can live with the uncertainty.

Milo has never mentioned what happened in the field. He has asked me—twice, because he's been more absent-minded than usual—if I think Huggler will ever make it into a courtroom or remain stashed in his isolation room.

"Or even shipped off to another loony bin. Maybe Kansas, huh? We owe them."

Both times I told him I wasn't feeling like a gambling man.

I've been a little edgy, though I think I've been handling it pretty well with Robin and Blanche, saying and doing the right things, play-acting a normal life.

For the most part, the dreams have stopped. I do think about the eyes, the four girls whose bodies haven't been found. Louis Wainright, Joanne Morton.

Belle Quigg was offered Louie but she demurred, telling Milo it was all she could do to make it through each day.

Louie and Ned were adopted by a family from Ojai, a Mormon clan with twelve kids and a long, honorable history of caring for old, ill castaway pets. I hear that both dogs have fattened up and once in a while, Ned's got the energy to play.

I've turned down several patient referrals, have increased my running time, spend more time listening to music, everything from Steve Vai to Bach's Brandenburg Concerto No. 6.

Every day I go into my office, close the door, pretend to work. Mostly I sit at my desk thinking, then trying not to.

I've contemplated recapturing my self-hypnosis chops. Or learning some new form of meditation that might succeed at emptying my head.

I think about meeting the parents of the four girls whose bodies haven't been found. Saying something to Dr. Louis Wainright's two adult kids.

No one has inquired about Wainright's nurse, Joanne Morton, and that bothers me more than it should.

I wonder about what created Grant Huggler. James Harrie.

At this point, I'm not sure I want answers.

ABOUT THE AUTHOR

JONATHAN KELLERMAN is the #1 *New York Times* bestselling author of more than thirty bestselling crime novels, including the Alex Delaware series, *The Butcher's Theater, Billy Straight, The Conspiracy Club, Twisted,* and *True Detectives*. With his wife, bestselling novelist Faye Kellerman, he co-authored *Double Homicide* and *Capital Crimes*. He is also the author of two children's books and numerous nonfiction works, including *Savage Spawn: Reflections on Violent Children* and *With Strings Attached: The Art and Beauty of Vintage Guitars*. He has won the Goldwyn, Edgar, and Anthony awards and has been nominated for a Shamus Award. Jonathan and Faye Kellerman live in California, New Mexico, and New York.

jonathankellerman.com